A Woman to be Loved

James Mitchell

HEADLINE

First published in 1990
by Sinclair-Stevenson Ltd

First published in paperback in 1991
by HEADLINE BOOK PUBLISHING PLC

10 9 8 7 6 5 4 3 2

ISBN 0 7472 3648 8

Printed and bound in Great Britain by
Collins, Glasgow

HEADLINE BOOK PUBLISHING PLC
Headline House
79 Great Titchfield Street
London W1P 7FN

For Delia
In loving memory

course. Mummy was not in favour of girls who screamed, or had nightmares. Come to that Mummy wasn't all that keen on girls who lived to be thirty-two years old, and had failed to acquire so much as one single, solitary husband. Really, Jane thought, from Mummy's point of view she had been a most unsatisfactory daughter. And perhaps from anybody else's point of view too. . . . The thought was a dreadful one, but it had to be faced, and, very tentatively, refuted. After all, her father liked her, and so did Aunt Pen. John had adored her. . . . But then her father was ailing, and so was Aunt Pen. And John, there was no denying the fact, was dead. She looked back again at the ceiling. White meant purity of course, but she'd read somewhere that for the Chinese it was the mourning colour, the colour of death. – *The blood had gleamed so red in the snow.*

But before the idea could develop there was a tap at the door and she called 'Come in' at once. Anybody would be welcome, even Mummy. But it was Peggy Hawkins with tea, and chocolate biscuits, the ones she liked.

'Beg pardon, Miss Jane,' the housemaid said, 'but your mother would like to see you in her bedroom, as soon as convenient.'

So mother was not avoided, merely postponed.

'Very well,' Jane said.

Hawkins hesitated, but in the end valour overcame discretion.

'I shouldn't hang about, Miss Jane,' she said. 'Not this morning I shouldn't. If you take my meaning.'

Then she bobbed a curtsey and was gone, and Jane Whitcomb looked at her tea and biscuits and knew that if she so much as touched them she'd vomit, and got out of bed instead.

Her mother said, 'You woke your father.'

Jane looked round the enormous bedroom, vast enough to contain a brass double bed, two wardrobes, two chests of drawers, a dressing table and a washstand, and still look half empty.

'Where is Daddy?' she asked.

'In his dressing room, where else?' her mother said. 'Recovering. You woke him with all that screaming.'

'I didn't mean to.'

'You know his heart is weak.'

Jane said, 'I do when I'm awake.'

Instantly her mother flushed. As always, Jane thought, it was a colour impossible to describe in words. Somewhere between magenta and vermilion was about as near as she could get to it. Her mother was in many ways a splendid woman to look at: tall, regular-featured, of good carriage, but when she took on that colour she was quite hideous. It was the colour, Jane thought, of East End sprees. Gin and stout, and charwomen on the loose.

'You must learn to control yourself,' her mother said.

'You mean I must learn to control my nightmares?'

'A little will power,' said her mother. 'Perhaps a more restricted diet.'

'I'm over-eating then?'

Her mother shrugged. 'Too many chocolate biscuits cannot be good for you. . . . And all this entertainment.'

'What entertainment, Mummy?'

'You know very well, Jane dear.' That 'dear' was a warning that she well recognised.

'All that theatre. . . . All that cinema,' her mother said. 'It cannot be good for you, not in the nervous state that you're in these days. I fear that we must cut it out.'

'I go to the cinema once a week and the theatre once a month.'

'Too much,' her mother said. 'Far, far too much.'

Really, Jane thought, one would think the cinema was whisky and I was Mummy's vermilion-magenta colour.

'We must cut it out, dear. All it needs is a little determination. In a few months you'll be thanking me.'

Not even whisky: gin.

'Yes indeed,' said Mummy. 'That's what we must do. Cut out all those rich bikkies that upset your poor tummy, and all those vile entertainments that bring on the dreams. . . . There? . . . What do you say?'

What could she say? She'd been tried, found guilty and sentenced, and there was no appeal: not to Mummy. Not to Daddy either, not since his heart attack.

'What can I say?' Jane said.

'What indeed? I'm glad you see things sensibly.'

Mummy was winning and knew it. Already the colour had left her cheeks; her face was rich creamy-milk now, with just a hint of pink rose in the cheeks.

'Kiss me, child.'

Apathetically Jane kissed her. Apathy, she thought, must be the only solace known to whores. Perhaps her mother thought it too, because her next set of questions were the ones she'd been summoned to hear.

'What will you do today, Jane dear?'

Jane began to shrug, then controlled the impulse. Mummy didn't like movements that drew attention to the female body, not even the female body encased in a flannel nightgown and robe.

'Go shopping – if you need any.'

'None, I thank you.'

Mummy still remembered the Indian days, when there were servants to do the shopping, the days when ladies – and their daughters – shopped only for pleasure.

'In that case,' Jane said, 'I think I shall take Foch for a walk in Kensington Gardens.'

'Foch,' Lady Whitcomb said. 'Such an odd name for a Sealyham.'

'Monsieur Foch is a very remarkable Frenchman,' said Jane, 'and my Foch is a very remarkable dog. And he's not a Sealyham. He's a Scotch terrier.'

'Whatever he is,' her mother said, 'I think he excites you too much.'

This was bluff of course. Foch was the one creature alive that she would die for, and if Mummy wanted to remove him then Mummy would have to kill her dear daughter first, and Mummy knew it. Even so it was not *all* bluff: if Mummy couldn't harm Foch she could most certainly complain about him. On and on and on she could complain. Jane supposed that she was being offered a contract: stop screaming and I won't complain. It was a contract she desperately wanted to make, but couldn't possibly honour.

'I won't let Foch excite me,' she said.

'I'm delighted to hear it,' said Mummy. 'A little will power, that's all it needs. – As in so many things. . . . Have you seen that doctor of yours lately?'

'No, Mummy.'

'Why not?'

'You told me not to.'

'Indeed?' said Lady Whitcomb. 'Why did I do that?'

'You said that he excited me too much,' said Jane. Like Foch, she added, but only to herself.

'Perhaps I was – '

Wrong? thought Jane. Let me have pencil and paper quickly so that I may note the day when Mummy said she was wrong.

' – a little hasty,' Mummy said. 'Perhaps after all you should call on him. Tell him I said so. Tell him I think you should have a tonic.'

'Yes, Mummy.'

She willed herself to seem submissive: as if to see Lockhart again were a chore, and not a delight.

'Do it today,' Lady Whitcomb said. 'At once, in fact. Your father has a weak heart. Your screams can only make it weaker.'

She glared at her daughter then, making no effort to hide the hatred in her eyes. 'I've no doubt you are about to tell me that you don't mean to scream,' she said, 'but that doesn't make the least difference to the harm you do to your father. Cut along.'

When she got back to her room Peggy Hawkins was there, come back for her tea tray, munching the last of her chocolate biscuits with a fascinating intensity: inflicting pleasure on herself as carefully as Mummy inflicted pain on others. She made no effort to hide what she was doing as Jane walked in on her, and indeed how could she? The two women looked at each other, Hawkins's ecstatic look fading, to be replaced by wariness. Jane taller, fairer, and far too thin, even by the standards of 1926.

It's really up to me to speak, Jane thought. But what am I to say? The best she could manage was, 'Do they – do *we* – feed you enough?'

'Yes, miss,' Hawkins said. She didn't seem to be lying.

'You just like these particular biscuits, is that it?'

'I've never tasted anything like them, miss,' said Hawkins.

'Then I'm obliged to you for helping me to finish them,' said Jane.

Hawkins, who had scoffed the lot, accepted this without a blink.

'That's all right, miss,' she said.

Then the two women smiled, before Hawkins went off to polish the brass.

Jane dressed carefully: nothing too gaudy, nothing that Mummy might veto on the grounds of frivolity, but nothing too slipshod either: Mummy could not *bear* untidiness, and neither could her daughter. The grey two-piece, she thought. Long-waisted, *of course*, but with a hemline low enough to satisfy even Mummy's exacting standards, though Hawkins would have thought it dull in the extreme. (Hawkins on her night off, Jane was sure, would wear skirts that showed her knees, would consider it eccentric not to.) But the grey two-piece did have pretty rose-pink buttons, and a rose-pink band round the waist and hem. Not bad, really not too bad, not when one was thin enough to be a professional mannequin. (And wasn't *that* an idea to try out on Mummy?)

She sat at the mirror and looked at her hair. The hair was good. Blonde, of course, which was not ideal, but thick and lustrous, and fashionably shingled. Blue eyes. Mary Pickford-heroine eyes, when what she really wanted was eyes that smouldered darkly. Theda Bara eyes; the eyes of the femme fatale. Still, blue was what she'd got, and now they'd acquired an interest of their own, the blueness intensified by the dark shadows beneath them. And anyway, who was there to notice? . . . Mouth too wide, and a rounded chin that should have been more determined than it was, and there you had her: Jane Victoria Whitcomb; born 1893, debutante 1912, ambulance driver 1916–1918, neurasthenic idler and unmarried widow thereafter.

She went to her bedroom door and peeped out. Cook was just disappearing into Mummy's room. With the whole day's menus to discuss, that would take care of half an hour at least. She went downstairs, to where Foch sat waiting at the foot as he always did: Foch who was compact yet burly, shaggy yet neat, cantankerous and yet adorable even so. She could take him into the breakfast room and eat before Mummy launched another day's offensive; she only wanted toast and coffee after all, and a chance to be alone, but she didn't get it. Her father was there, which was surprising. He never ate breakfast, wasn't eating now, just tea and a Turkish cigarette, a diet even worse than hers. He looked up at her.

'Hello little daughter,' he said in Hindi. 'You have come for hasri?'

'Hello, burra sahib,' she said in the same language. 'If my father says I may join him.' It was what her ayah had always said.

He smiled at her, a tentative, even apologetic smile, and looked around the breakfast room.

'Not much like the old days,' he said.

The old days meant her ayah, and servants in turbans, punkahs and a screaming mynah bird and the sun outside, waiting fierce as a tiger. It meant three brothers too, and now only one of them survived.

'Not much,' she said. 'It was always so noisy, then.'

Not just the mynah bird, but Guy and David laughing – or fighting – and baby Francis yelling to be fed.

'They were never quiet chaps – your brothers.'

'They were fun,' said Jane, and her father smiled again, but this time the smile meant only remembered pleasure.

'I agree with you,' he said. 'And it's only fair, wouldn't you say? After all, they didn't have much time.'

Second Lieutenant Guy Whitcomb, Leicester Regiment, missing believed killed at Ypres, 1916. Second Lieutenant David Robert Whitcomb, Royal Flying Corps, shot down over Arras, 1917. Both had been twenty-three when they died.

'All those years ago,' her father said, 'and your mother and I still miss the laughter.'

She poured tea for herself, buttered some toast, then added marmalade. Not that she wanted it, but to face Lockhart she'd need all her strength.

'And so do I, Papa,' she said. 'Honestly. Sometimes I think the war killed even that.' And then, before her courage could fail her she added, 'I can't help screaming, Papa. I mean I don't do it deliberately.'

'Of course not,' he said. 'Who could possibly – ' He dropped off the words, then said again, 'Of course not.'

Jane said carefully, 'What I meant was I'm sorry if my screaming makes you unwell.'

'It doesn't,' he said. 'It's my weak heart that makes me unwell. That and my memories. . . . Guy won a scholarship to Merton, do you remember? David couldn't even wait to try for one. No time, Papa, he said. And he was right, you know. He had no time at all before he was killed. Dear me, how morbid I am this morning. What are you going to do today?'

'Take Foch for a walk.'

'Lucky Foch.'

The dog heard his name and thumped his stubby tail on the floor. Sir Guy was one of the few people he could tolerate.

'And then?'

'See Dr Lockhart.'

'I'm delighted to hear it,' her father said. 'Sooner or later the good doctor will get rid of these dreadful dreams of yours. I'm convinced of it.'

She knew then why he'd joined her for breakfast. For her to go back to Lockhart was his idea, and somehow he'd persuaded Mummy to go along with it. It couldn't have done that poor heart of his any good. She rose.

'If you'll excuse me, I'd better telephone for an appointment,' she said.

2

Dr Lockhart. James Adrian Belmont Lockhart. J.A.B. Lockhart. Inevitably and forever known as Jabber. Tall and gangling, even in his fifties, his suit neat but his hair as usual looking as if he'd just dried it. Doctor of Medicine, specialist in mental disorders, patient, unyielding, demanding Lockhart, her friend for life. Whatever sanity she had left, Lockhart had preserved for her, and she knew it. She grasped the hand he offered all too eagerly.

'I thought you'd sacked me,' he said.

'You don't sack your hope of salvation,' she said.

'Sit down,' said Lockhart, 'and oblige me by not talking rubbish.'

She sat and looked about her, at his consulting room in Harley Street. It hadn't changed – not once, in all the years she'd been there. Pale green lincrusta wallpaper on the upper wall, dark green dado beneath it. Whitewashed ceiling mottled by tobacco smoke – (he and most of his patients smoked too much) – a college oar on one wall, with names lettered on the blade. (J.A.B. Lockhart had rowed number five.) No pictures, no photographs, no books except text books. A room with no memory of the past or vision of the future, because it had to be like that. Lockhart's business was with the shell-shocked, the ones driven mad by the unbelievable fury of the war the newspapers called Great; the ones whose only chance was to live from day to day.

'Can you tell me why it's been so long?' Lockhart asked.

'I'd rather not,' said Jane, 'but I can tell you why my mother hates me.'

'Why?'

'Because both my elder brothers died in the war, and I didn't. And I'm a girl. Or I was then.'

Lockhart pounced on the last sentence.

'And what are you now?' he asked her.

'An old maid.'

'That isn't strictly true, is it?'

He was the only one she'd told about John. She'd told him because unless she could share the secret with someone there was simply no point to her life at all and, as he was a doctor, she felt that she could tell him without fear of betrayal, as if he were a kind of priest. But to be reminded of John at that moment seemed in itself a kind of betrayal.

'You don't fight fair, do you?' she asked.

'I don't fight at all if I can help it,' Lockhart said.

'What are you doing now then?'

'Listening to you.'

She flushed. It was six o'clock, and she was his last appointment of the day, an appointment squeezed in because of the short notice she'd given him. All day he must have sat behind that mahogany desk with its cigarette box, ash trays and petrol lighter, and listened to people like her – young men for the most part – telling him about their terrors. But John – John didn't belong with all that.

'Why do you bother?' she asked.

'Because I care about you,' he said. 'It's not just that you're ill, and I'm trying to make you better. That's only part of it. It's *why* you're ill.'

'And why am I ill?'

'Because you began by doing a good thing and went on to do a better thing,' said Lockhart. 'You began by helping your country and ended by helping mankind, and so mankind owes you a debt. And I am that part of mankind which might – just might – be in a position to pay it.'

She surprised herself then, if not him, by bursting into tears. It was the first time she had cried for a long, long time.

Lockhart watched her carefully, yet with detachment, as if trying to decide what good her weeping would do for her. At last her fumbling hands found her handbag, came out with a delicate scrap of linen and lace.

'I doubt if that will do much good,' Lockhart said, and opened a drawer in his desk, then reached inside to hand her a vast square of anonymous cotton that at once absorbed her tears – though even as she wept she'd noticed a neat pile of handkerchiefs in the drawer. Those who came to see Lockhart it seemed did a lot of crying, young men or not.

'I'm sorry,' she said.

'Are you? Sorry that you cried?'

She thought about it. It was always best to think when Lockhart asked you a question.

'No,' she said. 'Not sorry. Surprised. It's been a long time since anyone said something nice to me so seriously.'

'Seriously?'

'"How pretty you look",' she quoted. '"That's a nice dress". . . . "You're looking better today" – which is usually a lie. But nothing about what I *do*. – What I did, I mean.'

'It's all in the past then, is it?'

'You know it is.'

He nodded, which meant that he'd heard her: not necessarily that he'd agreed, then pushed the cigarette box to her.

'No thank you.' Tobacco smoke might make her eyes water again, and there'd been quite enough of that. He lit one himself, and dragged smoke down deep.

'About your not being an old maid,' he said. 'How can you be? You're neither old nor a maid. You will be old eventually – time will take care of that – but maidenhood, that's over. Finished. Do you regret the fact?'

'No,' she said. No hesitations: none.

'And why do you not?'

'Because I gave – it, to a man who loved me. We were to be married.'

'But you're not married, are you?'

'You know I'm not.'

'Why aren't you married?'

'Because he . . . John . . . was killed.'

'And you weren't.'

'And I wasn't.'

'But before he died – you gave him the most precious gift you had to offer.'

'My virtue?. . . I gave him rather more than that. I gave him what he gave me.'

Lockhart nodded again. He was still listening.

'I gave him all my love and had all his. But we had no time to share it.' Before he could speak she hurried on. 'I know that happened to thousands of women. Millions. I know we've just got to get on with our lives. All that. God knows I've heard it said often enough. . . . But there's one thing I haven't told you about John.'

'Then tell me – if you want to.'

'For years I couldn't bear to think about it,' she said. 'But you know all the rest so you may as well know this. John was shot dead by a sniper at twenty to four on the afternoon of 10th November, 1918. The day before the Armistice. If he'd survived for nineteen hours twenty minutes more – the war would have been over. He would still be alive.'

'You can't possibly know that,' Lockhart said.

'Of course I can.'

'Don't be silly.' Lockhart ground the stub of his cigarette into the ash tray. 'What about car crashes and sailing accidents and runaway horses? What about the Spanish 'flu that killed even more people than the war?'

'I survived even that,' said Jane.

'Only the dead know whether you're to be envied or not,' Lockhart said.

Suddenly she realised that he was trying very hard not to yawn.

'You're tired,' she said.

He shrugged. 'It goes with the job. . . . If he'd lived, what would you have done?'

'Done?' It wasn't easy to answer; not in terms of 'doing'. 'Been his wife, had his children, looked after him – and them.'

'That would have kept you busy?'

She smiled then. Only a man could be naive enough to ask such a question.

'Oh yes,' she said.

'And instead of that, you're idle?'

'I don't want to be,' she said. 'Honestly I don't.'

Once more the nod, acknowledging, rather than accepting.

'Who said you could come back to me?'

'My mother,' said Jane. 'But I think my father said it to her. He's awfully sweet, my father – only he had a heart attack after the Spanish 'flu, and he hasn't been much good for anything since.'

'Did your mother say why you should come to see me?'

'She said you could prescribe a tonic – '

'For God's sake,' he said, 'I'm a specialist in nervous disorders.' Then he broke off and grinned.

'Why not?' he said. 'A tonic could be just what you need. – Maybe I do, too.'

He went to a cupboard and came back with a decanter and two glasses, poured out two measures of honey-gold wine.

'Amontillado sherry,' he said. 'Medium dry.' He passed one to her.

'Should I?' she said.

'Doctor's orders.' He raised his glass. 'Good health.'

'Good health,' she said, and sipped. The wine glowed sweetly on her tongue. 'Tonic is right,' she said.

'Every night before dinner,' he said. 'Tell your mother I said so.' He yawned, hugely. 'I'm supposed to be going to the ballet tonight,' he said. 'I hope the music's loud enough to keep me awake.'

'What's the ballet?'

'*Le Coq d'Or.*'

'You'll stay awake,' she said.

'You've seen it then?'

'I was going to,' said Jane, 'but Mummy thinks the theatre excites me too much.'

'Go anyway,' he said. 'Just forget to tell her.'

'Is that your professional advice?'

'No,' he said. 'I just want you to see the ballet.' He reached for another cigarette. 'You're coming back to see me next week?'

'I expect so,' she said. 'Mummy doesn't mind my drinking – if it's sherry.'

'Then it's time I made you one of my speeches.'

'Very well,' she said.

The lighter flared, and he squinted at her through a grey-blue haze. 'I may act like God,' said Lockhart, 'because that's the only way we'll get anywhere. But remember I'm human, Jane. I make mistakes, just like everybody else.'

'I'll just have to risk that,' she said. 'And anyway – I bet you God doesn't smoke.'

He laughed so hard that he choked and she had to pound his back.

'God wouldn't need that either,' she said.

Maybe it was the sherry that decided her against taking a bus. From Harley Street to Aunt Pen's in Mount Street by underground was difficult, and in any case the darkness made her nervous. A bus would have been more feasible but tedious, and a taxi just happened to be passing as she left Lockhart's rooms. . . . The real complication was the money. Daughters of good family, even ageing daughters like herself, simply weren't given enough. A tiny allowance had to take care of such things as coffees and face powder, as well as transport, and there was never enough, despite the fact that Aunt Pen bunged her the occasional fiver, or even tenner. Money just seemed to disappear. For Jane a stocking prematurely laddered was like a budget crisis, indeed *was* a budget crisis, – but fortunately Mummy had sent her shopping a couple of days ago and forgotten to reclaim her change. Not theft, she told herself. Spoils of war, and hailed her taxi.

London traffic since the war had increased enormously. Mummy called it impossible, but then Mummy's idea of comfortable motion was a tonga or a phaeton – or even an elephant, Jane thought. Certainly not a motor car, unless it was both big and expensive. A Rolls-Royce perhaps, or a Hispano-Suiza. . . . From inside the cab she looked at the Austin Sevens and little Morrises shooting by, and the occasional Rileys and Jowetts nosing among the buses. One of them would be fine to own, perfect even, she thought. And there'd be no problem in driving it. If you could drive a wartime ambulance you could drive anything, even a London bus. A little Morris would be as easy as pie. . . . But that would be pie in the sky if you like. Mummy had even vetoed a bicycle (so unladylike) and a horse (the *feed* bills, child).

The taxi arrived at Mount Street, and the figure on the meter meant she'd have to walk home, unless Aunt Pen sent her home in the Daimler. But even if she forgot, the warm spring night was fine and she would have Foch for company, so she smiled at the cabbie as she paid him off and went to lift the knocker of Aunt Pen's front door.

Mummy hated Aunt Pen's house – not because it was ugly, it

was in fact, rather beautiful in its own spare, clean-lined Georgian way – but because it was rich, as everything about Aunt Pen was rich, including her butler, Marchmont, now opening the door: tall and stout and stately as a bishop. A parlourmaid just wasn't the same. Not that they always had parlourmaids. Parlourmaids were difficult, according to Mummy, and had aspirations inappropriate to their calling. Parlourmaids were apt to speak their minds and leave. On a bad day the best you could hope for would be Hawkins in a clean apron. On a really bad day it would be Mummy.

Aunt Pen was Daddy's sister, a small, pretty woman with a dry and delicate wit who had married into trade in the reign of Edward VII. It had been, as Mummy never tired of saying, a quite shattering thing to do, but yet she'd done it, marched up the aisle of the Anglican Cathedral in Delhi as if, so she told Jane later, the massed ranks of her disapproving family were ranged between her and Walter. Walter Nettles. I mean what a name! And a box-wallah, a commercial traveller sort of fellow who travelled around all over India taking orders for machinery, with all his worldly goods corded up in a stout, termite-proof box: hence his nickname.

But Penelope Whitcomb had adored him from the time she first danced with him, adored him – and yet studied him critically too, and what she saw was a man stubborn and determined, with a gift for commerce, and family connections with an up-and-coming light-engineering firm. So she'd fluttered her fingers at the lancer subaltern and ICS administrator who'd seemed to be making all the running, and shoved her way to the altar, become Mrs Nettles, and never regretted it, not for a minute, except that she'd never had children. . . . What she had got was a house in Mayfair and a butler and a Daimler, and a much-loved niece who was all she had to worry about, now that her Walter had gone.

Marchmont led her into the drawing room, where her Aunt Pen's empty seat was flanked by Foch on one side, and her aunt's own dog, an Airedale called Rob, on the other. The two existed together in a state of armed neutrality, but would always combine against an interloper. When she came in, Rob yawned, but Foch was up at once, looking reproachful, and indeed she had been gone for a long time.

'I shall tell Mrs Nettles you are here, miss,' said Marchmont.

Jane looked about her. Always there were flowers, whatever the season, and that evening the room glowed with roses. There were the kind of chairs and settees that promised sleep without dreams, let alone nightmares, and a Persian carpet that must have made even her rich Uncle Walter think twice before he bought it.

She sat down and Foch, after peering at her through the thickets of his eyebrows, sat down too. There were Indian treasures about her: good, old ivory and brass, a few small Moghul pictures, some photographs in silver frames: Aunt Pen, and Mr Nettles (it was a long time before he could be called Uncle Walter), Mummy and Papa, Guy and David and herself, and baby Francis in the ayah's arms. Ootacamund, that must have been. 1905 or 1906. Snooty Ooty. The magic land. . . .

One went there because of the heat on the plains in summer time, the heat that really was what all the clichés said it was: heat that struck you like a blow; burned the strength out of you; drove you crazy – sometimes literally. Heat like hell, searing and relentless. Heat that was in effect an invincible army, her father used to say. One could either surrender – or take to the hills.

And such hills, the hills of Ootacamund, five thousand feet above the scorching plain. Hills where water flowed, and grass was green, and the roses bloomed on and on and on, and the climate was like a perfect English summer's day, each day and every day. Guy and David used to practise cricket, she remembered, and she being a girl and youngest of the three was condemned to being forever a fielder, whoever batted or bowled, until one day the syce told Papa – up in Ooty for a weekend visit, – that she, Jane, could outride her brothers. He'd demanded to be shown, and she'd proved it, and from there on she'd ridden her pony. It had been the servants' children who took her place at point or third man or deep square leg.

She had loved that pony. It had been a bay filly called Rani, kindly yet courageous, and she could close her eyes and see it as clearly as she could close her eyes and see Foch. And when she did close her eyes to see Rani, all the rest came back, too: the roses and the curry smells, the kites and the brown arms of her ayah. Twenty years ago and more, and all she had to do was close her eyes and remember. Just like the war. . . .

3

HER AUNT CAME in, small and bustling, always determined to be on time, and never succeeding.

'Jane, dearest,' she said. 'Forgive me. I had to practise.'

What was it this time, Jane wondered. The piano? The ukulele? The Charleston?

'Quite all right, Aunt,' she said.

'But you looked so serious,' her aunt said.

'I was just – remembering,' said Jane.

Her aunt said warily, 'Do you think that's a good idea?'

'Ootacamund,' said Jane, and at once her aunt relaxed. 'All those years ago.'

'Really Jane,' her Aunt Pen said, 'it wasn't all that many years ago. How could it be? You're just a girl. I mean look at you.'

'I'm thirty-two,' said Jane.

'Yes, but do you think you should say so?' her Aunt Pen said. 'Especially when you look like you do. . . . I hope you don't make a habit of telling people your age.'

'I told my doctor.'

'He'd know anyway,' said her Aunt Pen. 'Doctors always find out your age first thing. It's all part of the power they seek. . . . How was he?'

'Kind,' said Jane. 'He's always kind.'

Her aunt would have none of that. 'Was he any *use*?' she said.

Jane said, 'He can't help me. Nobody can. I've got to help him, it seems.'

'Well at least Guy's made sure you can go to see him. Maybe you can help each other. . . . I phoned your mother.'

'What about?'

'Dinner,' said her aunt. 'I thought you might have it with me.'

'Oh goody. – Is it permitted?'

'Well of course it is,' her aunt said. 'I wish you wouldn't talk like that.' And then, with one of those oblique exercises in logic Sir Guy called Penelope's knight's moves, she asked, 'Why did you bring Foch here? I mean he's perfectly welcome. – Just ignore what Rob says. But why?'

Jane said carefully, 'Mummy thinks that Foch excites me too much.'

'Oh dear,' said her aunt, and then, another knight's move, 'she adored Guy and David.'

And there it was. Thirty seconds, maybe even less, to reach a conclusion she'd spent all morning on.

'She adores your brother Francis too,' Aunt Pen said. To anyone but Pen it would have been a statement of fact, but Pen knew it was a warning.

They dined in the first-floor dining room, Marchmont and a footman in attendance even though there were only the two of them and the table reduced, and Jane watched delighted as champagne was opened and poured.

'How dashing,' she said.

'Your mother said you were in need of a tonic.'

'I had one at Dr Lockhart's.'

'Another one won't hurt you,' said her aunt.

They talked of India. It was strange, Jane thought. Both of them were homesick for it, and neither had the least intention of going back there. Of course with her, money was the obstacle, as always, but not to Aunt Pen. And yet, Jane knew, Aunt Pen would never go back. The homesickness was for an era, a state of mind, even more than for a physical place. For Jane it was the memory of a little girl her ayah said was beautiful, yet a little girl who could outride her brothers. Watching her take Rani over the jumps had frightened her ayah, frightened her so much that she'd taken her to a holy man, a saddhu, to find out whether she should continue to risk her neck – and her beauty. The saddhu was adamant. He'd spoken in Hindi, but she'd under-stood, and remembered, every word.

– 19 –

'She must go on,' he'd said. 'Great things await this child.'

'But will she be safe?' The ayah had no wish for greatness.

The saddhu smiled then. For the ayah it had been a smile of pity at such weakness, but for Jane it was more like complicity.

'To the leopardess you do not speak of safety,' he said. 'To be safe is the ambition of the deer.'

Jane pushed away determinedly what was left of her île flottante. Really, Aunt Pen's cook would make a gourmet out of even that saddhu.

'I wasn't much of a leopardess, was I?' she asked.

'You saved a lot of leopards,' her aunt said.

Jane said, 'Some were leopards of course. Even tigers. But there were deer too, and sheep, and monkeys. . . . All sorts and conditions of men. All they had in common was that they'd been hurt.'

She looked at her champagne glass.

'I'm beginning to talk nonsense,' she said.

'On the contrary,' her aunt said. 'You're beginning to talk sense. Fill Miss Whitcomb's glass, Marchmont, and mine,' she added as an afterthought, 'then later we'll take coffee in the drawing room. *Strong* coffee.'

Like many people who'd grown up in India, Mrs Nettles assumed that servants always knew everything about one's business. Even so she dismissed them before she asked her question.

'Did you ever see a painting called "The Judgement of Paris"?' she asked.

'I don't know,' said Jane. 'I don't often remember pictures.'

'You'd remember this one. It's frightfully rude. Three girls with no clothes on being stared at by a chappie in a sheepskin. He's supposed to be deciding which is the prettiest. I must say he seems to be taking his time about it.' She smiled then at Jane, and Jane remembered how incredibly beautiful her aunt had once been, not because of perfection of feature so much as that she was so alive.

'That was me or I or whatever it is,' said Aunt Pen.

'Standing about with no clothes on being stared at?'

'No, silly,' her aunt said. 'Doing the staring.'

'Oh the suitors,' said Jane.

'The suitors. Exactly.' Aunt Pen stared rather mistily into

the distance as if inspecting them. Clothed or unclothed? Jane wondered.

'Darling Jeremy,' said Aunt Pen. 'Beautiful Jeremy. He looked wonderful in full-dress uniform – and three thousand a year of his own. . . . And Richard. Clever *clever* Richard. Handsome devil. Scholar of Winchester, scholar of King's, double first. Bound to be a collector at least. Burra Sahib of Burra Sahibs. . . .'

'And Uncle Walter?'

'Not the most obvious winner of a beauty prize? No doubt you're right, though I never looked at him in that way. He was exciting, you see.'

'Exciting?'

Jane had drunk too much to hide her surprise, but then her aunt had drunk too much to be offended.

'Certainly exciting,' she said. 'He didn't shoot tigers or go pig-sticking like Jeremy, or make decrees and things like Richard. – He did more. He risked all his money, every penny he had, on deal after deal. And he shared it all with me. Every time. Exciting wasn't the word.'

'And he never went wrong?'

'Not after I met him,' her aunt said. 'Not until the very end, till the day he said to me, "It's only a bit of a cold. I'll be fine tomorrow."' Her voice took on Mancunian overtones in loving mimicry, then became her own again.

'They were the last words he ever spoke to me,' she said. 'Five hours later he was dead. The doctor told me he'd never known a case of Spanish 'flu so quick. But that was Walter. Always in a hurry. . . .' She shuddered. 'I've been lucky in love, wouldn't you say?'

'Extremely,' said Jane.

'There wasn't much luck the night he died on me. . . . People say that what you've never had you never miss. What do you think?'

'It's obviously true enough in logic,' said Jane. 'But it's a pretty negative attitude, isn't it? Cowardly even.'

'There speaks the leopardess,' said Aunt Pen.

Over coffee, hot and plentiful and very strong, her aunt said: 'I want to ask you something.'

'Very well.'

'I'm damn lonely,' her aunt said. 'If Walter were here he'd say

– 21 –

bloody lonely, but then if Walter were here it wouldn't be true.
Where was I?'

'Being lonely.'

'Well I am,' said her aunt, 'and I don't suppose your life's one
giddy whirl of pleasure, so what I was thinking was why don't
you come and live with me for a while? Be my companion?. . .
Not that I'd call you that. Companions always sound to me like
faded little women in sensible shoes and cotton next the skin.
Still it would be nice to have you here.'

'It would be lovely,' said Jane. 'But I can't.'

'Why not?' Aunt Pen asked. 'Guy could have no objection.'

'Mummy could – '

'Honoria,' Aunt Pen said. 'Of course.'

' – But it isn't her, either,' said Jane. 'It's me or I or whatever
it is.'

'What about you?'

'Sometimes I'm not entirely sane,' said her niece. 'Or you
could put it another way. Sometimes I'm as mad as a hatter. –
Dreaming and screaming all night long. That's not the way for
a companion to behave.'

'I could put up with it.'

'But I couldn't,' said Jane. 'I mean I couldn't put up with you
putting up with me.' She repeated the phrase in her head. *It
seemed* all right, but, 'I think I'd better have some more coffee,'
she said.

'There must be something I can do for you,' said her aunt.

'There's one thing.'

'Tell me.'

'You could let me have some money from time to time. I mean
you do already and I'm grateful – but if it could be more regular.
Ten bob a week say – or even a pound.'

'Well of course,' said her aunt, and then: 'But don't you have
any money?'

'Mummy thinks I don't need it.'

'She *can't* think that,' said Aunt Pen.

'She says she never did, when she was a girl in India.'

Aunt Pen said, 'India was different.'

'Well of course it was,' said Jane. 'In India Mummy never took
a bus.'

'Thirty bob a week do you?' her aunt asked.

– 22 –

'That's far too much,' said Jane. 'All I want is bus fares and cinema tickets and the odd pair of stockings.'

'Squander the rest then.' Her aunt searched in her bag, handed over two folded bank notes.

'You know Walter and I had a sort of ambition for you,' she said. 'Or maybe it was for us. One day we were going to spoil you rotten. I don't think he'd consider thirty bob a week was going too far.'

Foch and Jane went home in the Daimler, of which Foch approved, particularly its upholstery. For Jane its principal attraction was watching the chauffeur drive. On balance she thought that she herself was just a little bit better, but not after Dr Lockhart's amontillado and Aunt Pen's Krug.

Her mother said, 'Really your sister keeps most inconsiderate hours.'

Sir Guy looked at the bracket clock on the mantelshelf. It said ten seventeen and was always right.

'Hardly the middle of the night, my dear,' he said.

'When she *knew* that we would be anxious about Jane – '

'Well Jane's here now to tell us about it.'

'Do you mean about Dr Lockhart?' Jane asked.

'What else could your father mean?'

'Nothing Mummy.'

'Then get on with it,' Mummy said. 'We're your parents. You're our child. Does it not occur to you that we may be concerned?'

'Dr Lockhart considers that I've lost too much weight,' said Jane.

'It hardly needs a three-guinea consultation fee to tell us that.'

'He also considers that his fees should be paid by the War Department, if only I would fill in the necessary forms. He considers that what has happened to me is in the nature of a war wound.'

'Rubbish,' her mother said. 'You are quite unmarked.'

Unblemished, Mummy? Is that the word you seek?

Aloud she said, 'When my ambulance was strafed he considers that there may have been actual damage – physical damage – '

'It was nothing worse than a motoring accident,' her mother

said. 'You told me yourself – you carried on with your – job.'

'He considers that there may have been brain damage,' said Jane.

'Then he'll get no more three guineas from me. You may be nervous – that I do not deny – and you certainly dream too much, which is probably due to your diet – but you are not insane.'

'Oh hush, Honoria,' Jane's father said. 'Of course she's not insane. No one's suggesting that she is. But she served like a man in the war, and she's paying the price that some men are paying.' He raised his voice to drown out her interruption.

'Chaps I see at the club,' he said. 'Their sons – perhaps their nephews. Beddoes's boy, and Sinclair's. That young cousin of Brett-Lewis. All the same as Jane, except that some of them are a dashed sight worse.' He turned to his daughter. 'I don't say you're lucky, my dear, but you're luckier than some. . . . Shell shock they call it, don't they?'

'Yes, Papa. And it's true what you say. There are lots who are far far worse than me.'

For a moment Lady Whitcomb seemed outraged that her daughter should have a minor and therefore inferior version of any affliction that could affect the officer class, particularly one inspired by patriotism, but this was going too far even for her.

'You shouldn't have it at all,' she said.

Not for the first time Jane marvelled that this grotesque clown had once been the mother who loved her.

'If that dreadful man Nettles hadn't bought you an ambulance – ' her mother said. She made it sound like a superior kind of pram.

'Uncle Walter didn't buy me an ambulance,' said Jane. 'He paid for one. It was his contribution to the war effort.'

'He made you drive it.'

Jane said patiently, 'He didn't *make* me. I volunteered and was accepted. And Uncle Walter suggested it would be nice for the family if I drove *his* ambulance.'

Of course it hadn't been quite like that, not really. The odds were she wouldn't have gone to France at all if Uncle Walter hadn't paid. But that was none of Mummy's business.

'You should have asked permission,' her mother said.

All the old arguments were to be trotted out, it seemed.

'You and Papa were in India,' said Jane, 'and Aunt Pen said it was all right.'

'You are not Penelope's daughter,' her mother said, 'which makes it far from all right.'

'I was over twenty-one,' said Jane, 'and the war was going badly. By driving an ambulance I was able to release one more man for the fighting. Somebody had to do it, Mummy. It just happened to be me because I could drive.'

'That ghastly Nettles taught you, I suppose,' said Lady Whitcomb, then surprised her husband and daughter, and very possibly herself, by bursting into tears. The two of us in one day, Jane thought, and went to put her arms round Mummy because Papa was looking at her in a way that said, 'Don't ask me, – not any more,' – but Mummy didn't want to be comforted.

They were living in Kalpur, in an Indian state of middling size, and a population two thirds Hindu, one third Muslim. Papa was there as native adviser or resident to the maharajah, because the usual resident was being operated on for appendicitis. Kalpur was fine. They had a big bungalow, masses of servants and a vast maidan nearby where Rani could really go. And there was an elephant to take them on picnics and a Jersey cow that followed the elephant so that they could have fresh milk.

She and Guy and David liked Kalpur, but Mummy found it boring and Papa found it dreadful. The trouble was the maharajah. Officially he was a Hindu, but his real religion was cricket. Quite early in his career he had watched the great Ranjitsinhji bat, and had known, from then on, what his purpose in life was. (Ranjitsinhji had made one hundred and twenty-three not out against a British Army eleven, and both facts had their significance, Papa thought. The one two three struck some deep numerological chord, and to see the British Army thrashed by a princely Hindu held a more immediate significance.) The maharajah instantly caused a cricket pitch to be constructed at vast expense, as well as nets for practice, and a coach was hired from Bombay, a halfcaste who divided his time between cricket and the rajah's Scotch, and one who, drunk or sober, understood the maharajah's cricketing needs as poor Papa never had.

The trouble was that the maharajah played cricket so that he might appear triumphant. He didn't much care whether his side won, but it was vital, even inevitable, that he personally must triumph: a century in every game, and five wickets for fifty runs, or less. To this end the halfcaste, whose name was Hamish Buchanan, spent his working day rehearsing not only the maharajah's team mates, but the opposition also. (Opposing teams were invariably either the maharajah's subjects, or hired by him for money.)

Buchanan acted as a kind of ballet master or choreographer, drilling his white-flannelled corps de ballet in the mis-hits, dropped catches and fumbling on the boundary that would yet again allow the maharajah to raise his bat as a hundred was scored, or lead in the fielding side to a standing ovation (the spectators also were the maharajah's subjects).

At first the maharajah had been dubious of the potentialities of a cricketer called Hamish Buchanan. The Scots were not among the great names of cricket. But once Buchanan had demonstrated his talents as a régisseur all doubts were resolved, and cricket dominated the life of the state for at least five days of the week. The permanent resident approved thoroughly. Cricket was expensive, but not nearly as expensive as chorus girls or race horses or trips to Deauville and Monte Carlo. Moreover the maharajah would agree to anything, even sign anything, if one asked him just before it was his turn to bat. And so, as the resident knew his business, the state of Kalpur prospered and was happy, except for the inevitable gloom occasioned by the advent of the rains, and even that wasn't so bad when Buchanan rigged up an indoor practice pitch in the great hall of the palace, and the maharajah doubled his salary.

The trouble for Papa was caused by the fact that he too was a cricketer. The permanent resident had left careful notes of course, before he took the train for Delhi and the operation that King Edward VII had made so popular. The trouble was that Papa didn't get them – or at least not all of them. They had been censored. The permanent resident suspected Hamish Buchanan when they discussed it later, but Papa blamed the maharajah himself. Whoever it was, poor Papa had acted as he did out of an ignorance that amounted to innocence.

For Papa played cricket rather well. He was a goodish medium-paced bowler and a useful enough batsman at say six or seven, who had played for his college and had come close to a blue. It had seemed to Papa a good idea that he should turn out for a game at the first possible opportunity. Unfortunately, the maharajah refused to have Papa in his, the maharajah's eleven. His memory of his princely hero putting the Raj to rout was as fresh and green as ever. And so Papa turned out for the visiting eleven, the only man among the twenty-two – twenty-four if one counted the umpires, or several hundred if one added in the spectators – who did not know that he was foredoomed to lose.

The maharajah won the toss and elected to bat: the very coin he spun had been made to Hamish Buchanan's specifications. Even so, Papa bowled the maharajah first ball. The umpire called 'No ball', of course, even if it was a little late. In fact both umpires called 'No ball'. Hamish Buchanan had schooled them well. In the course of that innings Papa clean bowled the maharajah six times, and was no-balled every time. And yet Papa took six wickets for seventy-one runs. The maharajah was eighty-nine not out.

When it was his team's turn to bat, Papa scored seventeen runs in his first over, which was bowled by Hamish Buchanan. In his second over, when he faced the maharajah, he was given out lbw first ball, which he had touched with neither bat nor pad, nor any part of his anatomy. Papa left the pitch with an urgent need for a very large whisky and soda, followed by violent exercise. (The maharajah went on to take all ten wickets for seventeen runs.)

He took his stengah into his wife's sitting room, which was an unusual thing to do. His usual drink there was Earl Grey tea. His wife he discovered closeted with his daughter. They appeared to be grappling with French irregular verbs. Papa demanded an explanation, then looked at his whisky and soda, only to discover he'd just finished it, and yelled for another.

'Really Guy,' his wife began.

'An emergency,' said Papa. 'An absolute emergency, I assure you. His Highness has behaved in a way I had thought impossible for one human being to behave to another, always supposing he *is* human.'

He moved, rather stiffly, to a chair, and found he was still wearing cricket pads. He began to unbuckle them.

'That still doesn't explain the future perfect of "venir",' he said.

'It's young Guy,' said his wife.

'Oh Lord,' said their father. 'What's he up to now?'

'He's taken to speaking in Latin,' said their mother.

The bearer brought in whisky, soda and a glass on a tray, and Papa swopped them for his cricket pads.

'I thought only the Pope spoke in Latin,' he said.

'I hope he speaks it better than Guy. Ave mater dum est pabulum, indeed.'

'I *think* that means Hallo Mother, when is lunch?' said Jane.

'More or less,' said her father. 'Except it's more like when's fodder. Is David doing it too?'

'He says he prefers speaking in Greek,' their mother said.

'Quite right too. He's got a good chance of a scholarship to Rugby.'

'No doubt,' said her mother. 'But there isn't one single person in the place who can understand him – except you. So this young lady and I' – she stroked Jane's hair affectionately, 'decided to bone up on our French. At least we can talk to each other. – But why on earth aren't you playing cricket?'

'I've made the most extraordinary discovery,' said Papa. 'The bloody man cheats. At *cricket*.'

'Guy!' Her mother's voice was sharp enough, but there was the hint of a giggle in it.

'I apologise unreservedly,' said Papa, 'to both of you. But it's true.'

'Well of course it's true,' said Jane.

'And how do you know, miss?' her father asked.

'Everybody knows.'

'And who told you?'

'Ayah,' said Jane. 'She told me the first day we got here.'

'And did she tell you why he cheats?'

'Because he has to win.'

'Has to?' Papa said. 'What do you mean, has to?'

Really men can be awfully stupid, she thought. Even very clever men like Papa.

She said patiently, 'He's the maharajah, Papa.'

'Great God Almighty,' Papa said, but before Mummy could call him to order he began to laugh.

'All those players, all that crowd,' he said. 'And I was the only one who didn't know that in Kalpur cricket matches are preordained.' He bowed gravely to his daughter. 'Thank you for enlightening me. . . . Would you like to come for a ride, – or is the verb venir still unmastered?'

'Both of us have thought for quite long enough,' Mummy said. 'Jane's worked hard. She deserves a ride.'

So they'd changed while the syces brought the horses round, and for once ayah hadn't tweaked the elastic that held her solar topee in place. When the elastic snapped back it was very painful, but one mustn't cry, mustn't even call out. Her brother Guy had made that rule, and he was quite right. Her syce put her up and she settled at once, Rani ready to go, and yet responsive to her touch. They set off past the orange and lemon trees that encircled the bungalow with their nicely blended fragrance, on past the mangoes to the road that led to the palace, where the gardens ran wild because the gardeners spent all their time and skill on the cricket pitch, then turned off past the paddy fields where the kites screamed and soared high above them, and into the jungle. There was a path of sorts, worn down by the feet of villagers taking a shortcut from their village to their fields, a path that twisted and wriggled its way through undergrowth green as a bottle, unyielding and impenetrable except for the path. Dark, too. Not black but dark, like the inside of a church, because the trees grew dense and high and arched like a roof, and the creepers too grew dark with a green that was close to black; only the flowers held the glow of life, strong, vivid splodges of white and yellow and red; and all around them huge butterflies fluttered, birds sang or shouted or screamed, monkeys chattered and scolded and screamed back at the birds. And it would all have been jolly frightening, of course it would, except that Papa was with her, and with Papa beside her there was no need to be afraid of anything, because Papa was collector of Mussoorie District as well as acting resident of Kalpur.

Suddenly Papa reined in his horse, motioned her to stop, and pointed with his riding crop. Jane watched in silence as a herd of wild pigs crossed the path, a big boar in the lead, then a line of half-grown piglets with mamma pig following on behind nudging the others into a pack like the whipper-in of a hunt. Papa waited till the path was cleared, the sound of their progress through the forest faded, then he turned back to her.

'The Maharajah of Kalpur's Second Eleven,' he said, and winked, and Jane laughed aloud. Then afterwards they had a most wonderful gallop across the maidan and it didn't matter in the least that David and Guy were still spouting their silly old Latin and Greek, because now she could fight back with the future perfect tense of 'venir'.

Later over tea in the schoolroom David told them that he'd read somewhere that an American called Wright had flown off the ground in something called an aeroplane.

'Just the sort of stupid thing an American would do,' said Guy.

'That is xenophobic,' David said. 'I think flying's a good idea. One day I shall do it myself.'

'Like Icarus?' Jane asked. Not long before, Mummy had started her on Greek mythology.

'Certainly not,' David said. 'Icarus flew too high and was killed.'

Jane ignored the rebuke: she was happy. Despite that odd word 'xen-' something, they were at least speaking English.

4

I T HAD BEEN, she thought, one of the happiest days of her life
before John. It had stayed clear in her mind because Papa
had asked her to copy out the notes he'd made on it for his
autobiography: *Indian Days and Indian Ways. A Sahib Remembers.*
A book that would be for ever unwritten, she thought, but then
Papa didn't enjoy writing: he enjoyed remembering. . . . She
stretched out in the bed. A sliver of moonlight penetrated the
curtain, caught and held the eye like a magic sword, but she
made no move to pull the curtains together. If moonlight chose
to keep her awake, then thank you moon, because the only
alternative to wakefulness was sleep, and sleep, as the bard so
aptly put it, meant perchance to dream, except that there
wouldn't be any perchance about it, and it wouldn't be a dream
either. It would be the same bloody nightmare.

And of course it was. But this time she didn't wake up screaming. This time the nightmare went on and on. Which was absolutely right and proper, because this time the nightmare was the
retreat to the Channel ports, the 'backs to the wall' retreat of
1918, and that really had gone on and on, and the only way not
to see the wounded, malformed soldiers limping along beside
her was to stare straight ahead through the windscreen where
the night bombardment of our guns flickered like the light of a
cinema projector, flashing ever brighter so that she might see
the wounded horses.

But if she screamed aloud no one told her, or maybe, she
thought, the sound of the guns drowned out her screams. And

then she thought: now I really am going crazy. Now I'm treating nightmare and reality as if they were the same thing, and that could only be one more step down the wrong road. Now, she thought, I really have become useless. 'Surplus to requirement' the army called it. And so she was: beyond even Lockhart's skill and compassion. Now then was the time to die. It was obvious. Mummy detested her and Papa did his best but his heart was too weak, and if she were out of the way there were others to take her place with Jabber, more receptive patients, and probably more deserving, too. And even if Aunt Pen loved her, she didn't want to be saddled with a lunatic.

The trouble was how to do it. There was drowning, and the Thames wasn't far, but Papa had taught her to swim in the big tank at Kalpur, and Jane knew without doubt that she couldn't possibly find herself in deep water and not swim. Moreover she was a strong swimmer, and would almost certainly be rescued, probably with maximum humiliation: hair awry, wet clothes clinging, but not prettily. . . . She could, she thought, have shot herself had a gun been available, but it wasn't. Papa had given his away many years ago. Knives meant disfigurement like her nightmares and the only pills in the house were for Mummy's dyspepsia; Jabber had seen to that. Sleeping tablets were issued only on application, and never more than two at a time, and to save them up would amount to a kind of betrayal. Besides, who would take pills to bring on dreams like hers? Killing one's self was almost as difficult as keeping one's self sane, she thought.

And then she remembered Foch. It was wicked, it was downright sinful, that she had ever forgotten him. If she, Jane, died, Mummy would give him away. And maybe that would be a good thing, but only maybe. Mummy wouldn't worry about whether he went to a good home or not. She'd be too busy hating her dear daughter for the harm she'd done to the name of Whitcomb.

Then her obstinate honesty took over. And why not? she asked herself. Her suicide might solve her own problems, but it compounded everybody else's. She'd just have to go on living, she thought, then giggled in self-mockery. Goodness how decent I am. How brave. And all because a Scotch terrier needs me as much as I need him.

She went down to breakfast warily. Now that Hawkins was whacking into her chocolate bikkies she could at least manage some toast. Her father had already gone to his study to fiddle happily with notes and invitation cards and fading snapshots.

Her mother said, 'We have had a postcard. From Francis.'

'Oh yes?' said Jane.

'I had hoped for a little more enthusiasm,' her mother said. 'He is your brother after all. And he's away all term.'

'I hope he's well,' said Jane.

'You may judge for yourself,' said her mother. 'He has permission to come up to London – he and a friend. They are attending a meeting here, so naturally they will stay the night in London.'

Jane buttered her toast, and added marmalade. If she were to have a social life she must keep up her strength.

'What sort of meeting?'

'Political,' her mother said. 'Your father disapproves of it. – Naturally he would.'

'Why naturally?'

'Young men always adopt a political stance their elders disapprove of,' said her mother. 'Your father should be aware of that. In his younger days he twice voted Liberal. . . . I think perhaps we should have some cheese. Young men *need* a cheese course. Can I trust you to buy me some?'

'Of course, Mummy.'

'Then do so.'

'On account?' Jane asked. 'Or shall I pay cash?'

On account meant Harrods, which was far too expensive for undergraduate cheese. Reluctantly Mummy reached for her purse. . . .

Jane walked down the steps of Number 17, Offley Villas, and drew on her gloves. It was ridiculous to cover up her hands on a warm day, but Mummy had told her – and it was true – that no real lady ever went out without gloves, and so, 'Gloves will be worn.' But Jane rarely went out without Foch either, and there he was, briskly trotting beside her, the bushy eyebrows and enquiring eyes giving him the air of a cantankerous scholar. There was a look of self-satisfaction in his strut that day, she thought, and looked down at him.

'You needn't go giving yourself airs just because you saved

me from suicide,' she said. 'Jabber Lockhart helped you after all.'

Foch snorted, and strutted on.

Old Mrs Blyth-Tarkington, from Number 23, noticed the exchange and approved. A dog needed conversation like everybody else.

As Jane came up to her she said, 'They understand, you know, Miss Whitcomb.'

'Yes,' said Jane. 'I rather think they do.'

All the same, on the way to the High Street all she talked about was cheese, and on the way back, on the detour through Kensington Gardens, she didn't talk at all. Foch was too busy bossing every other small dog in sight to listen.

Instead she thought about Francis. She had never – the thought had to be faced – been close to Francis, as she had been to David and Guy. But then the reason was obvious enough. Lady Whitcomb's first three children had arrived at yearly intervals. She'd had to wait nine more years before Francis was born.

It must have been a struggle, she thought. The big three – so they must have seemed – always together, playing together, laughing together and, even though one was a girl, being siblings together, because they all looked alike. They really did. Tallish, fairish, loose-jointed, and all of them, all three, blessed with a marvellous co-ordination of eye and hand which made them good sportsmen, games players, equestrians. Laughing and effortless, that was the Whitcomb style, so David used to say. But he'd been quite young when he'd said it. David had never been anything other than quite young.

And then there was Francis. At first it had seemed to Jane that he wasn't a Whitcomb at all, for Francis was dark, rather short, and by no means slender. Not frightfully good at games, either, nor at laughing, and without the conventional good looks (what David had called 'the rather obvious prettiness') of the other three. Instead he'd been given a face to portray his moods: anger, gloom, despair, and occasionally a happiness close to ecstasy. But always he was beautiful. Not pretty. Beautiful. For one breathtaking moment Jane had decided that he wasn't a Whitcomb at all, and then she realised that of course he was. He looked very much as her mother must have looked at the time she met Papa.

He'd done well, no question of it. Head of his class year after year at school, then a Cambridge scholarship and a first in Part One last year, and almost certainly a first in Part Two in – when was it? – two or three weeks' time? The political meeting must be important. Francis had never been one to neglect his studies: they were too important to him. All he had, in a way, perhaps because they were all he wanted.

Pure conjecture, she told herself. You know nothing about Brother Francis – but that was because she'd hardly ever seen him. He'd always been in the nursery, or away at school, or Cambridge, or she'd been at Aunt Pen's or at the war. Even so, she ought to know at least *something* about her own brother, if only he'd let her. But all she had to go on was that he was going to a political meeting of which Papa would not approve.

Anarchists? she wondered. But anarchists were out of date. They belonged to before the war – wild-looking Slavs with beards and bombs. Bolsheviks, she decided. Still Russian, but with a passion for pamphlets and points of order before the actual trigger-pulling. Francis would approve of that. He believed in justice from on high every bit as much as Papa had done.

Firmly Jane separated Foch from the fox-terrier, the spaniel, the poodle and the pug that he was trying to form into a Soviet.

'It would never work,' she told him. 'Not in England. And even if it did the borzois would take over.'

Foch snorted.

'You intellectuals,' she said. 'You always think you can stay in control when the violence starts – but you never can.' Then she thought of Lenin. 'Well hardly ever.'

This time Foch said nothing. He knows he's lost, thought Jane, which is more than Francis ever did – or me, or Guy or David come to that. Poor Papa.

When she got back she rang the bell instead of using her key, because of the cheese. Hawkins answered, which surprised Jane. The parlourmaid – (Charlton was it? Railton? Lawson?) her notice given, still had a week to go.

'Good Lord, Hawkins,' Jane said. 'Has she run away?'

'No miss,' said Hawkins. 'She's serving tea. Proper tea. . . . Mr Francis came down early.'

'Oh I see,' said Jane. 'Did he bring his friend?'

'Not arf,' said Hawkins.

'What on earth do you mean?'

'You just wait and see, miss,' Hawkins said. 'I don't want to spoil it for you.'

Her eye flicked shut then open, fast as a lizard's, but Jane received the message. She had been warned. Slow and easy, she told herself. We can't have you screaming, not when there's company here. She opened the drawing-room door and went in, walking as the deportment school had taught her, and Foch trudged by her side, wary as John Knox at the court of Queen Mary, and there they were: Mummy and Papa and Francis and his friend: a large and muscular friend, a year or two older than Francis, with that look peculiar to Cambridge (according to Papa) of the man who had absorbed all the knowledge it was decent for one man to have, and now felt it to be his duty to pass it on to others. (Daddy had gone to Merton College, Oxford.)

'Ah,' her mother said. 'Jane. How late you are child.' Nevertheless there was relief in her voice. 'Come and meet Mr Pardoe.'

Pardoe stood up. There was an awful lot of him, thought Jane.

'Mr Pardoe – my daughter Jane,' Mummy said, and Pardoe's hand engulfed hers.

'I'm delighted to meet you,' he said.

'You're an undergraduate friend of Francis?' she asked.

'Pardoe took a first,' her brother said. 'Next year he'll be a PhD.'

He sounded petulant, as if he were being forced to state a fact that everyone should know, and Pardoe nodded in agreement, though without answer.

'I also played rugger for my college and got a half blue in boxing,' Pardoe said. 'I'm a naturally aggressive person.'

For perhaps the thousandth time Jane found herself wishing that Guy and David were there to share what looked like being a pretty good tea party.

'How fascinating,' she said.

'Not fascinating, precisely.' Pardoe's correction was kind, but firm. 'But I think one might call it interesting.'

'Oh indeed,' said Jane. '*Indeed*. And is your kind of aggression restricted to punching other very large men?'

'That and manhandling them on the rugby field. But both these aggressive acts are circumscribed by a set of strictly administered rules. The aggression is controlled.'

Jane took a cucumber sandwich from a plate the parlourmaid, Thomson? Withers? offered to her.

'And do you feel that all young males should take part in acts of controlled aggression? Francis, for example?'

Pardoe said, 'Francis is not a physically aggressive person. As his sister surely you must be aware of that?'

'I've always found him forceful enough in discussion.'

'A Marx rather than a Trotsky. Quite so.'

Jane leaned over to straighten Foch's eyebrows and whispered, 'You didn't tell me you'd invited friends to tea,' then Lady Whitcomb poured out a cup of Earl Grey, and passed it to her daughter.

'You approve of the current state of affairs in Russia?' she asked.

'Naturally,' said Pardoe. 'It's nice to see a country run by a set of logical principles for a change.'

'And long overdue,' Francis said.

'But it's moving now. On the march. You'll see,' said Pardoe. 'Russia's only the beginning.'

'You see it coming here?' Jane asked.

'You live in Kensington, just as Francis and I live in Cambridge,' Pardoe said.

As if he were very kindly explaining some difficult concept hitherto beyond my grasp, thought Jane.

'But you mustn't confuse Kensington, or Cambridge, with the United Kingdon – or Great Britain as I prefer to call it.'

'I never do,' said Jane.

Again Francis gave her that resentful look, but not Pardoe, who was in full cry.

'Great Britain is the Rhondda Valley and Glasgow and Tyneside,' he said. 'The tragedy of our present – and the hope of our future.'

Jane sipped at her tea. It was to be a sermon after all. She assumed the expression of polite awareness appropriate to Sundays and Morning Prayer, and was told all about the proletariat, the regrettable absence of a peasantry in what Pardoe preferred to call Great Britain, and the rôle of the intellectual in fostering proletarian aspirations.

When Pardoe paused at last for breath, Lady Whitcomb asked, 'Why do you prefer to call our country Great Britain rather than the United Kingdom?'

It was the first time that Jane could see the tiniest dent in Pardoe's armour of utter certainty, but then Mummy's action hadn't been controlled. She had asked the wrong question, used an alien set of rules, like Ludendorff attacking at random, probing for weak spots, in early 1918, rather than advancing on an entire front.

Francis said, 'Really Mummy, after what you've just been told, isn't it obvious?'

Sir Guy said, 'No' – just that one word and no more, but for a moment Francis became a small boy again. Pardoe sensed it too, and hurried in at once.

'You must forgive us, Sir Guy,' he said. 'Certain facts have figured so long in our discussions that we rather take them to be self-evident to everyone.' He turned to Lady Whitcomb, and shrugged on once more his kindly manner, as if it were an academic gown.

'We prefer Great Britain because it is a reality,' he said. 'The United Kingdom is no more than a concept.'

'You're a republican,' said Lady Whitcomb. 'I see.'

She made republican sound as if it were an affliction – like diabetes, Jane thought. Unfortunate, but containable, if one obtained the proper treatment in time.

'A believer,' Pardoe corrected her, 'a very *humble* believer, in the dictatorship of the proletariat.'

This, thought Jane, was the moment when Papa should explode, and perhaps even have a heart attack too, and she saw at once that her mother was aware of it without precisely understanding why – but the doorbell rang instead, and the parlourmaid went off to answer it.

'Who on earth can that be?' Lady Whitcomb asked.

Francis shrugged, Jane guessed that it might be the vicar because it nearly always was, but it was Pardoe who spoke aloud.

'Oh good Lord,' he said, and turned to Francis. 'I say I'm most frightfully sorry, but I rather think I asked her to meet us here – and clean forgot to tell you.'

Foch heard the unfamiliar note of apology in Pardoe's voice and stood up and glowered at him. He's got the eyebrows for it, thought Jane, and the kind of utter certainty that only the Scots possess and not even Cambridge can vanquish, but then the parlourmaid – *Moreton*, that was it – ushered in the visitor, and all thought of the Foch-Pardoe conflict was forgotten.

For what Moreton ushered in was the pantomime fairy, the one in the tutu who waves her magic wand at the Demon King and intones:

Your wicked plans be sure I'll thwart
And see your schemings come to naught –

while the innocent babes sleep on in the wood. . . . Or else it was the Sugar Plum Fairy herself, Jane thought, exactly as Tchaikovsky had first thought of her. An ice-maiden perhaps, though one, she thought after a second look, who would thaw, even melt, in the right atmosphere.

'Miss Georgina Payne,' Moreton said.

Hair of gold that positively gleamed. Could it be real? – And did it matter? Eyes of *such* a blue, and they were real enough, and a little rosebud mouth and slender figure that no one would ever call thin.

'Georgie!' Pardoe called, and moved towards her, then her mother and father rose, and last of all Francis. Foch ventured one tentative yap, then tried to pretend it had never happened. Georgina Payne was not the type to be snarled at.

'Pardoe,' she said. 'You're impossible. Why didn't you warn me I'd be interrupting a tea party?' Then she turned and smiled at her host and hostess: the sort of smile, thought Jane, that really merited the adjective 'dazzling'. Even her mother smiled back. Her father was positively grinning. She wore a blue blouse and a white skirt that showed her knees and Mummy smiled.

Pardoe said, 'I rather think that I owe you an apology, Sir Guy.'

Her father said, 'Not at all,' but Pardoe had recovered.

'Oh yes,' he said. 'In society as it is at present constituted, I owe you an apology.'

'Rules,' said Jane helpfully. 'Control.'

'Precisely,' Pardoe said. 'Miss Payne is to accompany us to our meeting – '

'Are you?' said Jane. It seemed incredible.

'Oh yes,' Georgina Payne said. 'There's to be music. I've been hired to play it.'

'Engaged,' said Francis.

'I beg your pardon?'

The blue eyes could have melted an iceberg, thought Jane, but her brother was concerned only with definition.

'Hired has rather a bourgeois connotation,' he said.

'Are you – ?' Sir Guy fumbled to find words not offensive. 'Leftist in your views?'

'Where I live,' said Georgina Payne, 'which is sort of Chelsea, one does meet rather a lot of them. It's – interesting.'

'And what sort of music do they play?'

'Experimental of course,' said Miss Payne. 'They're mostly Central Europeans no one has ever heard of. There's one called Béla Bartók whom I rather like, but the comrades never seem to be able to make up their minds about him. – Whether he's bourgeois or not.'

'And do you like playing that kind of music?'

'It keeps me up to scratch,' said Miss Payne, 'but the cinema's better.'

'The cinema?' said Lady Whitcomb.

'The Alhambra, Fulham, actually,' said Miss Payne. 'I play the piano there. It's lots of fun.'

'Indeed?' said Lady Whitcomb.

'Well I enjoy it,' said Miss Payne. 'A bit repetitive of course – lots of Tchaikovsky for the love scenes – and for the battles too, sometimes. "1812" you know.' She turned to Francis. 'Not your kind of Russian at all, I should think. . . . Then there's Suppé's "Light Cavalry", and "William Tell" and "In a Persian Market". And ragtime too of course, if there's a party. What I mean is you don't have to concentrate. Not like Béla Bartók.'

'And yet you play Béla – er – Bartók,' said Lady Whitcomb.

'Well of course,' said Miss Payne.

'May one ask why?'

'Because they pay me.' To Georgina Payne this was a silly question, but perhaps, thought Jane, she already suspected, and rightly, that Mummy was a talented amateur. 'They're not *madly* generous, but then I don't suppose they've got very much money, and every little helps as the old lady said, and I haven't finished paying for this skirt yet.'

Francis said, 'We ought to be going.'

'No no,' said Sir Guy. 'Don't rush away.'

Mummy continued to cross-examine.

'Don't you ever get bored, playing in a cinema?'

'Honestly, it's practically automatic, after a while, like breathing,' said Miss Payne. 'You hardly notice you're doing it.'

'But – ragtime,' said Mummy. 'I mean you must have been classically trained.'

'Just round the corner,' said Miss Payne. 'The Royal College of Music.'

'Then how – '

'Just after I took my diploma I went to hear Pachmann,' said Miss Payne. 'Three years ago it must have been. Did you go?'

'I don't think I – '

'He played Chopin *of course*,' Miss Payne said, while Jane marvelled that anyone, least of all a girl, could interrupt Mummy twice and get away with it. 'But even he must have been feeling good that day – the way he played. The "Revolutionary Study", and the Waltz in D flat, and the Fantaisie Impromptu in C sharp minor. They were like nothing I'd ever heard before – or since for that matter. But in the bus on the way home – I lived in Battersea in those days – I found myself thinking I couldn't even get close to Pachmann if he had rheumatism in both hands – never mind when he plays like that. So I gave up starving in a garret and went to work at the pictures instead.'

'Did you?' Jane asked. 'Starve in a garret, I mean?'

The wink she gave Jane flicked on and off so quickly that it might never have happened, like Hawkins's.

'Well where I lived was pretty much of a garret,' said Miss Payne, 'but I didn't actually starve. I adore my food.'

Foch got up from Jane's side and went to sit beside Georgina Payne, a rare mark of approval. Jane rather wished she could do the same. Being next to Miss Payne was like being bombarded with life instead of death.

'What do your parents think of your profession?' Mummy asked.

'They don't,' said Miss Payne. 'They divorced quite soon after I was born. Mummy married a penniless viscount and went to live in Kenya, – in the Happy Valley. I must say it sounds rather fun to be penniless there.'

'And your father?'

'He was killed quite early on, at a place called Le Cateau,' Miss Payne said. 'He was a regular.'

'I lost two sons,' said Lady Whitcomb.

Sir Guy said, 'We very nearly lost a daughter too.'

Miss Payne turned to Jane, astounded.

'You don't mean you were in it?' she said.

'Well – yes,' said Jane.

'Were you a nurse?' Miss Payne asked. 'Or was it a concert party? Oh God I'd have given *anything* to play in a concert party near the Front.'

'Nothing so glamorous,' said Jane. 'I drove an ambulance.'

'You *didn't*!' Miss Payne's voice now took on a sort of school-girl's squeak, and she looked at her as a third-former might look at a hockey captain. 'My dear how romantic.'

'Hardly that,' said Jane.

'And gallant.' Georgina Payne had no time for interruptions that clashed with her preoccupations. 'Driving those poor boys, through shot and shell – '

'For heaven's sake don't let's discuss the war,' Francis said.

'Don't discuss anything,' said his father. 'It is quite obviously time you left us.'

Pardoe charged in at once, spraying out oil over a potential tempest. 'What Francis means,' he said, 'is that there is simply no point in discussing such a vast and unnecessary slaughter.'

'Unnecessary?' said Jane.

'Certainly,' said Pardoe. 'This was a war to enrich the bourgeois – and it did. It also was intended to subjugate the masses by the intimidation of slaughter, and that too it achieved.'

'So that all those millions died for nothing?' said Jane.

'I think you're being just a little too pessimistic,' Pardoe said. 'It seems to me that without that ludicrous war the 1917 revolution could not possibly have succeeded.'

'So that in effect my brothers died to help the Bolsheviks murder their Czar?'

'I detect,' Pardoe said roguishly, 'the merest soupçon of irony. But in general terms the answer to your question is yes. And you are not alone in your loss, you know. I myself was deprived of a brother-in-law – and a cousin.'

'How ghastly for you,' said Miss Payne, 'but we really should be off now.'

She rose to her feet and the two men followed. Foch thumped his tail on the carpet in applause. Foch, thought Jane, is a superb judge of character.

Sir Guy too rose, and shook Miss Payne's hand.

'A pleasure to meet you,' he said. 'I mean it.' He turned to his son. 'Dinner will be at seven fifteen,' he said. 'Precisely.'

Georgina Payne crossed the room to take Jane's hand, and Foch came with her. 'So wonderful to meet you,' she said. 'I do hope I'll see you again.'

'I hope so too,' said Jane, knowing it was impossible, because seeing her again meant friendship, and no one wants a lunatic for a friend.

After they had gone and Moreton had cleared away, Mummy asked, 'Why did the old lady say that every little helps?'

Her father looked at Jane and then away.

'I've no idea,' he said. 'Some sort of idiom that the young people use, I suppose.'

'She did in fact talk rather wildly,' said Lady Whitcomb, 'but she was not without sense – though scarcely a suitable companion for Jane.'

Well at least we're agreed on that, thought Jane, as Mummy got to her feet.

'I shall lie down for a while,' she said. 'Visitors for tea and then dinner too. Just like old times. Quite ghastly.'

She left them then, and her father said, 'Oh dear,' and took out his cigarette case. 'Your mother often enjoyed old times,' he said when his cigarette was lit, 'but often one entertained dreadful people then, as now, and she has always found that to be an ordeal.'

'She finds Mr Pardoe dreadful?'

'I should think anyone would,' said her father. 'Don't you?'

'Decidedly,' said Jane.

'Then for once you agree with your mother. Did you like Miss Payne?'

'Very much,' said Jane. 'But Mummy was right about her, too. We wouldn't suit.'

Her father began to laugh, then choked on his cigarette smoke.

'Your jokes are often quite witty,' he said, 'but they seem designed to wound everyone: yourself most of all.'

'I think we should finish with Mr Pardoe first,' said Jane.

'You're running away.'

'From you, Papa, yes – but not from Mr Pardoe.'

'Very well. Then tell me about Mr Pardoe.'

'I find him awful, of course – '

'A sort of clown?'

'More like an enormously intelligent buffoon – if that's possible.'

'It obviously is,' said her father, 'since Mr Pardoe exists.'

'What makes him grotesque,' said Jane, 'is that he has no sense of humour. None whatsoever. It's as if he'd had it removed like an appendix. And yet, he's clever. And not just clever. He really wants the world to be a better place.'

'He wants rather more than that,' said her father. 'He wants to force the world to be better according to the one set of rules that he knows will work. To me he's a very dangerous man.'

'Francis thinks he's wonderful,' said Jane.

'That is Francis's privilege, after all,' said her father. 'You and I know he isn't.'

Foch snorted. He knew it too.

'Francis is in love with the idea of perfection,' her father continued. 'Nothing wrong with that, so long as you realise that's all perfection can be – an idea. Francis's problem is that he thinks his kind of perfection is achievable.'

'The Russian kind?'

'Russo-German, surely?' her father said. 'Lenin may or may not be doing the achieving, but it was Marx – Engels too of course – who had the perfect ideas.'

The phone rang, monotonous, repetitive. This is going to be a bad one, thought Jane.

'I hate that thing,' her father said. 'Back in India a bearer used to bring you a chit. That usually meant a chap had something to tell you, – because it was too damn hot to start writing chits unless you had to – especially in the monsoon season.'

Moreton came in. 'It's Mr Pardoe for Lady Whitcomb,' she said.

'Not possible,' said Sir Guy. 'She's resting.'

'Shall I go?' Jane asked.

'No,' Sir Guy said. 'He's bored you enough for one day.'

He moved stiffly off into the hall, where the telephone lay neatly centred between two draughts.

How old he looks, and how ill, thought Jane.

Foch came over to her, then slumped down heavily. Across his black back, one golden hair gleamed. Jack picked it up and looked at it: the root was gold too, and Jane found that she was glad. Foch sighed.

'Yes,' said Jane, 'I realise that you're in love again, but it won't do, Foch. She's much too wonderful for the likes of us.'

Her father came back in as she spoke, but he obviously hadn't heard a word. He was too busy being furious.

'That bloody man,' he said. ' – I'm sorry my dear, but what else can I call him? That *bloody* man has decided to cut dinner.'

'He told you so?'

'He did indeed. Then he handed the instrument to Francis, who also told me so.'

'But Papa – why be angry? Surely the loss of Pardoe is something to open the Bollinger for?'

'In an ideal world of course,' said Sir Guy. 'But in this one – in *ours* – there are forms and rituals and social obligations. And dinner parties are very much a part of all that.'

'But if something came up – ' said Jane.

'That's just the point,' her father said. 'Nothing came up. He told me so himself.'

'He didn't invent an excuse?'

'"I'm going to tell you the truth" he told me,' Sir Guy said, mimicking savagely. '"Always the best thing in the long run – believe me, Sir Guy." As if I'd been a liar all my life. – "The truth is," he said, "what with the flow of ideas at the meeting and the extraordinary music Miss Payne played, I find myself in an exalted state."'

'Papa, he *can't* have said that.'

'I quote him word for word,' said Sir Guy. 'Then he added, "That being the case I am simply not in the mood for dinner tonight. Indeed the very thought of food is unendurable. I'm sorry but I shan't be able to be with you – and I rather fancy that Francis feels the same."'

'What did you say?' said Jane.

'I said I wanted to speak to Francis, and when your brother came to the instrument I told him that Pardoe could do what he liked, but no son of mine would disappoint his mother by such ungentlemanly behaviour. . . . Francis at least will dine with us.'

Sir Guy got to his feet and smiled. 'You know – losing my rag like that did me good. What's that stuff they talk about nowadays? – adrenalin, that's it. It must be sloshing about inside me like beer in a barrel.' Then the smile died. 'Better tell your mother, I suppose.'

'I'll go if you like,' Jane said, hating the thought.

'You're a good girl as well as a clever one,' said her father. 'And I have to decline your second kind offer – but I must. We'll have things to talk about.'

He walked out then, and Jane considered the things that she might do. Read? Play the piano? Knit? Sew? Mummy always preferred her to choose the last two. Music and literature were far too exciting. What she really wanted to do was lament the fact that Pardoe had cut dinner. Pompous, boring and opinionated Pardoe certainly was, but he had one undeniable attraction: he was a stranger, and she didn't see nearly enough of them. It would have to be Francis after all, and all that cheese. . . .

Only it wasn't. Suddenly and magically it wasn't. As she sat in the drawing room flicking over the pages of the *Illustrated London News*, Moreton came back in and handed her a note.

My dear, [she read]

I told you that writing a chit was a serious business, and so you must consider this a serious invitation. Your mother and I have decided, since she would like to spend a cosy evening en famille with Francis and I would not, that I shall dine out.

If you would like to accompany me I should be charmed to have you as my dinner guest at the Hyde Park Hotel. If not, Francis awaits you and I dine alone. The choice is yours. I shall be leaving here at precisely 7.30.

Papa.

PS I find that chits are not only serious, but useful also. By sending you this, I do not have to go downstairs again, then up.

Jane looked at the parlourmaid.

'Tell Sir Guy I'll be ready at seven thirty precisely,' she said, and she was. Papa hated to be kept waiting.

5

SHE WORE HER blue dress because, if it was not exactly the most dashing, it was certainly the least demure, of her three evening dresses. With it went the pearls Mummy had given her, and the ruby brooch from Aunt Pen. It would have been nice to wear her engagement ring too, the dear little diamond John had given her – all and more than he could afford – but that was locked and hidden away for ever, even from Papa.

The Hyde Park Hotel was marvellous, and Papa was a marvellous host. He even ordered Bollinger because, as he told her, under the present circumstances she was right, and a total absence of Pardoe was a definite cause for celebration. There were sole bonne femme and lamb cutlets Reform too, and she managed to eat quite a bit of both, while Papa sipped his burgundy and remembered once again the maharajah who cheated at cricket; but Jane no more objected to its repetition than a four-year-old Jane had objected to the repetition of Goldilocks and the Three Bears, a ritual at once beloved and familiar.

Now and again she looked about her at the elegant room, skilful waiters, diners as elegant as the room itself, and she was glad that she had worn the blue, and the pearls that really were rather decent, and the positively opulent ruby.

Her father said, 'I should have done this more often.'

She smiled. 'I thought I owed it all to Pardoe.'

'The skeleton at the feast?' Sir Guy said. 'The rather substantial skeleton?'

'Too too solid flesh,' said Jane. 'I'm glad he's not here. I'm having a lovely time.'

'I too,' her father said. 'I love you very much, you know – '

'Please don't make me cry, Papa.'

' – But I find that I'm unable to help you.' Sir Guy went on as if she had not spoken.

'Jabber Lockhart does that. At least he tries to.'

'I do nothing.'

'There's nothing you can do, Papa.'

'I might – restrain your mother. But my heart isn't up to it.' He signalled to their waiter and asked for coffee.

'She doesn't mean it, you know. – Or did I say that before?'

'It's because of Guy and David, you said. Because they died and I didn't.'

'That's putting it very crudely.'

'I suppose it is,' Jane said, but didn't recant. Papa expected to be argued with. It was her right, and Francis's, as it had been David's and Guy's.

'I couldn't help being born a female, Papa.'

'It's my good fortune that you were,' her father said, 'but your mother – she misses them quite dreadfully. She was very proud of them, you know. – And of you.'

'We were sort of a set, like toy soldiers,' said Jane. 'Only two of them got broken.' She paused, then said, 'Now *that* is putting it much too crudely, and I apologise.'

'Accepted,' said her father, then, 'Forgive me – but I must ask you this. Has it ever occurred to you that that ghastly war took its toll of her too? She isn't the woman who taught you the future perfect of "venir". I doubt if she ever will be again.'

It never had occurred to her and she admitted it. But it was true enough.

'Does Lockhart – make any progress?' her father asked.

'He's helped me to know my illness for what it is, and to live with it. I suppose that is a kind of progress.'

'And just what *is* your illness?'

'The price,' said Jane. 'The bill if you like – for all the things I saw and did, and thought were going to leave me untouched. I was wrong.'

– 48 –

'There was a proverb I read somewhere,' said her father. 'Spanish, was it? "Take what you want, says God, and pay for it." Would that be it?'

'That's exactly it,' Jane said, and added sugar to her coffee. 'And anyway you know it's quite wrong of you to say you do nothing for me. You put up with me.'

'Please don't make me cry, either,' her father said. 'Not in a public dining room.'

'But it's true,' said Jane. 'You never tell me to pull myself together, as if I were lying all over the floor in separate bits.'

'Your mother does that, I take it?' Sir Guy said.

'Only because she's changed,' said his daughter.

Then the band came on, piano and banjo, drums and saxophone and violin, and Sir Guy said, 'I hope they won't play Pardoe's music.'

'Béla Bartók,' said Jane and giggled.

'At the very least,' said Sir Guy.

But the band played the waltz from *Floradora*, and some bits from *Chu Chin Chow*, and Sir Guy decided that that was worth celebrating too, and ordered port for them both. After it arrived the band moved on to more contemporary tunes: ragtime and one-steps and the newly arrived Charleston. Bobbed and shingled women, short skirts flying, jogged and jittered in their partners' arms while Sir Guy looked on smiling, for all the world, thought Jane, like an anthropologist who had discovered a new and fascinating, though perhaps rather naughty, tribe.

'Do you do that?' he asked her.

'This is all since my time,' she said.

'Pooh, nonsense,' said her father. 'One of these days we'll take a few lessons and amaze them all.' Then he swallowed more port and grinned at her.

'I'd have liked that,' he said.

They sat on and watched and marvelled, at the women who smoked, and the women who drank cocktails all the way through dinner, and the women who powdered their noses while still sitting at the table. Papa was enchanted, and it was she who had to remind him when it was time to go home. And even then, Mummy had gone to sleep, and so had Francis, so that she was able to kiss Papa goodnight and go upstairs without a row, take off her least demure dress and put on her oh so sensible nightgown. What were all those smokers and cocktail swiggers and nose-powderers wearing now, she wondered. Silken pyjamas? Nothing at all?. . . She'd be thinking of John in a minute and that would never do. This was still the best day she'd had since he died.

And then of course the nightmares came. This shouldn't have surprised her and in fact it didn't, except that this time a new fear was added: the fear that she might see Bridget O'Dowd. All the usual elements were there: the groaning wounded she knew were behind her, the shattered heavy artillery lit up by the star shells, the maimed and screaming horses, just as the dream always was – but the fear that one of them might be Bridget, this was new. For Bridget had been John's horse – or rather the horse that John had inherited.

Originally she had belonged to a captain in the King's Royal Irish Hussars, who had left her in charge of a trooper called O'Dowd while he, the captain, had gone off to reconnoitre outside Mons in October, 1914. He'd told O'Dowd to wait, but never came back, and the commander of B Company of John's Battalion found O'Dowd and his officer's horse and his own, hours later, all three of them hungry and dejected. O'Dowd had wanted very much to rejoin his squadron, but couldn't abandon his officer's horse. The company commander, Captain Heron, had gravely assured O'Dowd that he would take on the responsibility, and O'Dowd trotted off, leaving Heron the proud possessor of a promising three-year-old bay mare, known as Bridget. Heron added the O'Dowd in memory of his benefactor, and rode her till he was shot dead, early in March, 1915.

The mare was promptly inherited by the next commander of B Company, Captain Trevor, who lost a leg at second Ypres a year later. There was another, and yet another, before John took over the company in 1918, the last of Bridget's riders: two killed, one wounded, one missing believed killed. Or to put it another way: two DSOs, three MCs, two mentions in dispatches. For weeks John had practised riding before his promotion. Until that time he had never sat on a horse in his life, a donkey on the sands of Whitley Bay the height of his equestrianism. He'd taken a few hard falls too, the poor darling, but she'd taught him herself, he had naturally good hands, and he'd never once fallen off Bridget, not until that terrible day at La Basseé: the 10th November, 1918.

And now here she was lying wide awake and sweating at four in the morning, remembering that she'd had the horse dream again, and that this time she'd have seen poor Bridget if she hadn't wakened up in time. It didn't make sense, she thought, and it was no good saying that dreams and nightmares never did make sense, because hers always had a crazy logic of their own. But not Bridget. Bridget made no sense at all, because Bridget had never been wounded, not even a scratch. True, Bridget had never been in a trench during a mortar bombardment, or charged a German machine gun, but she'd lived right through the war. And when she'd left, Jane remembered, she was believed to be pregnant, which is more than I was. . . . Her last owner, Lieutenant Gurney, had mourned, and honestly, for John, but he'd coveted Bridget O'Dowd. Nor could Jane blame him. John had felt the same uneasy mixture of shame and delight.

I should read, she thought, but she knew it was no good. Her memories were stronger than words on pages, and anyway, they were all she had. Thirty-two years old, and only memories left for whatever years she still had to endure. . . . Sweat it out, the Tommies used to say. Once you've signed on you have to sweat it out. Well she was doing her share of that, lying all still in the dark, because if you moved and got comfortable you might fall asleep, and if you did *that* the bogeyman would get you.

But of course she did sleep. Champagne and port and exhaustion acted more effectively than tablets, but this time there was no sign of Bridget. This time it was a mule detachment behind the Australian line at Pozières, and German HE had landed smack in the middle of them, butchering, eviscerating. . . .

She was being shaken, and the dream faded, like a scene in a film, as her body rocked to the hands that shook her. Mummy come to tell her to pull herself together, she thought, but she opened her eyes even so. Even Mummy was better than the things her memories insisted she see. But it was Francis.

'I say,' he said. 'You were making rather a row.'

She lay back on the pillow and looked at him. Silk dressing gown, morocco slippers, and the most elegant pyjamas.

'How dashing you look,' she said.

'Never mind me,' said Francis. 'You were yelling your head off.'

'I was having a nightmare,' said Jane. 'I quite often do.'

'So Mummy told me.'

And why not? thought Jane. It wasn't supposed to be a secret. How could it be, when every servant knew? All the same, she wished that she had told Francis first.

Her brother took out a cigarette case from his pocket, and held it out to her. 'Want a gasper?' he asked. 'Or is it unladylike?'

'Yes to both,' she said, and took one. He lit up for them. She had smoked all through the war, like everyone she knew, but Mummy didn't approve. Francis watched her drag the smoke down into her lungs.

'You really needed that,' he said.

'I really did.'

'A lot of people at Cambridge say they're bad for you.'

'They're better than nightmares,' said his sister, and he looked at her with a kind of comprehending alertness that reminded her of David.

'You're seeing a doctor?'

'A man called Lockhart,' she said.

'J.A.B. Lockhart? The one they call Jabber?'

'That's right.'

She dragged smoke in, then blew it out again luxuriously. There could be no doubt that smoking was bad for you. It was so jolly soothing. . . .

'He's supposed to be the best,' said Francis. 'Lockhart, I mean. But isn't he the one who – doesn't he specialise in – '

'If you're asking me if he's the loony doctor the answer is yes,' said Jane. 'But with my particular kind it's known as shell shock.'

'Sorry,' said Francis. 'I didn't mean to imply that you're disturbed. Not for a moment.'

'But I am, love,' she said. 'Tremendously disturbed. That's why I have nightmares and scream.'

'And it's all because of the war?'

'I'm afraid so.'

'Please, Jane,' he said. 'Don't be ironic. I'd no idea – '

She looked around for an ash tray, and settled at last on the soap dish. 'I didn't mean to be ironic,' she said. 'It's just difficult for me to talk about it, that's all.'

'You must have thought Pardoe and I pretty beastly to discuss the war as we did. I'm sorry about that.'

'You said what you believed.'

'Certainly,' he said. 'But we must have seemed very insensitive. Though we weren't, you know. Not really. Just ignorant of the circumstances.'

'That's all right then,' she said. 'Did you have a nice dinner with Mummy?'

'Of course not,' he said, and she smiled. 'Mummy had bought about a stone of cheese.'

'And didn't you like it?'

'I can't stand the stuff.'

Cheese omelettes, thought Jane. Cheese soufflés. Cheese croquettes. Day after day after day.

'I say – ' Francis said. 'My friend Pardoe. He was jolly impressed by you.'

'He doesn't know I'm a loony.'

'It wouldn't make any difference if he did,' said Francis. 'Not to Pardoe.' Then he realised his own words and flushed. 'And anyway you're *not*,' he said.

'I think,' she said gravely, 'we'd better leave all that sort of thing to Lockhart.'

'Yes, of course,' he said. 'It's just that Pardoe thinks – I don't want to embarrass you – '

'As if you could,' said Jane. 'Please tell me what Pardoe thinks.'

'He thinks you have great potential.'

'Does he indeed?' said Jane. 'I should have thought Miss Payne was more his style.'

'I don't mean that,' said Francis. 'At least not just that.'

He was concentrating now, weighing up the words he must use, and the beauty was back in his face, a beauty that neither she nor Guy nor David had possessed, and she realised once more that when he was beautiful he looked very like their mother.

'It's all to do with the way the world must go,' he said. 'The world of the future – and how we're going to achieve it. Of course in the end the people will rule – '

'The dictatorship of the proletariat,' said Jane.

'That's the technical expression for it,' said Francis, 'though in itself it's a kind of paradox – because if the people rule, the world must be *more* democratic, rather than *less*, so that by definition

– 53 –

it will not be a dictatorship as we now understand it. But of course this will take time. The people must learn to govern.'

'And you must teach them?'

'Not just me. Us.'

'You and I and Pardoe?'

'Don't tease,' he said. 'You know what I mean. All the intelligentsia.'

Wit had no chance against Francis's singlemindedness. To use it was about as effective as throwing stones at a tank.

'Do I belong to the intelligentsia?'

'Pardoe thinks so. Pardoe thinks you've got a Beta-plus mind at least – once you've been trained to use it.'

'Never mind what Pardoe thinks. What does Francis think?'

'I think you're very clever indeed,' said Francis. 'But – '

'Go on.'

'I should have to be rude.'

'Go on all the same,' she said.

'I also think you're lazy. That's why you make jokes all the time, instead of making yourself useful. I also think you're not ready for the Party.'

'Party?' Her bewilderment was quite genuine.

'The *Communist* Party,' said Francis.

'Because I'm lazy?'

'Partly that.'

'What else?' He made no answer.

'Francis, I have to know,' she said, and it was true. She *must* know.

He said, 'You look back all the time. You never look ahead.'

'Look back where?'

'That war,' he said. 'That stupid war. It almost destroyed you and I'm sorry for that, honestly I am. But it's over now. Finished. And you won't let it go. Not even in your dreams.'

She said angrily, 'If you knew what my dreams were like – ' but he interrupted her.

'They're *your* dreams,' he said. 'Part of the you that exists now. You won't look forward – only back. The dreams won't change because you won't, and I don't think you ever will.'

'I thought we decided to leave all that to Lockhart,' she said, but even to say it was to admit defeat.

'You did ask me.'

'So I did,' she said. 'You'd better finish it.'

'You're no use to the Party so long as you cling to this stupid nostalgia,' he said. 'It's as if you'd had a love affair and it's finished and you won't let go.'

Somehow, by some strength of will she did not know she possessed, she neither jumped nor yelled. She had forgotten how perceptive her brother could be. If she gave herself away now he would know that what he'd used as a mere figure of speech had been the literal truth.

'Then you and Pardoe don't agree about me,' she said.

'He thinks you can change for the better and I don't,' her brother said. 'That's the only difference.'

'But then he doesn't know I'm a loony,' she said again. With Francis it was always best to be sure.

'You're not a loony,' he said. 'But he doesn't know Lockhart is treating you – not from me.'

Then Hawkins came in with the morning tea, and Francis saw the chocolate biscuits and ate one there and then, and Hawkins left in a huff.

'A bit of a tartar, isn't she?' Francis said.

'You just ate her biscuit,' said Jane.

'*Her* biscuit?'

'I always leave them for her.'

'Oh my God,' said Francis. 'Do you mean to say she doesn't get enough food?'

'That's what I thought,' said Jane. 'But she says she does. She just likes chocolate biscuits.'

'You don't think I should apologise to her?'

'She wouldn't understand why,' she said, 'and you haven't time to teach her, not if you're going back to Cambridge tomorrow.'

'Not tomorrow,' said Francis. 'Pardoe and I are going to a party tomorrow. Fancy dress.'

'Incidentally where *is* Pardoe?' Jane asked.

'Staying with a cousin in Knightsbridge.'

'I mean in the general scheme of things,' said Jane. 'His station in life. All that.'

'He's an economist. At Trinity,' said Francis. 'A junior fellow. Eventually he'll be a senior fellow.'

'Is that what you want to do?'

'It's what I must do,' Francis said, then added: 'Though not necessarily at Trinity.' He stood up. The conference it seemed was over.

'I say,' he said. . . . Not quite over.

'Pardoe really likes you,' he continued.

'Like Georgina Payne.'

'They all like Georgina Payne. But he really does like you. . . . He's something of a ladies' man. I just thought I'd better mention it.'

'I'm obliged to you,' said Jane.

'Not at all,' her brother said, and left her, passing Foch on his way in. Jane swung her legs off the bed, stretched, then looked down at Foch.

'What on earth was all that about?' she said. 'Pardoe likes me indeed. . . . And what about Miss Payne? "*They* all like her," he said. Not we. They. . . . I don't quite like the sound of that.'

But Foch was searching the carpet for chocolate-biscuit crumbs, and was too busy to answer.

6

HER MOTHER SAID, 'I understand that Francis came to your room this morning.'

It was eleven o'clock, and the two women were taking coffee together in the drawing room.

'Who told you that?' Jane asked.

'He did. I do not accuse him of impropriety – or you. I merely question the wisdom of protracted visits. Servants have the oddest notions of what is improper. Particularly housemaids. I have often noticed it.'

'Why did he tell you?'

'He thinks you're bored.'

Jane thought, well of course I am, you appalling old person. But that was not the way. Patience, tact and, above all, persistence.

'Why does he think that?' she asked.

'He is at Cambridge. He has his studies, his friends, clubs, meetings, sports. A life crammed with excitement. Yours by comparison *must* seem a little dull.'

How can you say so? thought Jane. Only two days ago I bought two pounds of cheese.

Aloud she said, 'Perhaps a little.'

'Francis is attending a fancy-dress ball tonight,' said her mother.

'So he tells me.'

'It occurred to us that you might attend it too, – as his partner. He has little opportunity to meet nice girls here when he spends half his life at Cambridge. There is, of course, the question of a costume.'

'Costume, Mummy?'

'It's a fancy-dress ball it seems. They almost all are these days, Francis says.'

'I'm to go then?'

'Have I not said so?'

'What does Papa say?'

'I broke it to him over breakfast. He could see no objection.'

'And the costume?'

'I thought the sari,' her mother said. 'With the choli of course, and those vulgar jewels, and those rather ghastly ruby ear-rings Nettles gave me one Christmas. You will not of course expose your midriff.'

Nor dance the Charleston, thought Jane, because I don't know how. And just to be on the safe side she thought it might be a good idea to find out if her father really wanted her to go.

It seemed he did. He even put aside his work (a viceroy's ball programme in New Delhi in 1918, with photographs of his party at dinner) to tell her so. 'And you're to wear the sari, I hear. Do you know how to do it?'

'Oh yes,' said Jane. 'Ayah taught me years ago when we used to dress up – Guy and David and I.'

'David was usually a Moghul emperor, I remember,' her father said. 'What was Guy?'

'Sir Arthur Wellesley defeating the Mahrattas.'

'And you?'

'Spoils of war,' said Jane. 'I don't think Sir Arthur Wellesley ever took spoils of war of that particular sort – but then Guy and David hadn't the faintest idea what they were. Nor did I – except I thought it rather boring. So I got hold of a helmet and spear – became a warrior queen instead.'

'That's much more like you,' said her father. 'And what will you be tonight?'

Her voice took on the demure sing-song intonation of a former acquaintance of theirs, a Mrs Lal, whose husband was a judge.

'I shall be examining with great curiosity the antics of these British people who are all the time finding it necessary to dance.'

Her father snorted with laughter, then asked, 'But won't you be dancing yourself?'

'Impossible to do so,' she said, 'lacking knowledge of correct procedure.' His laughter died, and she added in her own voice, 'I shan't wish to, you know. Not this new stuff. But I might risk a waltz if the sari can stand the strain.'

'We should have taken you about more once we got back from India,' he said. 'But I was ill – and after the boys your mother was distraught. But all the same we should have *tried*.'

'It's perfectly all right, Papa,' she said. 'Honestly.'

She lied of course, but she couldn't bear to hear him apologise.

Hawkins had ironed the sari while Mummy watched her, nervous of burn marks. But there were none. It was an old, and very beautiful garment, a gift to Mummy from the cricketing maharajah. Mummy had bitterly resented the insinuation that she might, under any circumstances, dress as a native, which was of course why the maharajah had given it to her, but for once Papa had been firm, and vetoed Mummy's immediate reaction, which was to cut it up for cushion covers. It was, he said, a work of art, and sacrosanct. It was certainly very beautiful; a great spreading sheet of wine-red silk, heavily embroidered in gold thread. The choli, the little jacket, was of white, with red and gold embroidery, and up in her bedroom after dinner Jane began the ritual that she and her ayah had performed so many times: long petticoat underneath with tapes tied tight, then the sari wrapped around, tucking it in as she went. Then she drew it over her shoulder, and fastened it with one of the 'terrible jewels', a ruby brooch set in heavy gold. There were bangles too, and a gold and ruby necklace, and Uncle Walter's terrible ear-rings which weren't terrible at all. They came from Cartier. Gold sandals with red drawn threadwork, and the dressing-up ritual was complete, and she remembered how it was to be nine years old again, to know the kites were screaming high over the garden, and the tame mynah bird was talking Hindi in Mummy's dressing room; that the smells were of jasmine and curry from the kitchen, and ayah's heavy perfume. And down in the schoolroom David and Guy were already duelling, scimitar against sword.

Then she looked in the mirror, and it was a woman who looked back, not an all-too-pert and precocious little girl. She looked at Foch, who seemed totally unimpressed by her Oriental splendour.

'You're just jealous,' she said. 'All the same I think Francis is right.'

Foch snorted.

'No honestly,' she said. 'I *do* live too much in the past. But I don't know how to get out.'

Carefully she used a little rouge to mark a beauty spot on her brow.

'I think you underestimate Francis,' she told Foch. 'Just because he can't laugh doesn't mean he can't think.'

Foch put out his tongue.

When she had done she went downstairs, back to Papa's study where he was once again rummaging happily among the material for his memoirs: this time a polo match on the Rawalpindi maidan; some kind of Indian Lancer regiment, it seemed, playing against the ICS. Papa had scored twice in the third chukka. Soon he would show her the photographs, but first she must be inspected. Straight and tall, shoulders back, her governess had told her. Girls can't be soldiers, a pert, precocious Jane had argued. Girls can still look smart, her governess had said, so straight and tall and shoulders back it was.

Her father walked round her as though she were a statue in a gallery. 'You look wonderful,' he said, and she started to giggle, then realised he meant it.

'Too tall,' she said. 'Too thin. Decked out like a Christmas tree.'

'Nonsense,' her father said. 'Jewellery suit you. Gold suits you. And riches.'

'They suit every girl.'

'Not as they suit you. Believe me. For some women wealth is a protective armour. Without it they're doomed. For you it's no more than a setting. You look wonderful.'

He said it that second time as if he were summing up the deliberations of a highly qualified committee. 'Let me show you.'

He rummaged among the fading sepia photographs he kept stored in shoe boxes, and came out with an envelope. Something special, thought Jane, as he opened it. There aren't many he protects so carefully. Not any more. . . . Her father laid a fading piece of cardboard down in front of her. A photograph was fixed to it, the photograph of a woman. The photographer had arranged some potted palms behind her, and she was standing on a tigerskin that had seen better days, but she was quite devastatingly beautiful. She wore a long skirted dress of forty years ago, and carried a parasol, striking a pose with it as a musical-comedy chorus girl might have done, and her figure showed up to perfection, even inside the enveloping folds of Victorian skirts. But her face had a beauty beyond fashion or custom. Jet black hair that flowed straight down, dark, unwavering eyes, straight nose, sweet mouth – one could tick off the list, Jane thought, and everyone would say Goodness! How pretty she must have been. But she wasn't pretty in the least. She was beautiful, just as Francis was beautiful.

'On her wrist there is a bracelet that a maharajah gave her. Round her neck is a necklace given her by a major in the Coldstream who was heir to a shipping fortune. The two together were insured for a hundred thousand pounds – forty-three years ago. Did you even notice them?'

'I didn't even know they were there till you told me. Who was she?'

'Her name was Posy Sanderson. – Ridiculous sort of a name. But with her a name didn't matter. She was an – Anglo-Indian we call them nowadays. Then we used to say Eurasian, if it wasn't "that bloody chi-chi".'

Carefully he replaced the photograph in the envelope, and put it back in the shoe box.

'What happened to her?'

'She died,' her father said. 'In childbirth. Poor darling girl. She lit up every room she entered. . . . The child died too.' He closed the shoe box.

'Better let your mother take a look at you,' he said.

Mummy was busy inspecting Francis, who had chosen to appear as a fox hunter: red coat, white breeches, top boots that gleamed. Mummy approved, as well she might, thought Jane. Any mother would approve such dark good looks, such elegant tailoring. . . . Then she checked Jane's midriff, was pleased to declare it adequately covered, and told them to enjoy themselves – though no later than twelve thirty. Jane must be home by one.

Moreton had found them a cab and they chugged off towards Knightsbridge. Two nights in a row, thought Jane. How fast I am becoming.

Francis said, 'The sari looks well on you.'

'Thank you,' she said. 'And you my dear – you're the young MFH to the life. Where *did* you hire that outfit?'

'I didn't,' said Francis. 'A chum of mine lent it to me.'

'A Cambridge chum?'

'Of course.' Francis sounded susprised that she could think that there were other kinds.

'He must be frightfully rich.'

'He is,' said Francis. 'He's at King's.'

She gathered that the two facts were connected.

'Is he a Communist?'

'Good Lord no,' Francis said. 'He's far too stupid.'

The taxi chugged on into the Brompton Road, then nosed its way past a crescent and a mews and finally settled at a house in a square.

'Somebody else who's frightfully rich,' said Jane.

Francis fumbled with half crowns and sixpences, and finally settled on a florin.

'Same chap,' he said.

'The one at King's?'

He helped her out and she rearranged her sari.

'Only rich chap I know. Only *really* rich chap. The house is his parents'.'

'Oughtn't I to know his name?' Jane asked. 'After all he *is* my host.'

'You're making jokes again,' said Francis. 'Being ironic – I've warned you about that. His name is Poynter. Richard Poynter. His father's in shipping.'

'His father owns the sort of ship that used to take us to India. – Francis Whitcomb – your chum's a capitalist.'

'You're hopeless,' her brother said. 'I knew you would be.'

They went inside.

It was a big, old house, built, she supposed, at the time of George III. There was a curving and very beautiful staircase, used, so it seemed, for sitting out; what was usually the dining room was a super room and bar, and at the back a marquee had been erected where a band was playing all over again the music of the night before: 'Varsity Rag' and 'The Charleston' and 'Get Out And Get Under'. Everybody present seemed to be drinking champagne, she thought, including the servants, but then she realised that they were for the most part merely carrying it and were comparatively sober. Meekly she accompanied Francis to hand over her coat to a maidservant, accept a numbered ticket in return and then, reminding herself that she was a Warrior Queen, prepared to join the party.

It wasn't as difficult as she'd feared. Francis, concerned, she told herself, not to embarrass her by undue attention, promptly went off and left her on her own. That gave her an excuse to wander, with that graceful carriage the sari seems to impose, and look at the people and think about Papa. She stared at Falstaffs and Nell Gwyns, Richard the Lionhearts and Madame Pompadours, but what she really saw was Posy Sanderson in a soubrette's pose, with a face so beautiful as to be scarcely real. Could it be, could it really be, that she had once had an elder brother – or sister – who had died at birth? And why had Papa waited so long to tell her? And if it were so, did it matter that it had happened? And did Mummy know? She wished that John were there to hear her questions, because there was no one else to turn to. But then it was just because there was no one else that Papa had shown her the photograph.

She wandered into the marquee to watch the dancing: a French sailor with a gypsy girl, a Felix-the-Cat with a Little Bo Peep, a gollywog with a Queen of Hearts. Then the band played a waltz and a Beefeater asked her to dance; she decided to risk it – like riding a bicycle, she told herself. Once you know the knack you never lose it, just one two three one two three. Watch-for-your-toes two three. For the Beefeater was nervous, and just a little drunk, but his place was taken by a Little Jack Horner who talked to her all the time in Urdu, and was enchanted when she replied in the same tongue. . . . Then there were a centurion, a sultan and a bull fighter, and then what she could only think of as a Cornet of Horse. That was what he had to be: a cavalryman of Wellington's time, all gold and scarlet and elegant frogging, overall trousers strapped under the foot. So young and dashing and pretty. But the band had grown tired of waltzes. It was 'I Want To See My Baby Do The Charleston' – and out of the question.

'I'm afraid not,' she said.

'Oh I say,' said the Cornet of Horse. 'I'm not that bad.'

'Of course you're not,' said Jane. 'It's just that I've had no supper.'

– 63 –

'Then I'll take you in,' the Cornet of Horse said, and offered his arm.

He had no difficulty at all in obtaining champagne for her, or lobster mayonnaise, though the crowd at the buffet had seemed to her impenetrable.

'You *are* adroit,' she said.

He flushed. 'Not really. I live here you see.'

'You're Richard Poynter?'

'We haven't met, have we? I feel sure I would have remembered.'

'No,' she said. 'We haven't. But I'm not a gatecrasher, you know.'

'I wouldn't mind,' Poynter said. 'Honestly.'

'Well I don't eat and drink so very much – '

'I didn't mean *that*.'

'But I *am* Francis Whitcomb's sister.'

'Oh good Lord,' said her Cornet of Horse. 'I say – would you mind if I got myself a glass of champers – '

'Get two,' she said. 'I'd rather like another myself. It's awfully good.'

'It's Bollinger,' said her Cornet of Horse.

'I bet you it won't work,' she said. But he was already gone.

And of course it didn't work, because after just two sips brother Francis appeared, and with him was Pardoe. But at least the awful moment was postponed, because before Pardoe could ask her to dance a woman dressed as Titania came up to him and said she simply must have a word with him about collectivisation. But then beastly Francis took her Cornet of Horse away, saying *they* must have a word about the Trinity May Ball. She sipped champagne and tried not to be jealous, until a tall man in evening dress appeared, the only person there not pretending to be someone else.

'May I join you?' he said. 'My name's Poynter.'

'Ah,' she said. 'The Colonel of Horse.'

He looked puzzled for a moment, then smiled.

'Actually I was in the Rifle Brigade, but I see what you mean. Young Richard's costume. He looks good in it, wouldn't you say?'

'If this were the Duchess of Richmond's ball before Waterloo he'd be just right.'

'I'm glad you like him, Miss Whitcomb.'

'He's – likeable,' she said. 'But how did you know my name?'

'I asked. Urdu-speaking maharanis are rather a rarity you know.'

'My friend Little Jack Horner?'

'He says you're very fluent.'

'So is he.'

The elder Poynter smiled. 'I'll tell him you said so. He's collector of the Bhopal District. Due back soon.'

'My father was in the ICS too.'

'So I'm told,' said Poynter. 'But not your brother?'

'Too young,' said Jane. 'He takes his tripos next month. And anyway he's an academic, not an administrator.'

'Is he, indeed? Not like Richard. Richard is not an intellectual,' Poynter said. 'In fact it'll take him all his time to take a pass degree, even with a following wind. But it doesn't matter.'

'Doesn't it?'

'Not in the least,' Poynter said. 'In a year or two he'll stop playing the fool at Cambridge and be what you called him – a Cornet of Horse.'

'I'm sure he'll do it delightfully.'

'He'll be a good officer,' said Poynter. 'Not over-burdened with brains, but good-hearted and conscientious.'

'May I wish him luck?'

'You certainly may,' Poynter said, then looked across the room, and rose. 'You must excuse me,' he said. 'I see young Millie Chetwynd over there. Richard's mother rather approves of her. Pretty little thing, isn't she?'

He bowed and went over to a dark girl dressed as Britannia, and not at all happy about it.

More heavy hints, thought Jane, though tactfully delivered. But there was no time to brood about it. The word about collectivisation had been spoken: Pardoe was upon her.

He approved of the sari. *Thoroughly* approved. Her wearing it went some way – some small and humble way – towards reparation due to a people who had endured almost two centuries of ruthless exploitation. Jane tried in vain to assure him that the inhabitants of the subcontinent had endured exploitation for rather longer than that; tried also to explain that no one was more adept at exploiting an Indian than another Indian. He didn't listen, perhaps didn't even hear: but then he wasn't made to listen. He was made to teach.

And teach he did, about majority rights and minority rights, self-determination and economic self-fulfilment, and Jane listened because although some of it was boring and some mere jargon, quite a lot of it was interesting and some even made sense. The fact did not surprise her. Pardoe was, as she had told her father, a very clever man. But she drew the line at being told about collectivisation. That was like being given another girl's box of chocs.

'But you can't mean you're jealous of Marigold,' Pardoe said.

'I might be,' said Jane, 'if I knew who she was.'

'Marigold Ledbitter. The girl dressed as Titania.'

'No,' said Jane. 'I'm not jealous of her.'

Pardoe seemed disappointed.

'She has a good mind,' he said, 'and is doing quite well at the London School of Economics, but she does have a tendency to put on weight, poor girl' – a tendency that Jane had already noted. 'Whereas you – ' He hesitated.

'Whereas I?' she prompted.

' – Are quite divinely slim,' he said and looked at her, – roguishly the only word. As if he expected me to roll over on my back with all four paws in the air, she thought. An impossible idea. Foch would never speak to her again.

'I think we should dance now,' Pardoe said.

The band was playing 'Love Will Find A Way' from 'The Maid Of The Mountains', so that she could not, like Mrs Lal, plead that she lacked knowledge of the correct procedure. Meekly she preceded him to the marquee, and his arms came about her.

He danced well, which surprised her. There was no hint of the rugger field or the boxing ring in the way his feet moved, his hands held. A little too inexorable perhaps in his decision on what line to take, but then Pardoe had been born inexorable. . . . For a few bars they danced in silence. He was assessing her, Jane decided; awarding her marks out of ten for responsiveness, awareness of rhythm, technical ability. To her own fury she discovered that she was exerting herself to dance her very best.

At last he said, 'Did your brother leave?'

'I think not,' said Jane. 'He went off with his friend Poynter.'

'Our genial host,' said Pardoe. 'You have met the father?'

'Briefly.'

'An almost perfect example of the genus capitalist. A man worth millions who thinks of no one but himself.'

'He thinks of his son.'

'A useless creature. Not even a capitalist. A parasite.'

'I think he's destined for the cavalry,' said Jane.

'And an obsolete parasite at that,' said Pardoe.

Jane, who had seen the effects of machine-gun fire at first hand, could only agree, but not aloud. With Pardoe one must never concede too much.

The waltz ended, and the drummer became busy with cow bells and cymbals, side drums, and what looked like a washboard.

'Cacophony will supervene once more,' said Pardoe. 'Let us talk.'

He took her arm and led her gently, politely, inexorably, back to the supper room. 'I shall get you some lemonade,' Pardoe said.

'Champagne,' said Jane.

'How many glasses have you had already?'

'One,' said Jane, and was furious with herself once more; this time because she lied.

'One more cannot harm you,' Pardoe said. 'There is a saying among the more convivial men of my college: "A bird never flew on one wing." There is a certain merit in it – particularly when applied to a bird of paradise.' He went to the bar.

Oh dear God, thought Jane. This can't be happening. And yet he was clever, he was strong – and he was a stranger. Talking with him was like a match of really hard tennis: exhilarating yet slightly frantic.

He came back with the Bollinger – like a disease bringing its own antidote, she thought, but that wasn't *quite* right. The antidote didn't work.

'Your brother Francis feels the need of a close emotional attachment to another male,' said Pardoe. 'Now please do not misunderstand me. There is nothing wrong with that.' He waited, but she made no answer.

'Nothing *intrinsically* wrong,' he said, 'though I could wish that he had attached himself to someone more politically aware.

– 67 –

However, that is not the point of my thesis. My needs are not his, and why should they be?'

'Why indeed?' asked Jane, dreading what was to come.

'My emotional needs are, and always have been, heterosexual,' said Pardoe. 'For as long as I can remember. Even at Oundle. Need I say more?'

'Well yes,' said Jane. 'I think perhaps you should.'

Pardoe consented to do so. 'You have a good mind – I think I mentioned the fact to Francis – ' he said.

'He was kind enough to tell me what you said.'

'I wanted it to be known. A good mind, as I say, and a refreshing willingness to learn. To take instruction. I also find you enormously attractive physically.'

'Is this by any chance a proposal?' Jane asked.

'Not of marriage,' said Pardoe. 'Situated as I am at the moment – a mere junior fellow – marriage is out of the question. What I *am* proposing is something more of a liaison, a coming together of kindred spirits, with no binding commitment on either side. I think I can say without flattering myself unduly that I'm not without experience in these matters. I can promise you fulfilment, both mental and physical.'

He looked away and his manner grew wary. Jane followed his gaze, to see that Titania was hovering.

'This is not the place to press you for a decision,' said Pardoe, 'though of course I shall be in touch quite soon. I shouldn't have any more champagne tonight. The thought of you tipsy is a profanation.'

Then he moved away, quickly and smoothly for a man of his size, with Titania stumbling after. Titania *was* tipsy. His women probably always were, thought Jane, and then: *His women*. What on earth is the matter with me? It was time to find Francis and go home.

But she could not find Francis. There were only three places to look: the supper room, the marquee and the stairs – but he was in none of them. She took another glass of champagne despite Pardoe's instructions, and sat in the darkest, quietest corner she could find. 'Horsey Keep Your Tail Up' was not the ideal music for self-analysis, but she would have to make do. Pardoe, she was sure, would insist on that.

The trouble was – or part of the trouble was – that she was

thirty-two, and it had been seven years since a man had embraced her with passion, and she desperately needed that embrace. Not just the sex part – with John that had always been something of a gamble – but the feel of a man holding her, the certain knowledge that a man needed her. She had to have these things. After all she *was* thirty-two now. John would never ever be thirty-two. John was dead and buried and twenty-seven when he died and she missed him but she couldn't have him, ever again.

Whereas she could have Pardoe, and that was the horrifying thing. Pardoe could be had. Moreover she was prepared to bet that Pardoe would be a good lover. Loads better than poor darling John, because Pardoe had told her he was good and he wouldn't lie. He probably had a diploma in it or something, and when they did it she'd get to like it so much she'd put up with everything, even his prose style. . . . And there would be other advantages. New people for example. The only one she'd seen so far was Titania, who would hate her, but there would be others, from LSE and elsewhere – she might even go there herself – and have jolly chats about the means of production, distribution and exchange. Because soon she'd be on her own, she knew that now. Papa would never have shown her that photograph unless he was sure he was dying.

And she couldn't be on her own with Mummy. Couldn't possibly. Any more than she could be Aunt Pen's toady. The only other offer she'd had was Pardoe, and even that one might be withdrawn if he found out she was a loony – and besides, he might start explaining to her that she was like that because of the war that should never have been. . . . She beckoned to a waiter to bring more champagne, because for some reason she felt disinclined to walk to the buffet, even doubted her ability to do so. She gulped at it when it arrived, and wondered what the time was. . . . If Pardoe ever tells me that I'm a loony because I fought in the wrong war I'll kill him, she thought. It was a splendid idea and seemed to solve lots of problems. Then the band played that tune from the show she'd gone to with John on his leave in 1917. When they got to the bit about

And when I tell them – and I'm certainly going to tell them,
That you're the man whose wife some day I'll be,

    They'll never believe me – they'll never believe me
    That from this great big world you've chosen me

she began to cry, very quietly.

When Francis came up to her at last he seemed angry.

'Where on earth have you been?' he said. 'I've looked every-where.'

'That,' said Jane, 'is a lie.'

He looked at her more closely.

'Good Lord,' he said, 'you're as tight as a tick.'

'And you,' she said, 'are as queer as a coot.'

She didn't shout, but her voice was a carrying one, and Francis looked about him, warily.

'Don't worry,' said Jane. 'I want it to be our secret. Just get me home.'

'How much have you had?'

'Five glasses of champagne,' she said. 'Not a lot for you varsity chaps – but too much for an innocent maiden. . . . You ask Pardoe.'

'Why bring Pardoe into it?' Francis asked.

'Because it's always bloody Pardoe,' said his sister. And then – 'What's his first name? Has he got one?'

'Of course he's got one,' said Francis. 'It's Cuthbert.'

'Cuthbert Pardoe.' Jane tested the name, and found it satis-factory. 'Cuthbert Pardoe. Cuthbert Pardoe and Francis Whitcomb. . . . Ruggery and buggery.'

'You're very rude,' said her brother.

'You were pimping for him,' said Jane, and fumbled in her handbag, found her cloakroom ticket. 'Go and get my coat.'

'What will you do?'

'Get up. Walk out. . . . Like a lady.'

'Do you think you can?' he asked her.

'I must,' she said. 'For both our sakes.'

Being biddable, he left her, and somehow she made her body do what she ordered it to do. An interesting exercise, she thought. One she had last performed eight years ago, when she had climbed out of her ambulance after the shell blast struck and helped unload the wounded, instead of lying still as any sane person would have done, and waiting for the next shell to land. Leaving a party wasn't nearly so difficult.

Francis found her waiting for him in the hall, and put her coat around her and took her arm, and together they walked out and nobody noticed, out into a London night already cold enough to make her feel it, and with a walk to the taxi long enough to help just a little. When the taxi came, she fell asleep – and snored, so Francis told her later. But she didn't dream.

Sleeping was a mistake, but then Francis hadn't had much experience of handling drunks – not like his big sister, Jane thought, one-time expert in bullying, coaxing, cajoling helpless young officers back to their billets. Francis had never done it before, admittedly, but when it came to holding up his sister with one hand and paying off a taxi with the other he was hopeless. No sense of improvisation at all. She told him so.

It was Hawkins who saved them, back from her night out, and with a skirt even further above her knees than Jane had thought possible.

'Are you all right, miss?' she said, and then, when Jane smiled at her, chuckled: 'No, you're not, are you?'

'Is it any of your business?' Francis asked – hacking away at our only lifeline, thought Jane, *and* he eats her biscuits.

'Please be quiet,' she said, and then to Hawkins: 'I have to go inside.'

'Yes miss,' said Hawkins.

'Only I don't think I can. Not just yet. I need a good sleep.'

She moved towards the doorstep, ready to sit, and Francis just stood there, but Hawkins blocked her off.

'Not now miss,' she said. 'There'll be a copper along in a minute.'

'Perhaps he can help,' said Jane.

'He'd wake the house,' Hawkins said.

'We can't have that,' said Jane, and then, 'Are you sure there's a copper?'

'Yes miss,' said Hawkins. 'He's keen on me.'

'I'm glad,' said Jane. 'You deserve a nice copper.'

She breathed in and out slowly, three long, deep breaths.

'You can get me up the stairs if my brother helps you?'

'Yes, miss.' She seemed quite sure.

'Open the door then, Francis,' said Jane. 'Put the prisoner back in her cell.'

They did it, too. Chaplinesque, the highbrow critics would call it: all that teetering and tottering and clinging to banisters, silent anguish from Francis when she stood on his instep, but at last they got her to her bedroom and Francis left without a word, but Hawkins put her to bed, folded her sari, left her and came back with aspirin and soda water, then forced her to watch as she shut each jewel in its case.

'Thank you Peggy Hawkins,' said Jane, and Hawkins turned the light off and tiptoed upstairs to the attic, cautious not to wake cook.

Jane slept. She didn't dream, but slept, on and on, so that when she woke her tea was cold and Francis, once more gorgeously dressing gowned, was eating her last remaining biscuit.

Jane thought: I should feel awful but I don't. Aspirins and soda-water. Peggy Hawkins, bless you. . . . She sipped her tea.

'Good morning,' she said.

Her brother said, 'I'm surprised you can still speak.'

'So am I,' said Jane.

'You couldn't much last night. Not at the end anyway.'

'There didn't seem much left to say.'

'No,' her brother said. 'I think you covered most of it. Ruggery and buggery.'

'Did I say that? I'm sorry.'

'Don't be. The chaps at college say I never make a joke. I shall borrow that one.'

'It's yours,' she said. 'With my compliments.'

'Who told you?' Francis asked. 'About me, I mean.'

'Pardoe,' she said. 'He saw nothing wrong with the way you make love – but he deplored your choice of partners.'

'He would,' said Francis. 'But he doesn't realise – '

'How lovely Richard Poynter is? But I do. I danced with him.' She sipped more cold tea. At the moment it tasted infinitely better than Bollinger. 'But Cuthbert wasn't the only one who told me.'

'Who else?'

'Richard's father. He came over specially to talk to me – give me a message, you might say.'

'What message?'

'You and the Cornet of Horse – Young Richard. His father forbids the banns, I'm afraid. Young Richard's earmarked for

Millie Chetwynd. He told me so very nicely – but I didn't enjoy it much.'

'He had no business to tell you at all.'

'Let's assume he thought I had a bit of commonsense,' said Jane. 'Let's further assume he's right. Who better to tell? Papa? Your college? The police? He's warning you off, Francis. What you do is your business I suppose – up to a point – '

'What point?'

'Upsetting Papa.'

She settled back among the pillows. Really a night without dreams was something she thought she'd never have again.

'We could be discreet,' Francis said. 'Damn it, we *have* been discreet.'

'Not enough,' said Jane. 'His father knows. And Papa is in no shape to take on Richard's father. And anyway – Richard's leaving Cambridge.'

'His father told you that?'

'He's going into the army.'

'No,' said Francis. 'Not the army. Nothing so vulgar. Richard's going into the Household Cavalry. The Life Guards.'

'How pretty he'll look,' said Jane. 'All that scarlet and horse-hair and burnished steel. You can go and watch him outside Buckingham Palace, and worship – from afar.'

'That sounds very like a command.'

'How can I command you?' said Jane. 'All I can do is tell you a pretty obvious truth. You're no match for Richard's father. None of us are.'

'Pardoe's right,' her brother said. 'You do have a good brain.'

'Why don't you call him Cuthbert?' she asked.

'Why do you make jokes as soon as you make sense?'

'But it wasn't a joke,' said Jane. 'At least I don't *think* it was. . . . Why don't you?'

'Because I don't want to.'

'Nor do I.'

'You said I was pimping for him.'

'Weren't you?'

'He likes you,' Francis said. 'Whether you like him or not is your affair.'

'I don't.'

'Do you want me to tell him so?'

She thought about that. Tipsy she might be able to tolerate him, but then he didn't want her to be tipsy, and she didn't either.

'Yes,' she said.

He rose. 'That's it then, I take it? We have a bargain. I keep your secret and you keep mine.'

'That's it,' she said.

He left her and she settled down to drowse and brood. Pardoe was out. O-U-T, but somebody else would have to be in and pretty damn quickly. Steps would have to be taken. . . . Taking steps was a phrase that Jabber used: she began to think of what she would tell him.

I used to think my whole life was predestined, she would tell him. But now I find I have a choice. I can either have nightmares or go to parties and get drunk on champagne.

Her eyes closed: she went back to sleep.

7

'S O I HAVE a choice, do I?' said Jabber.
       'Not you,' said Jane. 'Me.'
'Oh yes,' said Lockhart. 'It's your choice, I can see that – but
it looks as if I'm the one who'll have to make it. – Or maybe
condone it.'
'Not condone,' said Jane. 'At least I don't *think* so. I mean I
quite like champagne – adore it as a matter of fact – but I can't
go on shovelling the stuff down all day and every day. I mean
apart from anything else I couldn't afford it.'
'And you'd spend far too much time falling down,' said Lock-
hart. 'Perhaps in the street.'
'Mummy would hate that,' said Jane, and then more fairmind-
edly: 'So would I.'
'Better if we just get rid of those dreams,' Lockhart said.
'We?'
'Neither of us can do it on our own,' he said.
'But do you think we *can* do it – between us I mean?'
'Yes,' he said.
He had never before been so uncompromising.
'We'd better get on with it then,' said Jane.
'I have a colleague with me at the moment,' Lockhart said. 'Dr
Barker. He's from Sydney in Australia. He's doing pretty much
the same kind of thing that I'm doing, and just for now we're
exchanging ideas. One of these days we hope to do a paper
together.'
'And will I be in it?'

'A starring rôle,' he said. 'Dr Barker's here now. Would you mind awfully if he joined us for a chat? I appreciate that it's a lot to ask.'

'If it's in the interests of medical science I can hardly refuse,' said Jane, 'but I may get a little tongue-tied with a strange man in the room.'

'He's a doctor,' Lockhart said.

'He's a man,' said Jane.

'Ah,' Lockhart said. 'You're thinking of your love affair. I doubt if it will be relevant to our discussion.'

Now and again Jane felt a sudden, urgent need to slap her friend Jabber and this was one of the times, but even so it would be unfair, she thought. Punishing him for something he couldn't help – like not being a woman.

Lockhart rose. 'I'll go and get him,' he said. 'Help yourself to a cigarette.'

She took one at once. The war was coming back to her.

Lockhart returned with a tall, balding man in a blue suit, stiff collar, and what looked like a college or old-school tie. In his forties, just beginning to run to fat, but shrewd and alert-looking. A little browner than most, she thought, but very much the Harley Street type.

'Jane this is Dr Barker,' Lockhart said. 'Miss Jane Whitcomb – Ross Barker.'

She rose and offered her hand.

'Miss Whitcomb, it's very good of you to agree to see me,' he said. 'I want you to know that I appreciate it.'

And there it all was, in the voice. The tall, lean young men in the villages behind Pozières in the uniform coats that were cut like Norfolk jackets: gamblers who spoke an English all their own, and were homesick for outlandish places with names like Parramatta and Gundagai, Rottnest Island and Broken Hill. John had told her once that they were the most foul-mouthed troops he'd ever met: worse than the Liverpudlians even. But she remembered only how strong and handsome they seemed, until the shells burst among them . . . then they'd looked as dreadful as everybody else.

Barker said, 'From what I hear you had quite a war, Miss Whitcomb.'

Not that he'd heard it: he'd read it in her file. But a lot of men didn't like the idea of it all being written down, and maybe this young woman didn't either. She shrugged. The words refused to come easily, but it didn't matter. He was used to that.

'Miss Whitcomb went to France in 1916,' Lockhart said. 'She served through right till the end.'

'You drove an ambulance?' Barker asked.

'I did.' The words seemed wrenched out of her.

'Ever drive any of our boys? Australians?'

For some reason that got her started.

'I drove everybody,' she said. 'Australians, Canadians, New Zealanders, French, British, Portuguese. . . . Even Germans.'

'Did you find that difficult?' he asked. 'Helping Germans?'

'They didn't look like Germans.'

'What did they look like?'

'Men in pain,' she said.

He nodded, as Lockhart might have done: her words accepted, but no opinion offered.

'They also looked broken for the most part,' she added, 'and nasty. Disgusting.'

'And yet you helped them?'

'It was what I was there for,' she said.

He reached for a cigarette, a tired old trick that meant only that he wanted time to look at her, think about her. What he saw was a typical upper-class lady Pom: right sort of clothes, right down to the shoes and gloves, right accent, right way of sitting. Under weight, certainly, but then a lot of women were these days – and tired almost to the point of exhaustion, but too many nightclubs could be the cause of that. But he'd known that would be false judgement on this one, even without a look in Lockhart's file. This girl was what the blokes used to call a stoush-merchant: a fighter. You might break her, but she wouldn't bend.

'Tell me about the dreams,' he said, and she told him. It came haltingly at first, but he knew how to listen, how to coax, and out it all came at last: the wounded men that she must not see, and the wounded horses who were all too visible, until at last she got to Bridget O'Dowd, not yet seen, but somehow lurking, the most dangerous threat to her hard-won control.

'This horse – Bridget – belonged to a friend of yours?' he asked.

'Yes.'

'What happened to him?'

'He died,' she said. 'Like so many others.'

'And was the horse hurt?'

'Not a scratch,' she said. 'She was a very handsome horse.'

And you would know, Ross Barker thought. You're one who would know all about horses, and maybe all about your dead friend, too. But that's no business of mine.

Aloud he said, 'Thank you for your time and patience, Miss Whitcomb. I have no more questions.'

She shook hands with him then, and pulled on her gloves as if she were leaving a tea party, and walked with Lockhart to the door. When he came back the Australian seemed hardly to have moved, so intent was his concentration.

'Well?' Lockhart asked.

'That's a very determined lady,' Barker said.

'She's going to fight it out to the end,' said Lockhart. 'One way or the other she's going to finish it.'

'No question,' Barker said. 'When did her friend die?'

'Tenth November,' Lockhart said. '1918.'

Barker whistled: 'Couldn't be worse,' he said. 'And yet she's still fighting.'

'It's what she knows,' Lockhart said. 'What she's good at.'

'Too right,' said Barker.

'What sort of chance would you give her?'

Barker took his time about it. 'I wonder what the Freudians would make of it?' he said. 'All those horses.'

'I should think that's pretty obvious,' said Lockhart.

'Yes, but the most important horse is a *mare*,' Barker said. 'You know it's interesting. Not just the mare but the whole thing – all that imagery. Because that's all there is. The whole case is just one vast image. When she doesn't dream – she looks balanced enough, wouldn't you say?'

'Lonely,' said Lockhart. 'Frustrated. Lacking employment. Unfulfilled. But essentially sane and – ' He hesitated.

'Go on.'

'Sad,' said Lockhart. 'Heartrendingly sad. She was made the sort of woman who needs the right sort of man, the sort of man who needs her, and for a time she had him and then he was just – smashed down. Carted off. She's a woman to be loved if ever there was one.'

'We're talking about seven years ago,' Barker said. 'There are plenty of young blokes about these days.'

'For her seven years ago is still last week,' Lockhart said. 'If I could make it *feel* like seven years – she'd be cured.'

'I agree,' said Barker.

'So what's your prognosis?'

Barker snorted. 'Prognosis? After one little chat?'

'Look into your crystal ball then.'

Barker said, 'You're very taken with this lady, aren't you?'

'Yes,' said Lockhart. 'I am. Not because I desire her, at least I hope not, although if I were younger I think I would. But it isn't that. She's one of the ones to whom we owe a debt, Ross, and I can't rest till it's paid.'

'Always supposing you can pay it.'

'For God's sake,' said Lockhart. 'Tell me what you think.'

'I think she'll make it,' Barker said. 'In fact I think there's a part of her that's already made up its mind she'll make it. What do you think?'

'The same as you,' said Lockhart. 'But it isn't just what I think – it's what I want. And that terrifies me.'

She went home to find that she'd received a postcard, which meant that probably everybody in the house had read it from Peggy Hawkins upwards. Certainly her mother would have read it. Her mother read every communication she received, however much it had been stuck down or sealed. For her own good, was how Mummy put it, but where the good lay in knowing in advance what her daughter would tell her anyway Jane could never quite work out.

The reading of the postcard annoyed her. She accepted it from Mummy's disdainful fingers (it seemed a foolish way to put it, but somehow they *were* disdainful) and knew that it must be something good and it was, it was something gorgeous, and that was what annoyed her so much. She should have got the good news first. Be careful, she told herself. Be very careful. For this was an invitation to a reunion of ambulance drivers, and this time she knew she could cope with it. But Mummy didn't approve of even one ambulance driver, let alone a whole gaggle of them.

'You'll decline of course,' Mummy said.

'No,' said Jane. 'I don't think I will.'

Mummy flinched then, surprise and outrage blended. As if I'd jabbed her with a pointed stick, thought Jane.

'You'll become excited,' said Mummy. 'That is never good for you. We know that to our cost.'

Jane thought of the parties of three and four years before, the cinemas and theatres and restaurants when all was going well, with a nice young man hovering, then something would set her off: something trivial or even silly: a scrap of a tune, the sound of a man's laughter, even a smoke ring lazily rising – then off she'd go, leaving confusion and consternation behind her, and for her the tears and hasty exits and hours locked in the 'Ladies' while she cried and cried. But that had been before she'd begun to dream of horses, when she didn't know what was wrong. Now she did know, and all she did was scream out loud in the darkness.

'It might be fun,' she said.

'Fun?'

Really Mummy used the word as if it could mean only orgies. But there wouldn't be any men there, only poor old Fred, who, John had explained to her, was a lesbian, but not really all that good at it by the look of her.

'Fun,' Jane said firmly. 'You're always saying that I never see enough people, and these are my friends.'

'Odd friends,' her mother said. 'Odd *women*.' And then she added: 'Rude mechanicals, your brother called them.'

'David used to call them that because he was jealous. We could repair an engine and he couldn't.'

'It sounds most unwomanly,' said her mother. 'Couldn't you have got some man to do it for you?'

'Better to do it yourself,' said Jane. 'Then you know it's done right.'

Her mother ignored this, perhaps didn't hear it.

'David did write to me about all that,' she said. 'I remember now. But are you saying that he met you and your friends?'

'Certainly,' said Jane.

'But where?'

'Behind Wipers,' said Jane. '1917. The offensive had just finished and we were resting. David's squadron was quite nearby and he flew over.'

'Wipers?'

'The Battle of Ypres,' said Jane. 'The Tommies called it Wipers. I didn't think there was so much mud in the whole wide world.'

'And David flew to you?'

The question touched her for once. It was the way Mummy used the word 'flew'. It was to Mummy that the frightened child should fly. And David had been frightened, as well as brave.

'Oh yes,' she said. 'He landed in the field where we parked the ambulances. It was a good landing, good enough for him to be pleased – which didn't happen all that often with David, you remember what a perfectionist he was? – anyway he got out of the plane and he was smiling, and so of course all my friends fell in love with him.'

'He was a very attractive young man,' her mother said. 'So was Guy. So in fact is Francis.'

Better not go into that, thought Jane.

'Francis has left us?'

'For Cambridge,' her mother said. 'He has neglected his work for long enough, he tells me.'

'With Mr Pardoe?'

'I assume so. Your father has decided that we shan't receive him.'

Banished into outer darkness and a good thing too, Jane thought.

Aloud she said, 'His first name is Cuthbert.'

'Do stick to the point,' said her mother, but all the same she was pleased.

'The point is I'm going to this reunion,' said Jane. 'Unless you and Papa object.'

Mummy's pleasure vanished. 'Papa can see no harm in it,' she said. 'He rarely can when you seek some form of self-indulgence.'

'But you can?'

'I have already stated my fears of what harm excitement can induce in you.'

The next fence was a swine, but she had to take it.

'You let me go to the ball,' she said.

'You had Francis to look after you.'

'Does he say that I behaved badly?'

'No,' said her mother. 'He seems to feel that you behaved well enough. But you had his support after all.' Jane waited.

'Oh go if you must,' said her mother. 'But don't come crying to me if it all ends in tears.'

Jane could think of no answer that was neither cringing nor effusive, and the ringing of the telephone bell absolved her of the need to try, until Moreton came in.

'It's for you, Miss Jane,' she said.

Her mother could scarcely credit it. Who, she wondered, could feel the need to speak to her daughter on the instrument? When Moreton told her that it was Mrs Nettles, Lady Whitcomb's annoyance intensified. Mrs Nettles was *her* sister-in-law. She should have asked for Lady Whitcomb first. Moreton's only response was a silence so strongly indicating patient resignation that in the end Lady Whitcomb said no more, and Jane went into the hall and, standing between the two draughts, picked up the telephone.

'Yes, Aunt Pen?' she said.

'What a time you've been,' said her aunt. 'Are you in disgrace because I called you to the instrument?'

'It's more or less my permanent state,' said Jane, then added: 'Are you all right?' Telephone voices were often strange, but Aunt Pen's had sounded quite weird.

'I want to see you,' her aunt said. 'Can you come? Now?'

'Of course,' said Jane.

'It's urgent, Jane. Don't say you'll come if she won't let you.'

'I'll come,' said Jane.

'That's my lovely,' said Aunt Pen. 'When I say now – better make it teatime. There's a man I must see. And Jane darling, I'll need to know how your father is. Have you seen him today?'

'Not yet.'

'Do it, will you? Then come over to Mount Street. In a *taxi*, darling. Aunt Pen will pay.'

'You already have,' said Jane. 'I've got an allowance from you, remember? Thirty bob a week.'

'Goodness how generous I am,' said Aunt Pen, and then: 'Replace the instrument, my lovely. I must go.'

Jane hung up and returned to the drawing room. Foch had appeared and sat with his back to her mother. It was one of the days when he and Lady Whitcomb did not speak.

'Aunt Pen wants to see me,' said Jane.

'Has she a particular reason?'

'There's something wrong,' said Jane. 'I know there is. But she wouldn't say that. Not on the telephone.'

'Is she ill?'

'I think perhaps she is.'

'And did she ask for me?'

'No, Mummy,' said Jane. No one ever asked for Mummy any more, not even Francis.

'No,' her mother said. 'Of course not.' Her fists clenched. 'You'd better be off, hadn't you? To visit the sick and attend your reunions and talk with your nerve specialist. . . . You fade away, don't you, Jane dear? You're so good at it. . . . Like the Cheshire Cat.'

'Why should I do that, Mummy?'

'To leave me alone with your father,' her mother said. 'Darby and Joan. He on his floor and I on mine. I doubt if we exchange fifty words a day.' Her right hand unclenched. It held her handkerchief. 'Go away child,' her mother said, and Jane left at once. She had no wish to watch her mother cry for the second time. Foch felt the same: he came too.

In her bedroom she took out her writing case and fountain pen and replied to her invitation. Harriet had written it. Harriet Ryland she'd been then. Now she was Harriet Watson. Dr Harriet Watson. Nice for her: a husband and a profession. She looked down at Foch.

'I honestly believe that you're the only one here who doesn't know what Harriet wrote,' she said. 'Unless you heard Mummy read it out to Papa.' Foch looked hurt.

Dear Harriet, [Jane wrote]
    Your reunion seems a super idea. Do count me in. It will be marvellous to see the old crowd again. . . .

Will it? she wondered. Or will it be disastrous? But whatever it will be I shall have to go through with it. Then Hawkins came in with clean hand towels.

'I'm sorry, miss,' she said. 'I didn't know you were up here.'

'I'm just going out,' said Jane, 'but I'm glad I saw you. I haven't had a chance to say thank you for helping me up to bed.'

'A pleasure, miss,' Hawkins said.

'Hardly that,' said Jane, and smiled at her. Hawkins smiled back.

'It was a pleasure keeping you out of harm's way, miss,' she said.

'You've done it before I take it?' said Jane. 'Helped the helpless I mean?'

'My dad always gets a bit cheerful if he's had a good win on the horses,' Hawkins said.

'I wasn't exactly cheerful,' said Jane. 'In fact how or why I got like that I simply don't know. I wish I did.'

'You wasn't used to it,' said Hawkins. 'I could tell. And anyway it gets very hot in them dances. Weakens your resistance.'

'I'll bear that in mind,' said Jane, then opened her handbag, took out Aunt Pen's pound note and offered it to Hawkins.

'You don't have to miss,' said Hawkins.

'But I want to,' said Jane. 'I only wish I could make it more. But I can't. Please take it.'

Hawkins took it, and stowed it in the pocket of her apron.

'Thank you miss,' she said. 'It's rotten being hard up, isn't it?'

Then she left Jane to apply a little powder, very cautiously, then go along the corridor to her father's study. He was looking at more photographs, a haphazard pile tipped out at random on the desk. He passed one to her.

'Shikar,' he said. 'Bengal. 1911.'

Two men in pith helmets, armed with rifles that looked as if they could stop tanks. In the background an elephant, kneeling at ease, its mahout asleep in its shade, and in the foreground two dead tigers.

'Billy Smith-Hatton and me,' her father said. 'We were at school together then he came out to work in Lucknow. Legal chappy. Mad on shooting.' He took the photograph back. 'We measured the tigers. Can't think why. It was just something one did. His was a touch bigger than mine. Just as well, really. He'd have sulked for days.'

'Good afternoon, Papa,' said Jane. 'How are you today?'

Sir Guy chuckled. 'Teaching me my manners?' he asked.

'No, of course not,' she said. 'Just wondering how you are.'

'Because I said you could go to your reunion? Not that I would, if I were you. Boring affairs for the most part. I haven't attended one in years.'

'I'll risk that,' said Jane.

'I thought you would,' said her father, and then: 'Don't take any notice of what I've just said. It occurs to me that your reunions are probably the equivalent of what this pile of old junk is to me – ' He gestured at the fading photographs. 'The joy of my life. You go. With my blessing.'

'Papa,' she said, 'have you seen your doctor recently?'

He chuckled again. 'You sounded just like your aunt, then. One of her famous knight's moves in logic, remember? Let me see if I can work out how you got there.'

He groped for his cigarettes, found them, and offered one to her, and she lit them both with his little silver lighter.

'I support you in your struggle for independence, even though it means upsetting your mother,' he said at last. 'This leads you to suspect that I have given up worrying about my health, and the only possible reason for that is that I am a hopeless case. Therefore you ask me whether or not I've seen my doctor. Well?'

She looked at him steadily. It was what he wanted: needed even.

'Pretty good,' she said. 'Flawless, in fact.'

'The answer is that I do allow Mahaffy to call from time to time,' said her father. 'He's an amusing fellow, but it serves no purpose other than sociability. Where are you off to?' The subject it seemed was closed.

'To take tea with Aunt Pen,' she said.

'The incomparable logician. A delightful woman, my sister. Hidden talents, too. Do you know she was once Ladies' Croquet Champion of Uttar Pradesh? I've got a photograph here somewhere – '

He reached for a shoe box, then his hand drew back.

'But why bother,' he said, 'when you can visit the original? Give her my love.'

'Of course, Papa.'

Carefully she stubbed out the cigarette, then kissed him on the cheek.

8

As she walked towards the taxi rank on the High Street, Jane found that she was thinking of Vinney. It must have been Aunt Pen's call, she thought, that and Mummy dredging up memories of *A Midsummer Night's Dream*. Because the rude mechanicals had been Vinney's favourite Shakespearean characters. 'Because they're so endearingly stupid,' she'd explained to Jane. 'So characteristically male.'

Vinney – Miss Vincent on state occasions – had been most uncharacteristically female. She had been her governess, chosen by Aunt Pen, paid for by Uncle Walter, to be governess to Jane, tutor to Guy and David, when they were home from school and needed tutoring. Vinney was one of those rare and gifted beings who could teach anything: quadratic equations, leg-break bowling, anything. It was she who had first persuaded Jane to explore the engine of Uncle Walter's car – to the fury of the chauffeur, until she'd co-opted him as a teacher, too. He'd turned out to be quite a good one.

'The male sex,' Vinney told Jane, 'has its uses.' Always 'the male sex'; never 'men'. For Miss Vincent was a suffragette, committed, resolute, dauntless.

Guy and David had thought this exquisitely funny, though they never laughed in front of her. Few people dared. But for Guy and David there had been more to it than that. Grotesque as the suffragettes had seemed to them, they loved Miss Vincent. For Jane there had never been cause for laughter in Vinney: only love. Vinney did not *look* lovable. She was too big, too competent, and much, much too forthright. She was a former scholar of Somerville College, Oxford, who had missed a first, and therefore a fellowship, by a whisker, and was all too ready to tell people so. But she knew how to teach, and how to offer love – and how to accept it in return.

She had courage, too, Jane remembered, and a wit all her own. In 1912, long after she had left Jane, she had trained a group of young women in the art of artillery so well that they had loaded and fired a cannon captured in the Crimean War, and scored a direct hit on the local Liberal club where Lloyd George was due to speak the next day. No one had been hurt (the cannon was fired at dawn) but the meeting had had to be abandoned. She had even written to Jane to tell her all about it, quite certain that Jane would never betray her, and anxious to reassure her that the male sex were not having things all their own way, not even in Tunbridge Wells.

I have in many ways been lucky, thought Jane. John, of course, always John first, but Guy and David also, and Mummy as she was, and Papa always. And Aunt Pen and Vinney, so disgracefully forgotten, and Lockhart who would not let her give way. . . . Very lucky she had been. But how many of them were alive now? How many would there be in twelve months' time?

She shook her head angrily, and Foch at the end of his lead, sensing the movement, looked up at her.

'And there's you, of course,' she said. 'I hadn't forgotten you, honestly.'

Foch snorted. He knew precisely how unforgettable he was, and preened himself all the way in the cab to Aunt Pen's. When she paid it off she had exactly ninepence ha'penny left.

Tea was good. It always was at Aunt Pen's: cucumber sandwiches and éclairs and Battenburg cake, and all the biscuits that she and Foch and Rob liked most. Jane ate all that she could – Aunt Pen's cook was an artist of extreme sensitivity – and Foch and Rob ate all that they could scrounge. But Aunt Pen ate hardly anything at all, which was strange: her appetite had always impressed her nephews and niece. But this time she nibbled at one biscuit and watched her tea grow cold as Marchmont hovered and Jane told as much as she could of the Poynter ball.

'You must have looked divine,' said Aunt Pen. 'Saris are so lovely.'

But she said the words as if she were reading them, thought Jane. Reading but not quite understanding.

Champagne, said Jane, and 'Love Will Find A Way' and an odd young don called Pardoe. Aunt Pen smiled and nodded, but unconvincingly, as if Jane were delivering a highbrow lecture miles above her head, but she was too polite to say so. And then at last Marchmont left.

Aunt Pen said at once, 'Did you speak to your father?'

'Yes of course,' said Jane.

'And how is he?' Jane hesitated. 'Please tell me,' her aunt said. 'I must know.'

Jane said, 'He believes that he is dying.'

'Snap,' said Aunt Pen.

Jane had been ready for that, or something like it, and yet even so was horrified. For her to have bad dreams was one thing: but for Aunt Pen, glowing and gorgeous in her elegant and resolutely out-of-date tea gown to announce her own death: it wasn't possible.

'But surely – ' she began.

'You think I may be imagining things?'

'Of course not. But – '

'Listen, my lovely. If someone tells you you're going to die, you don't just take their word for it. You ask another expert, and another and another – and hope you'll finish up with one who thinks you might live after all.

'Well now I've tried five. You remember I said I had to see a man this afternoon? He was the fifth one. He left half an hour before you got here – and he's as big a hanging judge as the rest of them. He was very sorry, he said. But he still took my ten guineas.'

'But what's wrong?' Jane asked.

'Cancer,' said her aunt. 'Of the *most* unflattering kind. Breasts and things. I'd be no price at all in the Judgement of Paris Stakes now.'

'But can't they operate?'

'If I let them,' said her aunt. 'But I won't.'

'Darling, why not?'

'He did give me the odds on that. A one-in-seven chance of success he said. Radium and dressings and all the time being sick and then dying anyway. . . . And even if I lived I'd hate myself. My body, I mean. Or what was left of it. I know you young things are all for the boyish look – but I can't see any of you going that far.'

Jane got up then, went to where her aunt lay on a sofa, and embraced her. 'I love you,' she said. 'I always have. Since first I knew you. Uncle Walter, too. I loved you both. And so did Guy. And David.'

'The nicest thing about India,' said Aunt Pen. 'If it hadn't kept your father and Honoria there, we'd never have had you to love.'

'And now you're leaving me?'

'Like David? Like young Guy, you mean?'

'They had no chance,' said Jane. 'But even one in seven. I mean he could be wrong – '

'No,' said her aunt. 'The cancer's been kind to me so far. Dormant, Judge Jeffries called it. But soon it won't be.'

'What then?'

Her aunt shrugged. 'Narcotics,' she said. 'Stronger and stronger. Judge Jeffries does *not* approve.'

'Then how will you manage?'

'There's a man in Geneva who is more than willing to oblige me. . . . I shall be an addict, darling. What would your mother say?'

Jane's arms tightened round her and she rocked her aunt like a child. But Aunt Pen didn't cry. Not then. Not ever. Not for herself.

'Tell me about Guy,' she said.

'He's started doing what *he* wants,' said Jane.

'Defying Honoria, you mean. So that's how you know he's dying? What a macabre family we are. . . . Did he tell you he was dying?'

'He wasn't quite so forthright as you.'

Her aunt smiled. 'He was always the nicest man,' she said.

'We were talking about you,' Jane said. 'He told me you won a croquet championship somewhere. United Provinces, was it?'

'Yes,' her aunt said. 'And it's perfectly true. I did win it. Thanks to your father.'

'What did he do?'

'He showed me how to cheat,' said her aunt.

'The nicest man,' Jane mocked.

'Well so he was,' said her aunt. 'He knew I was dying to win. Dying. . . . What a stupid thing to say. . . . Has he got long?'

'He didn't tell me,' said Jane. 'If he had he wouldn't have dropped as much as a hint.'

'Poor Honoria,' her aunt said, and then: 'Posy Sanderson. Did he by any chance mention that name?'

'He showed me her photograph,' said Jane.

'Oh my poor sweet Guy,' said Aunt Pen, and that time, for her brother, she did weep.

Another of her famous knight's moves, thought Jane. Because Papa showed me the photograph, she knows he hasn't long to go. . . . Any more than she has. . . . How cosy Mummy and I will be together.

'It's all arranged, – going to Geneva, I mean,' Aunt Pen said. 'Or it will be quite soon.'

'You've spoken to your lawyer?'

'Not yet,' said her aunt. 'Though I'll have to of course.'

'Then – forgive me, aunt – but who's arranged it?'

'Why Marchmont,' said Aunt Pen. 'Butlers always arrange everything. He's going to marry Sophie.'

'Your maid?'

'The very same. One doesn't have to have one's hair done to be a dope fiend. He and the rest of them are going to buy a hotel in Hove. . . . I do hope Marchmont remains faithful, with all those housemaids in his power. So often butlers turn out to be positive pashas.'

'Do they indeed?'

'Sexual adventure has a great deal to do with opportunity. Haven't you noticed that?'

She has every right to an answer, Jane thought, and spoke at once.

'Opportunity is important,' she said. 'At least I found it so – but in my experience, my very limited experience, once the need is felt, the opportunity can be made.'

'Thank you for telling me, my lovely,' said her aunt. 'Somehow it was important to know.'

Jane said firmly, 'Talking of the male sex, I found myself thinking about Vinney today.'

Her aunt turned in Jane's arms to face her. 'What about her?'

she said, then began to laugh. 'Oh, darling, if you could see yourself. The picture of consternation. But there's no need to look so troubled. She isn't dead.'

'Where is she then?'

'In Delhi. Running a school for orphans. It was an ambition she had. . . . In almost anybody else one might have called it a vision. But Vinney didn't see visions. Only wrongs that must be set to rights. She came to see me, and told me exactly how much I must give her to help get the orphanage started. She was very nice about it.'

'She didn't come to see me,' said Jane.

'You haven't got any money,' her aunt said, and then – 'Don't let it distress you. Please don't. Vinney has no time to spare. Not even for love. So she opted for compassion instead. That means she sees only the very rich or the very poor. The middle classes are out.'

'I would have helped her,' said Jane.

'She doesn't need help. She needs money. And anyway – '

'Well?'

'She's fond of you. A lot of people are. But she can't afford to be near people she's fond of. They'd just get in the way.'

'Of the orphans?' Her aunt nodded. 'Girl orphans?'

'Whenever possible,' said her aunt. 'You don't approve?'

'Of course I do,' said Jane. 'In India an orphan girl needs every chance she can get. I hope you gave her a lot of money.'

'Yes,' her aunt said. 'I did. And speaking of money – how is your allowance holding out?'

'It isn't,' said Jane. 'I had to tip our housemaid a quid.'

'Rather a lot for a housemaid.'

'She did rather a lot for me.'

Her aunt nodded. 'Sounds like a story.'

'Oh it is,' said Jane, 'but – '

'But what?'

'Aren't you feeling tired?'

'No,' her aunt said. 'I don't think I shall ever feel tired again – until the pain comes. But let's get rid of this money nonsense first. How much have you got left?'

'Ninepence ha'penny,' said Jane.

Her aunt chuckled. 'You won't get fat on that. Unless – '

'Yes, aunt?'

'You could do me a favour,' her aunt said. 'Make yourself some money too.'

'Of course,' said Jane. 'What?'

'You could come here and stay with me. Until the pain comes I mean and I have to go away. I know I asked you once before – '

'And you were ill then, weren't you? But you didn't tell me.'

'I was still waiting to see Judge Jeffries,' said her aunt. 'But now we both know – what do you say?'

'I'd be glad to,' said Jane. 'That is – if Papa doesn't need me at home.'

'Let me talk to him on the instrument,' said Aunt Pen. 'I'm sure he won't mind sharing.'

'No. I'll do that,' said Jane. 'But I think I ought to tell Mummy first.'

'But you will telephone, won't you?' said Aunt Pen. 'And stay the night?'

'I haven't got any things,' said Jane.

'I have,' said her aunt. 'I'll set Sophie to find some that aren't too impossibly old.'

While she did so, Jane went to the telephone, which was in a sort of cloakroom in the hall, and enviably free from draughts. Aunt Pen, she told her mother, was not well, and had requested her company for the night. Her mother declared that the scheme was unthinkable and Jane said she must stay or else Aunt Pen would be left on her own.

'On her own?' her mother cried. 'The woman has seventeen servants.'

A slight exaggeration, thought Jane, but even so Mummy had a point.

'And what is wrong with her anyway?' her mother asked.

Jane lied without hesitation. A combination of Mummy and the instrument were not the means by which to break Aunt Pen's news to her father.

'That's why Aunt Pen wants me to stay,' she said. 'So that she can tell me about it.'

'It must be a most extraordinarily complicated affliction,' said her mother, 'if it's going to take all night to describe the symptoms.'

On the contrary, thought Jane, it's most fiendishly simple.

'Aunt Pen hasn't said so,' she said aloud, 'but I think she's a little nervous.'

'Then perhaps you had better stay with her,' said her mother, and went on to ruin the effect by adding, 'she always was a bit of a cry-baby.'

Jane said, 'Is Papa there?'

'Papa is extremely busy,' Mummy said. 'Upstairs. With his photographs.'

'Tell him I'll give him a full report tomorrow.'

'Very well.'

'Shall I give Aunt Pen your love?'

'Naturally,' her mother said, and hung up.

That evening they talked again of Vinney, and in particular of a day that Jane had forgotten, though not Aunt Pen.

'It was the summer that Walter rented that place in West Sussex,' she said. 'At one time he'd thought of buying it, but in the end I talked him out of it. West Sussex is too far from London, never mind Paris. – Marchmont was furious, I remember.'

'What on earth did it have to do with Marchmont?'

Aunt Pen glanced, rather furtively Jane thought, at the drawing-room door. It was shut. 'All good butlers are feudal at heart,' she said. 'And how can you be feudal without an estate? Walter had to raise his salary to make him stay on. Anyway it was a quite heavenly summer. 1907 would it be? 1908? You and I went to Paris in May, I remember. Vinney was furious because she'd spent so much time on teaching you to speak French properly, and she knew once we were away together we'd talk nothing but English.'

'I do remember,' said Jane. 'You bought me a blue velvet dress. . . . Didn't you have it made?'

'Of course,' said her aunt. 'It was very becoming.'

'It was for my fourteenth birthday,' Jane said. 'I adored that dress. . . . I wore it to the opera, didn't I?'

'*The Pearl Fishers*,' said her aunt. 'De Peszke was not in form. He made my teeth ache. . . . But we were talking about Vinney.'

'In West Sussex. The house was called Five Oaks, wasn't it?'

'You do remember. And there was a piece of grass miles from anywhere. Not the lawn – that was immaculate. This was just a great lump behind some cedars that somebody had decided would do for tennis courts and then hadn't bothered.'

'And then Guy and David decided it would do for cricket. For practice anyway. They used to bribe the second gardener's children to field for them. And then one day the fielders didn't turn up.'

'It was a Sunday,' said Jane, 'and the under-gardener was a Baptist.'

'You and Walter and I went for a walk and found them,' said Aunt Pen. 'And of course they had us fielding in no time at all.'

'They shouldn't have been practising and we shouldn't have been playing,' said Jane. 'It was a Sunday.'

'Guy and David had more than their fair share of chums,' said Aunt Pen. 'Like their sister. . . . It was just their bad luck that we had Walter with us.'

'He wanted to bat?' Jane asked.

'He *did* bat,' said Aunt Pen. 'It was part of the bargain he made – and Walter was very good at bargains. He had to be, being a box-wallah. Anyway he batted and Guy and David bowled, and they couldn't get him out, and being Walter he couldn't pretend to make a mistake and put himself out on purpose. No Yorkshireman could. So there he stuck and he wouldn't give way and neither would the boys – and then Vinney came looking for us.'

'She wanted to take me to Evensong because I'd missed Morning Prayers,' said Jane.

'Only she stopped to bowl at Walter instead,' said Aunt Pen. 'She got him in her second over.'

'It must have been a leg-break,' said Jane. 'She was awfully good at leg-breaks. Anyway I missed Evensong.'

'It's funny,' said Aunt Pen. 'Odd funny I mean. We were all so happy that afternoon but I can't remember any of us smiling – Vinney least of all. Not even when she bowled Walter. I suppose it's because cricket's sort of our second religion.'

Jane thought of the maharajah of Balpur and her father's rage.

'Oh it's much more important than that,' she said. 'One might miss Evensong, but one couldn't miss the Eton and Harrow match – not without a decent excuse.'

'You're a clever girl, my lovely, and Vinney would be proud of you,' said her aunt, 'but we *were* happy, weren't we?'

'I was,' said Jane, 'and I'm pretty sure that David and Guy were too, but that was because we were young and healthy, and quite adequately clever, and Aunt Pen and Uncle Walter were always there when they were wanted.'

'It was our – privilege, I suppose is the word I want,' said Aunt Pen. 'Or perhaps our good fortune. We were here, and Guy and Honoria weren't. Not their fault. We tried not to – '

'Take their place?' said Jane. 'You never did. You always had a special place of your own. So often – children like us – sent home to escape the heat – were just farmed out, housed on sufferance. Their lives were misery. Ours were magic, and we blessed you both for it when we remembered – which wasn't nearly often enough.'

Her aunt looked up at the clock on the mantelshelf.

'I hope it's nearly dinnertime,' she said. 'I'm rather hungry.'

After dinner they talked more of childhood, and Vinney's ability to insert knowledge into even the most reluctant head.

'And you never regretted not going to school?' her aunt asked. 'After all, your brothers – '

'They had no choice,' said Jane. 'One could almost say it was their fate – their karma if you like. But it was also what they wanted.'

'Did they?'

'Of course they did,' said Jane. 'It was what they were good at. Greek, Latin, cricket, football. Whatever they touched. . . . The shining ones.'

'The ones the gods loved,' said her aunt. 'Is that why they died so young?'

'Not too young to have known happiness,' said Jane. 'Every kind of happiness – like seeing their sister's governess clean bowl their uncle by marriage.'

'If they'd lived – ' her aunt began.

'If they'd lived they'd be here now, with you, just as I am.'

'And Honoria wouldn't hate either of us,' said Aunt Pen. 'Would you help me up, darling? Reliving one's life is quite exhausting.'

9

JANE WALKED UPSTAIRS with her aunt, and handed her over to Sophie. In her own room a small fire burned, despite the early summer, and on her bed were the night clothes Sophie had chosen: clothes her aunt must have long outlived: a negligée of quite outrageous frivolity, and a silk nightgown that Mummy would have condemned out of hand. Lucky Uncle Walter. She undressed and put on both, then sat in front of the fire and smoked a cigarette from the box on the bedside table.

It had been a happy evening, she did not doubt that, and yet it had been an evening devoted to death. None of the dead were perfect – how could they be? They were mortal or they would not have died – but there had been goodness in them, all three, a goodness that transcended their silly game, and yet somehow the game had captured the essence of all three of them, as it had of Papa when he raged about the maharajah.

They had been good people, but now they were gone, just as Papa would soon be gone, and Aunt Pen too, and she, Jane Whitcomb, still hadn't the faintest idea what she would do: what her mind would allow her to do, except that, like Aunt Pen, she would never cry out of pity for herself. Once she did that she really would go mad. . . . There had been a piece of prose that Vinney had been fond of: that she had made Jane learn by heart, and now it came back to her: 'O eloquent, just and mighty Death! whom none could advise thou hast persuaded: what none hath dared, thou hast done; and whom all the world hath flattered, thou only hast cast out of the world and despised. . . .'

She could hear Vinney's voice quite clearly. 'Sir Walter Raleigh wrote that, child. It's from his *History of the World*. He wrote it when he was imprisoned in the Tower, and had no hope of coming out. Not then. What courage he had. What style!'

'What praise for a member of the male sex,' Jane had teased.

'Male sex be damned,' Vinney had said. 'This was a *man*! There aren't too many of them, but he was one. You can jolly well learn it off by heart to remind yourself of that fact.'

So death was just, as well as mighty, Sir Walter claimed. That would take some thinking about. Had he been just to the soldiers in the war? That he'd been mighty was beyond dispute. . . . She woke up with a start. A coal in the fire had popped, and the smoke from her dying cigarette rose up like incense. It was time to go to bed. If she were going to have nightmares she might as well have them in comfort.

The mattress was firm, unlike the feather thing at home, and yet relaxing. Once, only once, she and John had shared a bed like that, when they went to Paris, and a room at the Ritz had absorbed their entire supply of spare cash. But it had been worth every penny: a night to remember. John had loved her quite beautifully. Maybe that was because the war was farther away. You couldn't even hear it except for the odd times when the Huns had used that incredible gun of theirs, the one called Big Bertha, to shell the city. Never more than a few rounds – even German technology wasn't up to a sustained bombardment – and it had been fun to watch the righteous indignation of civilians when they discovered that they too could be shelled. So John had laughed, and laughing had relaxed, and relaxing, loved her. The feel of his body had been wonderful, and hers enfolding his, until at last there had been neither his body nor her body, but theirs conjoined in one. And it had all been so wonderful she had yelled out loud.

Come come, she admonished herself. This won't do. You are guilty of what that incredible Girl Guide mistress used to call impure thoughts. (What Vinney had called them, apart from a bloody nuisance, she couldn't remember. They were just one more on the unending list of crimes the male sex would have to answer for on Judgement Day.) But she had called out aloud. She couldn't remember it, but John had told her so, looking smug. What on earth could I have shouted, she wondered. Howzat?

Another coal popped as the fire died. . . . Sometimes a nervous sentry, alone and vulnerable on the firestep, would imagine something moving, out in the angry dark, and loose off a shot without thinking. She'd heard it herself at a forward dressing station. . . . And then, John said, a sergeant or platoon commander would come running, swearing his questions to show how brave he was. And sometimes it would be nothing except a boy's need for his mother, or a man's for a wife deep breathing in a warm bed, and life, not death to look forward to. But sometimes it might be a raid, and the soldiers would come running from the sand-bagged shelters they called dug-outs, clattering along the duckboards to push back the Huns. Verey lights and machine guns and rifle fire, Stokes mortars and grenades. Or maybe Fritz got closer still and into the trenches, and then it would be rifle butts, bayonets, revolvers. John despised the British Army issue revolver for officers. It never hit what you aimed at. He'd bought a German Luger automatic from an Australian, instead. At least with that you had a chance. – Until 10th November, 1918. . . . The fire glimmered then died, like star shells falling.

And then it was daylight, and a bright and beautiful sun, and a much smarter maid than Hawkins, or even Moreton, brought her tea and biscuits, and Foch, who had spent the night in a kennel in the garden with Rob, ambled in and demanded his share.

'Good morning,' said Jane. 'I hope you slept well.'

Foch's tail twitched. Well enough, it seemed.

'I had a quite remarkable night,' said Jane. 'To begin with I am absolutely certain that I didn't scream, and I think you will agree with me that that in itself is remarkable.'

Foch waited for another biscuit, realised that he wasn't going to get one, and settled down to listen.

'And then I have no recollection of dreaming,' Jane said. 'I've no doubt I *did* dream, one of those sweaty fathoms-deep affairs Jabber talks about, but I don't *remember* it. And that's got to be a good thing, surely?'

Foch yawned.

'All very well for you,' said Jane. 'I expect all you ever dream about is rabbits, and the next Madame Foch – if I may so express it?'

Foch yawned again.

'I'm boring you, aren't I?' said Jane. 'You always get my problems. I know Mrs Blythe-Tarkington said I should talk to you – indeed she told us both, but dash it all Foch, there are limits.' Then almost shyly she added, 'What I mean is people might think that one or other of us was going crazy.'

She got up and stretched, and Foch, a diehard Presbyterian, averted his eyes.

'Breakfast first,' she said. 'Something nourishing for a change. And then we must go and see Papa. – Mummy too, of course.'

But it was Papa they saw. After a breakfast of devilled bones and kedgeree and toast and marmalade, it was late in the morning when Jane got back to Kensington. Papa was upstairs with his photographs, but Mummy was not at home. It was a second Thursday, Jane remembered, and every second Thursday Mummy took lunch with her old chum Miss Gwatkin, who speculated on the morals of the curate, who had, so it was said, been seen to one-step.

'Have a good evening?' her father asked.

'Yes,' said Jane. 'I did as a matter of fact.'

'You sound surprised.'

'I am surprised. . . . . Aunt Pen isn't well, Papa. In fact she's very ill.'

'I thought she might be,' her father said. 'Pen's always been furtive about bad news. What's wrong with her?'

'Cancer.'

Her father nodded, then very deliberately began to put away the photographs that lay on the desk before him, and took a cigarette.

'Help yourself,' he said, and Jane lit up for them both with his little silver lighter.

'She'll have seen the best men?'

'Yes, Papa.'

'Of course. With her money she'd be a fool not to. Will they operate?'

'She won't let them.'

'I see,' her father said.

'Do you?'

'Oh I think so. If she won't let them operate she thinks there's no chance. And my sister was never a fool.'

'She wants me to stay with her for a while, and I think I should. It isn't as if I'd be far away – '

'Of course,' her father said, and then: 'I want to see her.'

'She wants that too.'

'And your mother?' Jane was silent. 'She ought to see your mother,' her father said. 'For your sake.'

'Because Aunt Pen had me with her as a child and Mummy didn't?'

'It's a debt,' said her father. 'Pen will want to pay it. Tell me about her.'

And Jane told him, almost everything, because now that Papa was dying he was strong again.

'Drugging herself like that,' he said. 'Do you think that what she's doing is right?'

Jane thought of Penelope Nettles: witty and graceful and charming: most feminine of ladies.

'Oh yes,' she said.

Her father grunted. 'You'll have a hard time persuading your mother,' he said.

'Mummy would have chosen the operation?'

'Certainly she would,' said her father. 'She is not to be despised for that.'

'Of course not,' said Jane. 'She's to be admired. Perhaps feared.'

'Did you tell your aunt about me?'

'She asked,' said Jane, 'and I told her. And she wept.'

'It'll give us something to think about,' said her father. 'Wondering which of us will die first. An extra pinch of chilli in the curry.'

'You're not being very kind, Papa.'

He looked up at her then, and his face looked puzzled.

'No I suppose I wasn't,' he said at last, 'but dying makes one selfish I'm afraid. You'll have to allow for that.'

Carefully he shuffled together the photographs before him and returned them to their shoe box.

'Better start packing up,' he said. 'You know dying's rather like one's last school hols. I mean when one has finished sixth form and one doesn't know whether the university will accept one or not. All the same – everything must be left tidy.' He put the box back with its fellows. 'Not that there'll be a devil of a lot to leave.'

'Don't worry, Papa.'

'I'll try not to, because I'm a lazy feller. Always was. All the same I *shall* worry – because you're my daughter and I love you. Maybe Pen will help you.'

'She's done enough already,' said Jane.

'I wonder if she thinks so?'

'Papa you mustn't ask her. Promise me.'

He looked into her face, troubled, sad, and yet somehow the face of a much younger Jane.

'Promise, Papa.'

'Oh very well,' he said. 'You have my word I won't ask.' Then he rose to his feet. 'Do you wish to titivate at all before lunch?'

'Just a bit.'

'Then I shall go down to the cellar,' he said, and snorted. 'Cellar indeed. A cupboard with delusions of grandeur.'

He came up with Bollinger, and the toast was 'Confusion to Cuthbert', but nothing more was said of Pardoe, to Jane's relief. The food was good: far beyond the average, as, Jane remembered, it usually was on second Thursdays, when cook's decisions were her own. Papa ate heartily, almost greedily, and Jane did her best to match his enthusiasm. After lunch they went back to his study, and there Moreton brought up coffee, and they sat and smoked and gossiped and remembered. Especially Papa remembered ayah.

'She loved you, you know,' he said. 'You're lucky. So many people have loved you.'

You don't even know about the one who loved me best, she thought, and I can't bring myself to tell you, even now, and it may be my last chance.

'She took you to a saddhu,' Papa was saying. 'Got herself all excited, I remember. Came and told me all about it. Great things awaited you, the saddhu said. Called you a leopardess.' He smiled. 'Naturally we thought it was all mumbo-jumbo. You were pretty and clever and by God you could ride. But great things – '

'Maybe he meant the war,' she said.

'It was great enough, God knows,' her father agreed. 'But your part in it was not. Honourable and courageous, certainly. But modest, rather than great.'

'Then the saddhu was wrong.'

'I used to think so,' said her father. 'But now I'm not so sure. Great things. God knows you're clever enough – and capable. Far and away the most practical of the four. You get it from your mother.' This time her face showed dismay. He said gently, 'We're agreed, are we not, that the war hit her hard?'

'Yes, Papa. And you.'

'But you forget – I told you I was a lazy feller. Your mother is never lazy.' He smothered a yawn. 'There you see. . . . I'm drowsy now, and all I did was eat lunch.' He spoke in Hindi: 'Forgive me, little daughter, but I must rest.'

In Hindi she replied, 'I wish my father a refreshing sleep.'

She was almost asleep herself when her mother returned, yawning over the *Illustrated London News*, while Foch fumed and fretted, impatient for exercise.

'Miss Gwatkin is well, and enquired after you most kindly,' her mother said.

Gravely Jane replied, 'I hope you conveyed my best wishes to her.'

'Of course,' said her mother. 'You gave mine to your aunt, I assume.' Without hypocrisy, how could civilised communication survive? 'You have news of your aunt?'

'I'm afraid,' said Jane, 'that she's dying.'

'Impossible,' said Lady Whitcomb, then: 'No of course it's not impossible. – It's just that if anyone seemed to me to be indestructible it was Penelope Nettles. You had better tell me all you know.'

Jane told her, and when she had done her mother said, 'So she is determined to avoid pain, come what may?'

'Whether she avoids it or accepts it,' Jane said, 'she is convinced the end will be death, and so she has chosen to avoid it.'

'You don't find her decision cowardly?'

'How can I judge unless I feel her pain?'

Her mother said, 'That is a very shrewd answer, and a charitable one. All the same, one cannot help thinking that your aunt may in a sense have opted for suicide – a most unchristian decision.'

Jane said nothing.

'Even so I shall pray for her,' Lady Whitcomb said. 'You have informed your papa?' Jane nodded. 'Tactfully, I trust?'

'I did my best.'

'And he?'

'He's resting now,' said Jane, 'but we ate a good lunch. We drank champagne.'

'Indeed?'

'It was to celebrate the absence of Mr Pardoe.'

'There is a whimsical streak in your father which he appears to have passed on to you,' said Lady Whitcomb. 'Genes do they call them? I can never remember.'

'He wants to see Aunt Pen,' said Jane.

'And I am also to have that privilege?'

'Of course.'

Baulked of one source of combat, Lady Whitcomb at once found another. 'And you are determined to go on staying with her?'

'So long as I'm needed.'

'You are needed here,' her mother said.

'Papa says not.'

'After you made him tipsy with champagne, no doubt. . . . I am of course powerless to prevent this act, selfish though it is, and I can only hope that you will have no cause to regret it.'

She had packed a case to take over to Aunt Pen's, but Jackson, Aunt Pen's chauffeur, would take care of that. She could walk in Kensington Gardens with Foch, and think. And what she had to think about was Sir Walter Raleigh: 'whom none could advise, thou hast persuaded'. Very well. One could accept that. Death couldn't help being persuasive. Death was machine guns against fuzzy-wuzzys. He just mowed everybody down. After all he was *Death*. He held all the cards. No wonder he was persuasive.

And Death was mighty, all right. She'd already thought about that and it was true. She'd seen for herself. Seen what he did. Yes indeed Death was mighty. She'd carried enough of his samples in her ambulance to know just how true that was. But *just*? That was the one that had to be worked out, chewed over, the way Foch when a puppy had chewed at the corner of a rug Mummy had detested, which was why she still had Foch.

Raleigh had died on the scaffold. She remembered that now. He'd died the way Vinney had said he'd lived, like a man – even though the executioner had been nervous, taken two swipes, threatened the dignity of a brave man's death. But Raleigh's manhood had withstood even that. It was a standard too high for all but a tiny few. Aunt Pen, for instance. Maybe Mummy was right, and her aunt was embarking on a form of slow suicide. But even so, God might forgive her – let her win on a technicality so to speak. If she understood Raleigh correctly, Death certainly would, because Death came to everyone in time. It was in that fact that Death was just. He spared no one. Whether one died in agony, or in one's sleep all unaware, was no concern of his. . . .

Foch was confronting a Great Dane, rather as the poet had confronted what was left of Ozymandias. Foch had no thought of combat; Jane doubted whether he realised that he and the Great Dane belonged to the same species. 'Round that colossal wreck,' he seemed to be thinking. But the Great Dane might not see it that way. Jane hastened to intervene, and arrived at the same time as the Great Dane's companion. It was Dr Barker.

'Miss Whitcomb,' he said. 'Gooday. Is that your dog?'

'Yes,' she said. 'But he isn't quite so foolhardy as he may have seemed.'

'Brave little Belgium defying the Hun? But Horatio here isn't a Hun. The Danes were neutral.'

'Wise Danes. . . . What brings you here, Doctor?'

'The need for exercise. He belongs to my landlady and takes me out for a run occasionally. And you?'

'I can't think unless I walk. Foch is my excuse for thinking.'

'And how are you? Forgive me. As a consultation I realise that this is a little impromptu, but I have to go back to Australia shortly, and I should like to know – '

'I am better than I was,' she told him, 'but I could wish that others were the same.'

'You've had bad news?'

'Bad enough. Soon it will be worse.'

'You'll hold on.'

'You sound so certain.'

'How could you bear to undo all Jabber's good work?'

'You can always tell a psychoanalyst,' she said. 'They're the ones who never fight fair.' Then she whistled for Foch, but the wretched animal had decided to stand directly underneath the Great Dane as if sheltering from the rain. For some reason he found this amusing, and didn't want to come.

'That dog means a lot to you?' Dr Barker said.

'He means everything. . . . No. Not quite. There are still a few bipeds left I quite like – but Foch is – special.'

'Don't like him any less than you do,' said Dr Barker. 'But try to love the bipeds more.'

The Great Dane moved off then, exposing Foch to the summer sun. He disliked it, and joined her in the shade.

'You're ready to go?' Jane asked him, and he snorted assent. She turned to the doctor. 'It's a pity you're leaving us,' she said. 'You'd have enjoyed a chat with Foch. He's a psychoanalyst too. Perhaps rather more intuitive than most.'

They moved on, and after a while she looked down at the sturdy, small black shape beside her.

'There's no need to snigger,' she said. 'I was rude to the poor man. There was no *reason* to be rude. It's because he was right, of course. – Except he said "like" when he meant "love". But how can one measure out love? A quarter pound here, a half pound there, when you need a ton.'

10

IT WAS NEVER dull at Aunt Pen's, partly because Aunt Pen refused – had always refused – to consider dullness as a way of life, and partly because she decided that now, this very day, was the time to do what she and Uncle Walter had always promised themselves, and spoil her niece. Any protest on Jane's part was met with the charge that she was refusing to comfort the last hours of a dying woman. . . . Being spoiled it had to be.

Being spoiled meant dresses by Chanel and Molyneux, and hats from little shops in Mayfair, and hand-made gloves, and all one's stockings made of silk. Because time was short, it also meant flying in a specially hired plane from Croydon to Paris for fittings at Chanel's, and a room at the Ritz for an overnight stop. It meant boxes and stalls for the plays and operas they both liked, and the Russian ballet, where the Bakst sets sent them out to do even more shopping. It meant Cartier and Boucheron and a Riley two-seater.

But it meant more than that. It meant being involved with someone in a way that brought back the memories but not the pain: Guy and David and Vinney and Papa – and Mummy as she once had been, and even John. Aunt Pen dying brought back even the dead, and made their memory sweet. The money helped – of course it did – and she revelled in it, but no money could buy the love that Aunt Pen lavished on her, the knight's move logic, and the feeling that in spite of all the scarves and brooches and shoes, she had to stay and be spoiled, not only because Aunt Pen needed her and her love, but because she,

Jane Whitcomb, needed the need. It was there inside her, a great well of giving, and now once more she had found a taker that she loved. And again it would not be for long.

One accepted that, as one accepted the onset of her aunt's pain, variable still; as one accepted Papa's visit, and even Mummy's. Papa had been clever about that, and chosen a Second Thursday, which meant that there were three for lunch, and four for tea. They had every single dish Pen remembered Papa enjoying, and Bollinger because Jane had told Aunt Pen just enough about Mr Pardoe, and Château Leoville Barton because it was Papa's favourite claret. It was a noisy, happy lunch, and much of the talk was in Hindi. When it ended Papa declined port, and asked for brandy instead. His new doctor, he said, thought highly of brandy as a stimulant in cases like his.

'What a wonderful doctor,' said Aunt Pen. 'My dear you *must* stay with him.'

'Of course,' said Papa. 'Till the end.'

And the two of them smiled at each other like conspirators.

When the brandy came Papa cupped the goblet, sniffed and said 'Aah!' then raised the glass.

'You have a little wine left,' he said. 'I think I should propose a toast.'

'To your doctor?' asked Jane.

'To your brother,' her father said. 'He was good enough to telephone me this morning. He took a first, it seems. His college has offered him a junior fellowship. . . . To Francis.'

'Francis,' Aunt Pen and Jane echoed, and sipped, as Papa added: 'However there *is* news of a doctor. Cuthbert Pardoe has taken a PhD and is now *Dr* Pardoe. Shall we drink to that?'

'Certainly not,' said Aunt Pen.

'I quite agree,' said Jane.

'But we must talk, you and I,' Aunt Pen told Papa, and then to Jane: 'And in private too. . . . Boring stuff. Walter's study will be the best place. Your father can smoke a cigar there. We'll try not to be too long, my lovely.'

She sat in the drawing room between Foch and Rob, and read the *Morning Post* and listened to them sleep. And then her mother arrived, shown in by Marchmont. Mummy was not best pleased to be received by her daughter.

'Miss Gwatkin is well and sends you her best wishes,' she said.

'I have no doubt you gave her mine,' said Jane.

Really she thought, it's like chanting the responses in church. Rob and Foch rose, lay in a pool of sunshine by the window, and went back to sleep.

'You have become very fine,' her mother said.

Jane looked down at herself. Today's dress was of peacock blue silk, and designed by Erté. With it she wore a sapphire brooch from Asprey. It had not been her idea: knowing her mother was coming, she had suggested something in grey and with much longer skirts. But her aunt had been firm.

'Your father and I have to look at you too. So let's see something worth looking at.'

'A gift from Aunt Pen,' said Jane.

'I had not supposed you had purchased it out of your pin money. In fact I would have been happier if you had not purchased it at all.'

.'You find it revealing?'

'I find it vulgar.'

Before she could stop herself, Jane laughed.

'I have amused you?' her mother asked.

Nothing for it, but to soldier on regardless.

'Really Mummy,' said Jane, 'you could call this dress a lot of things: revealing, immodest, shameless, lascivious. . . . But not vulgar. It's by Erté. He has enormous talent.'

Disconcertingly her mother considered the statement on its merits, as she sometimes did.

'You are quite right,' she said. 'Your dress is superbly designed, exquisitely made, and quite indecent.'

'That's better,' said Jane.

'You have also become pert,' said her mother. 'Penelope Nettles's company is not good for you. And please do not remind me that she's dying. That is no excuse.'

'It's the only one she has,' said Jane.

Her mother ignored it. 'Are you – what is the expression – on the catch for some man?'

'Really Mummy,' said Jane. 'I'm thirty-two years old.'

'But you are quite healthy – apart from your nerves. . . . Well?'

'Not *some* man,' said Jane, 'in the sense of any particular man. But one appropriately qualified might be worth considering.'

Her mother snorted. She sounded not unlike Foch, Jane thought, though both of them would be appalled if I were to say so.

'Your nerves then are better, I take it?'

'For the moment.'

'Cured by kindness?'

'I am not in the least sure I *am* cured,' said Jane.

'You will be,' said her mother. 'Once you become rich, and the kind of young man you so aptly describe as appropriate makes his appearance, your nervous problems will vanish – though mine may not.'

So there it was, and it had to be faced now, this minute, before fear and rage and grief took over.

'I'd no idea that I was to become rich,' she said.

'Don't be naive, child,' said her mother. 'Walter Nettles was unpolished, plebeian even, but he had an enormous talent for making money. Penelope has no children. Where do you suppose her money will go?'

'To Papa, of course.'

'That would be foolish. – And your aunt, despite a great deal of evidence to the contrary, is not a fool. Why cause two sets of death duties to be paid in such rapid succession?'

Here was realism indeed: Papa reduced to no more than additional death duties on his sister's estate.

'It is far more likely,' said her mother, 'that she will leave the bulk of her possessions to her brother's children.'

'To Francis and myself in fact?'

'To the best of my knowledge you are the only ones,' her mother said, and Jane thought of Posy Sanderson as her mother continued: 'Your brother, of course, being the male, will no doubt receive the larger share, but even the smaller part should prove enough to attract an "appropriate" man.'

'You are on the warpath today,' said Jane.

'I called it pertness,' said her mother. 'Insolence might be more appropriate. But if you are hinting that I am displeased, I can only agree with you.'

'You haven't fallen out with Miss Gwatkin?'

'Certainly not,' said her mother. 'One does not – fall out –

with so trusted and valued a friend. Nevertheless it's true that I feel the need – '

She paused, and Jane, remembering the last Owen Nares matinée that she and Aunt Pen had attended, tried to be helpful.

'To be bitchy?'

'Is that how it sounds to you?'

'I'm afraid so, Mummy.'

'Oh dear,' said her mother, and Jane thought how unfair it all was. Just as the fight got interesting, her mother turned human on her.

'Want to tell me about it?' she asked.

'That, I'm afraid, is impossible.'

Definitely Posy Sanderson, thought Jane, and proceeded to move to cheerful matters. 'Papa told us the good news about Francis,' she said. 'A first *and* a fellowship. Jolly good.'

'Your brother is outstanding academically,' her mother said. 'The master of his college told me so himself. But he lacks stability.'

'Stability, Mummy?'

'Emotionally he is still immature. Friends like Pardoe and that Georgina whoever-she-is. He must settle down. Establish himself.' Then once more she became human. 'I worry about him, Jane. He needs help. Don't you think?'

Horror upon horror.

'Really Mummy,' said Jane, 'I see so little of him – but to me he always seems so successful.'

'You're not listening,' said her mother. 'I told you myself he was successful in his work. It's his life that's so – inadequate. You could help him in that. I'm sure you could. . . . If you wanted to.'

It was then that Aunt Pen and Papa came back, and Jane tried not to appear relieved. Rob went at once to Aunt Pen, and Foch, ever the gentleman, settled down by Jane, who watched as her mother and her aunt exchanged kisses and felicitations, and made not the slightest effort to conceal their dislike for each other.

' – such awful news,' her mother was saying. 'Is there no possibility of a mistake?'

'None,' said her aunt. 'How well you're looking, Honoria.'

'One of us must stay well,' her mother said. 'Though it was kind of you to take Jane off my hands, ill as you are.'

Her father said, 'Jane has been making herself useful, Pen tells me.'

'Really?' said her mother, as if such a thing were impossible; on a par with 'Jane has been piloting an airship,' or 'Jane has just finished repainting the Sistine Chapel.'

'I hope your lunch was as good as ours,' said Sir Guy.

'It was adequate,' said his wife. 'Sustaining even – but not a subject for discussion.'

'Ours was,' said Jane. 'We drank a toast – to Francis.'

Lady Whitcomb turned to her sister-in-law.

'You have heard of Francis's success?'

'Indeed,' said Aunt Pen. 'And I've asked Guy to convey my warmest congratulations.'

Lady Whitcomb thawed perceptibly. 'I shall do so myself,' she said. 'I am visiting him quite shortly.'

'You too, Guy?' Aunt Pen asked.

'Not to Cambridge,' he said. 'That might be going too far.'

Once again brother and sister smiled like conspirators, then Marchmont brought in tea, and the footman brought in cucumber sandwiches, and the sort of cakes that Rob and Foch liked, and the talk became social: why Lawrence of Arabia had found it necessary to join the ranks in the Royal Air Force; would the League of Nations work; why miners had to go on strike all the time. There was no more chance of anything more personal until Sir Guy declared that it was time to go, and Jane kissed her mother because she wanted to kiss her father, too. When she came back she found that Aunt Pen, for the first time, looked very ill and in pain. She went to her at once, but her aunt pushed her away.

'It's nothing,' she said. 'At least I'm told it's nothing. It doesn't feel like nothing.'

'They stayed too long.'

'Oh no,' said Aunt Pen. 'These things have to be endured, and one mustn't rush them. Besides – your father and I had a great deal to talk about. You and your mother too, I daresay.'

'We talked about Francis. Mummy's worried about him.'

'Despite his academic triumphs?'

'It's his private life – '

Aunt Pen said, 'I've no doubt it is, but I'm sorry, my lovely, I have literally no time to spare for Francis, and very little for your mother. Did you talk of nothing else?'

'My nerves,' said Jane, 'my frivolous way of life and my indecent clothes.'

'Goodness,' said her aunt. 'You did get a broadside.'

'I *think* we talked about Posy Sanderson too,' said Jane. 'If we did that would explain all the shot and shell. – Would you like to lie down?'

'Indeed it would,' said her aunt. 'Explain it, I mean. And I most certainly would not like to lie down.'

'If you're in pain –'

'I am *not* in pain,' said her aunt. 'The stuff that ten-guinea extortionist allows me still works. For the moment. . . . We addicts have our methods. Is Honoria unhappy?'

'Desperately,' said Jane.

He aunt nodded.

'You know the only man I ever slept with was your Uncle Walter. I had offers of course, some of them rather good ones – but somehow Walter became a habit – an addiction.' She shook her head suddenly. 'Addiction. . . . How inept of me. And so unkind. What I meant to say was I didn't ever feel the *need* for another man. He was really rather good at all that Judgement of Paris stuff. Am I shocking you?'

'No,' said Jane.

'Quite right,' said her aunt. 'It's far too late to be shocked. But what I'm saying is that Walter was so good he must have practised somewhere. I mean it's not something you're born with, like perfect pitch. *Someone* must have taught him those tricks of his.'

'Does it bother you?'

'No,' said Aunt Pen. 'It never did – because all that happened before we married. Never after. Don't ask me how I know – but I do know. Your mother's are a somewhat different set of circumstances. You must try to be nice to her.'

'She has Miss Gwatkin to do that.'

'Stir her up,' said Aunt Pen. 'Don't let her brood. You'll be able to do that.'

'I doubt it,' said Jane. 'But I'll try.'

'Of course you will,' Aunt Pen said, and then: 'Your father says I spoil you.'

Not a knight's move, thought Jane; not this time. More of a dive for cover.

'Is he angry?'

'On the contrary,' her aunt said. 'He thinks you look younger, more rested, and much, much prettier. In fact he wants me to spoil you some more.'

'You couldn't possibly.'

Her aunt took a deep breath. 'He wants me to buy you a horse,' said Aunt Pen, 'or rather arrange for you to rent one from those stables by Rotten Row.'

'I couldn't,' said Jane. 'You mustn't ask me.'

'I'm not *asking*,' said her aunt. 'Your father's asking. Why not accept? You were always such a good rider, for as long as I've known you.'

'If Papa asked you – then he must also have told you why I can't.'

'He said you dream of horses.'

'The horses I saw in the war,' said Jane. 'The ones that were hurt.'

'You haven't had those nightmares here.'

'That's true,' said Jane. 'But how do you know?'

'I would have seen it in your face,' said Aunt Pen, 'and perhaps I would have heard you, too.'

'I do yell a lot, that's true,' said Jane.

'But not here. Here your sleeps are dreamless. Rather boring, really.'

'Why does Papa want me to do this?'

'He thinks – he's thought very hard about this and he really does think – that it may help you.'

'Help me? How?'

'By showing you that a horse is just what you've always known it to be. A rather pleasant form of exercise with just enough danger to make it more exciting. To you, I hasten to add. Not to me.'

'The horses in my nightmares aren't like that.'

'The horses in your nightmares are all dead,' said her aunt. 'If the Huns didn't kill them then the army farrier would. It was his *job*, my lovely. Horses aren't allowed to suffer: not like their riders.'

'Why didn't Papa suggest this to me himself?'

'Because he couldn't,' said Aunt Pen. 'He thought – rightly or wrongly – that there were parts of your life during the war that he would never know about: that you would never tell. And I believe he's right. – So he asked me to do it, because two women can share secrets – or even conjectures – that a father and daughter would run a mile from. And he asked me to hire a horse for you on his behalf and I said No, I'd do that, because if there's any spoiling to be done, I'm the one who'll do it.'

'But I haven't any kit.'

It was a feeble objection, and they both knew it.

'Leave it to the Spoiler,' said Aunt Pen. 'Well?'

'Papa really wants me to do this?'

'He wants you to get well,' Aunt Pen said.

'Suppose he's wrong?'

'Can you become worse than you were when you first came to me? If you think that's possible, I'll tell Guy it's off. Of course I will.'

Perhaps she should talk to Jabber first, Jane thought, but with Jabber one discussed dreams, not horses.

'All right, I'll do it,' she said. 'Thank you, Aunt Pen.'

Aunt Pen said, 'By the look on your face you'd think I was offering you a dose of castor oil, but you're wrong, my lovely. You'll see. Now come and give me a kiss and we'll talk about what riding clothes you'll need – and then you can help me off to bed. I've had quite enough excitement for one day.'

She chose jodhpurs and a jacket of Lovat tweed, but there were also the right kinds of shirt and stock, a bowler hat, and the boots from Lobb. There were measurements and fittings and delays, but not nearly enough of them. Soon, far too soon, she was ready to go. Her aunt looked at her and smiled.

'You'll do,' she said. 'Will Jackson drive you?'

'No,' said Jane. 'I'll drive myself in the Riley.'

'Splendid,' said her aunt.

'Not at all,' said Jane. 'It's just that if you and Papa are determined I shall make a fool of myself, I don't want Jackson there to see it.'

But she didn't make a fool of herself. Not at all. All she did was park the Riley in the mews and take a look at the hacks for hire. Not exactly an exciting collection, but one of them, a bay gelding called Taff, looked as if he might have a little life in him. She used the mounting block and settled in the saddle, and Taff shuffled in an experimental sort of way to find out if Jane knew her business. Both of them discovered that she did, and after that it was just a matter of walking sedately across to the Row, and trotting when she must and cantering when she dared. Rather boring, really, compared with her childhood gallops on Rani. All the same she thought that Taff might be a goer, if only she could find some place where they could gallop enough to find out.

When she got back to Mount Street her aunt went to her at once, Sophie hurtled down to her, even Marchmont looked agitated. A bath, Sophie said. A bath was essential. And perhaps a preparation to guard against stiffness. As if she'd been riding in the National or something. But she took the bath and avoided the embrocation, and came down in a Chanel top and skirt that even Vinney would have approved, she thought. Liberated woman written all over it.

'How divine you look,' said her aunt. 'All Lysistrata and things. How did it go?'

'I rode a horse called Taff,' said Jane. 'Trotted a bit and cantered a bit. It was no more difficult than it ever was. I'm sorry I fussed so.'

'You think your father was right?'

Jane said gently: 'There isn't any point in thinking, darling. I'll just have to wait till bedtime to find out.' Then before Aunt Pen could worry about it, she asked, 'And just so that I don't spend half the night looking up the wrong reference books, tell me, please – who was Lysistrata? I feel I should know, but I've forgotten.'

'How upset poor Vinney would be if she found out. Lysistrata was that rather gorgeous Athenian lady who led a sex strike in Athens.'

'Gorgeous? Because she led a sex strike?'

'Gorgeous because it was to stop a war,' said her aunt.

'Is that how you see me? As a sex strike?'

'Not in that dress,' said her aunt. 'It's just that you look so – well – so in command of yourself.'

It was nice to have one's theories confirmed.

11

FOCH SAID, 'YOU realise that this is a significant breakthrough?'
Strange, thought Jane. This is the first time Foch has
actually *spoken* to me, and yet his voice does not surprise me. A
deep voice, rather precise, rather irascible, with educated-
Edinburgh overtones, like that surgeon in the advanced dressing
station at Arras. Major Buchanan. That was the one.

'I rather thought that might be so,' said Jane.

'Oh decidedly,' said Foch. 'Everything has changed now,
d'you see.'

Jane was lying on her side looking directly at Foch, who sat
on a gilt and velvet chair by her bed. Sophie or Mancroft, perhaps
even Aunt Pen, would have argued that he had no business to
be there, but they were unaware that Foch was not just her dog:
he was also one of her analysts.

'You're referring to my having ridden a horse?'

'Was there anything else of significance?' Foch asked.

'Not to my knowledge,' said Jane. 'Not if you include my
reaction to the outing.'

'Naturally I do.'

Really he was very like Major Buchanan, thought Jane. Bad
temper and all.

'You're not jealous, by any chance? – That I spent time with
another animal?'

'Of course not,' said Foch. 'My concern is for you. Have you
observed the time?'

She looked at the bedside clock. 'Seven forty-three,' she said.

'In the *morning*,' said Foch. 'You retired at eleven. Now tell me about your dreams.'

'I had none,' she said, then, remembering Jabber Lockhart's opinion on the subject: 'None that I can recall, anyway.'

'What you can't recall need not concern us,' said Foch. 'I've aye disagreed with Lockhart about that. But that horse and the absence of remembered dreams – that to my mind is a breakthrough.'

'Go on,' said Jane.

'It's my considered opinion that we were both afraid of regression when you got on that horse, but Sir Guy was correct in his conjecture. You slept well.'

'For one night.'

'The first of many,' Foch said. 'I am not saying that you will never dream again or undergo stress again – that would be absurd. But in the future it will be containable.'

'Are you saying I'm cured?'

'Insofar as you were ever ill – aye, I am,' said Foch.

It was the 'aye' that did it. Far too Harry Lauder for Major Buchanan, or Foch either, come to that.

She said aloud, 'This is ridiculous. I'm making this up, and I know I'm doing it.' Then she sat up in the bed and looked about her, and of course Foch wasn't on the chair. He was on the rug by the fire.

Jabber's going to love this one, she thought, and then – well yes. Maybe he is going to love it. Because I'm loving it. I mean I wasn't really asleep, just dozing and thinking, and I always talk to Foch when I'm trying to think. And what I was thinking was – *I didn't have that nightmare*. So maybe I am better. Maybe I'm even normal – whatever that may be. Then Foch opened his eyes and they looked at each other.

'Good morning,' she said. 'I'm sorry I gave you a voice like Major Buchanan. You deserved something much more grand.' Foch went back to sleep.

The next morning, early, she rode Taff again, and in the deserted tan bark she let him lengthen his stride and gallop. That night she dreamed not at all, nor did she talk with Foch. The next day she galloped once more, and that night she did dream. She was driving the ambulance, but it was nowhere near the Front. It was out in the foothills near Darjeeling, where she

– 117 –

had not been since her childhood, and yet there she was, driving an ambulance, which she knew to be empty, because where would she pick up wounded soldiers in West Bengal, in a summer of wild flowers and birdsong and tea gardens, with the ramparts of the Himalayas to guard them?. . . A warm and lazy summer. And then suddenly there *was* a soldier, and it was John, it had to be John, riding Bridget O'Dowd. He cantered across to her in the way she had taught him, and gracious how young he was; so young. . . . She pulled up and got out, and John dismounted, and they got into the back of the ambulance and made love that was like magic, and how could she begin to tell Lockhart about *that*?

But there were other things that she had to tell, and not just to Jabber. Her aunt first of all. Aunt Pen had to know that the nightmares so it seemed were gone. And of course she celebrated the fact by giving her niece a present: a little Cartier leopard of rubies set in gold.

'Souvenir,' said Aunt Pen.

'But you couldn't possibly have known,' said Jane.

'If not for that, then something else,' her aunt said. 'But I rather think I did know all the same. And by the way it's a leopardess, not a leopard. That's another thing I just know.'

'It's the most wonderful gift I ever had,' said Jane. 'But you've given me so much already – '

'It's the only thing I'm really good at – giving prezzies,' said her aunt. 'But I rather think that this will be the last one – for a while anyway.'

'It's getting worse?'

'It,' said aunt, 'is getting unbearable. It's Switzerland next week, my lovely.'

'I'll come with you,' said Jane. 'I must.'

'No,' said her aunt. 'That's the only thing you could do to me that I couldn't bear. Now go and tell Guy your good news.'

But when she phoned that afternoon it was to be told by Lady Whitcomb that her father was resting, and not to be disturbed, and then she enquired after her daughter's health. She received the news that Jane was better and Aunt Pen worse without comment, but promised to inform her father. Jane said that she would telephone again later, on her return: for this was the day of the reunion party.

What to wear was the first problem. It would have been a problem in Offley Villas where she had practically nothing that was pretty, and was certainly a problem in Mount Street, where she had nothing that wasn't. Expensive, too. She didn't want to arrive like some opulent show-off. . . . Then she remembered them: Harriet, the doctor, Louise, daughter of a baronet who farmed about half of Wales, and Sarah the actress who had grown to be famous – what they called a star. She and Aunt Pen had seen her just a couple of weeks ago. Smart clothes wouldn't be a problem for that lot: they'd be the only kind of clothes they had. And Freda, she thought. Would she be there? Lesbian Freda, known as Fred. When John had told her what lesbians got up to, she'd thought he was teasing her, but it was true, it seemed. No wonder Fred was always so miserable, but she was a marvellous driver.

12

HARRIET'S HOUSE WAS in Hampstead, not far from Well Walk, so she went in the Riley. Jackson and the Daimler really would be going too far. It was a nice house, set off the road by a garden, and there were already two cars there, and one of them a Rolls-Royce with a chauffeur who was reading the *Daily Mail*. Jackson would have been furious. She went to the door and a maid answered, and behind her stood Harriet with a cocktail shaker in her hand, darting at Jane to kiss her before the maid had asked her name.

'Darling, what fun,' she said. 'And how intrepid of you to drive all this way. Do come in. The others are all here.'

Jane went into a drawing room that seemed packed with women drinking gin, although in fact there were only three of them, and two were dazzlingly pretty. Being smart hadn't just been a good idea, it had been an essential idea. Sarah of course she knew about, she'd seen: tall and fair and elegant, and with that air of belonging to a different world that some theatrical people never lose. But Louise. . . . Had Louise always had those looks? Jane could remember her only with tousled hair, bedraggled clothes, a smudge of oil on her cheek. And now here she was: dark, intense, *glowing* with beauty, and in such a dress. . . . And between them Fred, a little thinner than she had been, and wearing a mannish sort of suit not all that different from the uniform she'd once worn. Hair cut short, but in a masculine way, not even an Eton crop. Collar and tie, too. And a monocle. Jane rather liked the monocle. She went over to them, and more kisses, and a glass brought by Harriet.

'It's a cocktail,' Harriet said. 'Mostly gin and different kinds of vermouth. At this time of day I couldn't think of anything else.'

Fred offered her a cigarette. Fred had always had cigarettes to offer, Jane remembered.

'Now I'm quite sure you know who these good people were, but do you know who they *are*?' Harriet asked.

Jane sipped her drink. My God it hit like hammers.

'Harriet and Sarah and Louise and Fred,' she said. 'And you're Harriet Ryland as was, and now you're Harriet Watson. Dr Harriet Watson. I remember you were half way through your course when you came out to France.'

'I qualified in '21,' Harriet Watson said. 'Married Neil in '23. He's a doctor too. Dr Watson. . . . It isn't a joke we encourage.'

'I should think not,' said Jane, and turned to the actress.

'You're still Sarah Unwin,' she said. 'That I do know because I saw it on a programme two weeks ago.'

'Ah,' said Fred. 'But she's also Sarah Beddoes and she used to be Sarah Timms.'

'I can't help it if I rather enjoy getting married,' said Sarah. 'Was it "Faint Hearts" you saw?' Jane nodded. 'And did you like it?'

'I liked you,' said Jane. Sarah laughed.

'The perfect critic,' she said. 'Darling, you look marvellous. Doesn't she, Louise?'

The dark woman smiled. 'Putting us to shame as usual,' she said.

'How can you say so and you so grand,' said Sarah. 'You know who she is, don't you?'

'I'm afraid not,' said Jane, and Fred hooted.

'What a comedown,' she said. 'Jane Whitcomb you are in the presence of Louise, Countess of Hexham.'

'Oh check it, Fred,' said the countess. 'How are you, Jane?'

'Well enough now,' said Jane. 'I hadn't been for quite a while.'

'So that's how you managed to keep out of the papers,' Sarah said.

'What on earth do you mean?'

'My dear, we all expected something really dashing from you,' said Louise. 'Driving racing cars at least.'

'And how about you Fred?' Jane asked.

'I run a publishing firm,' said Fred. 'Nothing grand. Mostly technical stuff and school text books.'

'She makes a fortune,' said Harriet.

'Not yet, ducky.' Fred screwed her monocle into her eye and looked stern. 'But I will.'

Like snakes and ladders, thought Jane. They all landed on ladders. I'm the only one who got a snake. But that's over now. Finished. . . . Harriet came round once more with the cocktail shaker, and drew her to one side.

'How splendid you look,' she said. 'You outshine even the nobility.'

'Borrowed plumes,' said Jane. 'Well – not borrowed exactly, but undeserved, which is worse.'

'Did I hear you say you'd been unwell?'

'You did,' said Jane, 'but I've decided to give it up.'

Harriet looked at her. 'I see,' she said. 'At least I think I do.'

'Of course you do,' said Jane. 'You're a doctor.'

'Come and see me at my surgery,' Harriet said. 'That is – if you want to talk about it. Or anything else for that matter.' Then Sarah came towards them to talk about the time the Ford's big end went at Abbeville, and they drank more cocktails.

It was that sort of party: reminiscence and alcohol, whatever-became-of and do-you-remember? There was a lot of laughter, and after the gin took effect rather a lot of tears, too, especially from Sarah, who wept even more, Jane noticed, when she remembered her eight-thirty curtain, and Harriet produced sand-wiches and coffee, strong and black as anything they had drunk in France seven years before. Jane drank coffee, too. She had no desire to telephone Jackson to come and drive her home. Aunt Pen would be sure to hear of it, and Aunt Pen must not be caused to worry.

When it was time to go they all kissed each other exuberantly and vowed to meet next year. And no doubt they would, thought Jane, though she doubted whether they'd ever think of each other again until the next time. Reunions were a bore really. Once she had thought that these women would be a part of her life for ever; supporting players in the romantic comedy that would star John and herself. And now she couldn't wait to get back to Mount Street to see how Aunt Pen was. But as she drove off in the Riley she knew it wasn't absolutely true. She would go to see Harriet again.

As soon as she walked into the house she knew that something was wrong. Aunt Pen wasn't in the drawing room but almost at once Marchmont appeared; stolid and competent as always, the way a good butler should be, but there was something else struggling to break through, something that didn't belong. Concern.

'Mrs Nettles is in her bedroom, miss,' Marchmont said. 'She asked for you to go to her as soon as you returned.' Jane raced for the stairs.

Her aunt was lying on the top of the bed. Jane, an expert now, could see at once that the pain was there, but that she'd taken enough of whatever it was to dull its edge.

'Darling,' said Aunt Pen. 'Did you have a lovely party?'

'Lots of gin,' said Jane, 'and too much remembering. But you didn't want to see me at once just for that.'

'No, my lovely,' Aunt Pen said. 'I didn't.'

There could only be one other reason.

'My father?' she asked.

Aunt Pen nodded. 'It was just after you left,' she said. 'We tried to find your invitation card so that we could call you, but –'

'I had it in my bag,' Jane said. 'Tell me about Papa.'

'I'm awfully sorry,' said Aunt Pen. 'There's no way I can make this easy for you. Your father is dead. Very suddenly it seems. He quite literally sat down and died.'

'Poor Papa,' said Jane. 'No more champagne on Second Thursdays.' Then she covered her face with her hands and wept, and Aunt Pen struggled from her bed to embrace her, and they comforted each other until it was time to go.

Jane had mislaid her door key and was obliged to knock – not a good omen – and the door was opened by Hawkins, which was even worse.

'Moreton?' Jane asked.

'Gave notice and left, miss,' Hawkins said. 'Last week. We haven't got another one yet.'

Jane looked about her: at the curtains drawn against the day-

– 123 –

light, the dark, unfriendly rooms. Who can blame her? she thought. Then she turned back to Hawkins. 'You won't do that, will you Hawkins?' she asked. 'We'll need you more than ever now.'

'Do me best, miss,' Hawkins said.

It was hardly an oath written in blood, but it would have to do. 'Where's my mother?'

'Upstairs, miss,' Hawkins said. 'The doctor's still with her.'

Jane went up at once.

It was Dr Somerville: white-haired, aged, and unmistakably Irish, but Protestant Irish, Church of Ireland in fact, which made him socially acceptable. He had had very little sympathy with her nightmares, Jane remembered, and had unhesitatingly blamed them on a faulty diet on the grounds that all young women ate the wrong food. His eyes took in the smartness of Jane's clothes, but he made no comment until Jane had gone forward to embrace her mother. Both women remained dry-eyed, which seemed to displease him.

'This is a sad business,' he said.

Jane could think of no adequate reply, and turned instead to the bed where her father lay, in pyjamas, hands folded over the sheet that covered him to his chest, eyes closed, the age-wrinkles already smoothed out by death. She knelt on the floor beside him.

'Dear Papa,' she said to herself, 'I hope you can hear me wherever you are. I'm most awfully sorry I wasn't here when it happened, but truly I didn't know, how could I? And you must realise that now. I loved you Papa, and I admired you, and now for the rest of my life I shall miss you.' Then she joined her hands. 'Dear God,' she prayed, 'have mercy on the soul of my father. He was human and by no means perfect, but he did his best for everyone who needed him. You know that that is true, dear God. Look what he did for me.' Then she rose to her feet.

'Perhaps you shouldn't stay too long,' said Dr Somerville. 'The sight of death is upsetting for young women.'

The old fool obstinately refused to remember, or maybe it was acknowledge, what she had done in the war, thought Jane. Maybe at his age the thought of what she had done was monstrous, as if the war had been the Crimea, and she one of Miss Nightingale's delicately nurtured young ladies.

Surprisingly her mother said, 'Jane has rather more backbone than that.' And then to Jane she added: 'You have finished your prayers for the moment?'

'Yes, Mummy.'

'Then we can go downstairs. Dr Somerville has signed the death certificate, and your brother has been sent for. There is no more that any of us can do until he arrives.'

Dr Somerville, having been told he wasn't needed, lost no time in going. As the drawing room door closed behind him, Lady Whitcomb said, 'He has become useless now, don't you agree?'

'I don't think he could have saved Papa,' said Jane.

'No one could have saved him. Naturally we called in a second opinion, and he too was quite sure. . . . What I meant was that we no longer need Dr Somerville.'

'You intend to change doctors?'

'Yes.'

'Who will you go to?'

'I have made no decison. First your brother must be consulted. After all he is head of the family now.'

And Mummy was quite serious, thought Jane, or at least had persuaded herself she was. The king is dead. Long live the king. But it was the queen who reigned. Determinedly she wrenched her mind away from these somewhat insulting conjectures. Now was simply not the time.

'You have informed the vicar?' she asked.

'Certainly. . . . He sent a curate.'

When one gives an evening-dress party and invites the governor, her mother's tone informed her, one does not expect to be fobbed off with an aide de camp.

'And the lawyers?'

'I shall leave all that to Francis,' said her mother. 'It was a pity you were not here at the end.'

'I'm sorry,' said Jane, 'but how could I possibly know?'

'I was here.'

'He must have been glad.'

'No,' her mother said. 'Not glad at all. He'd been upstairs all afternoon, fiddling with those – those *souvenirs* of his – then he came down to the drawing room. Hawkins finally informed me of the fact – a *most* unsatisfactory girl, but what can one do?

'Your father was reading *The Times* – or at least I assumed he was. When I came into the room he lowered it and looked at me. It was perfectly obvious that he resented my presence. . . . Then he lay back and I thought he was going to take a nap. In fact, he was dying, and his resentment was because I had impeded the process.'

Careful, now. Very, very careful, thought Jane.

'Why did you say that you *assumed* Papa was reading *The Times*?' she asked.

'Because he was holding it upside down. It would appear that he very much wished to die, and without interruption. Once he had arrived at that conclusion the whole faculty of doctors couldn't have saved him, let alone that dotard Somerville. You were drinking alcohol earlier today?'

'Yes, Mummy.'

'I could smell it on your breath. Not perhaps the most tasteful way of acknowledging your father's passing.'

Jane found that she was on her feet and yelling.

'I didn't know,' she shouted. 'How could I possibly have known?'

Her mother said, 'To look after us now we are reduced to a housemaid, a kitchen maid and a cook. Inadequate though they are, I consider them indispensable. You will refrain from conduct calculated to scare them away.'

'Indeed I will,' said Jane, 'if you will refrain from conduct calculated to enrage me.'

'Ah,' said her mother, and smiled: rather grimly, but she smiled.

'I have lost my husband in what I can only consider humiliating circumstances,' she said. 'Perhaps you are aware of them. I had thought they were forgotten, but quite recently your father revived his morbid interest in things past and best ignored.'

Then to Jane's relief she added: 'If you are aware of what I am referring to, you will oblige me by remaining silent.'

She waited, but Jane said nothing, and the grim smile returned.

'So this was a day of sadness – which I had anticipated – and of humiliation, which I most certainly had not. And on that day, refusing to live at home, living instead with a person she knows to be uncongenial to me, my daughter, indecorously clad, goes out with friends on a drunken spree. To say you couldn't have known is inadequate. Your place was here.'

'I had Papa's permission to go.'

'Naturally,' her mother said. 'He knew that it would annoy me.'

'He knew that Aunt Pen needed me too.'

'You are quite convinced that she is ill?'

'She's dying, Mummy.'

'So you and your brother are the only Whitcombs left.'

'Aren't you a Whitcomb then?'

'An honorary member only. You asked me to give your father a message.'

'Yes,' said Jane. 'Did you give it?'

'How could I?' said her mother. 'To do so would have meant interrupting his departure from life. He would not have thanked me for it.'

'I am sorry,' said Jane, 'that you were unhappy together.'

'I also,' said her mother. 'And I have no doubt that he was, too. I think we could have put up with each other had your brothers lived, but as it is – ' She paused, then deliberately changed the subject.

'You said you were well now, I believe?'

'It seems very likely.'

'That is good news, of course. Did I gather that your father was involved in the cure?'

'He gave me some advice,' said Jane.

'He was good at that,' her mother said.

It was a relief when Francis arrived, or rather it would have been had he not brought Cuthbert Pardoe with him. Mercifully she had changed from her Chanel suit to more appropriate mourning wear before his arrival. That he was pleased to see her was evident, but the bereavement prevented him from expanding on the subject, which irked him.

For a while he sulked, but at last Francis's inability to cope with the more practical aspects of death moved him to action, and even Jane found that he proved useful. It was he who interviewed the undertaker, and telephoned the vicar to make arrangements for the funeral – to such effect that the vicar, Dr Dodd, promised to call on Lady Whitcomb after dinner. He made lists, too, of people to be informed, such as *The Times*, and the India Office, and probable mourners, friends, colleagues, relatives – and reminded Francis that he must lock up his father's desks and files until his solicitors had called on him. But it was

Jane who remembered the heat of summer, and the need for ice in the room where the dead man lay, and told the undertaker to arrange it. Even Pardoe was slightly taken aback by that.

'It is necessary not to yield to grief, *of course*,' he said, 'but I really think – '

'An Indian background alerts one to such things,' Lady Whitcomb said. 'The dead could never be left for long. As for grief, I am in agreement with you that one should not yield to it, and so is Jane. She feels it, and suffers because of it, but she is aware that life must continue even so. I am quite sure that Francis feels the same way.'

'Yes, of course, Mummy,' Francis said.

'You feel that you will miss your Papa?'

'Anyone would,' said Francis. 'He had a first-rate mind.'

He'd had a body too, thought Jane, that had embraced his children – and Posy Sanderson and Mummy too come to that, or there'd have been no children to embrace: a body that knew precisely how to sit a horse, handle a gun, or a cricket bat; a body that had enjoyed champagne and claret and plovers' eggs and côtelettes Reform. But better not to mention that.

They went into dinner: Windsor soup, fillets of sole, roast mutton, summer pudding. No cheese – there had been no time. And no wine either, except that at the end of the meal Hawkins brought in port, on her mother's instructions, and Jane and she left the gentlemen to it.

'I expect they are used to it as they live in Cambridge,' her mother said. 'Your father seemed to think a sound knowledge of port essential to a university education.'

'I don't think Francis is much of a drinker,' said Jane.

'Probably not,' her mother said. 'Perhaps his friend Pardoe will teach him – though I doubt it.'

And indeed, Jane noticed, the port-drinking ritual did not take long, which was perhaps as well, as almost immediately after the gentlemen joined the ladies the vicar called. Dr Dodd was profuse in apologies for his earlier absence, fluent in references to a charity meeting in aid of the unemployed, a confirmation class, a visiting missionary lecturer, but his voice faltered when his eye met Lady Whitcomb's. She said nothing, except to introduce him to their visitor.

'Dr Pardoe – Dr Dodd,' she said, and waited.

Dr Dodd was small, plump, precise, and incurably inquisitive. He looked at Pardoe's flaming red tie.

'Your friend's field is not divinity, I take it?' he asked.

'Physics,' Pardoe said. 'I'm a PhD.'

Lady Whitcomb said, 'You must excuse us, Dr Dodd. My son and Dr Pardoe have just arrived from Cambridge. Under the circumstances I did not think it necessary to request that they change for dinner. I trust my conduct will not be considered disrespectful – or theirs either?'

'Of course not,' said Dr Dodd. 'At such a time – ' He looked again at Pardoe's tie, red as arterial blood, and then away.

'No indeed,' he said, and began to talk of funeral arrangements.

Lady Whitcomb had very clear ideas on the subject. Her husband would be buried not as he would have wished to be, but in his peers' eyes, how he ought to be. Pomp and circumstance, and all the old India hands that Jane's mother could winkle out of their Eastbourne or Cheltenham retirements. Hymns and an organ and floral tributes and notices in the newspapers. Francis, as head of the house, had little more to do than say 'Yes, Mummy', and Jane was not called upon to do even that. But she made no attempt to intervene: her father was beyond all pretension. . . . At last Dr Dodd said, 'Then everything is settled, I take it?' and Lady Whitcomb agreed.

'Then perhaps we can go upstairs to pray,' said Dr Dodd. Pardoe looked up, astounded. Really, thought Jane, he couldn't have shown more surprise if we'd all peed on the carpet. But she made sure he went, even so, by taking his arm on the way to the stairs. There might be pomp and circumstance at her father's death, but there would be respect, too.

They knelt around the bed, and the vicar launched into extempore prayer. 'Oh mighty and most merciful Father, trusting in Thy infinite love and mercy', and 'Thy servant Guy now departed', and on and on and on, while Jane thought of her father and knew that she was ready to weep, but would not while Pardoe could see her, and thought instead of Bollinger in the Hyde Park Hotel when the toast was confusion to Cuthbert.

At last the vicar paused for breath and her mother said 'Amen', very firmly, and clambered to her feet. Jane went to help her, and the others rose too, the vicar rather bewildered and not at all sure that he had finished. Lady Whitcomb advanced on him before he could make up his mind.

'I am very tired, as I'm sure you will understand,' she said. 'There is a spare bed in my husband's dressing room where I shall spend the night.' She offered her hand. 'Good night vicar,' she said. 'It was good of you to find the time to call on me. Come, Jane.'

They went together to the dressing room, where Hawkins had already laid out her mother's night clothes. Her mother looked about her.

'How nice it would be to get away from this place.'

'Are you going to move, then?' Jane asked.

'Certainly not,' her mother said. 'This is our home – yours and mine – *and* Francis's.'

'Francis will live in Cambridge.'

'He will need to visit London – and there are vacations,' said her mother. 'Then he will be married quite soon, and there will be children. A family needs a big house.'

'Has Francis told you he'll marry soon?' Jane asked.

'No,' said her mother. 'But it's what most people do, after all.'

'I must remember that,' said Jane, and her mother looked at her.

'You really are better,' she said, and added: 'Your aunt must of course be invited to attend the funeral. Will she do so?'

'If she's well enough,' said Jane. 'I doubt if she is.'

'Perhaps tomorrow you can make it your business to enquire. Good night, child.'

'Good night, Mummy.'

Once more the two women kissed, dry-eyed, then Jane went down to the drawing room where Pardoe waited for her alone.

'I sent Francis to take a look around your father's study,' he said. 'Very possibly there will be papers.'

'There's very little else.'

Pardoe beamed approvingly down on her, as if she were a beguilingly precocious child.

'Quite right,' he said. 'It's what studies are for, after all. You are bearing up rather well if I may say so.'

'Do smoke if you want to,' said Jane.

'I never do,' said Pardoe. 'I am convinced that nicotine would impede my form of exercise, which as I believe I mentioned to you tends to be violent.'

Jane took from her bag a cigarette case and lighter, selected a cigarette, and lit up, then ejected the smoke through her nostrils, a trick painfully acquired and rarely used. Pardoe watched her, censorious.

'I take no form of exercise whatsoever,' said Jane. 'Unless you count horse-riding at very infrequent intervals.'

'You should,' said Pardoe. 'In fact I'm going to insist that you must.'

Scrum-half? Jane wondered. Lightweight boxer?

'But not of course until the time of your grief is over,' Pardoe added more kindly. 'Talking of which I was sorry that you were subjected to that unfortunate piece of mumbo-jumbo upstairs.'

'Mumbo-jumbo?'

'The Tory Party at prayer,' said Pardoe. 'That ludicrous clerical placeman invoking his tribal God.'

'Oh the *prayers*,' said Jane. 'I rather enjoyed them. I usually do as a matter of fact. It gives one a chance to think one's own thoughts for a while.'

'And what did you think about this time?'

'God,' said Jane. 'And the fact that my father is dead.'

Even Pardoe took a little time to recover from that one, as if she'd clipped him a good un, she thought, not quite hard enough to knock him out, but sufficient to make him stagger for the ropes.

At last he said, 'I have not forgotten our last conversation.'

'Nor I,' she said. Nor had she.

'I'm delighted to hear it. It was conducted of course under much more agreeable circumstances than our present encounter, when custom demands a certain formality, even coolness, in our exchanges.'

It was clear that Dr Pardoe thought poorly of custom.

'That you should show a kind of coyness at this time is perfectly understandable,' he said, 'but when your gloom has lifted I shall come at once to discuss with you what sort of future we may expect together, wherever I may be. For the moment, naturally, I must say no more on *that* subject.'

And then Francis came down to interrupt them, which was perhaps as well, full of complaints about the fact that the study contained nothing but useless junk. Of the fact that it also contained much of their life, Jane thought, he seemed quite unaware.

13

NEXT DAY HER aunt telephoned. Her voice seemed as firm as ever, but she took her time in phrasing her words, as if conversation were an art she had not quite mastered. Penelope Nettles, once described as the most brilliant chatterer of her generation. That will be the drugs, Jane thought, and the pain.

'I was coming to see you,' she said.

'Not today,' said Aunt Pen. 'Not possibly. I want to ask about the funeral.'

'It's tomorrow,' said Jane. 'There's a notice in *The Times*. All that sort of stuff.'

'I shan't be there,' Aunt Pen said. 'I might disgrace myself. Not up to it, my lovely.'

'I understand.'

'Besides,' said Aunt Pen, 'your mother has enough sorrows to endure at the moment without the sight of me.'

One more knight's move, thought Jane. Perhaps the last.

'Will I see you before you leave?'

'You *must*,' said her aunt, with something like panic in her voice. 'Come and tell me about the funeral – but come alone, darling. Nobody else will be admitted. Tell them I mean that.'

She hung up then, and Jane went to visit the dressmaker who was altering the black coat she had last worn at Uncle Walter's funeral. She took Foch with her, which her mother considered indicated a lack of respect.

'Though why that should be,' she told Foch as they walked

down Offley Villas, 'I've no idea. Papa liked you very much, and anyway you're in black from nose to tail.'

Old Mrs Blythe-Tarkington stopped her then, to tell her how wise she was to confide her grief to her canine friend. They had their own way of giving comfort, and it was one of the blessings of God. Jane was surprised to discover how warmly she agreed with old Mrs Blythe-Tarkington.

The funeral was a kind of formalised horror that seemed at one point as if it would go on for ever. No mourners – except Miss Gwatkin – were invited to the house, not even to see the body, and Jane was glad of it; not that many mourners would have come. Mummy had managed to quarrel with most of Papa's friends, and all of his surviving relatives, but even so the cemetery was thronged and the church was packed.

It was the pomp that was hardest to bear, thought Jane. Papa had been the least pompous of men, and yet here it all was: the elaborate hearse, silver and glass and black wooden panels all gleaming in the sunshine: superb, perfectly matched black horses, coachman and footman in black livery with silver buttons – like a photographic negative of Cinderella's coach, she thought, except that it was Papa who rode in solitary splendour, flowers heaped around him, from those same relatives and friends, (Aunt Pen's great mound of roses, and the words 'Much loved, much mourned', shakily and laboriously written in her own hand); flowers from colleagues and clubs and societies; from the school where Papa had been a governor, and the examining board for which he had set questions in Hindi, from groups and individuals she had never even heard of, including one from R.J. Chatterjee LLB (Lond) inscribed simply 'To the man who helped me above all others'. So many flowers indeed that they'd had to bring in a second carriage, a landau, just to take the overflow, and then Lady Whitcomb and Francis and Jane in a black Rolls-Royce, and Miss Gwatkin and Dr Pardoe, attendant lady and lord, in another.

Then there was the church, crammed full with figures mostly male, elderly, distinguished, with here and there a female of the same generation. Many of them were obviously soldiers, thought Jane, some vaguely familiar, and the rest mostly ICS, the Indian Civil Service which had absorbed most of Papa's adult life. She could sense the stir of interest as the three surviving Whitcombs,

Jane and Francis on either side of their mother, walked down the centre aisle of the neo-Gothic church, Miss Gwatkin and Dr Pardoe behind them, and took their place front centre stage, to be assessed for their performance as mourners: marks out of ten for their portrayal of grief, bereavement, despair. But it seemed that they were not, after all, the stars of the show, far from it: that rôle was reserved for Dr Dodd.

The reason, Jane discovered, was that he had all the best lines. A parson reciting the burial service is a Hamlet: all the splendid soliloquies are his. Dr Dodd knew it, and did his best to be worthy of the lines he had been given. In the stark black and white of his robes relieved by an MA hood, somehow he managed to look taller, more spiritual. Even his voice had deepened.

'I am the resurrection and the life, saith the Lord.' 'I know that my Redeemer liveth, and that He shall stand at the latter day upon the earth.' 'Before the mountains were brought forth, or even the earth and the world were made, Thou art God from everlasting.' 'O spare me a little, that I may recover my strength before I go hence and be no more seen.' . . . Are you listening Aunt Pen?

The words worked their own magic, distancing Papa from the world he had known, – Oxford, India, Offley Villas, – into that existence beyond time and space that the Elizabethan prelates had evoked so superbly, that Dr Dodd invoked so well. Of the magic she had no doubt at all; she had lived too long in India: rhythmical invocation of superlative verse, and Papa fading, fading, as it continued. Neatly and without fuss, Jane began to cry.

Outside, the burra sahibs clustered, and the occasional mem sahib also, curious no doubt, thought Jane, to see how well Honoria Whitcomb had worn. Some, a few, remembered Jane, and one had even met her in France when she'd driven the ambulance. He had just been promoted to brigadier general, Jane remembered, and was not best pleased to meet a young lady he knew socially engaged in changing a tyre.

It was the Hammersmith cemetery after that, and Dr Dodd still dominating his stage, as well-drilled Yoricks lowered Papa's coffin into its grave: 'Man that is born of a woman hath but a short time to live, and is full of misery. He cometh up, and is cut down, like a flower; he fleeth as it were a shadow, and never continueth in one stay.

'In the midst of life we are in death: of whom may we seek succour but of Thee, O Lord, who for our sins art justly displeased.'

Until at last the incredible words for the moment ceased, and first Lady Whitcomb, then Francis, then Jane picked up earth to throw down on to the coffin, and Dr Dodd resumed.

'Forasmuch as it hath pleased Almighty God of His great mercy to take unto Himself the soul of our dear brother Guy here departed, we therefore commit his body to the ground; earth to earth, ashes to ashes, dust to dust.' And as he spoke the words the earth fell, clod after clod upon the coffin, and Dr Dodd continued: ' – in sure and certain hope of the Resurrection to eternal life, through Our Lord Jesus Christ.'

And that was the splendid thing about Dr Dodd, thought Jane: intellectual snob he might be, social snob he undoubtedly was, but his hope of the Resurrection was both sure and certain. Papa had a powerful advocate when we needed one.

And then, suddenly, it was all over, and more people came to shake hands and mouth the ritual words: 'so sorry', and 'fine man', and 'I hope it was peaceful', and so on: and even when it was kindly meant it didn't have the magic of those Elizabethan prelates, three hundred years or so ago. But she didn't want to cry any more: the magic of the words had put a stop to that. Papa had left her, and there was an end.

Miss Gwatkin and Dr Pardoe came back to Offley Villas for sandwiches and sherry. Bollinger would have been far more appropriate, thought Jane, especially with Cuthbert Pardoe sitting there. Papa would have enjoyed the idea of Bollinger, of Pardoe drinking to his own perdition. . . . But perhaps not.

Before she had finished her first sandwich Mr Binns arrived: 'young Mr Binns', who must have been fifty at least, of Binns, Barbour, Crofton and Binns, her father's solicitors. He wore a frockcoat and black satin stock without any visible signs of embarrassment, and Jane assumed that he attended a great many funerals. He was delayed, he told them, because he had been obliged to see to the remuneration of the gravediggers. The undertaker's services had also it seemed needed adjustment. But now he was entirely at their disposal. Which meant, Jane gathered, that he was ready to read the will. Rather hard on Miss Gwatkin and Pardoe, who were not invited, and who appeared to have absolutely no interests in common. Unless Pardoe attempted to – what was that splendid word? – debauch, that was it; unless he attempted to debauch Miss Gwatkin, but it didn't seem very much of a possibility.

The Whitcombs and Mr Binns moved into the dining room, and sat round the table as if about to conduct a séance, then Mr Binns opened his briefcase, coughed once and began.

'I do not know if you are familiar with the terms of this will, Lady Whitcomb?' he asked, in a voice at once plummy and precise, and very appropriate to the frockcoat and stock.

'Not in the least,' said Lady Whitcomb. 'My husband was always reticent about money matters.'

'I see.' Mr Binns looked from Francis to Jane. 'And you Miss Whitcomb? Mr Whitcomb?'

They shook their heads.

'It is a very recent will,' said Mr Binns. 'Made in fact on the twenty-third of last month.'

Jane said involuntarily, 'Two Thursdays ago,' and her mother winced.

'Precisely,' said Mr Binns. 'I attended Sir Guy here. We took sherry together.' He looked at the empty table, sighed and asked: 'Do you wish me to read the entire will, or would you prefer it in more general terms?'

'General terms, please,' said Lady Whitcomb. 'I am too tired for jargon.'

'The principal asset is this house,' said Mr Binns. 'Its lease has some ninety-two years to run. You, Lady Whitcomb, are to enjoy its occupancy for life, after which it reverts unencumbered to your son, Francis.

'In investments, money on deposit in the bank and other holdings, Sir Guy had some twenty-three thousand pounds – '

'*Twenty-three thousand?*'

For once, Jane noticed, her mother's voice was completely out of control: the incredulity and rage totally apparent.

Mr Binns consulted his papers. 'Twenty-three thousand four hundred and eighty-eight pounds seven shillings and fourpence to my nearest computation, taking the shares at their market value on Friday last.'

'But that's impossible,' Jane's mother said. 'I brought that – '
She broke off, her face once more became that horribly unpleasing mauve colour, but at least her voice was calmer when she continued.

'What sort of income would such a sum yield?'

Mr Binns pursed his lips. 'A thousand a year, perhaps,' he said. 'Sir Guy instructed me that he had a pension consequent on his services – '

'Two thousand a year,' Lady Whitcomb said. 'It died with him.'

'You receive some lesser sum, so I was informed.'

'Five hundred a year.'

'And there are insurances. Your income should be by my calculation somewhere in the region of two thousand five hundred pounds a year.'

'Fifty a week,' said her mother contemptuously.

A few months ago this to Jane would have been wealth untold, but since Aunt Pen's régime it seemed poverty indeed.

'Some people have to make fifty pounds support them for six months,' said Francis.

'I do not intend to be one of them,' his mother said, and then: 'Continue, please, Mr Binns.'

'You are to enjoy the interest on that sum for life – '

'*Enjoy!*' said Lady Whitcomb. 'Is that irony intentional?'

'Merely my instructions,' said Mr Binns. 'After which the principle reverts to Mr Francis Whitcomb.'

'The *entire* principle?'

'That was your husband's wish.'

'There is nothing for my unfortunate daughter?'

'His collection of Indian memorabilia,' said Mr Binns, 'and his pair of sapphire cuff-links, which he suggests should be turned into ear-rings. He does not however insist on that.'

'Dear Guy was always so thoughtful,' Lady Whitcomb said, then added: 'I think perhaps we should hear the will in its entirety after all.'

Mr Binns cleared his throat once more and began to read, and Lady Whitcomb sat upright, rigid with concentration, but when Mr Binns finished she was no richer than when he began. She turned to Francis.

'At least you have your fellowship,' she said.

'I'm quite comfortably off, Mummy. Really,' Francis said.

'Nonsense,' said his mother. 'You are not comfortable at all. You should have been. But you aren't. It won't take you very long to discover just how *un*comfortable you are. Even at Cambridge.' She turned to Jane. 'And you, my poor child, are quite, quite destitute,' she said, then added: 'For the moment.'

Jane said, 'I think we should offer Mr Binns a glass of sherry.'

'Yes, of course,' said Francis. 'I'll fetch it, shall I?'

He left the room a little faster than was necessary, and Lady Whitcomb advanced on Mr Binns.

'Sherry is something that you will no doubt always associate with the Whitcombs,' she said. 'I hope this will be a good one. It isn't something I shall be able to afford very often now.' Her face, Jane noticed, was severe again, the skin colour pale and clear.

'I lost control for a little while,' she said. 'I apologise for that.'

'Not at all, Lady Whitcomb,' said Mr Binns. 'Such experiences are always upsetting. I thought you conducted yourself very well. By the by, do feel free to call upon me if ever you need my services.'

'You are very good,' said Lady Whitcomb, 'but I fear that my means will preclude any prospect of litigation.' Then Francis appeared with the decanter. 'Come, Jane,' said her mother. 'We will leave the gentlemen to their drink.'

But of course there was still a gentleman in the drawing room. Pardoe sat on an upright and savagely uncomfortable chair, staring in horror at Miss Gwatkin, at ease on a sofa, prattling happily at an audience quite powerless to interrupt.

'Gloucester as I recall,' she was saying. 'Or had the dear canon moved on to Winchester at that point? Amelia had had a son – their third child. Such a *relief* after two daughters – he was destined for the church too, but went into the army. – The war you know. But one of the daughters married a missionary so that in the end there was a kind of fulfilment.'

Lady Whitcomb briskly turned off the unremitting flow.

'Francis and Mr Binns are taking sherry in the drawing room,' she said. 'Perhaps you would care to join them, Dr Pardoe?'

It was a kindly act, and Pardoe took advantage of it, leaving the drawing room with the air of a dog turned out for a run.

Miss Gwatkin turned to Lady Whitcomb. She was a short woman with iron-grey hair and a long, pointed nose which Jane considered she richly deserved. She was also, Jane noticed with satisfaction, rather plumper than the last time they had met, a fact all the more evident when she stood beside her stately and still elegant mother.

'I do hope it all went well, Honoria,' she said.

'Well enough,' said her mother, then turned to Jane. 'Wouldn't you say it went well enough?'

'Decidedly, Mummy.'

'Then you have no further plans?' Miss Gwatkin asked.

'None.' Miss Gwatkin pouted. There were to be no shared intimacies, at least not yet. Not when that very strange daughter of hers was present.

'I shall leave you now,' she said. 'You must rest.'

'Must I?' Lady Whitcomb said. 'Yes, I suppose I must. There'll be lots of time to do so now.'

'Rest is a great healer of sorrows,' said Miss Gwatkin.

'Then I shall rest a great deal,' said Lady Whitcomb. 'As an occupation it has the virtue of economy too.'

Miss Gwatkin turned to Jane. 'You must look after your mother. She's upset. Now please don't ring for your maid. I'll let myself out.'

But Jane showed her to the door, and on the doorstep Miss Gwatkin said: 'I take it everything really is all right? I mean your mother has always lived with a great deal of what she calls style.'

'I've no doubt she will continue to do so,' said Jane.

'She's not well you know,' Miss Gwatkin said. 'It's the strain of course. That's why she talks in that peculiar way.'

'Peculiar?'

'Rest has the virtue of economy,' Miss Gwatkin quoted. 'It doesn't make sense. Quite a lot of the things she said don't make sense.' She patted Jane on the shoulder. 'Try not to let it worry you,' she said, and was gone.

Jane went back to the drawing room, and her mother gestured to a chair. Jane sat.

'I've no doubt you find it strange that I should have made a friend of someone so utterly devoid of intelligence?' she said.

'Friendship has a great deal to do with habit, or so it seems to me,' Jane said. 'By observing others, I mean. I haven't made many of my own recently.'

'Would you put your Aunt Penelope in that category?'

'I wasn't counting relatives,' said Jane, 'but I should have done.'

'Let us hope so,' her mother said. 'Otherwise there is a problem. You may have gathered as much.' She waited, but Jane made no answer.

'You are an observant person,' her mother said. 'No doubt you heard me say "But I brought that much – "'

'Yes, Mummy.'

'I was referring to the fact that your father left twenty-three thousand pounds.'

'So I had supposed.'

'What I said was not precisely true. In fact when we married I had twenty-two and a half thousand pounds. Simple arithmetic informs us that I have inherited this house – and five hundred pounds in cash. After forty-two years of marriage. Say twelve pounds per year – a pound a month.

'And yet your father was fair, according to his lights. He gave me back what was mine – and squandered what was his. On what, you are at liberty to conjecture, but not in my presence.'

Posy Sanderson must have been as expensive as she was beautiful, thought Jane, and wished that she could love her mother more. To love her father less she rather thought would be impossible.

'I'm very sorry, Mummy,' she said.

'I believe you,' her mother said, 'but it doesn't heal the hurt. *Will* you turn those cuff-links into ear-rings? But of course you will. Your father decreed it.'

'They would make rather pretty ear-rings.'

'Charm,' said her mother. 'He had a great deal of charm. You must be careful. You may have inherited it. Heaven knows poor Francis hasn't. Yet perhaps not so poor after all. You see, charm must be paid for, child. If not with your money, then with someone else's. . . . Do you have any thought of marrying Pardoe?'

'No,' said Jane.

'He would marry you, I'm quite sure. Oh, Francis has explained to me that junior fellows have their way to make – though how he can equate that with being comfortably off is beyond my comprehension. . . . Where was I, child? I'm quite exhausted.'

'Pardoe,' said Jane. 'And me.'

'Out of the question,' said her mother. 'He is quite the most charmless person I ever met, and in no position to finance whatever charm you may have.'

'I have no intention of marrying Dr Pardoe.'

'I'm relieved to hear it,' said her mother. 'You feel trapped of course, and wish to escape. But Pardoe would prove an infinitely worse gaoler than I shall be.'

'I'll bear it in mind,' said Jane.

'Please do,' said her mother. 'Now your father was a most delightful gaoler.' Jane made no answer.

'He would dance with the prisoner, and serve champagne – which the prisoner helped to pay for. – And always the finest and softest silks wrapped round the chains and manacles so that they would not break the skin – though of course the chains and manacles were always there. That is what a woman is for. To be locked up, imprisoned, circumscribed, and occasionally stretched on the rack of what men are pleased to call love.' She looked once more at her daughter. 'You may not be so unfortunate as you may think,' she said, and rose. 'I shall follow Gwendoline's advice, and rest.'

'Gwendoline?'

'Miss Gwatkin,' said her mother.

'*Gwendoline* Gwatkin?'

Her mother smiled, very briefly, as if smiles were rationed, thought Jane, and must be used sparingly.

'Didn't you know?' she asked.

'No,' said Jane, 'but it was decent of you to preserve the secret for so long.'

'Poor Gwendoline,' her mother said. '*Her* life has not been precisely carefree either. . . . What will you do? Dine with the gentlemen?'

'Visit Aunt Pen,' said Jane.

'To be sure,' her mother said.

'She wants to hear about the funeral. I think I should go, Mummy. If you're sure you'll be all right.'

'Of course I will,' said her mother. 'And if I'm bored I can always get Dr Pardoe to teach me how to box. Tell Penelope that I send my best wishes. She won't believe it, but it will be true for once.'

14

MOUNT STREET WAS charming, as it always was, but there was an awareness in the house, an expectancy, that seemed to Jane rather more than servants anticipating death. Indeed, Marchmont, as he ushered her upstairs, seemed every bit as sure of eternity as Dr Dodd.

'Mrs Nettles is resting, miss,' he said, 'but she left word that you were to be shown up at once.'

Jane went into the bedroom, Foch at her side, and Marchmont left. Aunt Pen's Airedale, Bob, lay in his basket by the bed, and stood up at once when he saw Foch, the gesture of a host, no more, which Foch acknowledged by slumping down on the carpet as Jane went to the bed where her aunt slept.

This time she knew that her aunt was dying. Always slender, now she was emaciated, and her face had the yellow smoothness of ancient ivory. She breathed slowly and evenly, and lay quite motionless until Jane stretched out a hand to touch hers. At once her eyes opened.

'I've been with Walter,' she said. 'So naughty – '

And there you had it, thought Jane. The difference between the two women.

'I'm sorry I woke you,' she said.

'I wanted to be woken,' said her aunt, and then: 'Did I say something just now?'

'You said you'd been dreaming of Uncle Walter.'

'What a prude you are,' said Aunt Pen. Knight's moves to the end, it seemed.

'I have a nurse now,' Aunt Pen continued. 'She's downstairs having something called high tea. So far as I can gather, that's nursery tea for grown ups.'.

'It sounds rather a good idea,' said Jane.

'If I'd got better I thought you and I might try it,' said Aunt Pen, 'but now it looks as if you'll have to eat it on your own. Tell me about the funeral.' And then she smiled; an enormous, genuine grin. Where Mummy hoarded, Aunt Pen squandered.

'Oh dear,' she said. 'What a morbid speech that was. All the same I should like to know.'

And so Jane told her about Dr Dodd and the burra sahibs – all of whom had to be described so that Aunt Pen could name them – and Pardoe and Miss Gwatkin and the words that had helped her to bear it all. But when she had finished her aunt said: 'There's something else.'

'I don't think so.'

'Binns, Barbour, Crofton and Binns,' said her aunt. 'Which one did they send?'

'Young Mr Binns.'

'The frockcoat and stock one? He's done very well out of the burra sahibs, but he knows his job. . . . Go on, my dear.'

'Papa left it all to Mummy for life – and then to Francis.'

'And how much is all?' Jane hesitated. 'Come on, my lovely,' said her aunt. 'It may sound like morbid curiosity to you, but then everything about me is morbid now. But I'm not a Nosey Parker. I want to know.'

'The house,' said Jane, 'and about twenty-three thousand pounds.'

'How much will she have to live on?'

'About fifty a week.'

'Crikey,' said her aunt, and then: 'A lot of people would think that was a fortune.'

'That's what Francis said.'

'But to your mother it'll be what they used to call genteel poverty. Did she cut up rough?'

'A bit.'

'One can hardly blame her. It meant that Guy spent every penny of his own.'

'So she told me.'

'And Posy Sanderson? Did she mention her?'

'Not by name.'

'It was a kind of madness,' said Aunt Pen. 'Some women can do it at will. They seem to be born with it – like having perfect pitch. I had it with Walter.'

'And others too, no doubt,' said Jane.

'Nosey Parker yourself,' said her aunt. 'And anyway, it all stopped with Walter. *He* saw to that. Where was I?'

'Posy Sanderson.'

'He used to think she loved him – and maybe she did. Certainly she wanted him to leave Honoria and set up house with her. He couldn't of course, and she knew he couldn't. – It was just a way to make him feel rotten.'

'Were we alive? My brothers and I?'

'You were two, I should think. But it wasn't for the sake of the children.'

'What then?'

'It just wasn't done,' said her aunt. She was perfectly serious. 'Not even with another white woman. With a halfcaste it would have been unthinkable. So he gave her money instead. All he had, it appears. It turned out to be an inadequate substitute. He embezzled a bit, too.'

'*Papa?*'

'I told you it was a kind of madness. He came to me and told me about it.'

'But why you?'

'Why do you think, you goose? So that I could turn it on and drive poor old Walter mad, and get him to lend Guy the money, which he did. Guy's wicked deed was never discovered, thank God.'

'Papa,' said Jane. 'Of all people.'

'You never met Posy Sanderson,' said her aunt.

'Did she have his child?'

'Guy thought she did,' her aunt said. 'Certainly she had somebody's child. It killed her.'

'Does Mummy know?'

'About the embezzling? It's possible. Honoria's very clever, but on the other hand so was Guy. He covered it all up very discreetly. You know what those native clerks were like for prying.' Then, as if it were all part of the same chain of thought she added: 'I'm going away tomorrow.'

'So soon?'

'I can't take much more of this beastly pain,' said her aunt. 'Time I was off to the opium den. We shan't see each other again.'

'I suppose not.'

'It'll be marvellous if I catch up with old Walter. I've such a lot to tell him.'

'Tell him that driving the ambulance was one of the high points of my life.'

'You'll be able to tell him yourself when the time comes. I'm not being beastly, my dear. It's just that I'm going to miss you. . . . Or maybe there's only oblivion after all, and maybe it's just as well.'

'I used to think that too,' said Jane, 'but it was you more than anybody who persuaded me I was wrong.'

Her aunt said, 'Open the bedside table drawer,' and Jane did so. In it was a brown manilla envelope.

'One more present for you,' said her aunt. 'Just to tide you over.' Jane hesitated. 'And please don't be misguided enough to have what they call qualms. Not with me.'

Jane put the envelope in her bag.

'Will you take Bob with you?' she asked.

'All taken care of,' said her aunt, then her face changed, her jaw clenched as though she were biting on something hard to prevent herself from screaming. 'It's time for you to go, my lovely,' she said. 'I do so wish it wasn't. Kiss me good-bye.'

She couldn't go home. Even the *thought* of Pardoe was unbearable, so she went to the cinema instead, and drove the Riley to the Alhambra, Fulham, and Miss Georgina Payne. The place was two-thirds full, even though it was early, but this owed more to the fact that Lillian Gish was due to appear in the main feature, rather than Georgina Payne who appeared all the time, and thumped her way determinedly through the *Keystone Cops* and the *Perils of Pauline*, who finished the episode, as she so often did, being strapped to the railway line by the villain as the express chuffed closer and closer.

At the interval she stood up and turned in profile to stretch like a cat. It was done, Jane had no doubt, to ease her back after all that 'Hearts and Flowers' and 'William Tell', but it was a gesture at once so graceful and so lascivious that Jane found herself remembering what her aunt had said about Papa's little spot of bother. Whatever Posy Sanderson had had, Georgina Payne had, too. She looked at her watch. Seven thirty. Pardoe and Francis would be at dinner. Plenty of time for her to go to an ABC for a sandwich and a cup of coffee, which suddenly seemed far more important than Lillian Gish.

When she got back, Hawkins let her in, and she asked about her mother. 'Still in bed,' said Hawkins. 'Cook made me go up and ask if she fancied a bowl of soup, but she said no. Soup's vegetables, she says, and herbs. And you only get a dish of herbs where love is. She's not delirious is she, miss?'

'No,' said Jane. 'She was quoting the Bible.'

'Oh the *Bible*,' said Hawkins, as if that explained everything. 'Well she would, wouldn't she? I mean this day of all days.'

'Exactly,' said Jane, and hoped that would suffice. Apparently it did. 'Where are the gentlemen?' she asked.

'Gone out,' said Hawkins. 'They had a meeting.'

'They often do,' said Jane. 'It doesn't mean they aren't upset.'

'Maybe,' said Hawkins, 'but if you don't mind my saying so, miss – '

'We'll see,' said Jane.

'That Dr Pardoe could stand a bit of watching,' said Hawkins. 'Doctor or no doctor.'

'Oh dear,' said Jane. 'I hope he didn't – '

'Not likely,' said Hawkins. 'Only I just thought I better mention it.'

'I'm obliged to you,' said Jane, and turned away.

'Just one more thing, miss,' Hawkins said, and Jane began to panic. My God what now?

'Yes?' she asked.

'Can you spell parsimonious?'

'I *think* so,' said Jane cautiously.

'I mean will you, miss?'

'Will I what? Oh. – P-A-R-S-I-M-O-N-I-O-U-S.'

'Thank you, miss,' said Hawkins. 'It's for these classes I go to, you see. On my night off.'

'What classes?'

'Self-improvement classes,' said Hawkins. 'I wanted

"parsimonious" for next week's competition. It'll look a lot better than "mean".'

She left, leaving Jane to wonder who was parsimonious: cook, her mother, or herself.

Next morning she decided that the tea and biscuits Hawkins brought should serve as breakfast. It was not that she had gone back to starving herself, but Aunt Pen's boat train would leave at breakfast time and the thought of poached haddock revolted her. She lay in bed instead, and drowsed, then looked once more at Aunt Pen's present. It was a hundred five-pound notes – 'just to tide you over'. Ten weeks of Mummy's genteel poverty. . . . Tide her over till what? To think about that might be to wish Aunt Pen dead, so she thought instead how five hundred quid meant she wouldn't have to give up the Riley just yet, but that too was a shame-making thought. She sat up and lit a cigarette, and considered instead what to do that day. First there was Pardoe – at one time she had begun to think that there might always be Pardoe, but death and sorrow had reduced him to his correct proportions. Pardoe was a minor problem, and one that she could solve. Mummy was another matter.

She needed someone to talk to. That was obvious. And it couldn't be Francis. That was equally obvious. Francis would either be outraged, which was bad, or indifferent because the affair lacked social significance, which was worse. Or did it? Posy Sanderson had been Eurasian after all. That would make her an object of pity: of comparison even, and Jane wasn't having that. In any case Posy Sanderson was dead, and so was Papa. There was only Mummy, here in Kensington, and Francis was anxious to get back to Cambridge.

It couldn't be Lockhart either. She could only discuss this business with a man if he were her lover, as John had been, and for her and Lockhart to be lovers was impossible. They both knew that. They had been more and less than lovers, but without the bed there could be no confiding. So it couldn't be a man. But of course she knew who it was. Harriet Ryland as was. Dr Harriet Watson as is. She'd been invited. Any time. . . . There was a tap at her door. Jane stubbed out the cigarette in her soap dish as Hawkins came in for her tea things, and thought I must get an ash tray. Hawkins's eyes went at once to the money on the bed. It was indeed an interesting sight, thought Jane, and belonged in a bank, for Hawkins's sake as well as her own.

'We got a problem below stairs, miss,' said Hawkins.

'What problem?'

'Your mother, miss. Cook went up to get her instructions as usual, and all your mother did was give her that bit about the dish of herbs, miss. Same as she gave me. Only this time she threw in a stalled ox as well.'

'I'll go and speak to her.'

'I should miss,' said Hawkins. 'First chance you get. There'll be ructions if you don't.'

No time to get dressed, then. Clean the teeth and put on a dressing gown and put the filthy lucre in her dressing-gown pocket. For Hawkins's sake, and for her own. She went to her mother's room and tapped on the door, called out, 'It's Jane, Mummy' and went in before Lady Whitcomb could tell her to go away. Her mother was still in bed. She looked, and obviously was, exhausted, which was not surprising, thought Jane.

'I'm resting,' her mother said.

'Good morning, Mummy,' Jane said firmly, and kissed her.

'Good morning. Please go away. I'm resting.'

'As Miss Gwatkin advised.'

'Precisely.'

'First you must see the cook,' said Jane. 'Then you can rest. Perhaps you would like tea and toast first.'

'Ah,' said her mother, as if Jane had just confirmed a theory. 'You're taking over, is that it? Arranging my day? My life perhaps? No doubt you will give cook her instructions too.'

'Certainly not,' said Jane. 'There can only be one queen to a hive.'

Her mother smiled that same fleeting smile.

'And what are you? Worker or drone?'

'A bit of both, perhaps,' said Jane. 'But the cook's a worker if ever there was one, and she can't take instructions from biblical quotations, however apt.'

'You considered it apt?'

'Certainly,' said Jane.

'But you still love your father? He dishonoured his family,

stole from his wife, risked your very life to prove a theory – but you still love him?'

'I can't help it, Mummy,' said Jane.

Her mother turned her back to her. 'Tell cook I'll see her,' she said.

Jane dressed then, and went downstairs. She wore a suit that Captain Molyneux had designed: blue and white stripes, the blue as close to the colour of her eyes as the captain's fabric designer could get. Foch, fussing beside her, checked at the entrance to the drawing room. Pardoe was there, alone, reading a copy of the *Daily Herald*. Jane went into the room and Foch followed warily.

'Good morning,' said Jane. 'Where is my brother?'

'Gone out,' said Pardoe. 'Fascinating newspaper, this. Of course you don't take it. Not in this house.'

'I don't believe so. Can you tell – '

'Bet you a hundred you don't. Five hundred if you like. Any odds you want. And I'm not a betting man.'

I have five hundred in my handbag this very moment, but I'm not going to risk it.

Aloud she said, 'Can you tell – '

'It's a Socialist paper, you see,' said Pardoe. 'Designed *for* the workers, *by* the workers. Not always all that sound on theory – Marx, Engels, Lenin's plans for collectivisation – but very good indeed on union affairs. Wage claims. Hourly rates. All that. Fascinating stuff. Literary, too. They've even got a literary *page*. Not run by a worker, unfortunately, but a jolly good chap. Ex-army officer. Won an MC and chucked it away because he didn't agree with the slaughter.'

'None of us agreed with the slaughter,' said Jane, but Pardoe was not there to listen.

'Chap called Siegfried Sassoon,' he said. 'Perhaps you've heard of him?'

'I've met him once,' said Jane. 'He seemed rather a nice man, but somewhat bewildered, like the rest of us.'

That at least got through.

'Of course,' said Pardoe. 'I keep forgetting. You were in it.'

'And you weren't?'

'Too young,' said Pardoe. 'Missed it by a year. Too bad, really. It would have given me a chance to prove myself.'

'You would have fought?'

'Of course not.' Pardoe sounded outraged. 'I would have *refused* to fight. Gone to prison. For my principles.'

Another form of martyrdom, she thought, but not as permanent as John's. She took the gold Cartier cigarette case from her bag, lit a cigarette with the gold Dunhill lighter. A paper spill torn from the *Daily Herald* would have been even better, but the fire wasn't lit.

'I wish you wouldn't do that,' Pardoe said, and then: 'I say. . . .'

'Can you tell me where my brother is, Dr Pardoe?'

'Gone off to see that lawyer of yours in Gray's Inn. Shouldn't think he'll be back for ages. Rather convenient really. I've been longing to have a chat with you.'

'But yesterday you said that now was not the time.'

'No more it was,' said Pardoe. 'But that was yesterday. Your time of mourning. As you know I disapprove most heartily of the ritualistic way in which it was expressed, but for the moment I shall say no more on that subject.'

'Thank you.'

Pardoe ploughed on. Like a tank, thought Jane again. A huge, unstoppable tank, trailing barbed wire, straddling trenches, on and on for ever, spouting words instead of bullets, while one's own words smashed impotently on his armour-plated sides.

'After a – sadness such as yours, a bereavement as the jargon is – one needs reassurance. Comfort if you will – for the body as well as the mind. Now I know what you are going to say – '

As if I'm to be allowed to say anything, thought Jane bitterly.

'You are about to tell me that I am younger than you. And so, in terms of mathematical computation of age, I am,' Pardoe continued. 'But I hope you will agree that in terms of what we may call worldly experience I am infinitely more mature? It was, after all, inevitable,' he told her kindly, 'given the different milieux we were destined to inhabit.'

Jane blew smoke towards him, which made him stop so that he might wave it away.

'You are, I take it, inviting me to enter your milieu?'

'I am indeed.'

'Today?'

'This very moment – if you will only put out that beastly thing.'

'You are aware that my mother is in her bedroom, mourning, and that her bedroom is close to mine?'

'I am not, I hope, altogether lacking in tact,' said Pardoe reproachfully. 'We will not, as you so delightfully put it, share our milieu here. No worker would consider such a thing for a moment, and where the worker leads, the intellectual must follow. I have a small flat in Bloomsbury, and you, Francis informs me, are the owner of a motor vehicle. It will not take you long to drive us there. How delightful that you should own a motor vehicle. It will be very useful indeed – for political purposes every bit as much as the shared milieu.'

Jane then achieved the most successful theatrical feat of her life by bursting into tears.

'My mother warned me about men like you,' she sobbed.

The tank stuck fast, engulfed in tears.

'What can you possibly mean?' he said at last.

'All that talk of comfort, of sharing,' Jane cried. 'And all the time you belonged to another. *Lots* of others. A whole harem of others. You've been unfaithful to me before we've even begun.'

'That's preposterous.'

'I knew you would say that,' Jane cried. 'I'd have bet five hundred pounds you would say that. – Any odds you want,' – and sobbed louder than ever.

Pardoe glanced furtively – the only possible word – at the door, and then, as Jane's sobs grew even louder, he rose to his feet.

'I assume,' he said, 'that I am the victim of some despicable form of joke.'

Jane covered her face in her hands. For him to see her laugh might lead to violence, and he knew how to hit, and so, her face hidden, shoulders shaking, she made sounds that could be mistaken for grief.

'I'm not a fool, you know,' said Pardoe, and for some reason that did it. Her laughter died and she dropped her hands.

'And neither am I,' she said.

'Then why embark on this charade?'

'It was the only way to shut you up.'

But already the tank was mobile again: the armour absorbing all words but his own.

'If you are referring to Marigold Ledbetter I admit to a certain intimacy. As I recall I already *have* admitted it. We are adults, and being human she has certain needs and aspirations that I can help her to fulfil: not all of them physical, I may add. Your assumption that monogamy is essential to a relationship, while understandable, is erroneous. If you were to glance through the works of Sir George James Frazer for example – '

'If you don't shut up I'll yell again,' said Jane. The tank grew still.

'It wasn't Titania,' Jane continued. 'It was Peggy Hawkins.'

'I know no woman of that name,' said Pardoe. 'Is she at Cambridge?'

'She's here,' said Jane. 'In this house.'

'Then I can assure you,' said Pardoe, then paused for a moment. 'Oh,' he said.

'Oh is right,' said Jane.

'The housemaid?'

'The housemaid.'

'You consider it degrading that I should consider her in that light?'

'For her I do,' said Jane. 'She's not quite ready for your game yet.'

'Game? What game?'

'Doctors and Housemaids is it? Or Workers and Intellectuals?'

'The intellectual can always learn from the worker.'

'Not this worker,' said Jane. 'You try it again and I'll scream the place down.'

It was at this point that Francis returned, and for once his entry was opportune.

'Nice to see you two getting along so nicely,' he said.

'We are not getting along nicely,' said Pardoe. 'We are not getting along at all,' and left the room.

'What on earth have you been saying to him?' Francis asked.

'That he must stop making advances to Hawkins,' said Jane, and then, anticipating the next question: 'Hawkins is our housemaid.'

'He'd treat her the same as he treats everyone else,' said Francis.

'Me for instance? But that isn't the point,' said Jane.

'What is the point then, if it isn't snobbery?'

'Hawkins would leave, and that would upset Mummy.'

'It's time we went back to Cambridge anyway,' said her brother. It was a kind of victory.

He took from his pocket a pipe and tobacco pouch, a new departure. Probably something to do with his newly acquired status as a don, but any enquiry, however innocent, would be taken as sarcasm. She lit a cigarette instead.

'I've been to see my lawyer,' he said.

My goodness, thought Jane. That didn't take long.

'Mummy's lawyer too,' she said.

'Of course. And yours – should you ever need one.'

'Too kind,' said Jane.

'No need to be touchy. After all – why should you need a lawyer?'

'Destitute as I am?'

'I didn't make the will,' said Francis. 'And anyway, you'll be all right. Mummy will take care of you.'

'I'm to be her companion then?'

'Bound to be – since you'll live in the same house.'

'But what an enchanting prospect,' said Jane.

'Had you made other plans?' Francis asked.

'Dr Pardoe's the one who makes plans for me,' said Jane. 'Or rather he used to be.'

'You've really got your knife into Cuthbert, haven't you?'

'Not yet,' said Jane. 'But don't let's quarrel. I'm glad everything went so well at Cambridge. It meant a lot to you, didn't it?'

'It meant everything,' said Francis.

'Then you've no more worlds to conquer?'

'On the contrary,' said Francis. 'My wars are just beginning.' And then: 'I say – you'll be all right with Mummy, won't you? I mean it won't be exactly destitution, will it? I mean Aunt Pen must have given you a pound or two for you to dress like that.'

'I'll be all right,' said Jane.

She left him trying to light his pipe. He needed a lot of practice.

Before she set off for the bank she looked in her father's study. It was meticulously neat, far more so than when Papa had used it, but of Posy Sanderson and her beauty there was no sign. No sign at all. The bank was delighted to see her and her five hundred pounds, and suggested a deposit account, but Jane insisted that it be a current one, and left the bank shaking its head over the wilful irresponsibility of young women these days.

15

Harriet Watson's surgery was in Baron's Court, in a maze of dreary Victorian villas, each one surrounded by its neatly clipped wall of sooty privet. The privet outside Harriet's surgery soared to the skies, but the bell-pull gleamed. She tugged, and was answered by a furious clatter that died away at last as a bored maid opened the door, yawning, took in the glory of the Molyneux suit, the Paris hat, and more or less snapped to attention.

'It's free day, miss,' she said.

'I'm Jane Whitcomb.'

'Oh yes, Miss Whitcomb,' said the maid. 'The doctor did say you was coming. This way, miss.'

She led Jane down a passage covered in dark-green linoleum, the kind that's made to last, passing on the way a waiting room filled with ancient chairs made cheerful with cushions. There were pictures on the walls and a stack of magazines and children's comic papers. Two women sat there, with children, and a man whose head was bandaged. They all looked poor beyond belief.

Jane was shown into another room, smaller, smartly furnished, with rows of books on shelves, and a collection of photographs on a table.

'The doctor shouldn't be too long, miss,' said the maid. 'But you never know what might happen on free day. Shall I get you a cup of coffee, miss?'

But Jane was wary of coffee in such places as this, and asked for tea, looked at the photographs, then searched among the books, and took down a copy of *Pickwick Papers*. She was half way through Christmas at Dingley Dell when Harriet came in, dark and fiercely clever, as always, and kissed her.

'Darling,' she said. 'I'm so sorry. But I've had rather a rush.'

'I know,' said Jane. 'Anything can happen on free day.'

'Ah,' said Harriet. 'You've been talking to Minnie.'

'Bit of a snob, isn't she?'

'Appalling. But nobody can polish brass like she does. Pity she can't cut privet as well.'

'What is a free day?'

'What it says. The day when I treat people for nothing.'

'Anybody? You mean they just walk in off the streets?'

'Hardly,' said Harriet. 'The place would be crammed full. To qualify you have to be recommended – by a person or a health visitor or a councillor or something. I get quite a lot from Sally Ann officers.'

'Sally Ann?'

'The Salvation Army. Don't you know anything?'

'Not much.'

'They send too many actually,' said Harriet. 'More than I can cope with. I've told them I'll have to ration them if they don't ease up. I won't of course, but they don't seem able to get it into their heads that people who can afford to pay can be sick too. Will you stay to lunch?'

'Love to,' said Jane.

'Lunch is rather a grand name for it,' said Harriet. 'Actually it's poached eggs on toast, but I can offer gin to go with it.' She went in search of a bottle. 'Did you look at my photographs?'

'Yes indeed.'

'Recognise yourself?'

'It was the others I looked at.'

Harriet picked up a leather-framed photograph and passed it to Jane.

'Look at yourself this time.'

It was behind the lines of the Somme in winter; the snow in great ridges on top of the frozen mud, and all about the detritus of war: barbed wire, a pile of duckboards, a shattered gun limber; and in the foreground a motor ambulance, a converted Renault lorry, and in front of it five girls in knitted hats, mitts, and fur coats: two sables, a silver fox, a chinchilla, and a leopardskin. All five girls were laughing.

Jane looked at herself as she had been nearly ten years before. She was one of the girls in sables, a present from Uncle Walter and Aunt Pen. ('The most practical thing I ever gave you,' Aunt Pen had written. 'How can you drive our poor Tommies if you're laid up with pneumonia?') Grinning like an idiot, but dear God how *young* she looked. The photograph had been taken just three weeks after she'd met John.

'There we all are,' said Harriet. 'The Five Charioteers.'

It had been an RAMC colonel who had first called them that, when they'd ferried back the wounded to his field hospital.

'That's you in the silver fox,' said Jane.

'It was my grandmother's. She loaned it to me after I had 'flu and got home leave. She called it her war work.'

'Louise had the other sable,' said Jane. 'But she never liked it. I can't think why.'

'Because yours was better,' Harriet said, and poured two gins, then added Italian vermouth and passed one to Jane.

'I'm told it tastes better with ice,' she said. 'But it's the effect that counts. Cheers.'

Jane lifted her glass, and watched as Harriet sipped, then sighed in content.

'My God I'm whacked,' she said, and Jane stared.

'You used to say that in France,' she said. 'In just that way.'

'And I used to mean it. I still do.'

'You must be glad your work's over.'

'It isn't,' Harriet said. 'I've got the panel patients at six. They're the ones who *can* pay – but not a hell of a lot. And I've rounds to do before then.' She pointed to the photograph. 'That's Sarah in the chinchilla.'

'That was just about the time she got engaged to Billy Timms.'

'Of course it was,' said Harriet. 'Otherwise she'd have been the only one without a fur coat. . . . And there's old Fred in the leopardskin.'

'It was terribly her,' said Jane.

'Indeed it was,' Harriet said. 'It used to make me think of Tarzan. It's a terrible thing to say, considering what we were there for – but they were good days.'

'We were useful,' said Jane. 'That's always a good thing.'

'And you're not useful any more?'

'*Useless*,' said Jane, then Minnie brought in the poached eggs on a tray, and they sat down to eat.

Suddenly Harriet said, 'Daddy Howlett. Do you remember him?'

Jane giggled. 'Of course I do,' she said. 'He was battalion commander of the – Cumberlands was it?'

'It was,' said Harriet.

'That day they were marching back to the rest camp after that push at the Ypres salient.'

'Three hundred and sixty-something men,' said Harriet. 'Two weeks before they'd been eight hundred.'

'But we saved some of them,' said Jane. 'The Five Charioteers. We saved quite a few actually. And the ones that survived. . . . They were so happy. They just couldn't believe they were alive. They sang. My God how they sang.'

'They were on the road on the brow of the hill,' Harriet said. 'We were down below having a picnic. And they marched past us singing, and didn't even know we were there. It was a hot day – do you remember? – and Daddy Howlett had taken off his tin hat and knotted the ends of a handkerchief together like a tripper at the seaside to protect his bald spot.'

'And then the great man himself trotted past,' said Jane. 'Field Marshal Haig. Followed by his staff. And all of them mounted on the sort of horses they must give you to ride in Heaven.'

'And he looked down and saw us and we all stood up and he saluted and broke into a canter,' Harriet said. 'Because the Cumberlands were still singing. Do you remember what they sang?'

'Can I ever forget?' said Jane, and began in a husky contralto:

> Do your balls hang low?
> Do they dangle to and fro?
> Can you tie them in a knot?
> Can you tie them in a bow?
> Do they itch when it is hot?
> Do you rest them in a pot?
> Do you get them in a tangle?
> Do you catch them in a mangle?

Harriet joined in, her voice a small, true soprano. The two sang sweetly but softly together, because of Minnie.

Do they swing in stormy weather?
Do they tickle with a feather?
Do they rattle when you walk?
Do they jingle when you talk?
Can you sling them on your shoulder
Like a lousy fucking soldier?
Do your balls – hang – low?

They finished together then collapsed into helpless laughter, peal after peal. At last Jane gasped, 'And then Haig said, "I take it you are unaware that there are ladies present?"' – And the two women moaned again, until at last they could speak, and Harriet said, 'And now perhaps you can tell me why you came here? I don't want to rush you, but it's almost time for my rounds.'

Jane told her, and only once did Harriet interrupt, when she talked about Pardoe. 'Alistair knows him,' she said. (Alistair was her husband.) 'His work overlapped with some stuff Alistair was doing about X-rays. He may be a fool, but according to Alistair he's a learned fool. He's a physicist. The atom's his big interest. You've got to be insane to tackle the atom, according to Alistair, but you've got to be brilliant, too.'

'It's just that I can't stand him,' said Jane.

'Who could?' asked Harriet.

'Marigold Ledbetter for one.' Jane continued her recital.

When she had finished Harriet said, 'You've had your share – and maybe a little more.'

'I hope that's over now.'

'I hope so too. The horse-riding could have gone badly wrong. In a sense you risked your sanity to get better.'

'No,' said Jane. 'Papa did that.'

'I expect he had his reasons.'

'Mummy says it was all arrogance.'

'And he would have said it was all love. No doubt it was a bit of both, as usual. But at least you're here, and talking. Have you seen Dr Lockhart yet?'

'No,' said Jane.

'I should. You owe him that much.'

'I owe him everything.'

'What about your father?'

'Nothing would have worked without Jabber. I'll go to see him. Honestly I will. But not before I've heard about Aunt Pen. I couldn't somehow.'

'You'll just sit at home with your mother?'

'It won't be for long,' said Jane.

Harriet Watson nodded as if a valuable point had been scored. 'Then what?'

'Something useful,' said Jane. 'I can't do what you're doing, but I can be of some use, surely?'

'Find the right niche and you could be invaluable,' Harriet said. 'You're a very able woman after all. But be careful.'

'Of what?'

'You're looking for love, I think. And why not? But don't grab at the first offer that isn't Dr Pardoe. You're worth better than that. After all – you had it once, didn't you? That absolutely charming young captain in the Northumbrians.'

'You knew about us?'

'We all did,' said Harriet. 'You're not particularly good at hiding your feelings, you know.'

'But you never said – '

'We didn't think you'd want us to say,' said Harriet. 'Not then. Not the way things were.'

'We didn't have a day to spare,' said Jane. 'It was all used up so quickly. All the same, it was nice of you to stay quiet.'

'It was probably the hardest thing we ever did,' Harriet said. 'But we were fond of you, you see. We envied you too.'

'John was killed. The day before it ended.'

'And you were home on leave. We couldn't reach you, not then. There were still too many things to do. And by the time we could, it was too late. You'd shut yourself away. But you're back now.' She kissed Jane's cheek. 'Don't lose touch.'

After that she waited, because there was nothing else she could do. Books from the library at Boots, and furtive visits to the cinema, or theatre matinées; furtive because Mummy did not believe the cinema and theatre were either good for her nervous disposition, or appropriate to a time of mourning. Mummy practised her piano instead: mournful pieces by Chopin and Brahms, the more difficult passages played over and over, until

Jane would signal Foch to go for a walk, or bribe Hawkins to keep an eye on him while she watched a flickering screen or a West End stage, and tried to think of nothing at all. In the end she found that silent comedies were best: Charlie Chaplin, Buster Keaton, Mack Sennett's frenetic policemen. The furious car chases, fires, explosions, the frantic gyrations of pursuer and pursued, were like a mantra endlessly repeated, invoking oblivion. And if occasionally she cried, there was no one to see her in the dark, and if when the lights went up someone did, they would assume that they were tears of laughter.

The news came two weeks after Papa's death, while Jane was in the study, sorting out papers and photographs (still no evidence that Posy Sanderson had ever existed) for no good reason that she could see.

'A Mr Medlicott on the phone, miss. From Medlicott and Rubens. Says he's a lawyer,' Hawkins told her, while Mummy wrestled with the opening bars of a nocturne forever beyond her reach. Jane went to stand between the draughts in the hall, and listen.

At last, Medlicott said, 'I can come to you or you can come here, as you wish.'

'I'll come to you.'

'When will it be convenient?'

'Now,' said Jane.

'I shall look forward to meeting you.'

Jane went into the drawing room, where Mummy wrestled with Chopin. Never, never would Mummy give up, but Chopin was winning.

'Not now, child,' her mother said. 'Can't you see how busy I am?'

And so the hateful words could be left unsaid for a little while longer. She whistled for Foch, who deplored her whistling because it was unladylike, and took him to the Riley, which made him feel better. He adored being driven. Jane touched his head, where he sat perched, expectant, beside her in the two-seater.

'Bad news, I'm afraid,' she said. 'For your friend Bob and me – and maybe for you too. She was fond of you. She gave you bits of cake sometimes.'

Foch barked, softly. It was time to go.

Mrs Blythe-Tarkington watched the car pull out and nodded in approval. That nice young woman from Number 17 still talked to her dog, even if her clothes were rather too dashing for someone in mourning. But the poor child looked quite unwell, so she must be suffering inside. Mrs Blythe-Tarkington said a prayer.

Medlicott and Rubens had offices in Knightsbridge, not far from Harrods, which Aunt Pen had always considered very convenient. 'Whenever I have to visit my lawyers to see how much money I have, I can go round the corner and spend some of it.' These were lawyers who specialised in looking after the Aunt Pens of this world, thought Jane. Their offices reeked of money the way a pub reeks of beer. But that was unkind, she thought. At least Medlicott and Rubens were subtle about it. The only law offices she had ever seen before were those of Binns, Barbour, Crofton and Binns, and they had the sort of décor that matched young Mr Binns's frockcoat and stock. Deed boxes and leather-bound law books and sealing wax. Only Sidney Carton was missing.

Medlicott and Rubens would have none of this. Their offices were in one of the new office blocks, and their reception room was like the set of one of those plays she had stared at uncomprehending; all steel and leather, with an art nouveau carpet of multi-coloured squares, and the sort of sculpture, in welded metal, that could be anything. Foch looked about him. Apart from the sculpture he was impressed. The receptionist, pretty, with short skirts and shingled hair, said that Mr Medlicott would see Jane at once. She sounded surprised.

Mr Medlicott's office was rather as Papa had once described a gentlemen's club, thought Jane. Mahogany desk, worn leather chairs, a Turkey carpet and a parquet floor polished till it gleamed. Just the setting for Mr Medlicott, who wore tweeds and brogues, a shirt of fine check and a Balliol tie. He was tall and clean-shaven, ruddy-cheeked, silver-haired, and looked much more like a wealthy squire than a solicitor. Jane decided that he was probably both.

'Sherry, Miss Whitcomb?' he asked.

'Please.'

He gestured to one of the club armchairs, and poured them both a glass of amontillado, then sat on an armchair facing her.

No notes, no files, no deed box, only an envelope which he handed to her at once.

'I am instructed to ask you to read this before we begin our talk,' he said.

It was from Aunt Pen, of course, and written, obviously with great labour, in her own hand.

My dear, [Jane read]

By the time you read this I shall have left you. It's a very hard thing to do, leaving you. Remember how we both cried when I had to go to Glasgow with Walter for a sales conference and left you with Vinney and missed your birthday?

On the other hand I've kept poor old Walter waiting long enough. He's a darling darling man, but very impatient. . . .

I'm leaving you well off. I expect you knew it was going to happen, but I could see the thought of my money upset you, so I didn't mention it, though why you should be upset I can't imagine. It is *splendid* to be well off. There's a bit for Vinney and her good works, and a tiny bit for your brother, whom I scarcely knew, so that you won't let him come cadging. – He can't anyway. Medlicott's fixed that. Bit of a snob, Medlicott, and Rubens is much too fond of chorus girls, but they're both as clever as monkeys. I should stay with them.

The pain is becoming beastly again and I must finish now and go back to being a drug fiend. I shan't miss the pain, but wherever I'm going I shall miss you, my lovely.

Your very loving,
Aunt Pen.

For Aunt Pen, thought Jane, oblivion was out of the question. She folded up the sheets of paper, and put the letter in her handbag. It was not for Medlicott's eyes.

'My aunt says I'm a rich woman,' she said.

'There's a bequest of ten thousand pounds to a Miss Vincent, and five thousand to your brother Francis. The rest is for you.'

'And how much is the rest?'

Aunt Pen was right, as usual. It was silly to let money upset you.

'Approximately five hundred thousand pounds.'

She was not upset, she realised. She was astounded.

'Half a *million*?'

'Plus the jewellery, and the house in Mayfair. You're a rich woman, Miss Whitcomb.'

'Now? This minute?'

'There is the matter of probate,' said Medlicott, 'but I should be happy to advance whatever sums you may require in the interim.'

'I was thinking of her servants,' said Jane.

'Very proper,' said Medlicott. 'But that matter was attended to before Mrs Nettles left England. She financed their hotel venture.'

'And Bob? . . . Her dog?'

'He is now my dog,' said Medlicott. 'Your aunt asked if she might let me have a keepsake, and I asked for Bob. He lives in Berkshire now. He's become very fond of country life.'

'I'm delighted to hear it,' said Jane, and realised by that fact alone how much Aunt Pen had trusted Mr Medlicott.

Her mother, always unpredictable, provided none of the reactions Jane had expected. To begin with she expressed no surprise, except at the sheer size of the legacy, and the fact that Francis was now the richer by five thousand pounds.

'Thoughtful of her,' said her mother. Jane considered it unnecessary to explain precisely why Francis had inherited such a sum.

'You would not consider – er – augmenting it at all?' her mother asked.

'Aunt Pen has arranged things so that I can't.'

Her mother nodded. She might have been acknowledging a shrewd move in a chess game. 'You will move to Mount Street?'

'I shall sell it,' said Jane. 'It contains too many memories. . . . But I shall move out, if you have no objection.'

'I understand you, I believe,' her mother said. 'This house too is filled with memories of the dead.'

'Mummy, I didn't mean – '

'You will move away,' said her mother. 'Of course you will. You now have the means to do so – and as for: "If I have no objection" – I thank you for the form of words, because I'm quite sure that that is all it is.' Jane waited. There had to be more.

'I *have* no objection,' her mother said. 'None at all,' and had the satisfaction of seeing her daughter nonplussed.

'Use your brains, child. You do *have* brains, you know. How would you and I get on together here?'

'Badly,' said Jane.

'Of course. You are your father's daughter, after all, and your father was a man so accustomed to having his own way that on the few occasions when it was denied him he was not angry, not at first: he was amazed. And I too have been used to command the household at least. Impoverished, I might have been able to hold you at bay, but wealthy you would be invincible. Go with my blessing.'

Jane said, 'I should like to give you some of my wealth, if you will let me.'

'No,' said her mother. 'You are magnanimous – kind, even. But no. For some reason I consider that money not yours, but Penelope's. If she had wished me to have any part of it, she would have willed it to me. Will you be purchasing a motor car?'

'I have one,' said Jane.

'That ridiculous little box on wheels. I was thinking of something more spacious.'

'Like a Daimler perhaps? Or a Rolls-Royce? Too much trouble for me to drive.'

'One does not have to drive in order to enjoy comfort,' her mother said, and Jane knew then precisely what her mother would accept – in time. But for the moment there was only one thing she could offer.

'I know it's too early to go to a concert,' she said, 'but at least let me take you out to dinner.'

'We're still in mourning,' Lady Whitcomb said.

'We'd find somewhere quiet. No one need know.'

'God would know.'

'I don't think He'd mind,' said Jane.

'My God would,' said her mother. She paused for a moment, then hurried on: 'There is one thing you could do for me, if you would.'

'Of course,' said Jane. 'What is it?'

'I must warn you that it will cost rather more than a dinner – even a dinner at the Savoy.'

'Mummy, what is it?'

Lady Whitcomb said, 'There are these things called cruises. No doubt you've heard of them?' Jane nodded.

'Gwendoline Gwatkin has discovered one that goes to India and Ceylon. Bombay, Colombo, Madras. Gwendoline has planned to take this cruise for some little time now – was anxious indeed that I should go with her.'

'She is a woman of means?'

'Oddly enough, yes. She suggested that we go first class.'

'Well of course,' said Jane. 'How else would you go?'

'You will pay for it then?'

'Of course,' Jane said again.

'There is a boat leaving quite soon. In two weeks, I believe.'

Then God won't mind, thought Jane. The mourning will be over.

'I shall make sure you're on it,' she said.

'In a sense my absence will be useful,' her mother said. 'You will be able to engage in house hunting without my interference.' Then she flushed once more that unpleasing mauve colour.

'Please believe me,' she said, 'when I tell you that that remark was not intended to be malicious.'

And oddly enough, Jane did believe it.

16

S HE WENT TO call on Lockhart. Harriet Watson had suggested it, and Harriet had been right. Harriet so very often was right, Jane remembered. Strange how little her friends and acquaintance resented that fact. Jane knew that she too had something of the same pernicious habit, but achieved forgiveness far less often.

She had telephoned for an appointment and been given a time, but was asked to wait, even so. This was unusual. Jabber of all men knew how unwise it was to keep his patients waiting, to give them time to brood, and remember. Even more remarkably, someone else was waiting too in the small, ugly room with its faded carpets, insipid décor, cut steel fireplace and grey marble mantelpiece. Jabber did his best to ensure that his patients did not meet, especially his war patients. To meet might be to remember precisely where on the Ypres salient the German shell had landed; the spot where one had been buried alive. And yet there the man sat, immersed, so it would seem, in an *Illustrated London News* of four months ago. Foch's paws clicked on the linoleum and he looked up at once.

'Good morning,' he said.

Then, athletic-looking, of medium height, perhaps her age, perhaps a little older, with a scar that ran down his face from forehead to chin.

'Good morning,' said Jane.

'Nice morning.'

'Very,' said Jane.

'Rather a wonderful morning, really,' the scarred man said. 'Would you like a cigarette?' He produced a cigarette case. 'Only gaspers, I'm afraid.'

'Gaspers are fine,' said Jane. The young man proffered the cigarette case as if it were the keys of a city, struck a match as though to do so were a conjuring trick of incredible ingenuity.

Mad, quite mad, Jane thought. But content to be so.

'The reason I say it's a wonderful morning is that I've been declared sane,' said the scarred man.

'How wonderful,' said Jane. There didn't seem anything else *to* say. Then she thought: And there was I worrying about being right all the time.

'You're probably wondering why I'm sitting *here* if I'm sane,' said the scarred man, and flushed. Not mauve, like Mummy, she noticed, but a very bright red; almost crimson.

'Oh I say,' he said. 'I didn't mean you of course. You're obviously here on a social call. . . .'

'Coffee,' said Jane firmly. 'The poor man works much too hard. I interrupt him from time to time and make him give me coffee.'

'Jolly good,' said the scarred man. 'Interrupting him, I mean. Good for him. Chaps like me – we're jolly hard work. Or I was.'

'Shell shock?'

'Well . . . yes. Plus a few other odds and ends. I joined in 1915 straight from Cambridge. Infantry.'

'Which regiment?'

'Kicked off in the Gloucesters, then I was seconded to the Manchesters.'

Seconded meant he'd either been brilliant or terrible.

'What rank were you, may I ask?'

'Finished as major,' the scarred man said. 'I was commanding the battalion actually.'

He'd been brilliant: a battalion commander at twenty-four or -five.

'Jolly good,' she said.

'Yes,' he said. 'It was. It was jolly *marvellous*. I'd been reading law at Cambridge. God knows why – I'd have been a rotten lawyer – but I was a good soldier. Honestly I was. And one enjoys what one's good at, wouldn't you say?'

'Certainly I would.'

He smiled, and blew out smoke. 'You know you're a remarkable woman,' he said, then the smile died. 'I say – do you mind my saying that?'

'No woman minds being called remarkable.'

'But you *are*,' he said. 'You didn't ask me about the dead. Every other woman I know asks me about the dead. A lot of parsons, too. Do I repent? All that.'

'Why should you repent?' said Jane. 'You weren't committing a sin, you were doing a job.'

The scarred man stood up then, and so did Foch.

'It isn't like that,' the scarred man told the dog. 'This is homage.'

Gravely he bowed to Jane, and gravely she inclined her head in reply. 'I take it that killing was not what you enjoyed.'

'Killing,' he said, 'was the necessary means. The only way to get to the eleventh of November, 1918, if you like. To a soldier it was like killing sheep to a butcher, – it was what you had to do. But what I enjoyed was leading and tactics and looking out for men who needed me. Doing my best for them, and my best was what my don would have called alpha plus. Only of course three years in France was just too much. I should have been dead anyway. Only I went to pieces instead.'

'And now?'

'I decided I'd had enough of it. Being barmy I mean. So I sat down and tried to work out what I could do, and it wasn't all that much. Cambridge wouldn't look at me, and who could blame them? I'd tried going back in 1918. I lasted three days – and anyway as I say I'd have been a hopeless lawyer. All I knew about was madness and soldiering – and I'd given up madness; so soldiering it had to be.'

'You've rejoined the army?'

'Dear old thing,' said the scarred man, 'do you imagine for one moment that they'd have me? . . . I'm off to China.'

'China?'

'There are upteen war lords in China, each one fighting the next. They're only bandits, really. But there's a chap called Chiang Kai-Shek who's trying to put an army together to stop them. He needs foreign advisers and that's what I am. A foreign adviser. Signed up last week. Do you think they'll mind the scar?'

'The mark of a warrior, surely?'

'Not to boast,' the scarred man said. 'But you're absolutely right. They take you more seriously when you've got one of these.' He touched his cheek.

'When are you off?' asked Jane.

'Any minute, actually. Soon as I get a chit from old Jabber saying I'm sound in wind and limb I pick up my kit and get off to Liverpool. . . . I have enjoyed talking to you.'

'I too.'

'You make a chap feel awfully good.'

He said it, thought Jane, without the slightest hint of sexuality: as if I had been his governess, and he six years old. Then the manservant came in with an envelope on a silver tray, and told her reproachfully that Dr Lockhart was waiting.

'As if it were my fault,' said Jane, and Lockhart grinned.

'No doubt you appeared to be enjoying yourselves,' he said. 'Geekie could not possibly approve of that. He belongs to a very strict sect of some sort.'

'He had that look,' said Jane. 'Poor man.'

Lockhart glanced up sharply.

'*You* seem happy today,' he said.

'I am happy. Just like your splendid major. Tell me about him.'

'You know I can't.'

'Nothing about his illness, of course not,' said Jane. 'But did he do well?'

'DSO and bar.'

'Well enough,' said Jane. 'Wounded I see?'

'Four times. The last time was March, 1918. That's when I got him.'

'And cured him?'

'He cured himself.'

'That's what he told me. "I decided I'd had enough of being barmy." As if madness were something one gave up – like cigarettes for Lent. *You* did it.'

'Did he say so?'

'He didn't have to. It was enough to hear him say your name. . . . Jabber. . . . He loves you. I expect we all do.'

Geekie came in with coffee and biscuits, and Foch looked hopeful. Jane decided he'd been too indulged recently, but

– 169 –

Lockhart gave him a pink-iced horror after Geekie had gone.

Lockhart said, 'I rather think you've decided that you're cured, too.'

'The damnedest thing,' said Jane, then: 'Oh. . . . I *beg* your pardon.'

'Geekie is the one who deplores strong language,' said Lockhart. 'You can say what you like to me.'

'I always did,' said Jane. 'You knew my father died?'

'I read it in *The Times*,' Lockhart said. 'I'm very sorry.'

'It was very – peaceful. That's what people always say. "At Peace".'

'Or "At Rest",' said Lockhart. 'Sometimes clichés aren't just useful. They're essential. Tell me about the damnedest thing.'

She told him about riding Taff, and a suitably edited version of her dream encounter with John near Darjeeling.

'The dream was erotic, I take it?' Lockhart asked.

'Well yes it was,' said Jane, 'if you must know.'

'Of course I must know,' Lockhart said mildly. 'I may not want to, but I have to.'

'Yes of course you do,' said Jane. 'I'm sorry. It was just – a bit odd that's all. We were both so young and so happy in a place John had never even seen.'

'*You* were happy there. Perhaps you wanted to share it.'

'Yes, of course. It must be that.' She laughed. 'When I woke up – after the dream – my first thought was I could never possibly tell you, and now here I am – '

'Perfectly all right,' said Lockhart. 'Now tell me about the horse.' And she told him about Bridget O'Dowd.

When she'd finished, he said, 'That's all true, isn't it? The mare was handed on – like an inheritance?'

'All true,' she said.

'You lost a remarkable man,' said Lockhart. 'Once I thought the loss must be irreparable – but now – '

'I can go to fight the war lords in China?'

'You have a chance,' he said. 'A very good chance.'

'What did you think of my father's – experiment?'

'I think it worked,' Lockhart said.

'No more than that?'

'It was dangerous – it was a gamble, but it paid off. He must have been very sure of himself.'

'Well of course he was,' said Jane, then remembered her mother. 'He was always sure of himself. You would have liked him.' Lockhart was silent. 'Oh yes you would,' said Jane. 'You might not have wanted to, but you wouldn't have been able to help yourself.' She paused for a moment. 'Did I tell you about my chat with Foch?' she asked at last, and did so.

When she had done he said, 'And so I have a rival?' He bent to look at the dog. 'And a formidable one.'

'Do you think he got it right?'

'I've told you what I think.' The words were gently said. 'You're ready to face the world – more than ready. But you must stay on your guard – and you must find something to occupy your mind.'

'What kind of something?'

'Something useful,' Lockhart said. 'You'll never be content with frivolity, however elegant.'

Harriet Watson right again, thought Jane. Aloud she asked, 'Good works?'

'Why not? You don't have to be rich for good works. Just useful.'

'But I am rich,' said Jane. 'Enormously rich.' And told him about Aunt Pen's legacy.

He listened, delighted. 'But how marvellous for you,' he said, ' – unless you were very fond of your aunt.'

'She had cancer – the most dreadful pain.'

'Then it would be hypocrisy to wish her alive. Have you celebrated yet?'

'No,' she said. 'My mother thinks it would be inappropriate.'

'Do you?'

'No,' she said. 'Nor would my father.'

'Then perhaps you would like to accompany me to a party tonight.'

She looked at him. He was quite serious.

'I do *go* to parties, you know.'

'Part of the treatment?'

'If you like. But I do need a partner for this affair, and you're the only one I know who's free.'

She put her tongue out at him. 'What time?' she asked.

'We're asked for nine. I thought we might dine first. Say seven?'

'Seven,' she said, and thought: Now Mummy really will have something to grouse about.

But once again her mother surprised her, merely remarking that cook would be pleased if she had no dinner to prepare.

'Mummy,' said Jane, 'I want no more nonsense about dishes of herbs and stalled oxen.'

Her mother looked delighted. 'I told you that wealth would make you assertive and it has,' she said. 'All I meant to convey was that as I am alone I shall have a sandwich, no more than that. I really must get to grips with that Chopin nocturne. Will it be necessary to invite your friend in for a drink of some sort? He is not one of the "cocktail set", I trust?'

'Not if you don't wish it.'

'I do not,' said her mother. 'For me conviviality was always a problem. At the moment it is a virtual impossibility.'

She and her daughter ate lunch together, a perfunctory affair served by Hawkins at great speed. (She had the afternoon off.) When it was done her mother went to the drawing room to read the brochure of the P and O cruise which Miss Gwatkin had sent her, and Jane, bored, drove to Fulham and the Alhambra cinema. It was a hot and humid day and the place was more than half empty. And no wonder, thought Jane. The inside of the cinema was even hotter and stickier than the rest of London in high summer. But it was somewhere to sit and the darkness was soothing, the murmur of voices unobtrusive. Felix the Cat and Fatty Arbuckle and Mary Pickford in *Daddy Longlegs*, and the chance to yawn unobserved, and listen to Georgina Payne play the piano so much better than Mummy.

It occurred to her that it was because of Georgina Payne that she was sitting there. Not that she was going to set up as a rival to dear old Fred. Nothing like that. It was just that the woman fascinated her. And the reason was that she always looked beautiful. Even then, at that moment, thumping out 'In a Monastery Garden', adding more trills to coax more tears for the heroine's travail, even then she was beautiful; in last year's dress and too much lipstick and an audience that scarcely knew she existed. Beautiful. And what did it do for her? Jane wondered. Did that beauty give her power? Influence? Wealth? Obviously not, since she worked as she did. And did she regret it – the impotence of her beauty? Did she care about anything – apart from the fact of her existence? The question seemed to her important enough to keep her in her seat until the lights went up, but then she left at once, nervous that the blonde girl might see her.

Sitting in the Riley she thought the whole thing through again: the fascination of Georgie, the need to watch, and worry at a problem, like a much younger Foch with the corner of a carpet in his mouth. What was it the other girl had that she wanted so? Not her beauty – she was almost certain that that was so, though if she had possessed it it would have been no burden. But it wasn't that. Nor was it the way in which Georgina Payne wore clothes. Thanks to Aunt Pen she had no cause for envy there. And she was infinitely richer, though perhaps less free. And there was the answer. Georgina Payne's life was her own, to be lived as she wanted to live it, and nobody, nobody at all, would be allowed to get in her way. It was something to think about, perhaps even worry about: it was what she, Jane, wanted also.

The party was in Mayfair, but her host and hostess were interested in the ballet. Having been told as much, Jane dressed with a little more panache than Mayfair usually merited. (Stodge for Mayfair, Aunt Pen had said. 'All your most expensive stodge. Glitter for Chelsea, and just a *little* naughtiness.') So for Mayfair *and* the ballet a studied lack of ostentation, but rather a lot of décolletage, and some quite flawless diamonds. A dress by Patou and a cloak of white silk to cover all this glory until they got to the restaurant.

When Jane came out to his cab, ready to leave at once, Lockhart was much too good-mannered to look relieved, but she was quite sure he was. Evening dress suited him, she thought, emphasising his tall, lean physique. But in the restaurant she noticed that his sandy, thinning hair was unruly, his tie needed straightening. But to straighten it was a privilege she had neither earned nor wished for.

He ate with good appetite: potage Solferino, whitebait, poulet au diable, and as he shovelled down the chicken he looked at her and grinned.

'I never have more than toast for breakfast and I forgot to eat lunch,' he said, 'and Foch bagged my biscuit.'

And that was Jabber Lockhart, she thought. Too busy and too kind to eat.

'Tell me about my host and hostess.'

'They live in Berkeley Square,' said Lockhart, and Jane reminded herself that she need not be too impressed. She had a house in Mount Street.

'Sir Hugh and Lady Lessing. Isobel. What can I tell you about them? We were at Trinity together, Hugh and I. He read modern languages and hunted and wrote bad verse, in the manner, so he dared to hope, of Baudelaire. His family were bankers. *Are* bankers.'

'Lessing's Bank,' said Jane.

'Precisely,' said Lockhart. 'Small in number, vast in resources. Hugh was determined not to be part of it. Instead he was going to go to Paris and drunk absinthe and write verses and be decadent.'

'And did he?'

'He went to France all right, but not to Paris.'

'The war again,' said Jane. 'Guardee?'

'Artists' Rifles,' said Lockhart. 'I told you he was a poet.'

'And afterwards?'

Lockhart smiled. 'The family business, what else? After second Ypres he rather lost his taste for decadence.'

'But he likes the ballet?' Lockhart nodded.

'He's allowed to,' he said. 'He's a first-rate shot.'

'And Lady Lessing?'

'Isobel? She likes the ballet too. Adores it, in fact. My guess is she'd have been a dancer if she hadn't been born a lady.'

'That *is* a handicap,' said Jane.

'Insuperable barrier,' said Lockhart. 'Her father's a duke. What a damn silly world we live in. – Oh I beg your pardon.' He smiled.

'Granted as soon as asked,' she said. 'It *is* a damn silly world.'

'Damned unfair, too.'

'I've thought so in my time,' she said, 'and it seems I'm right. It *is* unfair. Even to dukes' daughters.'

Lockhart signalled for coffee.

'Have you thought of something useful to do yet?'

'I'm not sure,' she said.

'Because before you do, I think there's something else you should attend to.'

She stirred her coffee. 'Yes?' she said.

'That young man of yours. I think you should find out if he left any family – and if he did, whether they are in want.'

'Oh,' she said. 'I hadn't thought – '

'From what you told me, he wasn't born rich.'

'On the contrary,' she said. 'He was born poor. Really poor.' She thought, then realised that she had absolutely no idea what amount a workman might earn. 'Like a servant, I suppose. In the army all he ever had was his pay – but we managed between us.'

'Do you dislike the idea?'

'Of course not,' she said. 'But I know nothing about his family. We never talked about them. Or mine either. There wasn't time, you see. I don't even know where they live.'

'You're a resourceful woman,' he said. 'You could find out.'

It was one way to begin to live her own life.

'Yes,' she said. 'I could.'

'Come to me if you need any help,' he said, 'but I bet you a shilling you won't.'

She nodded, her mind busy with ideas for finding John's family, and for once Lockhart misread her mind.

'You look thoughtful,' he said. 'You're not worried about this little jaunt of ours, I hope?'

'Of course not,' she said. 'Is there any reason why I should be?'

'None at all,' he said. 'Believe me. No reason at all.'

'You approve of my dress then?'

'I do indeed.'

'I'm glad to hear it,' she said. 'It shows what good taste you have.'

17

S IR HUGH LESSING looked like a man who shot grouse and things, if by that was meant red-faced and moustached, with very sharp blue eyes, and the beginnings of a pot belly. When she was introduced to him and he saw her diamonds, he looked like a banker, too. He had not in the least the appearance of a ballet enthusiast, but when the subject arose it seemed to her that he was knowledgeable, and his French accent excellent.

Lady Lessing on the other hand looked so much a part of the ballet world that Jane would not have been surprised if she had worn a tu-tu. What she did wear was a dress that might have been, perhaps was, designed by Bakst, great splashes of colour on a soft, silken drape, with rubies round her neck and wrist. Aunt Pen might not have approved, because it didn't quite succeed, but never mind, thought Jane, she likes it. And that is precisely the point.

For a moment, after Lockhart introduced them, they talked, and almost at once the talk was of the ballet: not just *Scheherazade*, but *Spectre de la Rose*, and *The Rite of Spring*, and *Les Biches*. Jane had seen several of them in London (score six, she thought) and almost all of them in Paris (score ten and claim a prize. Any prize you like).

A footman brought champagne.

'Bollinger?' Jane asked.

'No. Krug I'm afraid. Does it matter?'

'Not in the least,' said Jane. This was one party that Dr Pardoe would not be attending. Lockhart led her away. There were more people to see.

So many. In a morning room, a drawing room, a music room where a man played a waltz on a grand piano, and already people were dancing.

'Do you dance?' Jane asked.

'When I must,' said Lockhart.

'You must now,' said Jane, 'before he plays a Charleston,' and turned to him, her arms lifted. For a moment he hesitated, and then he embraced her, firmly but carefully, as a man might grapple with a delicate piece of furniture.

It's gratifying, very gratifying, thought Jane, to know that I'm what he's after, but rather a relief to know he can't have me – and we both know it. I might not be his patient just at the moment but he knows too much about me, and he knows that, too. And understands.

When they had done Lockhart was instantly claimed by a girl in green, a tiny, vital girl who was obviously a dancer, just as another man came up to them, watched Lockhart take the floor, and spoke to Jane instead.

'One admires his courage,' he said.

'Does one?'

He turned to face her, and she saw a man even taller and leaner than Lockhart, fair-skinned and languid. Palely loitering, she thought. Not in the least like Jabber. Besides his hair was neatly brushed, and his tie immaculately tied.

'Indeed one does,' he said. 'That's Mirova.'

'Mirova?'

'Oh thank God,' said the languid man. 'Do I gather from that confession of ignorance that you can talk about things other than the dance, or are you just being a tease?'

The look he bent down upon her was one of earnest enquiry, and she found herself smiling.

'I shouldn't dream of teasing you on so short an acquaintance,' she said.

'Then that makes you unique,' said the languid man. 'But let me explain about Mirova. She belongs to the Ballet Russe of *course*, but quite recently she had the grippe or measles or some- thing – anyway something quite *lowering*, and she's staying with the Lessings to recuperate. Rather a smart way to recuperate, wouldn't you say? – My name is Lionel Warley, by the way.'

'Jane Whitcomb.'

'Delighted to meet you, dear Jane. . . . Whitcomb? Now *where* have I heard that name before?'

Jane said stiffly, 'In *The Times* perhaps? My father died quite recently. *The Times* published his obituary.'

'My dear I must own up at once to the fact that I never read *The Times*,' Warley said. 'All those dependent clauses. Too exhausting at breakfast.'

'I have a brother at Cambridge,' said Jane, wary still.

'Who doesn't?' said Warley. 'At some time or other. No it wasn't that. . . . Yes, of course. At Lady Hexham's. She was telling me all about the Five Charioteers.'

'You know Louise, Mr Warley?'

'My dear I don't like to boast but I know *every*body. And do please call me Lionel. Mr Warley sounds far too pompous.'

'Then you must know everybody here?'

'All that are worth knowing – now that I've met you.'

'Then come and dance and tell me who I should speak to.'

'Delighted, my dear,' he said. 'Enchanted in fact. Why is it we have never met before?'

'I've been rather out of the world just recently.'

Lionel glanced briefly at Lockhart, now being led very firmly by Mirova.

'Always a mistake to become too reclusive,' he said.

'So I have discovered,' said Jane. 'Now bring me up to date.' He offered his arm, but she hesitated.

'What's wrong?' Lionel asked.

'It's a Charleston,' she said. 'I can't do it.'

'That hardly makes you unique,' he said. 'Just look at all the galumphing clodhoppers about you and do something different.'

Firmly he grasped her, and she did her best, which was, she knew, barely adequate. Not till the next waltz could she listen while he reeled off a list of notable guests: the kind of actors, actresses, peers and musicians – even a couple of lawyers and a junior minister – who might be found in the gossip columns.

'Too many,' said Jane. 'I should have brought a note book.'

'And spoiled that lovely piece of nonsense you're wearing? Paton by the look of it.'

'Paton it is. How knowledgeable you are.'

'One must work jolly hard to be as frivolous as I am. But it's the only way I can be noticed. Now you achieve that blessed state with no exertion at all.'

'Do I indeed?' Jane said, laughing.

'You do, you do. Believe me you do.'

'The charm of novelty, perhaps?'

'Just the charm, my dear,' said Lionel. 'Though I can see you still don't believe me. But here comes Bower to prove my point.'

'Bower?' said Jane. 'You didn't tell me about anyone called Bower.'

'That's because he doesn't appear in the newspapers: he *owns* them. One, anyway. The *Daily World*.'

'Good heavens,' said Jane. 'He really *is* a tycoon.'

'He's worse than that,' Lionel said. 'He's an *American* tycoon. Not that he chews tobacco or anything. But – worth watching, my dear. Inordinately fond of his own way, Mr Bower.'

Oh my God another one, thought Jane, as the music stopped and they moved to where a man waited for them, older than she, but not old: shorter, more heavily built than Lionel or Jabber. Not that he was fat, she thought. His body looked hard and muscular, and restless, and his face reflected that same restless, perhaps masterful quality. Hard grey eyes, hard chin, enquiring nose. And yet not unattractive. Not at all unattractive.

'Lionel,' he said. 'You're neglecting your duty.'

A pleasant voice, baritone: the American accent intriguing, no more.

'If I but knew what it *was* – ' Lionel said.

'But aren't you the one, the only one, who knows everybody? And don't you realise that my paper gets to know everybody also?'

'Your gossip column does its best, but – '

'Certainly it does. We have our rivals of course, and they do their best too, but we're first more often than they are. And not just with gossip, let me tell you. But gossip is my business tonight.'

'You are here as a reporter?' Lionel asked.

'I'm here as the *Daily World*, because that's what I am.'

He means it, thought Jane. And he loves meaning it. Bower added: 'That being the case you should have introduced me before now.'

'Oh dear,' said Lionel. 'Have I been remiss? Jane my dear, this terrifying if pushy person is Jay Bower, owner of the *Daily World*.' – He turned to Bower. ' – And this is Miss Jane Whitcomb.'

They shook hands and she looked just a little upwards at eyes that were telling her to be interesting immediately, or expect no space in his newspaper.

'I'm pleased to meet you, Mr Bower,' she said.

'The pleasure is mine,' said Bower.

' – But I must disappoint you, I'm afraid. I'm not newsworthy.'

'How can you *say* that?' said Lionel. 'A friend of Lady Hexham, *and* Sarah Unwin. Childhood in India while your father served the Raj, drove an ambulance during the war – '

'Did you indeed?' said Bower. 'Then I must disagree with you, Miss Whitcomb. You are most definitely newsworthy.'

He bowed to her and moved away to where a red-headed girl waited, a very pretty girl indeed.

'That's the new musical comedy star, Suzanne de Lys,' said Lionel. 'She's about as French as I am but she can oo-la-la when she has to and sings in broken English rather well. . . . Bower liked you.'

'He hid it well.'

'Yes,' said Lionel. 'He did. It's his way.'

Lockhart joined them and watched as Bower moved through the crowd, the girl on his arm. Quite a lot of people spoke to him, all of them moved out of his way. It's a progress, she thought. A triumphal progress.

Lockhart too watched him go.

'You've been mixing with the mighty,' he said.

'Singled out,' said Lionel. 'Positively singled out.'

'You want to become a celebrity?' Lockhart asked her.

'It seems I have no choice,' she said, then turned to Lionel. 'Or do I?'

'Oh, none,' he said. 'Le roi le veult and all that sort of thing.'

'Then a celebrity I shall be,' she said, and Lockhart nodded his approval. Another hurdle sailed over, she thought. If I go on like this tonight will be a clear round.

'Talking of celebrities,' she said, 'you didn't do too badly yourself just now.'

'The Mirova? She is a good dancer, isn't she?'

'She leads awfully well,' said Lionel.

'Bitch,' said Lockhart, entirely without rancour, and took Jane into supper: lobster and chicken so frothed and swirled they seemed to evaporate rather than be chewed, but deadly for the waistline: and champagne; always champagne.

'Celebrities do live well, don't they?' she said.

'The good ones also do things.'

'Now that I've given up being barmy, are you going to be my conscience instead?'

'You'll do that yourself,' said Lockhart.

'How well you know me. – But of course you do.' She ate a vol-au-vent, then: 'I'm going to find John's relatives.'

'John?. . . Oh yes. . . . And do something for them?'

'If there's something I can do.'

Mirova came in amid a swarm of young men. Lockhart watched her. 'Terpsichore with attendant lords,' he said.

'More like attendant ladies,' said Jane, and Lockhart snorted. 'Did you enjoy dancing with her?'

'Lionel was right,' Lockhart said. 'She does lead awfully well.'

'How did you meet her?'

'She's staying with Hugh,' he said.

'And Sir Hugh is a friend of yours?'

'I've known him since Cambridge,' said Lockhart. 'I told you.'

Patient, thought Jane. I bet he was a patient and you're not telling. You'd never tell.

'As a matter of fact,' said Lockhart, 'he lends a hand with a charity I'm interested in, too.'

'What charity?'

'Helping ex-servicemen. The ones who were – disturbed.'

'Like me,' she said.

'Like you exactly. Except that they're poor too, and very often the only kind of doctor they can reach hasn't the foggiest idea what's wrong with them.'

'Pull yourself together man,' said Jane. 'All you need is a tonic and a spot of exercise.'

'Exactly,' said Lockhart.

'I'll send a cheque,' said Jane, 'as soon as my will's been through probate.'

'I wasn't hinting,' said Lockhart, then, 'That's not true. Of course I was hinting. There are so many. . . . As a matter of fact there's a chap I ought to speak to now – '

'Then go,' said Jane.

'But I don't like to leave you on your own.'

'We celebrities are never alone for long,' said Jane.

And in no time someone joined her, not the hopeful young man she had half expected, but Georgina Payne.

White satin, not in its first season, Jane thought, but I do like the ear-rings, and the necklace is charming.

'Do you mind if I join you?' she asked.

'Delighted.' Georgina Payne set down her plate and champagne glass, and sat. Every movement could have been rehearsed, they flowed so.

'But why are you on your own?' asked Jane. 'Are all the men here blind?'

'My own particular man is busy talking at the moment,' the blonde girl said. 'He won't be long. But don't let me mislead you. He's only my own particular man for the evening.'

'On approval perhaps?'

'Perhaps,' Georgina said. 'It won't be easy. It never is. But then I suppose you know that.'

'Why should you suppose anything of the kind?'

'Well you've done it, haven't you? Paid up in full, I mean. One never gets one's deposit back, but I suppose you know that too.'

She wasn't drunk, Jane decided at last, only in the condition that Miss Gwatkin described as overwrought; even so Jane was glad to see her begin on her food. She ate quite greedily, Jane noticed, and with an enjoyment that for a moment showed through the tension.

'I saw you today,' said Jane.

'You must have seen me six times at least since I came to your house. Are you fond of the cinema?'

'It's the solitude I enjoy most,' said Jane.

'We get a lot like that. Sit like statues some of them. No tears. No laughter. Not like you.'

'In what way?'

'You always watched. You were part of it.' She put her napkin to her lips. 'This – this friend of mine – I told him about the day I called on you. . . . That oaf Pardoe. . . . My friend reads *The Times*. He told me that your father had died. I was so sorry.'

'You liked him then?'

'Of course.' It sounded as if no pretty young woman could fail to like Papa. And then, 'How did your mother take it?'

To describe how Mummy had taken it was out of the question. 'She's over the worst now,' said Jane.

'She's tough all right,' said Georgina Payne. 'But sometimes one has to be. . . . You never came to speak to me at the cinema. It's allowed, you know, during the intervals.'

'I didn't know,' said Jane. 'And anyway – our acquaintance was so short – I didn't want to bore you, Miss Payne.'

'You could never bore me. And please call me Georgie. Please.'

'I'd be delighted to. My Christian name is Jane, by the way.'

'Thank you, Jane. But it wasn't just not knowing whether you could speak or not, was it? There was something else.'

'It was a time of great sadness for me,' said Jane, 'and worry, too. Hence my need to be alone. And just watching you – you were so alive – you did me a great deal of good.'

'I'm delighted,' said Georgie. 'Really I am. And I'd love to hear more.'

'I too,' said Jane. 'I'm – obliged to go away for a while – it's something I can't avoid, but as soon as I'm back in London – I promise – Where can I reach you?'

'I may soon be able to manage without the Alhambra,' said Georgie, 'that is unless they decide to manage without me first. I've had rather a lot of time off just lately.' She opened her handbag of silver mesh.

Cartier, Jane thought, or perhaps Boucheron, and very pretty. But its glimmer was uneasy against that gleaming white. She'd never have worn it if she'd possessed another.

'Here,' Georgie said, and gave her a card. 'Georgina Payne', it said, and beneath that, 'Piano Accompanist'; then in the left-hand corner in smaller letters: 'Recitals'. Top right contained a Chelsea telephone number and address.

'A bit of an eyrie,' Georgie said, 'but the stairs are good for the figure and it's near the King's Road, which is rather important – at least I think so. Oh my God.' She gulped at her champagne.

Jane followed her gaze. A man had just come into the room. He was pleasant to look at, smiling, by no means tall, and yet he looked strong: not with Bower's incipient burliness, but with a kind of whip-cord strength that was at the same time graceful, even when he was drunk, as he was at that moment. The evening clothes he wore were so old as to gleam in the electric light, the coat cuffs frayed. He moved towards Georgie with a massive concentration.

'Oh *hell*!' Georgie said, and stuck the last lobster patty into her mouth, reminded Jane, rather thickly, to call as soon as possible, then rose to her feet and grabbed the man's arm and turned him towards the door. He rotated easily, like some part of an engine designed to revolve, and allowed himself to be turned agreeably enough. He seemed quite happy to follow wherever Georgie led.

Once more Lockhart joined Jane.

'Did you get lots of money?' she asked.

'Eventually,' Lockhart said. 'You were watching Browne?'

'Was that who it was?'

'Michael Browne,' said Lockhart. 'He's an artist. Painter. Pretty girl he had to look after him.'

'She's a pianist,' said Jane. 'Works in a cinema.'

'You celebrities meet the most fascinating people,' said Lockhart.

'Is he any good?'

'When sober – first rate they tell me. He's here because he was in the Artists' Rifles like his host. His company commander as a matter of fact.'

'*He* was *Sir Hugh's* company commander?'

'Hugh rose to the full rank of private and stayed there,' said Lockhart. 'He reckoned poets as officers went out with Sir Philip Sidney – and look what happened to him.'

Jane nodded, warily. She had no idea what had happened to Sir Philip Sidney. 'But why is Browne so drunk?'

'No doubt he's borrowed money from Hugh. I gather he's ashamed to borrow.'

'Then why does he do it? He can work surely?'

'He's a painter, as I say. He reckons it's the hardest work there is, but it doesn't pay.'

On approval indeed, thought Jane, but then Georgie too led a buccaneering life. The point was that she lived it, which might also be the point of Michael Browne. 'Let's dance again,' she said. 'I promise I won't lead.'

Next morning she telephoned Medlicott. Her request surprised him.

'A private detective?' he asked.

'Don't you know one?' Jane asked. 'I thought all solicitors did.'

'Certainly I know one. He's endeavouring to trace Miss Vincent for me.'

'He should do very well,' said Jane. 'If you'll give me his address.'

'Perhaps I can be of assistance?'

'No no,' said Jane. 'Just a personal matter. More of a whim, really.'

Mr Medlicott sighed, but gave her a telephone number, and promised to arrange an appointment.

18

S HE CALLED ON him the next day. He had offices in a place
called Falcon Court, which, Medlicott assured her, was quite
close to the Strand. It was even closer to the Middle Temple, a
fact she found pleasing. The Temple was dedicated to the Law,
after all, and so, she supposed, was Mr Pinner. Moreover Fleet
Street was quite close, and Fleet Street meant mighty presses,
and creatures called Press Barons, and Mr Bower, who couldn't
be a baron because he was an American, and who in any case
behaved more like an emperor. . . . But the point was that Mr
Pinner belonged with Fleet Street too, and unidentified corpses
and Horror In Kensal Rise Sensation. Though perhaps that had
more to do with Sherlock Holmes and the *Strand Magazine*, she
thought, and hoped that Mr Pinner wouldn't turn out to be
like that. No opium, thank you very much, no violin. . . . She
reached Falcon Court and parked at last.

It was a neat little quadrangle of old and pleasing brick,
rendered dingy with soot. Inside it were an equally dingy lawn
and some roses that clung on grimly. Dickensian, she thought,
and hoped that Mr Pinner didn't blend with his environment
too perfectly. She found her way to Staircase Three, and consulted the information board. 'G. Pinner', she read. 'Confidential
Investigations'. Room Two. Floor Two. She climbed up stairs
surprisingly well polished and carpeted.

Mr Pinner had three rooms: a waiting room with a bell that
rang as soon as she entered, his own sanctum beyond it, and
behind him again another room where a typewriter clattered and

rattled as they talked. Mr Pinner took her into his own room at once, and sat her down in a leather chair as comfortable as it was elegant, while he himself sat at a mahogany desk. Neat and compact was Mr Pinner, much too small to be a policeman, in a discreet suit of blue serge, white shirt with a hard white collar, dark-blue tie in a tight little knot. A bowler hat and an umbrella hung on a hat stand, and the gold watch and chain across his waistcoat looked both substantial and real. A prosperous city gent was what Mr Pinner looked like, and Jane realised that he would indeed be prosperous if Medlicott and Rubens employed him. He had a round and curiously anonymous face, and grey receding hair. His only memorable features were his eyes: shrewd and brilliant and very dark, and a bushy Old Bill moustache of the kind that sergeants had favoured. In his left lapel he wore the lion-face badge, surrounded by blue enamel, of the British Legion, so the sergeant theory was likely enough.

'How can I help you, Miss Whitcomb?' Mr Pinner asked.

'It's a – sort of a missing person,' said Jane.

'Oh yes?' His voice was pleasing: deep, melodious and unhurried, the voice of a man who knew the importance of patience in his work. It made the stupidity of that 'sort of' even harder to bear.

'I say "sort of" because I want you to find out whether a friend of mine, now dead, has any surviving relatives, and if so where they can be found.'

'I see,' said Mr Pinner. 'May I have your dead friend's name?'

It was the most obvious question of the lot, and yet she found she didn't want to answer it. To do so would be to go back in time seven years; to dig up what she had so deeply buried. And yet she had to do it, if only to honour her dead.

'Patterson,' she said at last. 'Captain John Patterson.'

Mr Pinner made a note. 'Please smoke if you want to, Miss Whitcomb,' he said. She lit up at once.

'Where did Captain Patterson die?'

'La Bassée Canal,' she said. 'On the 10th November, 1918.'

Mr Pinner started, then at once apologised.

'Please don't,' she said. 'Everyone's surprised when they first hear. I'm quite used to it.'

'Nasty one, La Bassée,' Mr Pinner said. 'Piece of pie nine times out of ten, but the tenth one – ' He broke off. 'Sniper was it?'

'Machine gun,' said Jane.

'Then at least it was quick,' said Mr Pinner.

'Instantaneous,' said Jane, 'but then they always said that.'

'With a machine gun they had no need to lie,' Mr Pinner said. 'Honestly, miss. Infantry, was he?'

'Yes,' said Jane, and gave out the details.

'Second Battalion the Northumbrian Regiment,' Mr Pinner wrote. 'You wouldn't have his serial number by any chance, Miss Whitcomb?'

Miss Whitcomb had it by heart. It emphasised even more how besotted she was, but it didn't matter. Inside the few minutes that they had spent together, she had decided that she could trust Mr Pinner implicitly. She gave him the number.

'And where did he live, miss?'

'Just before the war he had lodgings in Bradford – he was a wool cloth salesman – but his family lived in the North East.'

'Did he tell you where?'

'Just the North East.'

Mr Pinner was looking surprised, and no wonder, she thought.

'I knew him for less than a year,' she said. 'Mostly we talked about ourselves. I told him I came from London and India – and he told me he came from Bradford and the North East. He may have mentioned a town, but if he did I've forgotten.'

'Did you talk about relatives?'

'Oh yes . . . of course, how silly of me. His mother and father – he called them Mam and Dad, and a sister – and I *think* two brothers. He mentioned a grandmother too, but I should imagine she'll be dead by now.'

Mr Pinner made more notes, then the door behind him opened, and the typist brought in tea, then left at once and closed the door.

'She can't hear us,' Mr Pinner said.

'I don't think that matters,' said Jane.

'If it ever does,' said Mr Pinner, 'she hasn't heard a thing – and these notes' – he gestured at his writing pad, 'I burn them once the investigation's over. You can ask Mr Medlicott, miss. Confidential means what it says.'

'In that case,' said Jane, 'I should like to offer you another job.'

'To do what, miss?'

'To find a missing horse.'

He took it without a blink. Jane decided that she liked Mr Pinner very much.

As she left Mr Pinner's office, Jane found herself confronting Miss Gwatkin, making her way along the corridor. She opened her mouth to speak, but Miss Gwatkin, staring glassily in front of her, moved on. Jane watched her retreating back with satisfaction. Really, Miss Gwatkin was becoming positively fat. If she persisted in her indulgence, the word obese might not be inadmissible. . . . She went to Harriet for gin and a poached egg, and a heart-to-heart about John.

When she returned Hawkins was waiting by the door, despite the fact that Jane used her latch key.

'Your mother's in the music room, miss,' she said, and made a curious sideways motion with her neck, thrusting her head up, and at the same time to one side. The only thing it seemed to signify was someone being hanged (at the end of the sideways motion, Hawkins's head suddenly drooped) and why should Hawkins be marked for death? She went towards the music room, and Foch emerged from the cloakroom and followed her. He had no more taste for badly played Beethoven (the E fantasy-sonata and well beyond Lady Whitcomb's range) than Jane herself, but he knew his duty.

Lady Whitcomb finished – for the moment – the passage that defied her, then rose to her feet, turned and faced her daughter.

'I should like to know,' she said, 'the reason why you found it necessary to visit a private detective.'

'Should you, Mummy?' said Jane.

'I should.'

'I suggest we sit down then,' said Jane. 'It may take you rather a long time.'

'You do not deny that you *did* visit a private detective?'

'What would be the point?' said Jane. 'You have a witness.'

Her mother flinched, a very little.

'It is true that Gwendoline Gwatkin saw you,' she said, 'and that she thought it her duty to acquaint me of the fact.'

'Why?' Jane asked.

'Ladies do not visit such creatures without a very good reason,' said her mother. 'An unmarried lady should have no reason at all.'

Suddenly, Jane understood. For most people, private detectives had but one function.

'*Divorce*,' she said. 'Oh goodness how priceless. Did Miss Gwatkin think that I was the other woman?'

'Heaven knows what she thought,' said her mother. 'But she saw you.'

'Of course she saw me,' said Jane. 'She walked right past me. How tubby she's getting.'

'Her over-indulgence is beside the point,' said her mother. 'Why did you go?'

'Why did she go, come to that?'

'She was visiting her nephew. He has an office there too. He works on behalf of the Christian Mission to the East Indies. *Why did you go*?'

'You know this is interesting,' said Jane, and then: 'I'm thirty-two years old.'

'I am aware of that,' her mother said.

'Old enough to attend to my own affairs.'

'No,' said her mother. 'Not if they involve private detectives.'

'If *you* went to see one, would you be answerable to me?'

'I can conceive of no circumstances that would impel me to see one.'

As if poor Mr Pinner were some sort of kept man. A – what was the word – gigolo.

'I am not the other woman in a divorce case,' she said.

'I'm delighted to hear it.'

'I give you my word on that.'

'No need,' said her mother. 'The courts would make it known soon enough. But there are other kinds of stigma.'

'Mummy,' said Jane, half amused, half exasperated. 'I hardly ever leave the house.'

'Not true,' said her mother. 'You spent weeks and weeks with Penelope Nettles, and even now that you live here – for however little time – you are rarely at home.'

'You think Aunt Pen corrupted me?'

'I consider it a possibility.'

She should have been on her feet then, yelling and screaming as once she had done. But what would have been the point? Aunt Pen had taught her that life was to be enjoyed rather than endured, but to protest that she had never played the rôle of amateur pimp would serve no purpose, and so all she said was: 'You're wrong.'

Her mother said, 'You rarely lie, but – '

'And never when there's no point,' said Jane. 'I hired the detective to find a horse for me.'

'Jokes are alien to me at the best of times,' said her mother. 'At the moment I find them unpardonable.'

'There's a horse I rather liked years ago and now I want to buy her, but first I must know where she is,' said Jane.

'But why in such an odd way?' her mother asked.

'Because I'm rich and I can afford to.'

'Are you reminding me that my cruise depends on your bounty?' Lady Whitcomb asked.

'Of course not,' said Jane. 'I went to Thomas Cook on my way home. Here.' She opened her bag, and handed over a P and O ticket. Her mother looked at it.

'At least you will have your revenge,' she said at last.

'Revenge?'

'I shall be sharing a state room with Gwendoline Gwatkin for eight solid weeks,' said her mother, and then: 'You have not lied to me? This person really is seeking a horse on your behalf?'

'A mare,' said Jane. 'A bay. Fifteen hands or thereabouts. Reared in Ireland.' The truth, but not the whole truth.

'I do so hope,' her mother said, 'that you will not become wayward.'

'I promise I'll do my best,' said Jane. 'Have you enough clothes? – For your cruise, I mean.'

'Perhaps not,' her mother said.

'Then we must go and buy some. Harrods, I think, since there's so little time.' For a moment, Jane thought her mother would cry, then the moment passed.

'I told you I would not accept Penelope Nettles's money,' she said at last.

'This isn't money. It's fripperies. I can't have you sharing a cabin with Miss Gwatkin and looking like a dowd.'

'You are vehement again,' said her mother.

'I'm sorry.'

'Please don't be,' said her mother, and smiled as she had not smiled in years. 'You have overborne me. May we go tomorrow?'

'Of course,' said Jane, and Hawkins came in.

'There's a Mr Warley on the phone, miss,' she said. 'Asking for you.'

'Tell him I'm coming,' said Jane, and when Hawkins had left: 'Mummy I promise you this has nothing to do with private detectives.'

Lionel said, 'So my dear, you *are* a celebrity?'

'Am I?' said Jane.

'The *Daily World* thinks you are. Or haven't you read it?'

'I'm afraid not.'

'My dear you must,' said Lionel. 'Not a dependent clause from first page to last. Are you free?'

'At this moment?'

'It really is rather important.'

'What is?' Jane asked.

'I must teach you to dance. Don't tell me it's a bore – I *know* it's a bore, but it's what one does. There's no escape, I'm afraid.'

'I would like to be able to dance – ' Jane said cautiously.

'Splendid. Then it's agreed. Take a cab.'

'But why should I?' said Jane. 'Why should you for that matter? We've only just met after all.'

'Tell that to Jay Bower,' Lionel said.

'But what on earth has it got to do with him?'

'Buy a copy of the *Daily World* and find out. Do say you'll come. It's the sweetest little mews just off Cadogan Gardens.'

She went back to the music room to tell her mother she was going out.

'Mr Warley?' her mother asked.

'He's quite safe, Mummy.'

'How reassuring,' her mother said. 'What does he do?'

'Amongst other things,' said Jane, 'he appears to be a dancing master.'

'How very odd,' said her mother. 'Is it all because of that appalling war you were involved in?'

Jane found herself wishing, in the cab, that Mummy and Dr Pardoe could have a long, long chat about the after-effects of that appalling war, and that she might be permitted to eavesdrop unobserved. And then, as it seemed most unlikely to happen, she stopped the cab by a news-stand, bought a *Daily World*, and turned to the gossip column, 'This Wicked World', to learn that of all the rich and famous at the Lessing party for Mirova, she,

Jane Whitcomb, was the only one who had made the evening memorable. Grace, beauty, a singular wit, and so on. All very great nonsense of course, but a powerful weapon in the hands of her mother.

Lionel's house was all that she had expected. A neat little gem all in stone, with window boxes full of geraniums on every available ledge. And inside a décor quite ruthlessly white. 'So virginal and improbable,' said Lionel. 'You've read the *World*?'

'Oh my,' said Jane.

'He did go on a bit, didn't he? All that *stuff* about grace and wit and not a word about charm.'

'I have charm then?'

'Obviously you must have,' said Lionel, 'or Jay wouldn't have gone on so, and I would not be about to teach you how to Charleston.' And he wound up the gramophone with grim determination.

They stopped briefly for tea and cucumber sandwiches, served by a parlourmaid of rigidly conservative bearing, whom Lionel addressed as Pott.

'Hasn't she a first name?' Jane asked.

'My dear I don't know,' said Lionel. 'I'm much too afraid of her to ask. And she deplores my friends. Deplores and despises. She thinks of them as quite unsuitable, which of course they *are*.'

Then they practised some more until friends dropped in and Lionel mixed cocktails and Jane was able to put into practice what she had been taught, as she danced with the friends. Unsuitable didn't do them justice.

But at last she had to go home. There would be other visits, other lessons, but her mother's moment could be postponed no longer, Jane thought. She must go back and face the opening salvoes of the long-sustained bombardment that would precede an annihilating charge.

As she removed her coat in the hall she thought how gloomy the house was, after all that glittering white, white wood and glass and chromium, she remembered, a heavy white rug rolled back from floorboards polished to sherry-gold so that they could dance. Even the gramophone had been white. She went into the drawing room.

'Why Francis,' she said. 'How nice to see you.' The *Daily World* lay on a table between Francis and her mother.

'I had no idea,' said her mother, 'how famous you were, until Francis brought it to my attention.'

'It is called "being a celebrity", Mummy,' said Jane.

'Is it indeed? I thought celebrities appeared only in the pages of journals read by housemaids. But perhaps that *is* the sort of journal read by housemaids.'

'Oh I shouldn't have thought so,' said Francis. 'They do a sound financial page – very sound. Well worth a look while capitalism lasts.'

'And its views of celebrities?' Lady Whitcomb asked.

Francis shrugged.

'I really know very little about such things,' he said.

'Nor I. I could wish to know less,' said her mother. 'Really Jane. How you could consent to give an interview to a journalist – '

'But I didn't,' said Jane. 'Of course I didn't.'

'You cannot possibly mean that they invented this rubbish without consulting you?'

'Rubbish' really was a bit hard, Jane thought. What about all that beauty, grace and singular wit?

'All I did was talk with Mr Bower,' she said. 'I'd no idea – '

'Bower?' said Francis. 'J.W. Bower?'

'I expect so,' said Jane. 'Everybody called him Jay.'

'He owns the *Daily World*?'

'So they tell me.'

'That's him,' Francis said. 'J.W. Bower.' Then to their mother: 'He's the most ghastly reactionary, but extraordinarily able.'

'If somewhat fulsome,' Lady Whitcomb said. 'Can you explain to me why he should choose to write such stuff, then print heaven knows how many million copies?'

Jane took her time thinking about it. At last she said: 'I rather think it's because he *can* print it. What I mean is he has the power to engage a perfectly ordinary female in conversation then make millions of people read about it next day and believe it's important.'

'He sounds most disagreeable,' said her mother.

'I am quite sure he could be.'

'And Gwendoline Gwatkin has already telephoned me about it. Try not to appear in the public print again before I am on shipboard.' She got up and left them. Soon there came the sound of the piano: Beethoven matched against Lady Whitcomb, no quarter given. Jane knew at once that the field was left clear for her brother, and was glad.

Francis took out his pipe and filled it, a slow and slightly uneasy ritual still. When it was drawing comfortably he said, 'You were right about Richard Poynter. He's gone down from King's. It seems he prefers the Life Guards.'

'He'll look very well in all that scarlet and horse-hair and burnished steel.'

'Yes,' said Francis. 'He will. I shall miss him.'

'I can understand why,' said Jane, then, as her brother jerked upright, 'That is merely a statement of fact. Sympathetic, if anything.'

Francis sat back again.

'Mummy's off on a cruise, she says.'

'India,' said Jane. 'With Miss Gwatkin. She'll enjoy it.'

'She says you're paying.'

'I can afford to. I'm a rich woman – as I've no doubt Mummy told you. Have you heard from Medlicott?'

'The solicitor? He said five thousand.'

'Congratulations.'

'You got rather more.'

'Just a bit,' said Jane.

'Don't you think I'm entitled to some of it?'

'No,' said Jane. 'Neither did Aunt Pen. She said I mustn't share with you. That's why you got five thousand. And anyway, why are you so worried about money? When Papa died, you said you had all you needed.'

'I was wrong,' said Francis.

Jane waited, but all that her brother added was, 'I need money now. And I've got to wait for this blasted probate.'

'How much do you need?'

Francis shrugged. 'I want to go to Germany with a friend of mine.'

'Dr Pardoe?'

For a moment he looked incredulous. 'No,' he said at last. 'Not Cuthbert.'

'A holiday?' she asked.

'You might call it that. Two or three hundred should do it. I could pay it back as soon as I got my whack.'

'I'll speak to Medlicott. He'll arrange an advance.'

'That's very nice of you,' said Francis, then smiled. 'At least we'll both be out of your way – Mummy and I. It won't matter what Bower puts in his paper.'

'How long will you be in Germany?'

'Five or six weeks. Till just before term starts.'

'Berlin?'

'I expect so,' he said, and was suddenly angry. 'I don't see why I have to be cross-examined. After all it's only an advance on my own money.'

'I didn't think I was cross-examining you.'

'What then?'

'Friendly interest. Obviously I was wrong. Let's drop it, shall we?'

'But you'll speak to that lawyer?'

'Of course,' she said.

19

HARRODS AND DANCING took up much of her time. There was more to it than the Charleston, she discovered. The foxtrot, blues, Black Bottom, one-step and tango had also to be mastered. But the Charleston was always the Charleston. 'Controlled dementia', Lionel called it, but she didn't fear the dementia because the control was hers too. And there was never a shortage of places to practise: from the Embassy or the Savoy, to the conscientious wickedness of clubs like the Cave of Harmony or Ma Meyrick's 43. Or else you could simply give a party and roll back the carpet. Not in her own house, of course. 17, Offley Villas belonged to her mother, and Lady Whitcomb, who made no great objection to her going out to dance, merely smiling grimly and inspecting what Harrods had just delivered, could never, Jane admitted fairmindedly, have countenanced such cavortings in her own home.

That they *were* cavortings Jane did not doubt for an instant. Frenetic, energy-consuming, angular and loud for the most part. And difficult, that was the odd thing. For a long time one had to concentrate very hard to perform these graceless antics, until at last it became as simple and natural as breathing. But how good one felt, whether concentrating or not. Always it was fun. And not just at the time, but when it was over too. One sat – or flopped to be more honest – and grinned at one's partner in triumph as if together the two of you had just constructed a work of art, and 'Goodness that was fun' one said.

And it was. That was the point. Fun in the music, fun in the movement of the dance, the cocktails, the antics of the band. Fun that had been deserved and earned. A right. Rows of young men in stiff white shirts and evening-dress coats, and oneself in diamonds and chiffon. A gardenia corsage, and the King of Roumania at the next table, and the Somme had happened on another planet.

She became popular and was not surprised. Half a million is a big secret to keep, and Lionel must have known because he knew everything, and Miss Gwatkin, who did not dance but had relatives, almost certainly knew too. So she was wary, and when a couple of her new male friends became rather too urgent in taxis – a strange mixture of correct behaviour physically and urgent passion vocally – she rang Mr Medlicott.

He said, 'Can you hold on a minute? I think I know but I'd better ask Rubens.' Divorce courts, chorus girls and an uncle in a commercial bank had all trained Rubens well.

'Your lord's about to go bankrupt,' Medlicott said after his consultation. 'As a matter of fact you're rather out of his class. All he needs is a hundred thousand quid.'

'How disappointing,' said Jane. 'Should I feel insulted?'

'Oh I don't know,' Medlicott said. 'He was reckoned to be rather a catch before he set up the racing stable. The other one –'

'The vicomte,' said Jane.

'That's as maybe. He's after your – ah – virtue.'

'But he can't be,' said Jane.

'Why can't he?'

'He's so frightfully well-behaved.'

'That's because he hasn't got it yet,' said Medlicott.

'What a gentleman you are,' said Jane. 'What would happen if he did get it?'

'Exposure,' said Medlicott. 'Or else a payment in cash – a large one.'

'Suppose I wouldn't pay?'

'He'd produce his wife,' Medlicott said, 'and start divorce proceedings.'

'What odd ways people choose to make a living.'

'Don't they though?' said Medlicott. 'You'll be careful, won't you?'

'No need to worry. I don't think either of them will be able to afford me much longer,' said Jane. 'But thank you for your concern, Mr Medlicott.'

'Not at all,' said Medlicott. 'Glad to help. And by the way I've arranged three hundred for your brother.'

'You're very kind.'

'How easy that is with other people's money. Going to Germany, you said?'

'I did.'

'Sensible feller.'

'Why sensible, Mr Medlicott?'

'Cheapest place in Europe just at the moment. Cheaper even than France.'

'So he should be able to live there for some time?'

'With three hundred pounds he could live like a rajah for six months.'

I do hope not, thought Jane, but she kept the thought to herself. It would take too long to explain.

Next day she received a letter from Mr Pinner. In the top right-hand corner were the words Confidential Investigations and his address. Below in precise typescript was written:

Dear Miss Whitcomb,
    I shall be glad if you will find it convenient to call at my office at any time between nine and five thirty on Thursday of this week.
    With best wishes,
    Respectfully yours,
    G. Pinner.

The signature was written in a clear, almost copy-book hand. Jane was quite sure that the 'G' stood for George.

'I hope he has found your horse,' said her mother, who had seen the letter first.

'He intends to surprise me if he has,' said Jane easily. 'But then he does describe himself as "Confidential", doesn't he? Where's Francis?'

'At work in the study,' Lady Whitcomb said. 'He claimed not to want breakfast. Most unwise.'

'Then he'll have to get out of the study,' said Jane. 'I still haven't finished doing that stuff of Papa's. I told him so.'

'Jane dear,' said her mother. 'This is my house – or had you forgotten? One day it will be Francis's house, but it will never be yours.'

'I'm aware of that, Mummy.'

'Then how can you order your brother out of a room I choose to allot to him?'

'I can't,' said Jane. 'Obviously.'

'And yet you do. Will you apply pressure of some kind?'

'Pressure? On whom?'

'On me,' said her mother. 'I am very much in your debt at the moment.'

'You owe me nothing,' said Jane. 'Presents aren't debts. But Francis knows about the request in Papa's will. He was there when it was read out – and I told him I was almost finished. I can finish today.'

'Not if he chooses not to move,' said her mother.

'Then I shall go and ask him,' Jane said, 'if you'll excuse me.'

'Certainly,' her mother said. 'But there's no great rush. You'll find nothing unsavoury among your father's papers, I assure you.'

'Thank you,' said Jane, 'but I want to finish this job now.'

'Very well,' her mother said. 'I think however that you should tell your brother that whether he leaves or stays is entirely up to him.'

As she climbed the stairs Jane pondered the fact that she didn't mind in the least that Mummy had opened Mr Pinner's letter – she had assumed she would, and arranged matters accordingly – but that the thought of Francis among her father's papers was unendurable. She flung open the study door, and Francis put down the pipe he was cleaning.

'Come to do a little work?' he said. 'Mummy said you wouldn't need this room today.'

'Mummy was wrong,' said Jane.

Francis shrugged. 'I'll leave you to it then.'

He picked up a couple of texts and a notebook, and prepared to leave.

'Where will you work?' Jane asked.

'My bedroom. The table there's just right to work on.'

'Thank you,' said Jane.

'Not at all,' Francis said. 'I expect you'll be glad to finish with all this stuff?'

'I expect I will,' said Jane.

'Is it any good?'

'It was his life,' said Jane, 'but I doubt if it has any commercial value.'

'I was thinking of it as history. You know, socio-political stuff.'

'Not unless you want to know who played Tum Tum in *The Mikado* at Amritsar in 1897.'

'I'll be off,' said Francis.

'Have a good morning's work,' said Jane. 'You should. I didn't have a chance to tell you yesterday, but Mr Medlicott's arranged the advance you wanted.'

'Two hundred?' Francis asked.

'Three.'

'That's absolutely marvellous,' said Francis. 'Thank you,' and rushed out and forgot his pipe.

Jane looked at the neatly docketed piles of photographs, letters, invitation cards. She knew her mother was right. They contained nothing unsavoury. No bills for jewellery, no letters of love, no photographs of Posy Sanderson. Nothing unsavoury at all. She set to work on the last unsorted pile. One big tea chest should do it, she thought. Store it all away, and when she moved house she would take it with her. After lunch, (mulligatawny soup, poached haddock, stewed pears) she returned Francis's pipe to him and their mother watched as if they were children still, and Jane giving back a much-valued toy.

'I hope you haven't been quarrelling?' she said.

'Not at all,' said Jane. 'The information you gave Francis about the study was wrong, that's all – and he left without his pipe.'

'Oh dear,' said her mother. 'Bear with me, children. I'm growing old, you see, and quite unreliable.'

But the smile she gave her daughter was brilliant. Just because you're rich, the smile said, doesn't mean I can't still give you a game.

Mr Pinner had asked permission to smoke a pipe, something he did much better than Francis. Jane had the feeling that he needed to smoke, that he had bad news to deliver.

'I've found your family,' he said at last.

'But that's marvellous,' said Jane.

Mr Pinner didn't look as if anything was marvellous.

'They live in a town called Felston in County Durham. They're at – ' he looked at his notebook, – 'Number 36, John Bright Street. The father's a widower now. There's two sons and a daughter and a grandmother.'

'The mother?'

'She died in 1919,' said Mr Pinner. 'Spanish 'flu. About four months after your friend.'

'How did you do it?'

'Army list,' said Mr Pinner. 'I took what I could from that. I could have asked his regiment for a look at their records – they'd have listed his next of kin and so on – but I knew you wanted this done discreetly so I went up there instead and got on to a local man. He'll cost you ten pounds but he was worth it – *and* he'll keep his mouth shut.'

'That's all right,' said Jane.

'Then we got on to the electoral rolls, but there's an awful lot of Pattersons in Tyneside, and so I went to the British Legion.'

'But John died before it was even thought of.'

'War memorials,' said Mr Pinner. 'The Legion knows all about War Memorials – and we found the right one at last. With his name and rank and regiment. That's where they are, miss. Number 36, John Bright Street, Felston. But if I were you I wouldn't go there.'

'Whyever not?' asked Jane.

'It's the most terrible place I've ever seen,' Mr Pinner said.

'But – but that's not possible,' said Jane. 'The war – '

'Well of course I saw a bit there,' Mr Pinner said. 'Arras and Nueve Chapelle and Wipers – all of that. But that was the *war*, miss. In Felston – ' He hesitated. It seemed as if the words were just not there. At last he said: 'It was like they'd just had a war of their own, miss. And they'd lost it.'

'And the Pattersons?'

Mr Pinner didn't shrug because he was too polite to shrug.

'No worse than any of the others I saw,' he said.

'But no better, either?'

'No, miss. . . . Of course I didn't get in too close – seeing you didn't want anybody to know about it. But they didn't look good, miss. They didn't look good at all. None of them did.'

'But in God's name what's wrong?' Jane asked.

'No work,' said Mr Pinner. 'And no prospect of work. Not this year – not next year, not never. My colleague in Newcastle he put it a bit different. Blasphemy you might call it, but not if you'd been there: not if you'd seen it. "As it was in the beginning, is now and ever shall be, world without end, Amen." He was talking about no hope, miss. – And no jobs either.'

'You're saying the whole town's like that?'

'The whole area's like that,' said Mr Pinner. 'And it's not the only one. You should try taking a look down the East End. But I reckon Felston's worse. You see it's *all* East End there, miss. They wouldn't know what the West End was.'

'I must go there,' said Jane.

And show them what the West End is? Mr Pinner wondered. A fat lot that's going to do for them – or you.

'You want me to go with you, miss?'

'No thank you,' said Jane. 'I once drove an ambulance through Ypres. I don't think I'll need a bodyguard in Felston. Any news of my horse?'

'I've got a couple of leads,' Mr Pinner said, 'but it's a funny thing – horses is a lot harder to find than people.'

'But you won't give up?' said Jane.

'Course not,' Mr Pinner said. 'I've never had to look for a horse before. It's what you might call a challenge.'

Jane rose and offered her hand. 'Thank you for your help,' she said.

Mr Pinner took it. 'Been a pleasure,' he said. 'Mind you take care of yourself, miss.'

But before she could set off, first her brother, then her mother, packed their bags and left. Francis, hopeless at packing, called on her for assistance, and she helped him arrange in his suitcase a great many books, which did not surprise her in the least, and a dinner jacket and full evening dress, which surprised her a great deal. After that he left, with sixty five-pound notes in his pocket, to meet his friend on the boat-train platform at Waterloo. He told neither Jane nor their mother who the friend was.

Her mother's packing took rather longer. There was a vast cabin trunk from her Indian days, there were valises and a Gladstone bag which had belonged to Papa, and a sort of vanity case that contained everything from curling tongs to a packet of pins, and functioned as a sort of portable safe as well, for her mother took with her every piece of jewellery she possessed, since dining at the captain's table, which might well happen, Gwendoline Gwatkin or no Gwendoline Gwatkin, was a serious business. To transport this vast mass of stuff to the train for Southampton something roomier than the Riley would be needed. A taxi would be considered banal, a van ironic. Jane hired a chauffeured Rolls-Royce for the day, and her mother was enchanted.

The enchantment survived even the bundle of newspapers she sent the chauffeur to buy for her mother to read on the train, for among them was the *Daily World*, and once more the name of Whitcomb appeared in the column called 'This Wicked World'. Not that to have avoided it would have made the slightest difference, Jane saw. For as her mother sat in her first-class carriage, reading and snorting, Miss Gwatkin arrived, brandishing her copy, thought Jane bitterly, like a Turk with a scimitar.

For this time Lady Whitcomb was mentioned too. She was the gallant and gracious widow, recently bereaved, off to visit India, scene of her former social and artistic triumphs. 'Artistic' thought Jane, must refer surely to her mother's unremitting attacks on the piano. Not that she escaped completely. She, the witty, elegant daughter, most unlikely of war veterans, continued to be seen in all the smartest places, the ones patronised by aristocracy both native and foreign.

'What can they mean?' Miss Gwatkin asked.

'I expect it's the Embassy nightclub,' said Jane. 'The Prince of Wales goes there once a week, so the rest of them feel they have to go.'

Miss Gwatkin was delighted. Here she was sitting in a railway carriage with someone who had actually been on the same dance floor as the Prince of Wales, *and at the same time*. Miss Gwatkin was a great disappointment to Mummy, for, as she said, if the dear prince was there, how could she disapprove? And when Mummy ventured to suggest that aristocrats, whether native or foreign, were often notorious fortune hunters, Miss Gwatkin once again invoked the sacred name.

'But not those who sit near the Prince of Wales, surely?' she said.

Mummy looked at Miss Gwatkin, then at Jane, and smiled, rather ruefully, Jane thought; the carriage doors began to slam, and she kissed first Miss Gwatkin then her mother, stood on the gritty platform as the guard's green flag waved, his whistle shrilled, and the cream and chocolate train slid out towards the west.

Jane looked in her purse and found two pennies. The first thing, she thought, was to ring darling Lionel and ask him what the hell he was playing at, for that it had been darling Lionel she had no doubt. But she stopped short of the phone booth. What had the poor man done anyway, apart from say apparently very nice things to be quoted or misquoted by whichever *Daily World* hack Bower passed them on to? Nothing offensive about Mummy, and who could object to being witty and elegant in the *Daily World*'s estimation? True, Mummy had been on to the aristocrats like a knife, but she could hardly explain the implications to Miss Gwatkin, and in eight weeks' time no doubt there would be other things to fight about. Like a visit to Felston, perhaps. And anyway, she was seeing Lionel at lunch.

Instead, she went in the Rolls to a jeweller's shop in New Bond Street, and showed him Papa's cuff-links. Ear-rings, she learned, *beautiful* ear-rings would present no problems. That *would* be a change, she thought, and was driven to Lionel's house in the mews.

20

H E WAS ALONE except for Pott, and the treasure in the kitchen and her satellites, which surprised Jane. Lionel liked an audience at lunch as much as any other time. But he explained it all to her as soon as Pott had gone from the room.

'I knew you'd be wanting a row with me,' he said. 'So much easier to have it without witnesses.'

'Well I must say – ' Jane began.

'Of course you must,' said Lionel, and picked up the cocktail shaker. 'White Ladies all right?'

'White Ladies are fine,' said Jane. 'Lionel, how could you?'

'Oh *easily*,' said Lionel. 'I ran into Jay at a party some maharani or other was giving – we all tried on saris. Such fun. Have you ever tried on a sari?'

'Only my own,' said Jane. 'Get on with it.'

'Well he was *asking* about you,' said Lionel, 'and I'd had rather a lot of champagne and crème de menthe – '

'A lot of *what*?'

'Champagne and crème de menthe. Really much too much.'

'But you can't have done,' said Jane.

'But I *did*,' said Lionel. 'Stop interrupting. Jay kept asking me what you were up to and what your mother was like, and what with the drinks and the saris I'm afraid I told him.'

'You don't mean to say that he tried on a sari as well?'

'The day he does,' said Lionel, 'I shall progress down Piccadilly in a tu-tu. Did you find it awful – all that gossip?'

'Not awful, exactly,' said Jane. 'I mean I do go to smart places and Mummy is off to India.'

'Well then?' said Lionel.

'The trouble is,' said Jane, 'that Mummy and I don't always get on all that well – and any stick's good enough to beat a dog with and if it's a bitch so much the better.'

'Do you mean me?' Lionel asked.

'I mean me,' said Jane, and looked at her glass. 'These White Ladies are lethal. . . . What I mean is, Mummy's awfully good at pained rebuke, and getting a mention in "This Wicked World" because of *me* gives her rather a lot of scope. If it hadn't been for – ' She broke off and giggled.

'Laugh your girlish laughter then,' said Lionel. 'Don't mind me.'

'Mummy's friend,' said Jane. 'She's called Gwendoline Gwatkin.' Lionel snorted. 'But that's not for publication,' she added.

Lionel winced. 'Touché,' he said, and then: 'Am I forgiven?'

'How can you be?' said Jane. 'You've committed no crime. You've convinced me of that – you and all that Cointreau and lemon juice and gin. You're lily-white, as usual. It's just – '

'Mummy?'

'Not only Mummy. Me too. The well-known Jane Whitcomb – observed at the Embassy, spotted at the Café de Paris, seen at the Savoy. I mean what am I well-known *for*? If I don't watch out I'll be well-known for being well-known, and where's the sense in that?' She looked again at her glass.

'Would you like another?' Lionel asked.

'Good God no.'

'Very wise,' said Lionel, and helped himself from the shaker. 'What you're saying is that you're not a completely frivolous person like me?'

'I don't know about you,' said Jane, 'but sometimes I have this urge to be very serious indeed, if only I could find something to be serious about.'

'Good works?'

'Jabber suggested that,' said Jane, 'and it may come to that, yet if – ' She broke off. 'I used to be a patient of Jabber's,' she said. 'Did you know?'

'I guessed,' said Lionel.

'Of course you did,' said Jane. 'You're as cute as a box of monkeys.'

'I'm what?'

'It's what a friend of mine used to say. It's sort of a Tyneside expression, one gathers.'

'Does one indeed? And why have you decided to tell me?'

'Because you're my friend,' she said. 'Such a bore, trying to hide things from one's friends.'

'What a devious person you are,' said Lionel. 'Nice, of *course*. But devious without a doubt. As a matter of fact I'm devious, too. I've invited someone for coffee.'

'Bower?'

'Who else?' said Lionel. 'Shall we eat?'

'I doubt if I could swallow a mouthful,' said Jane.

In fact she ate rather well, partly because Lionel's treasure could have been weighed in rubies, and partly because she had to do something about that lethal cocktail. As they ate, they discussed her other – problem. Could she call it that? Her need to get away; to find a house before her mother returned from India.

'You want me to help?' Lionel asked.

'Oh please – if it wouldn't be too much of a bore.'

'Not in the least,' Lionel said. 'I was born nosey. Few things give me more joy than poking about in other people's houses and knowing they can't do a thing to stop me. . . . Expense no object, as they say?'

'I don't want grandeur,' said Jane. 'Comfort yes, but not grandeur.'

'Mayfair is out of the question, then?'

'Completely,' said Jane. 'I'm selling up in Mayfair.'

'How grand you are,' said Lionel. 'All the same I'm delighted. I know far too many people in Mayfair as it is.'

They were still discussing possible areas when Pott announced Jay Bower.

The weather was still hot, but he was dressed with a more than British correctness. White shirt; discreet tie; blue suit. And yet he looked cool, easy and relaxed, even though, according to Lionel, he already would have done six hours' work at least, and have six more to go.

'Sorry I couldn't make lunch,' he said.

'Perfectly all right,' said Lionel. 'There were compensations.'

Bower looked at Jane with an eye that missed nothing.

'Yeah,' he said. 'I could see there would be. How are you, Miss Whitcomb?'

'Well, thank you.'

'That's it?' said Bower. 'Just well?'

'In my own estimation, yes,' said Jane. 'To say that I am witty and elegant would be extremely rude.'

'Even though you are,' said Bower.

'Even then.'

Lionel chuckled, and after a while Bower did so, too. 'OK,' he said, and then, 'At least you read the right newspaper.'

'Why do you say it's the right one?' Lionel asked.

'Because it's the only one that mentions me, of course,' said Jane.

'It won't be for long,' said Bower. 'You'll see.'

Jane smiled. To do anything else would only make her more vulnerable.

'What makes you so sure the others will take Jane up too?' Lionel asked.

'You tell him, Miss Whitcomb,' Bower said.

'I'll do my best.' She took a cigarette from the box beside her, lit it and said, 'My guess it's like covering a bet. Mr Bower has singled me out for attention, which may just be his particular form of naughtiness, or it may be because he has some sort of premonition that I may do something interesting at some point.'

'That's kind of a puny word, that interesting,' said Bower. 'You were going great till then, but cut out puny. Try exciting – maybe even sensational. And there you've got it.'

'And that's why Mr Bower's doing this,' said Jane to Lionel. 'You and I know it's all nonsense, but the *Mail* and the *Express* don't.'

'It may not be nonsense at all,' said Bower.

'People like me simply aren't "sensational",' said Jane.

'Driving an ambulance was.'

'That won't happen again.'

'Why not?' Bower asked.

'There won't be any more wars.'

'Then I'll be out of business,' said Bower.

'What nonsense,' said Lionel. 'You out of business indeed. How could you be? You fulfil an indispensable function.'

'I do?' said Bower. 'Tell me about it. I thought all I did was sell wood pulp for money.'

Lionel put down his coffee cup. 'You do rather more than that,' he said. 'You've taken the place of the Roman Colosseum. Wild beasts and gladiators and sacrificial virgins, scantily clad, throng your pages.'

'I grant you the sacrificial virgins,' said Bower, 'though they're not so scantily clad as all that – but gladiators?'

'Footballers,' said Lionel. 'Boxers. What else would one call them? In fact if I had your sort of money I'd start two newspapers. The *Daily Bread* and the *Daily Circus*. Perhaps the *Daily Bread* would have a little popular religion, too. Why don't you try it?'

'One daily's enough,' said Bower. 'Believe me. And if you'll excuse me I'd better go back to mine. Can I give you a lift, Miss Whitcomb?'

It was a challenge she could not refuse, but she would not make it easy for him. 'I have my own car with me,' she said.

'Send it away,' he said. 'I'd be glad of the chance to talk with you.'

'Very well.' She rose and kissed Lionel's cheek. 'I'll telephone you,' she said, and Lionel knew that he must hold his tongue, and did so.

Together they walked out on to the road that seemed hotter than ever.

'Aren't you going to get away out of this?' Bower asked.

'I intend to quite soon,' she said.

'Now that your mother has gone? At least we'll be cooler in my car. It's really very comfortable.'

They turned a corner to where Jane's car and chauffeur stood waiting. Behind them Bower's car was parked. It too was a Rolls-Royce.

'Never mind,' said Jane kindly. 'Yours looks bigger than mine.' Then, when they moved off she added, 'And mine's only hired after all. I drive a Riley.'

'I heard you were rich,' Bower said.

'Well of course you did. You hear everything. But I like to drive myself.'

'You reckon that's because of the ambulance in the war?'

'It's because I like driving,' she said. 'I always have.'

'Most women of your class stick to horses,' said Bower.

'Oh I like them too,' said Jane. 'But in London a car makes more sense. And how about you, Mr Bower?'

'Not cars,' said Bower. 'Mostly I prefer being driven, but horses sure. My father's got a ranch in Wyoming. I'd like to show it to you some time.'

'Oh how divine,' said Jane. 'Have you ever met Tom Mix?'

'Not in Wyoming,' said Bower. 'In Hollywood.'

'Does your father own a studio, too?'

'No,' said Bower. 'I do. A piece of one anyway.'

Game and set to Mr Bower, thought Jane. But not match. . . . Not yet. . . .

'How long have you known Lionel Warley?' he asked.

Jane thought: he asks questions like the reporter he is. The only thing important to him is one's answer. Good manners and hurt feelings don't come into it at all.

'Not long,' she said.

'You're kind of making your début, aren't you?' he said. 'I mean there doesn't seem to be anybody you have known for a long time.'

'I'm hardly making my come-out, however.'

'That's true in a way, but not in another way. I mean you're not a flapper exactly, but so far as I can gather – this is your first season.'

'I came out in 1914,' she said. 'But soon after that I had more important things to think about.'

'For eleven years?'

Not just a reporter, but a persistent one.

'I lost two brothers,' she said. 'My mother was quite ill because of that fact.'

'And your father?'

'Reclusive,' she said. 'We all were.'

'And yet you go to the Embassy. And the Bag O' Nails. That's a noisy ambience for a recluse.'

'My father died. My mother decided to travel, and I became rich. Shutting myself away no longer appealed to me.'

'Became rich, huh?'

'You know I did. You said so just a little while ago.'

'And I was right?'

'Of course you were,' said Jane. 'You know you were. My aunt's will was recorded. One of your staff must have shown it to you. That's how you know.'

This he ignored. It was not relevant to the line he was taking.

'And going to the Embassy's what you like doing?'

'Sometimes.'

He said, 'You don't much like talking about yourself, do you?'

'Not much.'

'That's OK.' He waved his hand as if she had just received his permission to stay silent. 'What I mean is – you're interesting because of what you are, now, this minute. Not because of what you used to be. Only going to nightclubs isn't going to sell my paper much longer. It's time you moved on to something else, Miss Whitcomb.'

'I must remember that.'

'You don't have to remember it,' said Bower. 'Either you'll do it or you won't. My guess is you will, which is why we're talking. And when you do it, whatever it is, I want you to let me know about it first. Not Beaverbrook. Not Rothermere. Me.'

'That wouldn't be exactly reclusive,' she said.

'No . . . but it could be useful.'

'For you?'

'For both of us.'

'You think that what I do will be newsworthy then?'

'Oh sure.' Another wave of the hand, but this time dismissive, as if she'd said something banal.

'You have been a reporter, I take it. As well as a newspaper proprietor?' she asked.

He looked at her in mild reproach, as if for her to ask questions were a breach of etiquette.

'*Los Angeles Post*,' he said. '*Chicago Messenger*. Then I was a sub on the *New York World*. . . . Then I was a war correspondent for the Bowers Group.'

'You own a – group?'

'My father does,' said Bower. 'Among other things it's the *Los Angeles Post* and the *Chicago Messenger* and the *New York World*. I never had too much trouble getting a job on a newspaper, but I had to be good at it or my old man would fire me. Except being a war correspondent.'

'Your father didn't approve?'

'My mother. She didn't approve of the fact I might get shot.'

'My aunt and uncle had exactly the same prejudice when they bought me an ambulance.'

'And yet you drove it in France.'

'And you went out as a war correspondent.'

'You got shot, too. Well – not shot, I guess. But blown up anyway.'

'Who told you that?'

'Never ask a newspaper man to reveal his sources,' Bower said. 'He'd just as soon show you his entrails. It's what I heard. I haven't printed it.'

'Please don't,' she said.

'OK. . . . There's a fellow I want you to meet. In Paris. Would you like to go to Paris?'

'Not immediately,' she said. 'I have something rather important to do.'

'After you've done it?'

'We'll see,' she said, and he said, 'OK,' once more, as unperturbed as if he'd asked for change for a pound and she hadn't got it, then looked out of the window. They were on Kensington High Street.

'Soon be home,' he said, and reached out to touch the little jewelled leopard she wore pinned to her blouse.

'He's pretty,' he said.

'The person who gave it to me said that it's a leopardess,' said Jane, trying her best to make her voice sound matter-of-fact.

He hadn't touched her breast. Perhaps it was the exercise of scrupulous care, perhaps it was just that he was a rotten shot, but the point was that he shouldn't have done it, yet seemed totally unaware of the fact. He was not, she thought, the kind of man to force his attentions on an innocent maiden – well woman then – in a taxi at night, let alone in his own car with a chauffeur driving and the sun beating down for all of Kensington to see. He had simply wanted to draw her attention to the leopard, so he'd touched. If she'd complained he'd have looked bewildered and serve her right.

'Any idea where it came from?'

'No,' said Jane. She had no wish to see its twin sister embellishing Suzanne de Lys. Anyway, he'd get to Cartier's soon enough: Miss de Lys would see to that.

'You look good in pretty things,' he said.

'Thank you.'

'My pleasure. But it happens to be true. You're one of the ones who make money look good. You choose what's right and you wear it with style. And so of course you look rich. Which means that now and again somebody may get ideas above his financial station, if you follow me.'

'I'm listening,' she said.

'Birth and breeding, and a very pressing need of money.'

'Oh, those two,' said Jane, and at once Bower smiled. It was a grin of pure delight, and so unlike any other expression he'd used that she smiled back. I knew you wouldn't let me down, the smile said, and you haven't, and it's great.

'There'll be others,' he said.

'I'll keep you posted,' said Jane.

'You'll let me publish?'

'Maybe. Not the most flattering light for a young female, the cold glare of greed.'

The car pulled up. Her own hired car was already there waiting.

'It's ridiculous,' she said. 'Travelling in two Rolls-Royces.'

'It would make a nice piece.'

'Print it then,' she said.

'How can I?' he said. 'I'd have to say you were with me.'

'I don't mind,' said Jane.

'I do,' said Bower. 'Or rather my father does. Newspaper proprietors should be read and not seen. What do you think?'

'Up to you,' said Jane. 'It's your newspaper.'

The grin came again. 'When can you go to Paris?' he asked.

'I'll telephone you,' she said.

'I'll look forward to that,' said Bower, and offered a hand. His grip was every bit as strong as she'd expected.

'May I have a word, miss?' said Hawkins.

Jane looked up from the bed. On it were an evening dress of a soft and subtle pink, fresh underwear and, reprehensibly, evening shoes of a deeper pink. Hawkins looked in her turn, and gasped.

'Oh it's lovely, miss,' she said. 'Paris?'

Jane nodded. 'Balenciaga,' she said, and reached for the shoes. 'Sorry about that. I wanted to see how they looked together.'

'They look lovely, miss,' said Mr Hawkins.

'Yes, they do rather. What can I do for you, Hawkins?'

Hawkins said, 'That's rather up to you, miss. If you take my meaning.'

'I'm afraid I don't,' said Jane. 'Not yet, anyway.'

You asked for that one, Hawkins, the maid told herself. Go ahead and explain, you silly cow. She won't eat you.

'I wouldn't want you to think I was eavesdropping, miss,' she said at last.

'Why on earth should I think that?'

'Because I've been hearing things,' said Hawkins. 'But when you're in service you're always hearing things.'

'And what have you been hearing?'

'That you'll be leaving, miss. Setting up on your own.'

Jane went to her bedside chair and sat. 'Yes,' she said. 'It's true.'

'And what with your mother being away we thought – me and cook – it'll be board wages for us once you move. Till your mother comes back.'

Left to their own devices, thought Jane, with their own food to find. 'No,' she said. 'I wasn't considering that. I mean I haven't even found a place for myself yet – haven't even *looked* – and by the time I've found one and it's ready it'll be almost time for Lady Whitcomb to come back.'

'And it'll all be just like before, miss? Except you won't be here?'

'This is my mother's house, after all,' said Jane. 'She'll be here as usual, and my brother will look in from time to time.'

'In that case, miss,' said Hawkins, 'I should like to give two weeks' notice.'

'Hawkins!' said Jane, and rose to her feet.

'I've thought it over very careful – carefully I should say,' said Hawkins, 'and while I don't mind admitting I need the money, I can't see my future here. It isn't congenial, miss.'

'Isn't what?'

'Congenial, miss,' said Hawkins. 'Isn't that the right word?'

'Well yes,' said Jane. 'That is to say – yes. But what will you do?'

'Find another place, miss,' said Hawkins. 'That is unless you would care to take me with you.'

'I?'

'In your new place, miss. You'll be needing a housemaid. Maybe a parlourmaid even. I could do that. I've been doing parlourmaid's work ever since Moreton left. And I've given satisfaction, haven't I, miss?'

'Of course you have, but – '

'And – you'll excuse my mentioning it, but I do know how to be discreet, miss.'

'You do indeed,' said Jane. To herself she wondered: 'congenial', 'discreet', 'carefully'. How much self-improvement did Hawkins feel she needed? How much did any parlourmaid need?

'Well, miss?'

'How does cook feel?' Jane asked.

'She quite likes it here, miss,' said Hawkins. 'Being used to it, she'll stay here.'

'In that case,' said Jane, 'I'll take you with me – since you're determined you won't stay here.'

'Thank you, miss,' said Hawkins. 'Would you like me to help you to dress?'

'I'll manage,' said Jane.

She needed time to think about how to say goodbye to a couple of blue-blooded optimists at the Café de Paris, and what to wear on a visit to Felston.

21

THE NORTH EAST meant the Great North Road: Watford and Grantham and Doncaster and York. It also meant easing her way through parts of London of which till then she'd been to dancing classes there, with a girl who came from Highgate – but Hornsey? Muswell Hill? Edmonton? The Riley chugged on, past rows and rows of identical houses with identical chapels, past soot-blackened terraces with no gardens at all: past small shops and big shops, laundries and public baths, schools and cinemas and tiny chapels and mock-Gothic churches so huge as to hint at dementia.

And people. Not too many children: she'd set off late so the children were in school for the most part. But there were policemen and postmen and tram drivers and railwaymen – and nursemaids and housemaids too, where the money was: odd how the uniforms persisted, seven years after the war was over. But for the most part it was men and women in civvies (though that was uniform too, depending on which regiment you belonged to), bowler hats and smart suits if you were wealthy, caps and blue serge if you were poor. And, this being England, there were all sorts of subtle gradations in between. Uniforms for officers, for sergeant majors, for NCOs and, down at the bottom of the ladder, for other ranks. Upper class, middle class, lower-middle class, and working class, each had a way of telling you where they belonged as soon as they put on their clothes. They didn't even have to open their mouths and speak.

And it was the same with the women, she thought. Their uniforms might be more subtle – hadn't she herself worn a sable coat to drive an ambulance? – but they were there if you knew where to look, especially if you were another woman. . . . She drove on to a sort of scrubland that was neither London nor anything else. Long roads of semi-detached houses with newly planted saplings in front of them, then more waste land, refuse dumps, and then another long, neat road. London pushing out, feeling its way towards more land, more space, until at last even London gave up, and she was in the countryside.

Fields and hedges, and very nice too, she thought, when one's idea of unlimited open country had been restricted to Kensington Gardens. Here were pasture, and corn land already golden, and cows and sheep and occasional horses. There were hay waggons too, with massive Clydesdales easing them along like ships through a brown-gold sea, and if she stopped the Riley and got out there would be the sight and smell of hedge flowers, birdsong, a glimpse of rabbits, or even a fox. The England she'd read about in India, she thought, and seen and learned about with Vinney in her uncle's rented mansion.

But she couldn't stop. She had to get on. This journey of hers was using up all her courage; if she dawdled and wavered she would never see it through, and she knew it. Yet still the countryside was beautiful. It was hard to put her foot down and keep on going. And still there were the villages, too: houses and people sleepy in the heat, where to hurry seemed a profanation as the Riley chugged grimly on. When she did stop at last it was at the top of a hill, with common land beside her. She got out and stretched, and spread a motor rug beneath a chestnut tree, took out her sandwiches and a vacuum flask.

Beneath her the common land gave way to a park, and in it the local great house, not huge, but big enough: grey stone, dark slate that sparkled in the sunshine. Money. And nearby, just far enough for a Sunday stroll, a church of the same grey and sparkling stone; no spire, but a most elegant bell tower. And beyond the spiritual and temporal power, the village, pictur-esque and straggling; duck pond and smithy and pubs; and the wrong sort of diet and chilblains in winter and rheumaticky cottagers, she had no doubt, but oh how beautiful it looked that day.

She poured out coffee and began on her sandwiches, and wished she had brought Foch with her. She knew it was impossible – she was going among strangers who might not like dogs, and Foch disliked strangers, besides being an unabashed snob, but all the same it would have been pleasant to watch him roam the scrubby grass, worrying about what he would do if he encountered a rabbit. It was just as well that he had Hawkins to wait on him hand and foot, she thought, and Foch would certainly see that she did wait on him. After all, she had nothing else to do.

Jane heard the soft thud of a horse's hoofs only just in time. She had begun to doze, but looked up at once. Coming towards her was a man on a mouth-watering roan gelding: a man quite old, with a white moustache, who wore, despite the heat, a buff-coloured riding coat, dogskin gloves, white breeches and boots. As he came up to Jane his sharp blue eyes took in the Riley, the motoring rug, the young woman at her picnic in one glance, touched the rim of his hat with his riding whip and cantered on, and Jane knew that despite the fact that she had with her neither chauffeur nor companion she had been accepted, she belonged.

Time to move on, more than time, but the heat made her lazy, and besides there were the aristocrats to think about. Cramming them both into the one night might have been clumsy, even tactless, she thought, but she really had had to get rid of them and get on with her life. The English one had really been quite grateful, she remembered, glad of the tip off that gave him the chance to look for somebody else before the pheasant season. But the vicomte had been more difficult and demanded a loan of five hundred for time and money wasted. For all the world as if I owed him a week's wages in lieu of notice, she thought. She had had to be quite sharp with him. It was the mention of Medlicott and Rubens that had done it. When she invoked them, he had gone like a lamb. Aunt Pen was right. It would be madness to go elsewhere.

She went back to the Riley and set off once more, through more enchanting country, pretty villages, neat and handsome little towns, through Huntingdonshire and Lincolnshire and into South Yorkshire, and at last the landscape began to change. Suddenly there were more railways, and factories, the first winding engine wheel of a coalmine, then another and another as she moved further into Yorkshire. No more cows at grass, but the narrow rows of pit cottages and soot-smeared waste land beyond, where children raced and shrieked, or else played grimly at a kind of cricket with rules of their own devising. The easy rolling hills too were gone, and in their place great jagged ones of slag and pit waste. And yet the sun still shone.

She reached York at last, looking down at its great cathedral – Minster, they called it – from a landscape grown kind once more. 'The Vale of York', the guide book said, where they grew fruit and raised cattle, and tended cows for the milk that they made into chocolate, a gentle, kindly sort of industry compared with the battlefields she had come through. She would stay there for the night, she decided. No point in arriving at Felston exhausted.

There were plenty of hotels, and she chose the best she could find, old and comfortable, and not far from the cathedral. The landlord seemed surprised that she was on her own, and looked at once at her left hand. No rings, at least not on the relevant finger.

'Come far, miss?' he asked her.

'London,' she said. 'Have you a room with a bath?'

'Not a room, miss,' said the landlord. 'Private baths is only with a suite.'

'I'll have a suite, then,' said Jane.

'On your own, miss?'

'I certainly don't intend to share it.'

'No, miss, of course not,' the landlord said. 'It's only that suites is expensive.'

'How much is expensive?'

'Three to five guineas a night, miss. Including breakfast.'

He made it sound like a lakh of rupees, she thought. A hundred thousand glittering coins poured out of great leather sacks at the feet of a maharajah. She took out a five pound note from her note case, and added two half crowns. 'I'll have five guineas' worth,' she said.

When she was taken up to see it, she understood his reluctance. It was the bridal suite. Rather more gloomy than one would wish on one's honeymoon, but the furniture was comfortable, and the bath huge, with loads of hot water. She wallowed happily, and soaked the stiffness from her bones. Really it would have been better to have someone to share it with, she thought. He could have dried my back, too.

As it was all she could do was be a tourist, and walk round the old city walls, squeeze her way up the narrow medieval streets and stand at last in the cathedral itself. Evensong was just finishing, and the clear sweetness of boys' voices, the richness of men's, blended in the great space of the nave, and she dropped on her knees and stared at the incredible stained-glass window that faced her. 'The Seven Sisters', so the hotel's guide book told her. 'A masterpiece of medieval craftsmanship.' The guide book didn't tell her that it was also a creation of a quite overwhelming beauty, the declining sun turning the coloured glass into the shining richness of jewels: rubies, sapphires, emeralds heaped up into the shapes of prophets and saints. But John had told her that, she remembered, one day as they looked at the stained glass in Nôtre Dame, told her then boasted, because he was a chauvinist, that the great Rose Window in Durham Cathedral was even better. . . . She went back to the hotel, and had dinner. The dining room seemed packed with clerics of one kind and another, all doing themselves well, and taking peeps from time to time at the young female bold enough to be dining alone. Jane wondered how many sermons she would appear in the following Sunday. It was obvious that neither they nor her waiter approved of her.

But next morning she found a garage with a young mechanic who approved of her very much, and even more of the Riley. He checked it for her carefully, filled it up with petrol, then asked where she was going, and when she told him he wished her luck for all the world, she thought, as if I'd said Passchendaele.

At first it was pleasant – up into the North Riding, and what was called the Dale Country, wild and open, with sheep wherever one looked, and the remains of ancient abbeys that had once existed because of wool. 'Bare, ruined choirs', Vinney would have called them, and as for John, they would have reminded him of the cathedral at Ypres that was just as impressive a ruin when he had last seen it. The sheep would have made him think of his civilian job in Bradford, and his prospects, and the career he was going to make for her and the bairns. If he'd lived he'd have been a rich man by now, she thought – if Aunt

Pen had liked him, and of course Aunt Pen would have liked him. There would have been no need for her to frighten off impoverished young aristocrats, either; then she vigorously repressed the thought that she'd rather enjoyed frightening off impoverished young aristocrats.

The Dale Country ended. As she crossed the border at Darlington more slag heaps appeared, the great steel mills stood strong as fortresses, then the landscape grew bleak indeed, the little iron towns and pit villages blending into their grimness. Only once more did that kinder England show itself, at Durham. She looked down at it from above, massive, enduring, beautiful, and remembered what John had told her and drove into the town for sandwiches at a teashop, then on to the cathedral; another glory of Gothic. And John hadn't been all that chauvinistic. The Rose Window too, glowing as if its light were all within, proclaimed its utter certainty in God's glory. Jane knelt and prayed. She had no doubt that there was a lot to pray for.

If Durham was the city of God, she thought, the country between it and Newcastle had long gone over to the Devil: pit heaps instead of downland – colliery wheels for spires. And so it was all the way to Newcastle, which was like an island of cheerfulness: trams and shops, and people who looked as if they were going somewhere, doing something, before at last she fumbled her way to a sign that said 'Felston', and left the city, and went back into the nightmare.

Dismal streets yielded to more pit heads, narrow-gauge railways held row upon row of waggons that looked as if they hadn't moved in months. Now and again the tall, gaunt shape of a factory appeared, a factory where no one worked, and then she was beside the river, – the Tyne it must be, – dark and filthy, crusted with rubbish, and lined with shipyards that were just like the factories, because no one worked there either. There were cranes and engines, the great stages where ships' hulls were assembled, the machine shops where engines were made, the whole intricate life of a steamship constructed, and all were empty. The only living things were the planing seagulls, and even for them the river held no hope of life.

The men who should have been in the shipyards and factories, down the pits, she saw in the streets of Felston. Because the weather was fine they lounged out of doors, most of them with their backs to a wall or seated on a doorstep: the miners – so she learned later – squatting down, easy as Cossacks, the way they squatted at their work in the narrow seams deep down below. None of them moved very much. When she had last seen a group of men like that, they had been in khaki, behind the lines, and they'd been skylarking, scuffling, playing impromptu football. But these men had learned that exercise makes you hungry, and it's foolish to make yourself hungry when there's nothing to eat.

Every one of them, she noticed, wore the uniform of the working class: the cloth cap, heavy blue-serge suit, white scarf and boots, even in the sunshine. There weren't so many women as men, but the ones there were wore a uniform of their own: old dresses with a pinafore over them, scarves or shawls round their heads, cotton stockings, enduring, clumsy shoes. Jane remembered the old gentleman in the buff-coloured riding coat she had seen the day before. He could have belonged to another country – even another planet. The thought that nagged her was that she belonged with the old gentleman (he'd known at once that she belonged) and not with Felston at all. Even so she had to find John Bright Street.

She pulled up beside a group of men at a crossroads, and they looked towards her at once. A woman, smartly dressed, driving her own car in a town where practically nobody owned a car apart from the more successful doctors, that was a sight to be savoured. Jane wound down her window and called out 'Excuse me.' At last a man came up to her.

'Yes, miss?'

'I'm looking for John Bright Street,' she said. 'Can you direct me?'

He began to speak in his turn, but apart from his pointing finger she understood nothing. His dialect was so thick as to seem like a foreign language, but how could she say so?

A voice from behind the first man said, 'Are you lost?'

She twisted in her seat. Looking at her was a small man with a bicycle. He seemed Jewish and, unlike every other man she'd seen, was bare-headed and wore a coat of some light material that could even have been silk.

'I'm looking for John Bright Street,' she said.

'Straight on till you get to the town hall,' said the bare-headed man. 'Left there and up Norman Purvis Street past the Labour Hall and second right.'

The other man beside her made noises that appeared to mean 'That's what I told her.'

'I'm obliged to you both,' she said.

The bare-headed man said, 'May I ask what number you're looking for?' He spoke with what Jane took to be a Lancashire accent, but not exaggeratedly so. He was also asking a question that was no business of his, but he was pleasant about it, and he'd helped her.

'Number 36,' she said.

'I hope the Pattersons aren't in any trouble,' said the bare-headed man.

'So do I,' said Jane, and drove off and left him. The invitation to gossip was a little too much.

22

J OHN BRIGHT STREET was where the bare-headed man said it
was, and she drove carefully along it, easing her way past
children newly out of school, who played games involving skip-
ping ropes and lamp-posts, and a great deal of chalking of
pavements, and who were liable without warning to run out on
to the cobbled road that rarely saw anything more lethal than a
horse-drawn milk cart.

Number 36 was exactly like the others: sooty brick and fading
paint, but in common with the others too its windows were
washed, its door handle gleamed, its front step holystoned. She
got out of the car, went to the door and knocked, and the children
flocked like sparrows as the door opened, and she found herself
looking at John. The right age, the right expression, the right
sort of cockiness, even in shirt sleeves, and no shoes.

'What is it?' The voice was brusque, harsh even, yet there was
no hint of cruelty. It was a voice familiar to her, and yet quite
new. For a moment she found it impossible to answer, for this
was John looking at her and John was dead.

'Mr Patterson?' she said at last.

'Bob Patterson. . . . Aye. . . . What is it?'

Bob. The younger brother. 'Our kid.' She wished that John
had warned her how much alike they were. Perhaps it wouldn't
have hurt quite so much.

'I'm awfully sorry to bother you,' she said, 'but I once knew
your brother you see and as I was passing this way – '

Behind her she could hear one of the children mimicking her

– 'awfully sorry' – 'as I was passing this way' – No wonder they mocked her, she thought. Her excuses were pathetic.

'You know our Andy?' Bob asked.

'Not Andy. . . . No. . . . Your brother John. . . .'

'Oh,' said Bob. 'I see.'

And maybe he did see, she thought, for he had John's quickness too.

'Not Andy. . . . No. . . .' the child mimic said, drawling out the vowels in a way that sent his fellows into ecstasies.

'Excuse me, miss,' said Bob, and went outside, stockinged feet and all, and roared once. The children scattered.

'Is that your car, miss?' he asked, and she nodded. 'It's a bonny un. You'd best come in.' He pushed the front door wider.

'Sorry I was a bit sharp,' he said. 'When you get a caller this time of day it's usually somebody selling something. Though where they think we can get the money to buy – this way, miss.'

He led the way up a steep flight of stairs. Their carpet was threadbare, Jane noticed, but the brass rods gleamed. At the head of the stairs was a tiny landing. Bob opened the door on the right.

'In here, miss,' he said. 'I'll just go and get Grandma – if you'll give us your name, please.'

'Jane Whitcomb,' she said. That it meant nothing to Bob was obvious.

'Right, miss,' he said. 'If you'll just take a seat. . . .'

He left her, and she sat down on a black, horse-hair sofa. It was flanked by horse-hair armchairs. Four indentations in a worn carpet marked the place where a table had once stood. The fireplace was filled with crinkled red paper, and in front of it was a wooden screen papered with scraps, then varnished over. On the mantelpiece there was one photograph, John in the uniform of a lieutenant, the ribbon of his DSO looking very new against the whipcord cloth. It could have been Bob dressing up. She got up and picked up the photograph, looked at it more closely. 'My but you are a bonny lass.' She remembered the words, and how and where he had said them, and the tears were very close.

Behind her a voice said, 'Aye, that's him all right,' and she turned to the door, and the old woman framed inside it. Quite small, the old woman, and stooped, but ablaze with vitality.

Formidable too, with a strong little chin and a nose like the beak of a predatory bird. Luxurious white hair, thick and gleaming, coiled in a bun. Only the dark eyes that should have gleamed with the power she had, did not belong, but looked milky, languid even. Going blind, thought Jane, but she's not giving in to it.

'Mrs Patterson?' she said.

'John's grandma. . . . He used to call me Gran.'

'I'm Jane Whitcomb. I used to know John.'

'So Bob tells me,' the old woman said. 'You've got him gawping like an idiot. Anyone would have thought there was a giraffe on the doorstep. Mind you I can't say I blame him now I've seen you.'

'Giraffe?' said Jane.

'How many young women do you think come knocking on our door – dressed the way you're dressed and driving their own cars?'

And she was wearing her oldest, plainest suit.

'As I told you,' Jane said, 'I used to know John, so I thought I'd look you up.'

'You took your time,' the old woman said. 'He's been dead seven years.'

Gently, Jane admonished herself. Gently. . . . She wouldn't talk like this if she hadn't loved him, too.

'Not quite,' she said. 'There's rather more than two months to go first.'

The old woman's face thrust forward towards her, then her fists clenched. She wants to see my face because I said that, Jane thought, but she can't.

'You know the date then,' she said at last.

'Tenth of November, 1918,' said Jane. 'At La Bassée Canal.'

The old woman's head bowed, but came up again almost at once.

'And where did you meet him?'

'In France. . . . Autumn. 1917.'

'Nurse, were you?'

'I drove an ambulance.'

The old woman seemed not to have heard. 'Our John was wounded the year before. 1916 it was. Just a scratch, he said. Some scratch. He was in the hospital six weeks.'

Some scratch indeed, thought Jane. A great curving scar from his collar bone to his ribs. A shell splinter that had hit him just right. A little more of an angle and it would have killed him. She used to stroke it. It was hard, ugly, compared with the smoothness of the rest of him, but it was a part of him and so she loved that too.

'You drove an ambulance, you say?'

'That's right. I met John at a dance.'

The ruins of a little château with one wooden floor surviving and a wind-up gramophone. . . .

'John was fond of a dance.'

'I too.'

The old woman said, 'Come over here a minute, will you? My eyes aren't what they were.'

There was a stool with a cushion by the old woman's feet. Jane went to sit on it. Now, she thought, you can look down on me.

Grandma Patterson said, 'Driving an ambulance – you'd be near the battlefield. The what-did-they-call-it?'

'The Front,' said Jane. 'Yes. I was.'

'And weren't you frightened?'

'Of course,' said Jane. The old woman waited. 'But somebody had to do it,' Jane added at last.

'It must have been nasty sometimes, chaps knocked about like they were.'

'Ghastly,' said Jane, but this time she added nothing.

'You didn't pick up our John when he was killed?'

'No,' said Jane. 'I was at home. On leave. But I did make enquiries. He was hit by a machine-gun burst. It was a clean death. Quick too.'

'It was still a death,' the old woman said. 'His colonel wrote and told us the same and we were grateful, but it won't bring John back.'

The old woman sat for a long time among memories more real than the sounds of the children outside, thought Jane, and she could understand that, but even so it had been a mistake to come. Better if she left and found a place to spend the night then drive back to London and go dancing with Lionel.

'I think I'd better go,' she said. 'I'm sorry to have bothered you like this.'

'You haven't bothered me,' the old woman said. 'It's just come as a bit of a shock after all these years. Our John. An officer. Dancing with a lady.'

'With an ambulance driver,' said Jane. 'And I'm sorry it's been so long, Mrs Patterson, but I've been rather ill for a long time – too ill to get about much, I'm afraid.'

'But you're all right now?'

'Oh yes. I'm fine.'

'And you came from a long way, likely?'

'From London.'

'You drove yourself all that way just to come and see us? His family?'

'To see whether you were all right.'

'You must have been fond of him.'

It was like being out to hounds, Jane thought. Either you went for the fence no matter how high it was, or you pulled up and turned away and went home.

'Fond isn't quite the word,' she said.

'I was hoping you would say that.' The old woman folded her hands in her lap. 'Would you mind telling me what the word is then?' she asked.

'I loved him,' said Jane.

'I was hoping you would say that, too.'

'We were engaged,' Jane said, and she opened her handbag, took out the little box and opened it too. 'When the war was over we were going to marry.' She took the ring from the box and gave it to the old woman, who held it close to her face.

'By it's a bonny un,' she said. 'Why don't you wear it?'

'Would you mind?'

'Our John gave it to you,' she said. 'And you chose to take it. Why should I mind?'

Jane slipped the ring on to her finger. It still fitted.

'That's better,' said Grandma Patterson, and added: 'So now you've come to see how the Pattersons are getting on.'

There was irony in her voice, but Jane thought she heard sympathy too.

'It's bad?'

'There's plenty worse. We've no bairns here, you see. – What you would call children. – Bairns eat money. Always hungry: always wearing out their clothes. And then we had the bit cash

John left – him having put Minnie down on his next of kin. – Minnie was his mam.'

She waited for a moment, but all that Jane said was, 'Of course.'

'But it didn't last for ever – and one by one they were out of a job – first Andy – that's the other brother. Then Stan, the father – then Bob. So there was nowt coming in and only John's money and the dole going out. And now it's only the dole.' She looked at Jane. 'Unemployment Benefit you'd call it, though where the benefit is in under three pound a week to feed three grown men and two grown women I'm blest if I know.'

'Two women?'

'There's his sister. Bet.'

'Oh yes of course. John used to talk about his little sister.'

'She's not little any more. She helps me look after the place. . . . No. . . . That's a lie. I help her when she'll let me. . . . I'm gettin' past it.' She looked up, at once puzzled, and irritated. 'Where was I?'

'The dole,' said Jane. 'Trying to manage.'

'Well you can't,' said the old woman. 'Not on two pounds twelve and six a week you can't. Not even if you were that financial genius our Andy's always on about. . . . What's his name? German would he be?. . . . Oh aye.' She looked at Jane in triumph. 'Karl Marx himself couldn't do it.'

'I believe you,' said Jane. 'So how *do* you manage?'

'Go on a diet,' the old woman said. '*That's* how we manage. The Wednesday and Thursday diet.'

'Why then?'

'Because the men's dole's paid on a Friday, and by Wednesday teatime there's nowt left. . . . Oh aye. And we simplify our lives an' all. Leastways that's what Bob calls it.'

'And how do you do that?'

'Get rid of stuff we don't need.'

'Like the parlour table?'

The old woman looked at once at the carpet, to the place where the four indentations were.

'You've a sharp pair of eyes on you. So did I, once upon a time. . . . Aye. Like the table. Solid mahogany that was. A proper good un. I could have cried when it went.'

'Why didn't you?'

– 230 –

'Where's the sense?' the old woman asked. 'You can't eat a table.'

'Very true,' said Jane, and Grandma Patterson made again that peering lunge. 'Are you mocking me?' she asked.

'Of course not,' said Jane. 'I want to know, that's all. But I just don't know what words to use.'

Surprisingly, the old woman accepted this. 'Bit of a novelty,' she said. 'Meeting with folks that are hungry.'

'Well not exactly,' said Jane. 'I was brought up in India – but of course only the natives were hungry there.'

'Your father in the army?'

'Indian Civil Service actually. He died earlier this year.'

'And your mother?'

'She's gone back to India on a visit.' How could I possibly use a word like 'cruise' after what she's told me? Jane thought.

'Mr Whitcomb would be a high-up, likely?'

Jane answered without hesitation. 'Very high. He was knighted for it.'

'You mean – ?'

'Sir Guy Whitcomb,' said Jane.

'And your mother?'

'Lady Whitcomb.'

'Sir Guy and Lady Whitcomb,' the old woman said. 'And you'd have a big house and servants and all that?'

'Our house in India was very big,' said Jane. 'Almost a palace – and as for servants – we must have had twenty at least. In Kensington not nearly so many. Never more than four. But of course the house is smaller.'

'Well I'll go to France,' the old woman said. That she was amazed there could be no question, but she was also lapping it up.

'And our John,' she said, 'you and our John – '

'He gave me this ring,' said Jane. 'We considered ourselves as good as married, and we acted accordingly.'

The old woman sat silent for a moment, then: 'I'm obliged to you,' she said.

'For what?'

'For being honest. There's a lot between us, but we'd get nowhere if we aren't honest. You've no bairn?'

'No,' said Jane. 'Perhaps it's as well.'

'Perhaps. . . . John was my favourite. I've never denied it and God knows I've been punished for it. But there wasn't many like John.'

'I know that,' said Jane.

'Well of course you do. Man and wife you were and I'm glad of it. The minister might not be, but I am. . . . For John's sake. Yours an' all. You had a good man while it lasted. Not that I'll be telling anybody else about it. You've my word on that. They're a prim and proper lot round here. Chapel mostly. – Though mind you the Catholics is just as bad. . . . Where was I?'

'Being glad for us,' said Jane.

'Well so I am,' the old woman snapped. 'And glad you've told me an' all. Our John and a proper lady. . . . But what took you so long, lass? I know you said you were poorly, but at my age – I might have died not knowing.' The thought was so appalling that for the only time her voice faltered. Her John had been happy and she could have died in ignorance of it.

I can tell only the truth, thought Jane, and if it's too much for her I can still drive back three hundred miles, and dance tomorrow with Lionel at the Savoy.

'I wasn't just poorly,' she said. 'I was mad. What they call shell shock. Maybe you've heard of it?'

'Heard of it?' said the old woman. 'I only have to walk out of that door to see it. . . . Sarah Barlow's lad. Back home for seven years and he thinks he's still in France. . . . Bad for you, was it?'

'Bad enough,' said Jane. 'I saw a lot of things I still don't believe – I was hungry and exhausted and blown up by a shell – but it wasn't that.'

'What then?'

'It was John,' said Jane. 'It was losing John.' Her hands came up to her face, and she sobbed, not yelling, the way she used to do when things were bad, but quietly, containedly almost, emptying out grief like water from a basin. The old woman's hand came out to touch her hair, and gently, softly stroked.

'Whisht, me bairn. Whisht now,' she said, over and over, and even as she wept Jane was aware of the power in that old and work-hardened hand, the grim strength still remaining in the worn-out body. When at last she had done, she looked up.

'I bet I look a mess,' she said.

'You looked better when you came in,' said the old woman, and smiled.

Jane took the mirror from her handbag, and examined her face that was blotched and tear-stained and smeared with make-up.

'Oh dear,' she said, and began to clean herself up with a handkerchief soaked in the cologne she carried.

'That's a good lass,' the old woman said, then watched in silence as Jane produced powder compact and lipstick and got to work, and showed to Grandma Patterson at last a face that might never once have wept.

'Well I'm blessed,' the old woman said.

'You've seen a woman make up before,' Jane said.

'No,' the old woman said. 'That's just it. I haven't. Like a conjuring trick. You look just like when you came in. And to think the minister's always going on about painted harlots.'

Jane said defensively, 'John liked me to look pretty.'

'I'll bet he did,' the old woman said, and then: 'What time is it?'

No clock on the mantelshelf either. Jane looked at her watch. 'Nearly five o'clock,' she said.

'They'll be wanting their teas,' said the old woman. 'There's fresh herring and potatoes. You're welcome to stay.'

'You'll have to excuse me,' said Jane. 'I had a huge lunch in Durham.' This was a lie, but she knew beyond doubt that the herring would have been allocated already. 'Besides – I'll have to think about finding a place to stay.'

'The Eldon Arms,' said the old woman at once. 'It's the only place that's fit. But if you don't mind my asking, pet – what are you going to do after that?'

'Pet' Jane thought, meant a concession, and not a small one either.

'I'd like to stay for a while,' she said. 'This was John's birthplace. He lived most of his life here. I'd like to look around. See what I can do to help.'

'You?' the old woman said. But it wasn't anger, merely amazement.

'I'm quite young – and healthy nowadays, and I'm not poor exactly. There must be something – '

'We'll talk about it tomorrow,' said the old woman. 'Now you better come and meet the family before they start chewing the oil-cloth.'

She got up and led the way into what was the centre of the household: kitchen, dining room and workshop, too. The room was dominated by a fireplace with an oven beside it, and even on that hot day the fire burned. The only source of power they had, thought Jane, for on a bar across the fire a kettle simmered, and on a ring beside it a pot of potatoes steamed.

Facing the fire was a deal table, its top covered with some kind of artificial material: what Grandma Patterson had called the 'oil-cloth', well worn and shiny, and decorated with unlikely flowers. There was a mat on the floor, and another, half finished on a frame. For the rest there were a set of kitchen chairs, a rocker, a wooden Windsor chair, a couple of stools, and a sideboard that looked homemade. A man and a woman sat at the frame, working on the mat. They had a supply of strips of cloth, cut from old clothes by the look of them, which they knotted with the aid of steel hooks into a canvas backing. The two were obviously father and daughter, and both looked like John and like Grandma Patterson. Only then did Jane realise that John too had resembled his grandmother, but he had inherited her combative self-reliance, too. The man and woman before her both bore the marks of defeat.

At the table another man sat, mending a boot on a boot last, banging in the nails with a sort of monitored aggression. He too had the family look, but in him the fierceness was apparent at once. This must be Andy, the reader of Karl Marx. Red Andy, John had called him. In a corner Bob, the only one she knew, fiddled with the earphones of what she assumed must be a crystal set.

Grandma Patterson said, 'Now then. Stan, Bet, Andy. You can stop your fidgeting. I want you to meet our John's fiancée.'

23

B OB HAD OFFERED to show her the way to the Eldon Arms, provided nobody pinched his share of the herring. He wants a ride in a car, thought Jane, and a chance to see and be seen beside a smartly dressed woman, and to talk about a place, *any place*, that wasn't Felston. He was in a fever to leave it, as John had been, but John had acquired skills, shorthand, book-keeping, that gave him a start in a booming industry. Bob had trained as a printer, and been fired the day after he'd finished his apprenticeship, because skilled men cost money, and appren-tices soon got the hang of things.

They drove, at Bob's suggestion, by the sea coast, a roundabout way to get there but at least she could see the gleaming yellow sands, the lazy-rolling waves, green as wine bottles, roaring softly in. Jane pulled up to watch.

'So there's something beautiful in Felston,' she said.

'I come here every chance I get,' said Bob.

'May one ask why?'

'It's the way out,' he said. 'It's escape, the sea is.'

'Escape to where?'

'Anywhere,' said Bob. 'There's the colliers for a start. They take coal to London. There's one. Look.' He pointed at a stubby, weathered little ship.

'I thought the pits were closed?'

'There's too much coal, that's why,' said Bob. 'When the stocks is low they'll let them back in – if they've a mind to go. Pitmen is gluttons for punishment. But that ship's off to London and I can get a place on her for ten bob – cheaper than the railway.'

'Won't it take a long time?'

'Three or four days,' said Bob. 'Too far to walk.' He hesitated. 'Don't let Andy upset you. He gets a bit sharp sometimes – but he doesn't mean it.'

'Doesn't he?'

Bob smiled. 'He's going to change the world, you see. God knows it needs changing. But it's a bit hard on the temper.'

'He didn't spare you, I notice.'

'That's because of me crystal set. Most of it's second hand – or ninth hand or tenth hand mebbes. But batteries is only for cash.'

'He thinks you should spend it on food?'

'He thinks I should spend it on pamphlets,' Bob said. 'He's got a pal with a printing press and I set it for them – "Workers of the World Unite" and all that. But now and again he runs out of paper and ink, and he expects me to give a contribution. Me.' He shook his head, miming amazement at such idiocy.

'Two nights ago I heard Ambrose's band at the Café de Paris,' he said. 'That was before the earphones went.'

'Then you heard me,' said Jane. 'I was there that night.'

'You never,' he said, and turned towards her, as delighted as if he'd been at the next table. 'Was it marvellous?'

How could she tell him she'd gone there to get rid of a couple of millstones?

'Wonderful,' she said. 'They played "Mean To Me" three times.' She took one last look at the waves. 'Shouldn't we get on to this pub now? They might eat all your herrings.'

Andy Patterson said, 'She has no business here.'

'Well of course she has,' said Bob. 'Don't talk daft.'

'How has she?' Andy asked. Bob went on eating herring. The walk from the Eldon Arms had made him hungry. It was true that Jane had given him threepence for a tram ride that cost a penny, but that would go for a pint.

'You can't, can you?' Andy said.

Stan Patterson leaned forward. 'What Bob means,' he said slowly, 'is that that young lady was our John's intended.'

'That's what she says,' said Andy.

Bob speared his last potato and looked up. 'For God's sake man,' he said, 'why on earth would she lie about it?'

Stan Patterson said, 'No language Bob,' but his eyes were on Andy.

'What I mean,' said Andy at last, 'is that it's all wrong. Them clothes. That car. . . . They don't belong here. There's nothing about her belongs here. What did she come for?'

'To help,' his grandmother said. 'I asked her straight and she told me. She wants to help.'

'To help us starve?' said Andy. 'We can do that on our own.'

'She's got money,' the old woman said. 'Anyone can see that.'

'We don't want charity.'

'Don't we? We don't seem able to get anything else. But I wasn't thinking of her on her own. She couldn't keep the whole town.'

'She's got money all right,' said Bob. 'She was in the Café de Paris two nights back.'

'And what that might be?' his father asked.

'Nightclub,' said Bob. 'I heard it on the wireless.'

'You would,' said Andy.

'From what I hear nightclubs is sinful,' said his father. 'We don't want any of that.'

'We couldn't afford it,' said Bob, 'and anyway, she didn't look like a sinner, now did she?'

'She looked like a nice young woman,' said his grandmother, 'which is what she is. If she wasn't she'd still be in London going off to a dance.'

'I still don't see what use she'd be to us – or Felston,' Andy said.

'Then you need glasses like me,' said his grandmother. 'Look. She wants to stay here and look around for a bit. What's wrong with that? She's got a car. She can make herself useful taking folks to the clinic – and that way she'll get an idea what housing conditions is like.

'And when she's seen for herself – if she still wants to help – we can set her on going round her rich friends with the collecting box.'

'Collecting for what?' Stan Patterson asked.

His mother sighed. 'For what Felston needs,' she said. 'Free milk for bairns, and medicine and specs and winter coats for poor old bodies like me.'

'Charity,' said Andy. 'I've told you before – we don't want charity.'

'You might not,' said Bob. 'I'll take whatever's going.'

Andy jumped to his feet then, angry, ready to hurt, but Bob sat tight. No sense in him having a barney with Andy, not when he had the price of a pint.

'You're forgetting something else, Andy,' Grandma Patterson said.

'What?'

'Sit down and I might tell you,' said his grandmother, and Andy sat. 'That's better. She was going to marry our John. No sense in making a mystery out of it – there's his ring on her finger, and like Bob said, why should she lie?'

'I still don't see – ' said Andy.

'You wouldn't,' said Bob. 'But I do. It means she's got a right to come here.'

'It means more than that,' his grandmother said. 'It means she loved him and he loved her. It means they would have been married and had bairns by now.'

'Posh bairns in a posh school,' said Andy.

'Your nephew – or your niece mebbes,' said his grandmother. 'Wouldn't you have wanted to see them given a better start than you had?'

Stan Patterson said, 'You make charity sound like a sin, Andy. But you're wrong. Charity's a wonderful thing. Remember St Paul.'

Bob watched, and chuckled inwardly as Andy bit off his reply. Nobody could tell his father what St Paul could do, least of all in Da's own house.

'"Though I speak with the tongues of men and of angels, and have not charity, I am become as sounding brass, or a tinkling cymbal." First Book of Corinthians that is. And then a bit later on: "And now abideth faith, hope, charity, these three; but the greatest of these is charity." The *greatest*, Andy.'

His mother had sat listening as he quoted, her hands folded in her lap. 'Very nice, Stan,' she said. 'Words of comfort, which is no more than you would expect from the Bible. And being the Bible it also makes sense. The best sense yet.'

Bet said, 'We can't turn her away. We just can't.'

These were the first words she had spoken, and the whole family turned to her. She blushed, but went on: 'She was very nearly one of us. How can we tell her we don't want her?'

'That's all very well,' said Andy. 'But we're forgetting one thing.' They waited. 'How is it it took nigh on seven years for her to come and find us? And how did she know where to look?'

'She's got a tongue in her head,' said Bob. 'There's ways.'

'All right,' said Andy. 'She found us – or had us found. But why did it take so long?'

'She was ill,' his grandmother said.

'For seven years? What on earth was wrong with her?'

'Never you mind,' his grandmother said repressively, and this time it was Andy who blushed. Women's ailments were a taboo subject in the Patterson household.

'The important thing is she's all right now,' Grandma Patterson said. 'Fit and well and ready to have a look round. I've asked her to call in on us here tomorrow morning, unless anybody objects?'

She looked about her and waited, but nobody objected.

Jane was taking stock of her room. It was the best room in the house and comfortable enough, with a view of the deserted market place and the river beyond. Faintly she could hear the clang of tramcars, the rumble of an occasional horse-drawn cart. Not many motor cars. Hers was the only one in the yard of the hotel, a yard cobbled and deserted, that had once been busy with horses when the Eldon Arms had been a coaching inn, and people had posted there to make money from iron and shipping and coal. But now nobody and nothing came to Felston, money least of all. Her treatment at the reception desk had made that all too clear. The Highlanders at Lucknow could not have been made more welcome.

She had dined well enough on lobster caught that day and a chicken that had died, she thought sadly, only because of her arrival. But it was quite delicious. The coffee however was not. The hotel waiter, and the manager, who brought the brandy she asked for, tried and failed to hide their surprise at such an extraordinary guest. If it hadn't been for the money. . . . But the money, they had no doubt, was there, and perhaps for some time to come.

The telephone was housed in a sort of cupboard by the stairs, and the manager acted as telephonist. Lionel was out, which didn't surprise her, and although she longed for conversation, it wasn't yet time to talk with Sarah Watson. There was too much to explain and it was far too soon, always supposing that she would be allowed to stay. She telephoned Offley Villas instead, and Hawkins answered almost at once.

'Lady Whitcomb's residence.'

'Hawkins? This is Jane Whitcomb.'

'Yes, Miss Jane?'

'I'm just telephoning to find out if everything's all right.'

'Everything's fine, miss.'

'Cook's all right?'

'Oh yes, miss.'

'And Foch?'

'I took him out for a walk like you said, miss. And he finished off the stew we had for supper.'

Foch was all right. He was very fond of stew.

'That's good. Take care of yourself, Hawkins. And give cook my best wishes.'

'Very good, miss. Thank you. I hope you're enjoying yourself, miss.'

'Well enough,' said Jane, though 'enjoy' was not the word.

'Only it's very quiet without you, miss. The house is like a graveyard.'

'Perhaps my brother will look in on his way to Cambridge,' said Jane. 'His term must start soon.'

'Yes, miss.' Hawkins didn't sound exactly elated. 'Will you be away long, miss?'

'Not long, I hope,' said Jane, and what else could she say? For all she knew Hawkins could be packed and ready to leave. 'I'll telephone, soon. Goodbye, Hawkins.'

'À bientôt, miss.'

À bientôt? What the *hell* was Hawkins up to? She hung up, and looked at her watch. It was only just nine o'clock. As she looked the town hall clock began its slow and utterly certain chime. She would need Lionel's help to work out what to make of that town hall, she thought. It had the frontage of a palazzo, and a clock tower like a campanile. It – and the Eldon Arms – were the only evidence she had seen so far that Felston had ever known wealth. But that was not exactly true. The shipyards, the factories, the mines said it also.

She thought of the Pattersons. Grandma was the inspiration and the source of all that energy, so much was obvious. It had skipped a generation, for Stan, her son, was of a different mould. Stubborn and enduring, but slow, so slow. Not like the three grandsons, all of whom had that same restless energy, that combative quickness. John. Andy. Bob. John had wanted to improve himself, she remembered, and Andy wanted to improve the whole world – provided the world saw eye to eye with him about what constituted improvement. But who or what did Bob want to improve? Not the world. . . . Not even Felston. He wanted to leave the place. And not himself either, not in the way John had done it: night school and competitive examinations, and the ladder of progress climbed rung by rung. His *lot*, that was what Bob wanted to improve. He wanted to dance at the Café de Paris.

She looked out of the window again. Below her a lamp-lighter moved from one lamp to the next, and as he moved the gas lamps glowed. There were still people about, and from the market place she could hear a steady thumping sound that might be music.

The people on the street – Queen Street it was called, (and who could the queen be but Victoria?) – were for the most part better dressed than the ones she had seen so far, but even so they stared at her, especially the women. She would have to do something about that, but for the moment she walked along the street of uneven flagstones while the trams swayed past, and passersby stopped to stare into the windows of shops long since locked and bolted – some of them for good, she thought. On across more tramlines to a great cobbled square, with a church on one side of it, and for the rest, pubs, stacked together like the stones of a wall, for this market was near the old harbour, so the manager had told her, and a harbour meant sailors and sailors meant pubs, pubs for the kind of sailor that would never be allowed in the Eldon Arms.

By the door of one pub, the biggest, with a great flaring gas lantern of its own high above, stood the source of the music: the

Salvation Army. Two cornets, two trombones, a tuba and a drum: in a raging glory of blue and scarlet and gold. And beside them three women, equally splendid, with tambourines and poke bonnets that Lionel would have adored, and a standard bearer with the army banner. A crowd stood in front of them in two concentric semi-circles, the poor at the front, the better off further back. There could have been a fence between them she thought, and went to stand with the well-to-do because it was where she belonged. She knew her place. The standard bearer had just finished his sermon, it seemed.

'We'll have a bit of a hymn now,' he said equably. 'I know very well that's what you've come for most of you and it'll do your souls good anyway, so let's be hearing you.' And he nodded to the cornet player who seemed to be acting as leader. The music was the first sound of joy she'd heard, clear and sweet, and with the rich power that only brass can give; then suddenly the tambourines were shaken, struck, and the singing began:

> Shall we gather at the River
> Where the angel-feet have stood?
> Shall we gather at the River
> That flows by the Throne of God?

Three sopranos, the standard bearer's tenor, the drummer's bass to begin with, but soon the whole crowd was singing:

> Yes we will gather at the River,
> The beautiful, the beautiful, the River.
> Yes we will gather at the River
> That flows by the Throne of God.

They sang it quite seriously in the main, each one enjoying the opportunity to be part of such a splendid noise. Here and there she could hear a hint of exaggeration, rather too much gusto, as she had during the war near the railway stations when the soldiers waited for the time to board the train that would take them back, and the Sally Ann offered hymns and tea – and a prayer if anyone was interested. John had told her it was usually the mockers who gave most when the collecting plate came round. And there was superstition if you like: buying off a sin with silver. The hymn ended, and the crowd waited for another, but first, the standard bearer announced there would be a collection 'from those who had the money to give'. A woman with a tambourine moved among the poor, a trombonist with a cloth bag headed purposefully towards the well-to-do, and quite a few of them left – absentmindedly for the most part, though some strode off purposefully as if they'd just remembered an appointment. Those who stayed, paid up: Jane dropped a half crown into the bag, then wandered across the square as the music followed:

> Yes Jesus loves me, Yes Jesus loves me,
> Yes Jesus loves me, the Bible tells me so.

Across the cobbles she went, God at her back, and facing her, not Mammon – these men had no faith in wealth – but Reason, Justice, the Egalitarian Society. No brass bands, no military ladies with tambourines, just three men in the shabby uniform of poverty she already knew so well, grouped around a speaker. One of them was holding a banner, and holding it all wrong. It was Andy Patterson, and she knew at once that he had seen her. It was too late to move away.

She joined the crowd confronting them – if you could call it a crowd, she thought. Not much more than a handful, and nearly all of them poor. No concentric circles. The speaker was the Jewish-looking man who had directed her to John Bright Street, still bare-headed, and this time he wore no jacket, but the shirt he displayed also looked like silk. He seemed to be quoting statistics.

'The way we live is not only evil but senseless,' he was shouting. 'This world of ours is a bounteous place. There's enough for everybody – more than enough – and yet in this country alone ninety per cent of the wealth is owned by five per cent of the population. People like you die ten, fifteen years earlier than people in Mayfair – '

Except in the war, Jane thought. Then we all died together.

'Fifty times more tuberculosis, a hundred times more rickets, and a million times more malnutrition – because the rich never starve. They'd take the bread out of your mouths first – or send their servants to do it.'

The crowd stirred, but without enthusiasm. It was an old theme, and no help to them. How could the rich take the bread out of their mouths? Their mouths were empty.

From across the square the little brass band exploded into 'Onward Christian Soldiers', jaunty, triumphant, and at once a couple of spectators slipped away. The man in the silk shirt acknowledged defeat.

'Now I want you to think about what I've told you,' he said. 'That's all I ask. Just think about it. And in the meantime I'll pass you on to Comrade Patterson.'

Andy came forward at once, body thrusting towards his audience, fists clenched, like a man running to a fight. For a moment he glowered at them in silence, then his voice sounded in an effortless roar.

'You don't look as if you've got any fight left in you,' he said. 'Well I'm not surprised. You've had more than your share these last few years. Lock-outs. Strikes. Dole money. Starvation. – And none of it your fault. . . . *Well of course it wasn't.* But that doesn't make it any better. Now does it?

'And there's nowt you can do about it, I hear you say. Nowt. Not a thing – except go across the road and join the army of God over there, and promise Him you'll give up the sins of the flesh, like eating four-course meals and drinking champagne and dancing all night at the Café de Paris.'

And that's one for me, thought Jane. But she couldn't move away because to do so wouldn't be a retreat, it would be a rout.

'The remedy's in front of your eyes, but you won't see it,' said Andy. 'It's within your grasp but you won't take it.'

'Tell us then,' said a voice from the front.

'I'll be glad to. Join us. . . . Is that so difficult? Be one of us. Help us grow to a majority, an overwhelming majority, a majority so great that we take back what is ours by right. Not just a bit here and a bit there. – Everything. The whole country. The entire means of production, distribution and exchange. The lot!'

His voice grew gentle.

'Comrades I tell you,' he said, 'there's a part of that religion over there that we are proud to copy – and that is the part that the boss Christians – the ones in fancy clothes and fancy cars – have forgotten. Well they would. Of course they would. Because there's nowt in it for them. – And that's their way of life when they first started. Share and share alike, and no man, no woman, holding back. Everything for everybody. You know what we call that? From each according to his ability: to each according to his need.

'Isn't that simple? Isn't it honest? Isn't it right? No private fortunes, no grand houses and flocks of servants. None of that. All done away with. Finished. And in its place – enough for everybody – aye and more than enough – when men work out of a need to serve, and not fear of the sack. Can't you see? – When that day dawns – there'll be more for everybody: for every one of us that works and makes his contribution to the community of the workers – but none at all for the boss exploiter with his selfishness and greed – and none for his women neither with their silks and their jewels and their idle, useless lives.'

Now it really was time to go, she thought: now she knew precisely where Andy stood.

24

NEXT MORNING AFTER breakfast she went shopping. There was one store, the breakfast waitress told her, that might have the things she wanted. Otherwise it would have to be Newcastle. But the store contrived to supply her needs. She bought a suit, a dress, blouses, gloves, hats: but not stockings or shoes or underwear. She was doing this for Felston, she told herself, but not even for Felston would she give up the feel of silk against her skin, the comfort of handlasted shoes.

When she had changed she went back to John Bright Street, and this time it was Bet who opened the door for her. Her eyes went at once to her clothes, and she seemed disappointed, but conducted her to the kitchen even so. Grandma looked up from the potatoes she was peeling.

'Come a bit closer, lass,' she said, and Jane did so. Grandma smiled. 'Bought yourself new clothes, have you?'

'This morning,' said Jane.

'I liked the old ones better,' said Bet.

Jane turned to her. Bet was blushing, and looked the prettier for it. With less hardship and better food, thought Jane, she would be pretty all the time.

'I'm sorry,' Bet said. 'That was rude.'

'Not really,' said Jane. 'The other ones were nicer – but if I'm going to look round Felston these make more sense.'

'You mean – ' Bet sounded incredulous, ' – you just went into a shop and bought all that? It must have cost pounds.'

'Well – yes.'

Bet looked at her, saucer-eyed. 'Andy's right,' she said. 'You *are* rich.'

'Well what of it?' her grandmother asked.

'Nothing,' said Bet. 'Only I've never met anybody who was rich before. None of us have.'

'Well now you've had a good look at her you can help me with the potatoes,' said her grandmother. 'She's not a wild beast from the circus.'

That raised a point of etiquette. She ought to offer to help, but she'd never peeled a potato in her life. Grandma vetoed the idea at once. There was, she said, no time to teach her just then. So she watched instead as the peel came away tissue-paper thin on to the newspaper spread on the table: a trick as far beyond her reach as pulling rabbits from a hat.

'Where are the others?' she asked.

'Andy's at the library,' the old woman said, 'reading books about setting the world to rights. Stan's at the allotment.'

'Allotment?'

'Bit of ground,' said Grandma. 'Sort of a garden. He grows potatoes, onions, cabbages. Keeps him happy and keeps us fed.'

'And Bob?'

'Loafing somewhere.' The old woman sat up straight for a moment. 'He misses the printing – he was a good un at his trade they tell me. He loved it and now it's gone. We can't all be potty about putting the world to rights or growing cauliflowers, but I wish he could find something. He's ripe for mischief, that lad.'

Jane stopped for lunch, or what the Pattersons called dinner, because Grandma insisted that to do anything else would be insulting. And so she sat and waited, until one by one the men came in: first Stan, with leeks and beans and potatoes, and marigolds and sweetpeas brought, Jane was sure, because his mother had demanded them; then Bob, empty-handed and yawning, but cheered at the sight of Jane; and last of all Andy, books under his arm, head up, body forward, because he knew at once that the fight wasn't over.

'It's broth,' said Grandma. 'And don't waste your breath telling us it's too hot for broth, because that's all there is.'

It was a good broth, too. Onions and vegetables and bones and scrag, and the potatoes she had seen peeled that morning. But Grandma was right. She had been generous with the pepper, and served it piping hot. When she had finished Jane wondered if she would ever feel hungry again. The others pushed away their empty plates, and looked towards her – in gratitude, or so she thought: as if she were the reason why they had eaten so well.

Andy said, 'You'll have to excuse us, Miss Whitcomb. We realise it's not what you're used to, but we do our poor best.'

'*We?*' said Jane. 'I thought your grandmother and your sister cooked a delicious meal.'

'Now look here – ' Andy began.

'Now you be quiet,' said his grandmother. 'I've made a jelly – and we'll have a bit of peace till it's finished.' She glared at Andy, who opened his mouth. 'Now mind, I mean it,' she said, and her grandson shrugged and was silent.

From the street there came an odd, wailing sound that some-how seemed to promise delight rather than pain.

'What on earth – ' Jane said.

'Ice cream that'll be,' said Bob. 'Crespo's Neapolitan Ices. They're good an' all.'

'Couldn't we have some?' said Jane. 'They'd be nice with jelly.'

The silence seemed to reach out to punish her.

'What I mean,' she said, 'was that you've been so kind. If I buy the ice cream it gives me a chance to say thank you.'

'No,' said Andy.

'But whyever not?'

'You wouldn't behave like that in London.'

'In London I'd send flowers,' said Jane. 'It just seemed that ice cream might be more sensible. And anyway your father's just brought the most marvellous marigolds and sweetpeas.'

'And nobody can eat *them*,' grandma said. 'Take the basin, Bet. Fetch some ice cream – if Jane'll give you the money.'

'How much?' Jane asked.

'A tanner.'

'Sixpence?' Jane opened her bag and offered the coin, careful not to offer more. Bet took it and was gone.

'Is he in the street?' Jane asked. 'The ice-cream seller?'

'Back lane,' said Bob. 'Look out the window and you'll see him.'

She looked, and saw a little, two-wheeled cart that held a white-painted tub with a brass lid. The cart was pulled by a piebald pony, and driven by a fat, sallow man with a flopping moustache who from time to time called out that weird, encouraging cry.

'Fascinating,' she said.

'You mean you've never seen that before?'

It was Bob who spoke.

'Of course she hasn't,' Andy said. 'Miss Whitcomb's a lady. She's never seen a back lane in her life.'

'She hasn't missed all that much,' said Bob.

Grandma said, 'It's time she did see a back lane or two.'

'Where's the sense?' said Andy.

'We went into that yesterday,' said his grandmother. 'If she doesn't see for herself she'll never believe what *I* tell her.'

'No reason why she should,' said Andy. 'It's none of her business.'

His grandmother sighed. 'I was thinking you might show her round,' she said. 'There's no one knows this place like you do.'

'You thought wrong.'

'Then it'll have to be Bob,' said their grandmother, and Bet came in with the ice cream.

'Bob?' said Andy. 'What does he know?'

'He knows where the hardship is,' said his grandmother.

'He couldn't know much else; not in Felston,' Andy said. 'But does he know how to cure it?'

'You think you're the only one knows that? You and Manny Mendel?'

'We *do* know,' said Andy. 'And if the rest of you would learn we could *do* something.'

'Manny Mendel,' said Jane. 'Is he the one who was with you last night? The one who directed me here?'

'That's him.'

'You had a good go at me last night,' she said.

'Did you?' Grandma Patterson turned on Andy, ready to let fly.

'Not her personally,' said Andy. 'She was just a representative of her class.'

'Idle and useless,' Jane quoted.

'Aye. I said that.' Andy was still unperturbed.

'You had no right,' said Stan. 'She's our guest here.'

'No bourgeois is *my* guest,' said Andy.

'Idle and useless.' Jane stuck to her point. 'Well sometimes I am and sometimes I'm not. I don't think I was useless when I drove an ambulance.'

'I wouldn't know,' said Andy. 'I wasn't in the war.'

'Why not?'

'I was on me holidays,' said Andy. 'In Durham Gaol.'

'Conchy,' said Bob.

'And was Mr Mendel a conscientious objector too?'

'No, he was in France,' said Andy. 'He hated it.'

'Not many of us didn't. Is he *very* rich?'

'Manny? He's secretary of Felston Labour Party. He'd do better on the dole.'

'He dresses rather well, wouldn't you say? For a poor man? Silk jackets. Silk shirts. And those shoes he wore last night – they could do with a cleaning but they were made by hand – by some poor exploited worker, no doubt.'

Andy said nothing, and the others watched in silence.

'And his cuff-links,' Jane continued. 'Real gold were they? Paid for by exploitation to satisfy selfishness and greed? Those *were* your words. A typical bourgeois, Mr Mendel. Surely. And has *he* ever come to this house at your invitation?'

'He has,' said Andy. 'Though why I should answer your questions I'm damned if I know.'

'I'll have no language,' said Stan, and when his son made no answer: 'I'm talking to you, Andy.'

'All right. I'm sorry,' said Andy. 'But she's got no call to talk about Manny – '

'She?' said his grandmother. 'She? And who is "she" when she's at home? Where's your manners?'

'I left them at the shipyard gates last time they paid us off,' said Andy. 'Along with my illusions.'

Bob's head nodded. It was if if he were watching a fist fight, thought Jane, and acknowledging a good punch landing square.

'And where did Mr Mendel leave his?' she asked.

Andy shrugged. 'It's true his parents have a bit of money,' he said.

'A bit?' Bob's voice was mocking. 'His da owns a wholesale tailoring factory – the only place round here that's open full-time – so he doesn't exactly have to pay union rates, does he?'

'That's his da,' said Andy. 'Manny isn't like that.'

'Left the fold, has he? Or been thrown out, perhaps?' asked Jane.

'No,' Andy said. 'Neither. You know what Jews are like when it comes to family.'

'And not just Jews,' said his father.

'Personally he admires them,' said Andy. 'But politically – he knows they're wrong. Knows they're bound to fail for that matter, the way the whole rotten system will fail.'

'So he's a worker?'

But Andy's dogged honesty would not accept that.

'He's never worked,' he said. 'Not like us. He's an intellectual.'

According to Cuthbert Pardoe, that made him a second-class revolutionary at best.

'University man?'

'Manchester. He studied history.'

'And his parents paid? Really Andy – he's no better than I am.' Bob chuckled.

'Oh yes he is,' said Andy. 'He believes in what we're doing.'

'But so might I – if you'd give me the chance to find out.' Andy said nothing. 'Is it because I'm a woman?'

'Of course not.' He looked and sounded outraged, but Jane thought that perhaps he might be lying, even if he were unaware of the fact.

So it was Bob who acted as her guide to Felston. Queen Street she knew, with its shops and cinemas and theatre, all somehow clinging on to life, and the town hall she knew, and the tram sheds, and the grim, well-scrubbed poverty of John Bright Street. Bob was to show her better – and worse. Better, far better, was Westburn Village, the suburb where the wealthy lived; neat, Georgian houses for the doctors and lawyers and works managers. Comfort marooned in poverty, she thought. Gentility shut in on itself, like some little station in an Indian state, where the sahibs entertained each other to dinner in strict rotation, and listened to gramophone records of shows long forgotten elsewhere.

'Do the Mendels live here?' Jane asked.

'That big one there,' Bob said, and nodded to a sturdy piece of Georgian brick: solid and enduring: set in a couple of acres or thereabouts: neat lawns and flower-beds, a tennis court with fading lines.

'Three of them,' said Bob. 'In *that*. . . . Not counting the servants, of course.' Then he disconcerted her by adding, 'Man it must be marvellous.'

Jane said severely, 'Now let's look at the worst,' and he smiled at her the way John used to smile, when she'd wanted to be serious and he'd needed her laughter.

The worst was very bad, as bad as anything she had seen in India. Courts and places and lanes that straggled up from the river in clumsy sweeps and inclines, and the older they were, the worse they were. At last they had to leave the car, and Bob struck a bargain with a man who lounged nearby to guard it. Bob settled for sixpence, and the man spoke quickly in the dialect that Jane found so hard to understand.

'For a tanner he'll watch it all day,' said Bob. 'He was wondering if you were from the council.'

'Why should I be?'

'Folks in cars that comes round here has to be from the council,' said Bob. 'They're the only ones who'd bother. He says if you're going to condemn any houses you can start with his.'

Jane walked down the steps and looked about her and could sense the despair all around. Dwellings in the last stages of dilapidation, broken windows patched with cardboard, no paint, no polish, no gleaming doorsteps; several of the houses leaned out of the vertical, slum towers of Pisa: one was even shored up by a baulk of timber that looked as if it were worth more than the house.

'You'd think it had been shelled,' she said.

'From what chaps that were in the war tell me, the Germans would have been more thorough,' said Bob.

All around the tenements, men and women, children too young – or too old – for school, were looking at them. They too wore the uniform of the poor, but this was a battalion that had been defeated once too often. They would never stand and fight again. Dirty, stinking, ragged. But what could you expect, Bob asked her, with one stand-pipe to a yard and an outside privy with no flush toilet? He looked at them with pity, but with interest too, as if they were some sort of a show, thought Jane. Near-human creatures that could never quite achieve humanity: chimpanzees in a cage waiting for food that never came. . . . A rat appeared from nowhere, snatched up a piece of cabbage stalk and disappeared down a gap in a crumbling wall.

'I bet it makes a change from Mayfair,' said Bob.

'Just a bit. I have to ask them some questions,' said Jane.

'They'll be a bit shy,' said Bob.

'But why on earth should they?'

'The only ones that comes asking questions is the Guardians. The Poor Law, you know. And they only come to see if they've got any money to stop out of their dole.'

'But how could they have money?'

'The man from the Guardians isn't paid to ask how, he's paid to look,' said Bob. 'Because if he didn't look he might get the sack and be like them. But you're too well-dressed for the Guardians. They'll think you've come to condemn their houses.'

'Surely they'd be glad if I were?'

'All right in the summer, mebbe. They could sleep on the beach. But what about the winter?'

'They wouldn't get somewhere else?'

'Not unless they can pay for it. And all this lot can afford is a slum.'

'Would they talk if you ask them?'

'Yes, of course,' said Bob. 'Might cost you half a dollar.' He saw her bewilderment. 'Half a crown.'

'All right.' She gave him one, then went back to the car. Its guardian still stood by. He was gaunt with undernourishment, she noticed, but shaven and clean, his boots were brushed. As he came towards her Jane saw that he limped as he walked.

'All present and correct, miss,' he said.

From a distance a group of children watched and waited.

'Thank you,' said Jane. 'I wouldn't want the paintwork damaged.'

'No miss,' said the man. 'She's a nice job.' He moved back to take in the Riley's splendour.

'You were in the army, weren't you?' Jane asked.

The man smiled. 'No prizes for guessing. It's my gammy leg, isn't it? Name of Laidlaw, miss. I was a corporal in the Royal Northumbrians.'

'I knew someone in that regiment,' said Jane.

'Half our street was in it,' the man said. 'The half that wasn't in the navy.'

'His name was Captain Patterson,' said Jane. 'He commanded B Company. Did you know him?'

'I was D Company,' Laidlaw said. 'Captain White. I don't

think – wait a minute. He was killed, wasn't he? Just before the Armistice?'

'That's right.'

'And he lived round here?'

'When he was younger. John Bright Street.'

'Bit better than this, John Bright Street.'

'Yes,' said Jane. 'It is. I'm – anxious to help the people round here.'

'Yes miss?'

I'm going too fast, she thought. The shutter's just dropped with a clang.

'There's a group of people in London,' she said, lying furiously – but at least there would be soon – 'Sort of a charitable trust. They want to help people in places like this. Only first we need to have the facts.'

'Facts, miss?'

'Housing conditions, health, diseases,' she said. 'Is there any-where I can get any information? I suppose the town hall – '

'Them,' said Laidlaw. 'They wouldn't tell you the time of day. Stobbs and Messeter, miss.'

'I beg your pardon?'

'It's a report: *Felston* – by Stobbs and Messeter. You'll get it at the public library.'

He waved his hand and limped away as Bob came up. With him was a stunted man, a woman she took to be his mother and a cluster of children, one of whom looked ill indeed, too ill to walk.

'This is Mr Richardson,' said Bob, 'and his wife. He's Albert – she's Nan. The bairns are Frank and Les and Maude.'

If one judges by the age of the children, Mrs Richardson can be very little older than I am, thought Jane. She looks fifty at least. And her daughter seems very ill.

'You shouldn't have brought the girl,' she said aloud. 'She's exhausted.'

'She wouldn't be left,' said Bob. 'She wanted to see you close to.'

Maude could have been twelve, thought Jane. She looked up at Jane through blue eyes made big by the pinched and hungry face, her gaze devouring the make-up, the clothes, the neatly tended hair. Health and wealth together in one body.

'Ask your questions,' Bob said, and she did so, and at times Bob acted as interpreter as she fitted the pieces together. Man, woman and children shared one room, one bed. The room cost five shillings a week, on the occasions when they had five shillings. They lived mostly on bread and jam and weak tea – and fish if Albert managed to get a place in a boat, and broth when they could afford vegetables and bones. Albert hadn't worked in three years, and now he didn't even bother trying. The dole was starvation, but it was all there was. None of them had ever had a proper bath, or even seen one, except at the pictures, and Maude had pulmonary tuberculosis. Both parents were sure that she would die of it, and were equally sure that there was nothing they could do about it. The questions ended at last, and Bob handed over the half crown and they left.

'What will they do with it?' Jane asked.

'Eat if they've got sense; drink if they haven't.' As they watched the little girl was racked by a fit of coughing.

'There's a lot worse off than me,' said Bob. 'Wouldn't you say?'

'How on earth do you manage?' Jane asked.

'Blowed if I know,' said Bob. 'But I do.'

Mind your own business, Jane Whitcomb.

They drove to the public library, where 'Stobbs and Messeter', stencilled on cheap paper, was available price sixpence, Proceeds in Aid of the Shoeless Children's Fund. She took Bob back to John Bright Street, then returned to the Eldon Arms for tea.

Tea was in the lounge, which looked, thought Jane, like a room hired for a funeral where the corpse had only just been taken out to the hearse. Dark blue carpets, dark blue curtains more than half drawn, artificial flowers grey with dust. . . . She entered on tiptoe, and a waitress took her order for tea and biscuits. She gave it in a whisper.

It was a big room, not quite empty. In a far corner, beneath potted palms huddled like relatives waiting for the will, two men and a woman were taking tea, and doing it in style. Sandwiches, cream cakes, some kind of tart. One of the men wasn't eating much. It was Andy's friend Mendel, she noticed. The other two tucked in with good appetite. They had to be his parents. Their talk, which had been loud when she entered, had diminished to whispers, the hissing kind used when one had to conduct one's quarrels in public, but then her tea arrived and it was too late to leave.

Stobbs and Messeter believed in realism. Their prose was simple, their message plain, and there were graphs and charts to underline the message. Felston's casualty rate was the equivalent of a battalion in the Lines: at Loos say, or Ypres. If something didn't happen soon the battalion would be at the Somme. But here it was mostly the very young and the ageing (ageing meant fifty, sixty meant old), who suffered most, though tuberculosis attacked at any age, and childbirth too demanded its share. Malnutrition and rickets, scarlet fever and pneumonia, operations that succeeded and patients who died because they were too undernourished to heal, and the old ones who died just because they were cold and there was no way to make them warm. . . .

'You find it interesting?'

Jane looked up at Manny Mendel. Today a suit of light material, she noticed, and a tie.

'Horrifying,' she said.

He nodded. 'Stobbs and Messeter know how to diagnose,' he said. 'It's cures they find difficult. They just won't see it.'

'See what?'

'That there's only one way.'

'Your way? And Andy's? Oh – my name's Jane Whitcomb, by the by.'

'Mendel. Manny Mendel. My way and Andy's, that's right. . . . I sent you to him.'

'So you did. You saved me a lot of trouble.'

'You. . . . Yes. . . . Andy, I'm not so sure. You worry him, Miss Whitcomb.'

'He worries about many things, Mr Mendel. And with reason. He has absolutely no cause to worry about me.'

From the doorway the elder Mendel called out to his son.

'Excuse me,' Mendel said. 'I have to go.'

Over the pamphlet she watched him leave, mother and father moving in close to protect him. He'd been talking to a Gentile woman, which was bad, thought Jane, and what was worse – *she'd been smoking a cigarette.*

25

S HE WAS GOING through the pamphlet again when someone
else came in: a man in a grey suit, white shirt and a tie, the
complete uniform of the businessman in summer fatigues, but
ruddy-faced and heavy-shouldered as a farmer. He carried a
whisky and soda and came straight up to Jane.

'Do forgive me,' he said. 'But Nellie told me you were reading
our little effort and I hope you won't mind if I ask what you
make of it?'

'Nellie?' said Jane.

'The waitress. She helps in the bar as well.' He lifted his glass.

Clipped white moustache, Jane noticed. Very clever and rather
bloodshot grey eyes. He looked like a colleague of Papa's they
had met once in Nagpur, but the voice was different. This wasn't
a sahib's voice – or a servant's. If such a thing were possible, his
voice was classless.

'I'm Dr Stobbs. Frank Stobbs. I wrote that piece with Canon
Messeter. Do tell me what you make of it.'

'It's like the blueprint of a nightmare,' said Jane. 'I'd no
idea – '

'So many of us don't,' said Dr Stobbs. 'Up on a visit, are you?'

'Oh,' said Jane. 'Excuse me. My name is Jane Whitcomb.'

She offered her hand and Stobbs took it warily, as if he had
to think hard to remember how the trick was done.

'I suppose you could say I'm here on a visit,' she said, and
looked at the ring on the third finger of her left hand. There
could be no denying it, nor did she wish to do so.

'I was engaged to a man who once lived here,' she said. 'He was killed in the war. I suddenly had this urge to see what the place was like.'

'And now you know.'

'Dear God yes,' she said.

'May I ask – what was your fiancé's name?'

'John Patterson,' she said.

He thought for a moment. 'Don't know him,' he said at last. 'I know an Andrew Patterson – '

'His brother,' said Jane. 'But my John doesn't belong here.'

'Because he's dead you mean?'

'And so escaped from Felston? No. When you die, you escape from rather more than Felston. John had made his escape long before.'

'Like me,' said Dr Stobbs. 'But I came back.'

'But why – ?'

'My father was a ship's captain,' said Dr Stobbs. 'What they call a master mariner round here. He saw I had a few brains and sent me off to the grammar school at Newcastle, and from there to London because I wanted to be a doctor. My father thought that no man in his right mind would ever want to be anything but a sailor – but he'd decided I was a madman long before, so it didn't matter.'

'And your mother?'

'She was proud of me – and prouder still when I qualified, – and just about ready to burst when I set up in Harley Street.'

'You specialised?'

'Certainly. A lot of chaps seem to think you can only find gold in South Africa or the Yukon, but don't you believe it. The rest of London may not be paved with gold, but Harley Street is. Appendixes. . . . That's what made me. His late majesty King Edward VII had had his out not long before, and by the time I came along the queue was round the block. It was snip snip snip and fancy stitching right up to the war.'

'And then?'

'RAMC,' said Dr Stobbs. 'Advanced Field Dressing Station. It was just as well I'd kept my general surgery up to date as well.'

'You served for long?'

'Four years,' said Dr Stobbs, 'but I was lucky. Not a scratch. . . . Not like my dad. He'd retired, but he went back as soon as he was needed. Torpedoed in the Atlantic second voyage. But I came back.'

'Here?'

'Harley Street. Appendixes were still popular. And then my mother died. Cancer. I watched her but I couldn't help her.' The sharp grey eyes looked more closely at Jane. 'You've seen it too?'

'Yes.'

'Ghastly, isn't it? And yet Messeter still goes on about God. . . . But once my mother died – in her home in Westburn Village – you know – where you were earlier in your car – '

'How did you know that?' asked Jane.

'Felston's a shocking place for gossip – the biggest village in the world the locals call it – and there isn't much gossip escapes the doctor. Anyway, when my mother died I took a walk round the town – just as you did this afternoon round Crawford's Buildings – and I ran across Messeter trying to set a broken wrist for a child who had fallen off a coal cart – trying to steal coal, most likely. They can't help it, poor little devils – not in the winter. But there was Messeter with an old ruler and some rags and not an idea in his head – him being a parson – so I did it for him and one thing led to another and we've been here ever since. We run a clinic.'

'It must keep you busy.'

Dr Stobbs smiled. 'Full-time job. Trouble is, Messeter's away just now.'

'Oh,' said Jane. 'Why is that?'

'It's a damn nuisance, but his doctor says he's been overworking. He has to rest.'

Jane had the feeling that she was being gently but very efficiently backed into a corner.

'And does Mr Messeter – '

'Canon Messeter.'

'Does he have a good doctor?'

'Of course he does,' said Dr Stobbs. 'It's me.'

'Can't you get another parson?'

'He's more than that,' said Dr Stobbs. 'He's auxiliary nurse and cook when there's nobody else, and clerk and storeman and ambulance driver.'

'Oh,' said Jane. 'I see.' And then: 'Dr Stobbs – who told you that I had driven an ambulance?'

'You know how these things get about,' Dr Stobbs tried and failed to look guileless.

'No,' said Jane affably. 'I'm afraid I don't. Do tell me.'

Dr Stobbs finished his whisky, and tugged at a bell pull.

'Well as I understand it,' he said, 'one of the Patterson lads was in the Ring of Bells last night and somebody happened to ask him who the posh lady was that came calling. But please don't ask me who "somebody" was. I don't know and it isn't relevant.'

'Then I won't,' said Jane.

'But the barmaid at the Ring of Bells is Elsie Edwards, and her sister's eldest had tonsilitis – I took them out last week. She brought him in this morning for me to see how he was getting on and she just happened to mention – '

'I see,' said Jane. 'And I suppose it was ex-Corporal Laidlaw of the Royal Northumbrians who told you about my visit to Crawford's Buildings.'

'What makes you think so?'

'He told me about your pamphlet.'

'You're no fool, Miss Whitcomb,' said Dr Stobbs.

'No,' said Jane. 'I'm an ex-ambulance driver.'

Nellie came in, and Dr Stobbs ordered another whisky and soda, and sherry for Jane.

'Smart chap, Laidlaw,' he said when Nellie had gone. 'He just happened to say you'd been to Westburn Village, too.'

'I congratulate you on your intelligence service,' said Jane.

'It's efficient,' Dr Stobbs said, 'because it has to be. There are still far too many people who are afraid to come to me, so when I hear about them, I have to go to them.'

'Why won't they come to you?' Jane asked.

'Because the damn fools are afraid that I'll charge them money.'

'And you don't? Not ever?'

'What would be the point?' said Dr Stobbs. 'They haven't got any.'

'But how on earth do you manage?' asked Jane.

'We shame people into helping us.'

Nellie came back with the drinks, and Dr Stobbs paid, and was silent until she had gone, then: 'Now the point is this,' he said. 'We have an ambulance and you are an ambulance driver.'

'I *was* an ambulance driver,' said Jane.

'You can't expect me to believe that you've forgotten how to do it. And anyway it isn't precisely an ambulance. Not *specifically* an ambulance, I should say.'

'And what is it specifically?'

'A motor car. An Armstrong-Siddeley, as a matter of fact.'

'The large one?'

'The very largest, according to Messeter. Odd, really. He bought it when he rarely drove anybody but himself.'

'It seats five?'

'Good Lord no,' said Dr Stobbs. 'Eight at least.' He went into his old duffer act, which would have been so much more effective had his eyes not been so clever. 'It has to, you see.'

'And I am to drive it?'

'If you would be so kind. But only for a few days. I shall have a relief driver next week.'

'Does he know it yet?' said Jane, and Dr Stobbs chuckled.

Jane lifted her glass. 'I drink to you, Doctor,' she said. 'I do indeed. . . . And I'll start tomorrow.'

It *was* the biggest Armstrong-Siddeley, and a pig to drive, which was what she had expected. Nothing wrong with it precisely, just heavy and awkward. What it really needed was a man of Bob's size at least. But Dr Stobbs was right about one thing: it could hold eight people, if some were children and almost all were undernourished.

She drove about Felston and scooped up the people on the list that Dr Stobbs gave her, and discovered that Dr Stobbs was right. Most of them didn't want to come, but all of them did, because they were terrified of Dr Stobbs, and having seen him in a rage the fact did not surprise her. To help her find her way and lift the ones who couldn't walk she had Bob to help her. For money. She had insisted on that. Not that Bob had needed any persuasion. Ten bob a day and not a word to the man from the Guardians, he settled for. It was too much – but oh how he looked like John.

Dr Stobbs's clinic was in an old, decaying mansion by the riverside. Here he and Messeter lived and ate and worked together in rooms panelled with worm-eaten oak, plastered ceilings that seemed forever about to collapse, an elegant, fast-rotting staircase of carved mahogany. Jane asked him about it on the second day.

Dr Stobbs looked at the house as a king might look at his palace.

'There was money here once,' he said. 'All built out of coal this little lot.'

'I doubt if you'll have it much longer,' said Jane.

'You're wrong,' said Stobbs. 'I can make this place last as long as I need it. I've got plumbers and bricklayers and carpenters any time I want them.'

'Then why not rebuild the place?'

'Because then I'd have to pay rates,' said Stobbs, 'and where's the sense in that? No. This place is safe enough – just about. But it doesn't look safe.'

And it didn't.

'But if it looks unsafe shouldn't the corporation demolish it?'

'Of course they should,' said Dr Stobbs, 'but how can they? They'd have to turn me out, and my patients. Not to mention Messeter. Look good at election time, wouldn't it? Vote for the men who turned the sick and afflicted out on to the streets.' He turned to the nurse who waited beside them. 'I'll see the little lad with the earache now,' he said.

That was another thing, thought Jane. Dr Stobbs always had nurses, relays of them, all efficient, all highly trained. Most of them spoke better English, all were better nourished, than the people they treated. She supposed that it must be the doctor's favourite weapon – shame. He had other helpers too. Platoons of women who appeared like genies from bottles, women who brought buckets and brooms and scrubbing brushes; women in the uniform of the good poor, fanatic in their devotion to cleanliness. They scrubbed and polished the crumbling ruin till it gleamed.

'All the same,' Jane said to Bob, 'if he's got a house in Westburn Village I don't see why he doesn't use it. He'll have to pay rates on it anyway.'

Bob chuckled. 'One of the nurses was telling me about that,' he said. 'He rents his house out and gets money for the clinic, and also he goes round his posh neighbours with a collecting box. Lets them know what'll happen if they don't cough up.'

'And what will happen?'

'He'll get rid of his lodgers and put the clinic in there. Westburn Village invaded by scruffs and beggars, TB and body lice. And all of it catching. The toffs'd sooner pay up. Every time.'

Jane chuckled. 'What now?'

'Lord Nelson Street. A chap with some kind of a cough it says here.'

What the chap had got was the effects of a lifetime in the coal mines. He was a big chap too, with a body so exhausted that he couldn't even walk to the car. Bob had to go out to recruit another two men to help Jane and the man's wife and himself load him into the Armstrong-Siddeley.

At the end of it all, Jane found that she was trembling from the effects of sheer, physical effort, as she had not done since the war. Bob looked at her.

'You're not built for the job,' he said, 'and them blokes was very near useless. Not their fault, mind you. There's no strength left in them.'

Jane waited till the trembling ceased and drove to the clinic.

When they got there, they had to call in Dr Stobbs to help with the lifting, and the nurse on duty looked shocked. *Doctors do not help with the lifting.* But Stobbs had to, or leave the patient in the car. Somehow between them they got him out and stretched him on a bed in what had once been the house's dining room. The man wheezed and gasped as they lifted him, and strange bubbling noises came from his chest, like the sound of a vat in which cider was fermenting.

'It's George Habbershaw, isn't it?' Dr Stobbs asked.

The man gasped and made the strange, bubbling noise, and his wife had to answer for him.

'That's right, doctor.'

'Been seeing me off and on for three years now, haven't you George?'

Habbershaw settled for a nod of the head, and Stobbs turned to Jane.

'He's got a form of pneumoconiosis,' Stobbs said. 'Too much coal dust and not enough filtered air in the pit where he worked. Too much coal dust up here come to that. I spoke for him at his compensation case. How much did I get you?'

'Twenty-two shillings a week, doctor.' It was the wife who answered.

'Better than the dole – but not all that much – not when you need eggs and milk and a lot of expensive treatment and a holiday in Switzerland. And so three months ago you got worse. Right, George?'

Again Habbershaw nodded.

'So I went to court again and told a few truths and a lot of lies. Right?'

'Yes, Doctor,' Mrs Habbershaw said.

'And I got his money up to twenty-five bob and a lump sum of fifty pounds. *Fifty pounds.*'

He glared at Jane, who recognised her cue.

'That's a lot of money, Dr Stobbs,' she said.

'It is indeed, Miss Whitcomb. A hell of a lot for an idle, time-wasting, good-for-nothing I wouldn't trust with fifty pennies – not to mention the lies I told.'

The big man on the bed wheezed and gasped, his breath bubbled, until at last he said, 'No lies.'

'Don't you contradict me, you lying, conniving, useless lump of sub-humanity. You wretched, foolish, surplus-to-requirement Neanderthal – '

'No lies,' the big man wheezed again. 'I was poorly. Still am.'

'Certainly you are,' said Dr Stobbs. 'In fact you're worse than you were when you went to court. At least you could sit up then. Now why are you worse, George Habbershaw?'

After a struggle the big man managed the one word, 'Dust.'

'Dust be damned,' said Stobbs. 'There's no more dust in you now than there was three months ago. But a lot more fibrosis. Inflammation's up too, by the look of you.'

His hand moved, quickly and accurately to Habbershaw's coat pocket, and came out holding a packet of cigarettes and a box of matches.

'Wild Woodbinitis,' said Dr Stobbs. 'That's what's wrong with you. Cough cough cough. Tobacco smoke mixed in with the dust to give it a bit of help. And you Mrs Habbershaw – ' he turned on the woman. 'You went out and bought them for him.'

'I never,' said the woman. 'Honest, Doctor.'

'Who was it then?' Dr Stobbs asked. 'Santa Claus?'

'Marrer,' the big man gasped. 'Me marrer got us them.'

'Marrer means friend among miners,' Stobbs told Jane, then returned to Habbershaw. 'A fine friend you had to bring you the means of killing yourself. And I've no doubt you gave him a few coppers for his trouble? Why didn't you tell him to fetch you a cut-throat razor or a loaded revolver while you were at it?' He turned to the woman. 'Is he eating much?'

'He can't,' said the woman. 'Not with all that coughing. He manages a bit broth and a custard. Stuff he can drink.'

'Stuff he can drink,' Dr Stobbs echoed. 'Stuff you can get at the Ring of Bells and the Boilermakers' Arms and the Durham Ox – eh, George Habbershaw?' He waited for an answer, and waved the woman to silence.

'I might have had the odd one,' Habbershaw managed at last.

'The odd one? Man you were infesting the pubs the way rats infest sewers. When you couldn't walk you had yourself carried by those wonderful marrers of yours.'

'No!' This time it was a yell: a great cry of fear thought Jane: fear of what had been, and even more of what was still to come.

'It's "Yes" and I can prove it's "Yes",' said Dr Stobbs. 'Why do you think I had you brought here – to look at your shining, rosy face – the picture of health? To feast my eyes on your happy, smiling wife, singing away because she hasn't a care in the world? I'll take no more "Noes" from you, George Habbershaw.'

'Bit of company,' Habbershaw wheezed. 'A man needs a bit o' company.'

'A man?' said Dr Stobbs. 'Call yourself a man?' His voice slashed Habbershaw's self-esteem to shreds. 'Drinking the money I lied to get for you? Oh yes – you were every bit as ill as I said you were – no disputing that, but they asked me if you were doing everything you should to help yourself and I said "Yes". And if there's a God in heaven as Canon Messeter says, there goes my chance of salvation.

'You were smoking then and you were boozing then, and damn me if you're not smoking and boozing now – on the days when you've got strength enough to swallow. Do you imagine that's why I committed perjury? Do you?'

'No, Doctor,' Habbershaw gasped.

'That's one "No" I'll accept. I did it for that wife of yours and those children of yours so that they can have a little bit put by when the twenty-five shillings a week stops, and that won't be long now – will it George? Not at the rate you're going.'

'I'm bad then?'

'You're killing yourself,' said Dr Stobbs. 'With the help of your marrers of course.'

'What if I gave up the drink? And the smokes? Will I still die?'

'We all die,' said Dr Stobbs, 'but if you die teetotal you'll last a bit longer. I'll tell you how much longer after I've examined you.'

'All right,' Habbershaw wheezed, and then: 'Who shopped us, Doctor?'

'Shopped you?' Dr Stobbs roared. 'It was common knowledge, you cretinous hominid. Birds fly. Fish swim. George Habbershaw goes on the beer. Watching you carried home was a show for the whole street.' He turned to the woman. 'You'd better wait outside, you and the others while I take a look at him,' he said, then threw the cigarettes and matches to Bob, who fielded them neatly. 'Compliments of George Habbershaw,' said Dr Stobbs.

They went outside, to a cup of hot, sweet tea for Mrs Habbershaw, and a yawning wait for Jane. Bob offered her a Woodbine, but she declined. She could still hear Habbershaw's cough. Soon it would be time to take Habbershaw home, and then she would be finished for the day. A bath, she thought, after a nurse had checked her hair for nits. She herself would take care of the search for fleas. She looked at her hands that were grimy and beginning to blister. She really was back with the Ambulance Service.

When at last she had finished, Dr Stobbs was still writing up case notes. 'Same time tomorrow?' she asked him. Stobbs grunted and continued to write.

'Habbershaw wasn't any lighter going back,' she said, and Stobbs looked up.

'That's the beer,' he said. 'Beer and no exercise. What he eats wouldn't fatten a flea.'

'He's still heavy.' He sat still, waiting. 'I can't understand why you didn't go to him,' she said. 'I could have driven you.'

'He wouldn't have let me in,' said Stobbs.

'But he came here.'

'In a posh car,' said Stobbs. 'Carried on a stretcher. Making a lot of fuss. Driven by a lady. Of *course* he came here. There's not much in life he enjoys. He enjoyed that.'

'He enjoys beer.'

'Not any more,' said Stobbs. 'His life isn't much, but *he* thinks it is. I've frightened him off. Besides, his wife and children will need what's left more than the brewers. . . . Good night.'

'Not yet.' He sighed, and laid down the pen. 'I didn't mind lifting Habbershaw,' said Jane. 'It isn't that.'

'What then?'

'I'm not very good at it,' she said. 'I never will be. Any more than I was good at getting an eight-stone woman down three flights of stairs. You need stretcher bearers – ambulance men. Fellows with a bit of muscle.'

'Of course I do,' said Stobbs. 'I also need an operating theatre and an X-ray machine and a couple of Jersey cows. And there's only one reason why I haven't got them. There isn't the money. And anyway the fellers round here don't *have* muscles. Not any more. Not on their diet.'

'You've got a kitchen in here with water and electricity,' said Jane. 'It's got a kitchen range as well, but Bella tells me it's useless.'

'Bella?'

'The Queen of your Harem,' said Jane. 'The one who organises all the cleaners.'

'Oh. . . . Mrs Docherty.'

'That's the one. She used to be a cook in service. What that kitchen needs is a modern stove.'

'And what I need is a hundred thousand pounds,' said Stobbs. 'One's just about as likely as the other.'

'I'll buy the stove.'

Stobbs put down his pen. 'Why should you do that?'

'So that Mrs Docherty can cook meals for your coolies and keep their strength up.'

'They'd want paying.'

'Not if you fed them,' said Jane. 'They'd be queueing up.'

'There'd be food to pay for.'

'I'd pay for that, too. Bob Patterson's grandmother is the shrewdest person I've met round here. I'll arrange things with her. She and Bella will take care of things between them.'

'Under my direction?'

'Of course. I'll leave enough to feed the harem, too. We can't have the men eating while all the women do is watch. Not even in Felston.'

Dr Stobbs said genially, 'You know I'm glad you're not here

for long. Damn glad. It's not that I don't like your ideas, but if you were here a month I get the feeling I'd be working for you, and we'd neither of us like that.'

'I'll speak to Mrs Patterson,' said Jane.

'And Mrs Docherty?'

'I've already spoken to her. She says she can't wait to start.'

Dr Stobbs opened his mouth to yell, then burst out laughing instead.

26

GRANDMA PATTERSON LIKED the idea, but then Jane had been quite sure she would. It appealed to her every instinct: her quickness, her need to organise, her compassion – and her bossiness.

'Broth,' she said, as soon as Jane had finished. 'That's what we'll have for a start. It's cheap and filling – and it does you good an' all.'

'Have you met Mrs Docherty?' asked Jane.

'No,' said Grandma, 'but if you're happy with her she'll know what she's doing. We'll get on fine.'

Her son said, 'Docherty? She'll be a Catholic, likely.' He sounded uneasy.

'She'll be the cook,' said his mother firmly. 'Just like I'll be the supplier.' Then after a pause she added: 'Fish on a Friday?'

'Almost certainly,' said Jane. 'Is it cheap?'

'It will be where I'll go,' the old woman said. 'My – I'm really looking foward to this.'

It was Jane who formally introduced Grandma Patterson to Bella Docherty. There could have been nothing like it, she thought, since Queen Victoria met the Empress Eugénie, and Grandma Patterson was in no doubt which one of them was Queen Victoria. Even so, thought Jane, they got on surprisingly well, largely because they shared a contempt for the male sex that was almost total, including as it did men like Dr Stobbs, who did their best, which was no excuse. They settled down to a pleasurable and exhaustive discussion of the inadequacies of the male, and provided a list of dishes almost as a postscript:

broth, Irish stew, baked herrings, oven-bottom cake, and something called pan haggerty. Jane made a silent vow that she must, very soon, taste pan haggerty, if only to find out what it was.

Andy disapproved because it was charity, but then she had been sure he would.

'Don't you be so sure,' said Bob. 'Not till you've tried humping a twelve-and-a-half-stone man on a stretcher.'

'That isn't the point,' said Andy.

'It is when there's only two of you to lift him. Right, Miss Whitcomb?'

'We had to send out for help,' said Jane.

'No question,' said Bob. 'It wasn't all that easy even with four. A bowl of broth's not all that much for work like that.'

'It's still charity,' Andy said.

'It's commonsense,' said Jane. 'To do work like that you have to be properly fed – and the sick have to be healed, after all.'

'Do they?'

'But surely – ' said Jane.

'Healed for what, Miss Whitcomb? To get better again so they can go back on the dole in Felston?'

'But if there's no alternative – '

'Who says there isn't?' said Andy. 'They can protest, can't they? They can march and demonstrate.'

'The police and the special constables, and the mayor reading the riot act,' said Stan. 'That's where demonstrations get you. We saw it in the market place two years back, remember? That time the seamen were out and the ship owners brought in blacklegs.'

'Nowt wrong with demonstrating for your rights,' said Andy.

'Not even when you lose?' said Bob. 'The sailors lost that day, I remember. You could see the blood in the gutter.'

'That's enough,' Grandma Patterson said. 'Miss Whitcomb's only trying to do us a good turn, and if we're not grateful for that we should be.'

'Gran, I understand that,' said Andy. 'Honestly I do. But what *you* don't seem to understand – any of you – is that charity only makes you more dependent. Charity's never more than just enough to keep you alive – why should it be? – but as long as it's there folks accept it, and because they accept it they won't fight.'

'For a feller that was a conscientious objector you talk a lot about fighting,' said his father.

'That war was for the bosses,' said Andy. 'I wouldn't fight for them. But for my family, my friends, my union, my class – I'd fight for them all right. By God I would.'

'And what's more if you fought as well as you take the name of the Lord in vain you'd win,' said his father.

'I'm sorry, Da,' Andy said. But – '

'And so am I,' his father said. 'But it's the Lord you should apologise to.'

Andy walked out.

'Where's he off to this time?' said Bob.

'Off for a word with Manny Mendel,' said his father. 'Doing a bit of staff work for the Workers' Armageddon.'

'That's not very nice, our Stan,' said his mother.

'No Mam,' he said. 'I know it's not. But I've only one other cheek to turn.' He looked towards his younger son. 'Fancy a walk, Bob?'

'Suits me,' said Bob. 'Not too far, mind. I've a day's work to do tomorrow. How about taking a look at the Mafeking Hall? I hear the Colliery Band's rehearsing.'

'I'll put my boots on,' said his father. 'I've got nowt against music properly played. . . . Good night, Miss Whitcomb.'

'Oh please,' said Jane. 'I think it would be better if you called me Jane.'

'Would it?' said Stan. 'I'll have to think about that.' But his son had no such hesitations.

'Good night, Jane,' said Bob.

'Impudent thing,' said Grandma automatically, but without rancour. 'Still, you can see the sense in it.'

'What's the Mafeking Hall?' Jane asked.

Bet looked astounded that anyone should be ignorant of the Mafeking Hall. 'Why – there's everything there,' she said. 'Concerts, leek shows, pantomimes.'

'Sort of a Welfare Hall,' said her grandmother. 'Where folks can have a bit of a get-together. Though how they managed these days I'm blest if I know.'

'Short of money?'

'Like everything else in Felston.' She smiled, ruefully. 'Sorry, pet. Money's the only song I sing these days.'

Bet said, 'Now they're all out can I have a word with – Jane? You said I could.'

A grown woman, thought Jane. Long past her majority. But still Gran's word was law.

'There's nowt to stop you,' said Grandma. 'If she's a mind to.'

'Of course,' said Jane.

'In the bedroom,' said Bet. 'Please.'

Jane followed her into the bedroom. A double bed, and a vast wardrobe that seemed somehow uneasy in such a small room, the cheapest of dressing tables, neatly painted white, and a couple of small, hard chairs. Above one side of the bed was a page torn from a magazine and framed in passe-partout, a photograph of a mannequin in a gown that looked like Lanvin. Bet followed her gaze. 'That's my side,' she said.

'I beg your pardon?'

'My side,' Bet said again. 'Of the bed. I share with Grandma.'

'Oh,' said Jane. 'I see.'

'Sit down please,' said Bet. 'If you wouldn't mind.'

'Of course not.' Jane sat. 'What can I do for you?'

'It's about – about face cream and that. Make-up.'

'What about it?'

'I'm twenty-four,' said Bet. 'I reckon at my age I'm entitled to use it.'

Twenty-four. I'm eight years older than she, thought Jane – and I look eight years younger.

'Of course you are,' she said.

'Gran says she wouldn't object – not if there was money coming in. And I doubt if me dad would even notice. And as for Bob and Andy, it's none of their business.'

'Then why don't you do it?'

'I don't know how,' said Bet. 'I was hoping you could teach me. You always look so nice. I mean that suit you wore when you first came – '

'You liked it?'

'I loved it. Best clothes I ever saw.'

Nothing wrong with your taste, thought Jane, and said aloud, 'Would you like it? To keep, I mean?'

'Oh,' said Bet. 'Oh no, miss. I mean Jane. I couldn't.'

'Whyever not?'

'It doesn't belong,' said Bet. 'I'm not being silly. Honest . . . I don't mean I *shouldn't* have it. I mean I *can't*.'

'I still don't understand,' said Jane.

'How could I go about dressed like that when every other woman in the street dresses like this?'

She swept her hand down the front of her old and fading dress.

'You could say you bought it in a jumble sale.'

'Even if they believed me they wouldn't forgive me,' said Bet. 'It's – it's just too much, that suit. Like a bit of heaven.'

'Then take this one,' said Jane. 'I bought it in Queen Street. Don't tell me you couldn't have found that in a jumble sale?'

'I don't want you to give me things – ' said Bet.

'Not even if I want to give them?'

'Just tell me about make-up.'

'Very well,' said Jane, and opened her bag. 'Let's have a look at you. You've a lovely skin, thank heaven. That's half the battle won already.'

'That's as maybe,' said Bet, 'but when you're after a chap – claes like yours would be better.'

'Claes?' said Lionel.

'It means clothes,' said Jane. 'Sort of a dialect word.'

'Their dialect is very broad, I guess,' said Bower.

'Almost incomprehensible,' said Jane, and stirred her coffee.

Jay Bower dropping in like this was a nuisance in a way. Lionel had invited her to lunch because he was *almost* certain he'd found her a house, and at the end of lunch Bower had dropped in and demanded coffee and asked endless questions about Felston. Definitely a nuisance, except that she had found in herself this deep need, this compulsion even, to talk about Felston, and the horror and pity it awoke in her.

'Different landscape, different language,' said Bower. 'Creatures of another country?'

'It would be easier if one could believe it, but I can't,' said Jane.

'Was there nothing pleasant there?' Lionel asked.

She thought for a moment. 'There was a beach that was quite beautiful,' she said.

'A plage do you mean?' asked Lionel. 'Deauville? Cap d'Antibes? That sort of thing?'

She could see the beach quite clearly: the sand of palest gold, the high cliffs flecked with lichen, the bottle-green sea that even on the calmest day showed fast-darting whitecaps. And all so cold, even in summer.

'More beautiful,' she said.

'And no one goes there?' Bower asked.

He was wrong. The poor went there, as they went everywhere: to scavenge for driftwood, sea coal, coins if they were lucky. The poor were very seldom lucky.

'It's cold,' she said, 'even when the sun shines. And no one has the money for pleasure.'

'I have to know more about this,' said Bower. 'Come back to Fleet Street with me.'

'No.' Now was not the time. It was all too close, too real. 'I have an engagement – with Lionel.'

'Something important?'

'I think so.'

Near the Brompton Road. . . . A divine little terrace, just off Thurloe Square. Harrods virtually on your doorstep, my dear. Not cheap, of course. I should be very suspicious if it were cheap. But I shall not allow you to be robbed.

'It could be very important,' said Jane.

'This evening, then. Come and dine with me this evening.'

'You seem in rather a hurry,' Lionel said.

'I always am,' said Bower. 'It's the only way I can work. It's the only way a newspaper gets published, for that matter.' He turned to Jane. 'Café de Paris suit you?'

He got up then, and Lionel rang for Pott to show him to the door, then smiled at Jane.

'Too exhausting,' he said. 'Do you think you could stand a whole evening with him à deux? And what possible connection does he hope to make between you and the newspaper business?'

'I'll tell you tomorrow,' said Jane. 'Now I want to hear about the house.'

But they went to see it instead: the tall, narrow house on a corner, with a garden of lime trees and rose bushes, and inside enough room, more than enough, but never too much. Dining room and drawing room and book room, two bedrooms – (Quite sufficient, said Lionel. For once inside a house like this, no guest would ever want to leave). And a bathroom that he knew he could convert into something positively sybaritic. Heliogabalus himself would feel at home there.

The house was empty of course, and the floor boards creaked, the sun sought out the dust: but the rooms were light and gracefully proportioned, the house itself an elegant, up-ended box of Georgian brick. Aunt Pen's furniture would fit in awfully well, but she would have some modern pieces too. Lionel couldn't monopolise London's art-deco furniture completely.

'Certainly not,' said Lionel. 'And we must have a look at new fabrics too. Lady Lessing cannot be allowed to possess the monopoly of Bakst designs either.'

'Bakst? In a house?'

'Bakst.' Lionel was firm. 'Discreetly but inevitably. Now. . . . Is there anything else you would care to see?'

'I don't think so,' said Jane.

'The servants' quarters perhaps?'

'Oh my God.' Jane's hands went to her face. 'After all my fine talk of Felston. It was just – '

'The taste of freedom?'

'Exactly that,' said Jane. And so it had been, but it was a poor excuse.

The kitchen was roomy and well enough lit but the stove would have to go, said Lionel. The kind of cook he had in mind would never tolerate such an ageing monstrosity. Scullery and pantry as they should be, tradesmen's entrance in good repair. At the top of the house the servants' rooms, that seemed all right, so Jane supposed, but how was she to know? The only way was to show them to Hawkins and accept her judgement.

It couldn't be the Café de Paris she decided, not that night, and telephoned Bower to tell him so. She could stand up to an encounter with a discarded lordling – English *or* foreign – and even if she couldn't, Bower could. It wasn't that. What she couldn't stand was the thought of Bob listening in on his crystal set up there in Felston. It would have to be somewhere else. In fact the Café de Paris had been Bower's first choice.

'What's wrong with it?' he asked.

'Too loud. I thought we were going to talk.'

It was a reason that made sense to him.

'We can't go to the Embassy,' he said. 'Not on a Thursday. The Prince of Wales will be there and we don't want him to think the press is spying on him. I know it sounds banal, – but what about the Savoy? Pick you up at eight thirty?'

'I'll look forward to it,' she said, and was reasonably sure that she spoke the truth.

27

SHE HAD A fire lit in her bedroom – extra work, but Hawkins was all in favour. And this time she allowed Hawkins to help her dress: a gown by Paquin, of a warm, almost glowing pink and cut loose. Too loose, she had thought, but Aunt Pen had been sure she would grow into it, and she'd been right. Prescience, it must have been. Was that the word? Foreknowledge. Just the sort of thing Aunt Pen would be good at. Anyway the dress didn't hang on her like a sack any more, but went out and in precisely where it should. Soon it would be time to say 'no' to potatoes.

Hawkins loved the dress and said so, and Jane welcomed her approval. More and more she was beginning to appreciate Hawkins's intelligence. The maid began to brush her hair, and Jane told her about the new house.

'South Kensington, miss?' said Hawkins. She sounded dubious.

'I honestly think we could call it Knightsbridge,' said Jane.

'And would you still want to take me with you?' Hawkins asked.

'Of course,' said Jane. 'If you still want to come.' And then, before Hawkins could speak: 'Best wait till you see it.'

Then she sat in the drawing room and waited for Bower. She had no doubt that he would be prompt, and how right she was. The clock was still chiming as his chauffeur knocked. Hawkins helped her on with her cloak, then opened the door.

'Au revoir, miss,' said Hawkins.

'Hasta luego,' said Jane.

For once Hawkins looked puzzled, and not before time.

The chauffeur's presence meant that she was on parade, thought Jane, and was glad that she had chosen the Paquin dress (smart but not *too* revealing) and at the last moment pinned on the Cartier leopardess. It was unlikely that any other woman would be wearing such a thing, even at the Savoy.

She got in beside Bower, and the scent of Roger et Gallet cologne and Havana cigars. He made no move to come closer to her, nor had she expected it. Instead he at once began to talk politics: Gandhi and self-government in India – and why the British couldn't hope to prevent it (because they weren't tough enough): this guy Mussolini who everybody said would stop the Reds (but what was the point when he behaved just like them?): and why the Prince of Wales should get married (the popular press needed the story. The pictures alone . . .). They had got on to the subject of the Little Man's latest mistress and why they always had to be so goddam mature when the car pulled up and the doorman came scurrying. And two nights before this she had been eating fish and chips at Dr Stobbs's clinic.

When the champagne had been tested and approved, Bower said: 'Now I think *you* should talk for a while.'

'My innings? Is that what you mean?'

'Of course not.' He gestured impatiently: she had made a remark unworthy of her, it seemed. 'Tell me some more about Felston.'

'But why on earth should I?'

'Because I want to know.'

She gave him a kindly look, one modelled on that used by Vinney when she was about to correct a lack of manners.

'First you're supposed to ask me to dance, you know,' she said.

He glared at her, then threw back his head and laughed.

'May I have the pleasure of this dance, Miss Whitcomb?' he said.

'But of course,' said Jane.

He was no Lionel, but aeons ahead of Cuthbert Pardoe, and his presence on the dance floor set up a buzzing like bees.

When they had eaten and the coffee arrived, Jane said, 'Please smoke a cigar if you wish,' and this time he grinned at her, a grin of simple pleasure in her company. When the cigar was drawing easily she asked, 'What would you like to know about Felston? I don't have too many statistics. I did get hold of a pamphlet, but it's at home somewhere.'

'Not statistics,' Bower said. 'What I want is a story. An anecdote.'

She thought for a moment, then said, 'George Colley.'

'What about him?'

'He's a dustman now, but ten years ago he was Private Colley in the Tyneside Highlanders.'

'You mean he wore a kilt?'

'Just like all the others,' said Jane. 'He fought at Passchendaele.'

'Otherwise known as the third Battle of Ypres,' said Bower. 'I somehow get the idea this isn't going to be a very happy story.'

'I forgot,' said Jane. 'You were there too. I don't have to tell you what it was like.'

'It was hell,' said Bower.

'Private Colley thought so. He wasn't a very religious man, but he knew hell when he saw it. . . . He'd served eighteen months by then. Once promoted to lance-corporal, once reduced to the ranks for drunkenness. On the other hand he'd won himself a Military Medal for rescuing an officer under fire.'

'Not much of a story so far,' said Bower.

She looked at him. He was perfectly serious: a news editor rebuking a junior reporter.

'I think you'll find it gets better,' she said, ' – or at any rate more interesting.

'On 10th August, 1917, he and his platoon were in a communications trench moving up to attack, when the trench received a direct hit from a shell. Private Colley was buried alive, covered in mud and what was left of his comrades. He lay upon the body of his closest friend. The body was headless. On top of him was his corporal who was dying, and screaming as he did so. When they dug Colley out he was unmarked, so of course he was simply transferred to another platoon that was short of men. They gave him rum in his tea that night, and he slept well, moved up with the others, ready to attack. Another communications trench, another platoon, another shell: the mixture precisely as before, except that this time he was buried for rather longer. – His battalion had gone into the attack. There was no

– 278 –

one to spare to hunt for Private Colley. This time when they brought him out he was quite mad.'

'You don't surprise me.'

'Only he didn't stay that way. He recovered in a month, returned to his battalion, finished his war and went back to his dustcart. When I asked him how he'd done it he said, "I had a wife and a bairn, miss – bairn means child – and another on the way."'

'A man of strong will,' said Bower.

'Perhaps even a fortunate man,' said Jane. 'But not entirely. The madness came back from time to time – mostly in nightmares. But he and his wife and children have learned to live with it. He has a job, you see.'

'A job is that important?'

'A job in Felston is life itself.'

'Even collecting other peoples' dust.' Bower examined the ash on his cigar, and decided to let it stay for a while. 'And how did you come to meet him?'

'I'd been having lunch with a friend.'

Baked herrings – again – and home-baked bread, and Dr Stobbs writing up case notes as he ate.

'When it was over I was going back to the car we used to bring patients to our clinic – '

'Sounds like another story,' said Bower.

'Perhaps. Let me finish this one first. I took a short cut to the car down a lane behind the house – what they call a back lane – and George Colley was going by with his dustcart.

'A child – a girl of about ten I suppose – had got one of those rattles, the kind that makes a noise like a corncrake. You swing them and they make a rattling sound very fast. You know.'

'I know,' said Bower. 'Swing it really hard and it could be a machine gun you're hearing.'

'Exactly,' said Jane. 'It was a machine gun that Private Colley heard. He was out of that dustcart and under it in about three seconds, and on the way down he'd collected a spade from the side of the cart and was there under cover, holding the spade like a rifle. It was – you may find this ridiculous – but it was rather beautiful to watch.'

'Not ridiculous at all,' said Bower. 'Extraordinary though. That you should see it – and remember.'

'Like an athlete,' she said. 'So quick. So elegant. So perfect. There in place, armed and ready – except that there was no enemy.'

'This cart?' Bower asked. 'What about the motor?'

'The motor was a Clydesdale mare called Mavis,' said Jane. 'Chestnut. Twenty-three hands at least. When Private Colley stopped, she stopped. We females have some sense.'

'So what did *you* do, being female and sensible?'

'I gave the little girl tuppence to fetch a man I know – an ex-corporal called Laidlaw who helps in the clinic – and told her there'd be another tuppence when she brought him. I even showed her the other two pennies. After all, she's a sensible female too. When I got under the cart beside Private Colley and said, "That was a close one." And he looked at me and said, "What in the name of God is a woman doing here?"'

'I said, "Driving an ambulance. What else would a woman be doing here? Now stay still. Our relief is coming."'

'And was it?' Bower asked.

'Of course,' said Jane. 'The little girl had come for her extra tuppence, and brought my friend Laidlaw, and a doctor called Stobbs. I told them both what had happened, and they talked him out in the language of Passchendaele because they'd both been there, and for a while it was 1917.'

'And then?'

'Suddenly George Colley said, "I'm being barmy, I know that. I'll be all right if I can have a bit of a lie-down but I have to take the horse and cart back – I've finished my shift. Trouble is I'm that tired." And he leaned against the wall of a yard and closed his eyes and slept.'

'So your friend Laidlaw took the dustcart back?'

'No,' said Jane. 'I did.'

'You?'

'Well of course me,' said Jane. 'Laidlaw had never handled a horse in his life – nor had Dr Stobbs. But Mavis and I got on very well. Two sensible females.'

'And George Colley?'

'Had a nap and a cup of tea at the clinic and went back to his wife and bairns. . . . Oh listen, they're playing a Charleston. I *adore* the Charleston.'

He got up and danced well enough to escape censure. When they sat down again he said, 'You told that well.'

'Thank you.'

'Do you think you could write it?'

'Write it?' said Jane. 'Why on earth should I? I'm not nearly old enough to be thinking of my memoirs. You're not very flattering.'

'I want you to write it as a feature for the *Daily World*,' said Bower. 'You won't get it right first time, – nobody does; but you'll soon get the hang of it.'

'But why should you want to print a story about Felston?'

'What I was looking for was a story about poverty.'

'Then I chose the right place.'

'Sure you did. But I also needed an angle. An attention grabber.'

'And you think you've got one?'

'Certainly I have,' said Bower. 'You. . . . You and Felston. A diamond among the coals.'

'I see,' said Jane. The idea revolted her, but she couldn't just abandon it. Not yet. 'And *why* do you want to print my story?'

'Because poverty's going to be fashionable,' said Bower. 'Not just poverty. The workers, the class war, Socialism. All that.'

'And you care about it?'

'Of course I care,' Bower said. 'It'll sell newspapers.'

'Oh I see,' said Jane, and indeed she did. 'And if I wrote this piece for you, would I be paid?'

'Certainly,' said Bower. 'Going rate. That's ten guineas for a thousand words – even if you are a beginner.'

'Then I'll do it,' said Jane, 'on one condition.'

'I better warn you,' said Bower. 'The editor's decision is final.'

'Well of course,' she said. 'All I want you to do is say in your newspaper that the ten guineas goes to the Felston Relief Fund.'

'I've never heard of it,' said Bower.

'That's because I've just opened it,' said Jane.

'And how are you going to organise it?'

'I'm not going to organise it,' said Jane. 'I'm simply going to ask people for money and pass it on to a man I know in Felston. A doctor.'

'Are you going to ask me for money?'

'Of course.'

'How much?'

'All you can spare. After all, you're the richest man I know.'

'I'll give you some,' said Bower. 'And some free advice. Plus your writing fee. Aren't I generous?'

'Depends how much you give. Let's have the advice.'

'Get yourself talked about. That way Felston will be talked about too.'

'And how do I do that?'

'You've a brother at Cambridge,' said Bower. 'Go and talk about it there. See if they can't discuss Felston in that debating society of theirs.'

'The Cambridge Union?'

'That's the one. If they do, the Oxford Union's bound to follow and then maybe some of the other newspapers will take it up. Then when you ask people for money they'll be bound to give because you're a celebrity. Would you like to dance again?'

'No thank you,' said Jane. 'But I must say you asked me very nicely. To the manner born, almost.'

Once more he gave her that friendly, almost conspiratorial grin.

'I think I may want you to go to Paris,' he said, 'if your article works out.'

'But why on earth should I?'

'Partly for Felston,' he said, 'but mostly for yourself. Save it for now, humh?'

She saved it, but she was curious. Any woman would have been.

Next morning there were letters: bills for the most part, and a postcard from Mummy: a picture of Bombay. 'Miss Gwatkin remains garrulous,' Mummy wrote, 'despite the heat, but the motion of the ship is soothing. I find that I think of Papa more often than I could wish.' There was a letter from Jabber's secretary too. Dr Lockhart would like to see her at her earliest convenience. Her ear-rings were ready, too. Jane telephoned Jabber's rooms and made an appointment, then rang for Hawkins.

'I think perhaps we should look at the house in South Terrace this morning, unless you've made other plans?' she said.

'None, miss.'

Jane was relieved, yet perhaps disappointed also, that Hawkins spoke in English.

'I want to call at Bond Street first,' she said, 'but it won't take long. We'll have to take Foch, I'm afraid.'

'Be a pleasure, miss,' said Hawkins. 'We get on very well, Foch and me. Foch and I, I should say.'

And it seemed that they did, though whether this was due to approval on Foch's part for self-improvement, or a sure source of extra stew, Jane was not sure. She and Foch had celebrated their reunion immediately on her return. Now he had reverted to his more formal manner, but consented to be squashed between two women with reasonable grace.

Hawkins accompanied them into the jeweller's shop. She had always wanted to see inside a shop like that, she said, but had never had the nerve. Once inside she stood deferentially by Jane and a little to one side, but her eyes, Jane was sure, took in everything. The assistant brought out the ear-rings. They were for evening wear, each of two stones, one beneath the other, and set in platinum.

'Very nice,' said Jane, and turned to Hawkins. 'What do you think?'

'They're lovely, miss,' said Hawkins. There could be no doubt that she meant it.

From the West End they drove to South Terrace, and this time they were met by a man from an estate agency. Somehow Lionel had managed to avoid his services, but Jane was not so fortunate. Round the garden they went, and then from room to room, from basement to attics, while the estate agent's man chanted his litany of praise; a remorseless flow that even Miss Gwatkin might have envied. When they had done, he asked if she had questions, and Jane turned to Hawkins.

'Have you?' she asked.

'I should just think I have, miss,' said Hawkins.

'Go ahead and ask them,' said Jane. 'Foch and I will wait in the garden. The sun is still quite warm.' Foch quite liked the house, she knew, but was even more pleased with the garden, not so much because of the sunlight, as because of the shade of the lime trees. A compromise, as usual. Jane thought that perhaps she was rather good at compromises, but that Hawkins was not: at least not with estate agents. At last Hawkins emerged to prove her right. The estate agent followed her, thoroughly cowed, and it was Hawkins who did the talking. The estate agent lifted his hat to Jane, then left, not quite running, but walking very briskly indeed when one considered the mildness of the weather.

'What *did* you say to the poor man?' Jane asked.

'Told him about the stove, miss.'

'Yes. Mr Warley spotted that.'

'Also the broken sash cords and the crack in the servants' washbasin and that bit of parquet near the garden window that needs renewing. And that loose moulding in the second bedroom and the light switch on the second landing and the radiator going rusty in the dining room.'

She didn't ask if Mr Warley had spotted them, too. She didn't have to.

'And what did the man say?'

'Said he'd report it, miss. I told him to look sharp about it. Not that he'll have it seen to, but it should bring the price down a bit.'

'You seem to have impressed him very much,' said Jane.

'I think he sort of got the idea that I was your adviser, miss,' said Hawkins.

'It's an idea I seem to have got, too.'

Hawkins said, 'Yes miss,' and left it at that.

'Shall I take it?' said Jane. 'I rather liked the central heating.'

'The last lot who had it were Americans, miss,' said Hawkins. 'Still, it'll come in handy in the winter.'

Jane took this for consent.

'What staff shall I need?' she asked.

'Well there's me,' said Hawkins, 'and I'll need a girl under me – a house that size. And we'll need a cook and a kitchenmaid and a jobbing gardener part-time and a couple of charwomen for the rough, and that's about it, miss. Always assuming we use the steam laundry.'

'Oh I'm sure we will,' said Jane. 'Poor part-time gardener and so many women. . . . There's no bath for the servants.'

'No miss,' said Hawkins.

'We'll have to have one fitted.'

'You mean a real bath – with taps and hot water?'

Jane thought of the zinc tubs in Felston that the miners used, laboriously filled with hot water boiled in pans on the fire.

'Of course,' she said.

'Golly, miss,' said Hawkins.

28

LUNCHTIME BROUGHT A note from Bower. He had a cheque for the Felston Fund as he called it, and looked forward to presenting it to her that evening over dinner at Ciro's. If it was convenient there was no need for her to reply. He would pick her up at eight thirty. He doesn't say how much, thought Jane, but it's bound to be pretty decent, then took Foch to call on Lockhart. He ought to be good for at least a guinea.

For once in his life Jabber acted as if he were angry with her. Well perhaps not that, exactly – Jane doubted if he could ever be really angry with anybody – but nervous and distressed. He sat her down, gave her a cigarette, then went to the window.

'You've been away,' he said.

'Certainly,' said Jane. 'You sent me. Don't you remember?'

'So I did,' he said. 'You're saying it's my fault, and of course you're very probably right – '

'Fault?' she said. 'You talk as if it had all gone wrong. But it didn't. Honestly. *Dear* Jabber – I had a wonderful time.'

'No more dreams?' She shook her head. 'No screaming?'

'Of course not. What on earth is this all about?'

'I had a letter from a colleague of mine. We both had consulting rooms in the same house years ago. He sent me some case notes. A man called Colley.'

'Dr Stobbs,' she said. 'You've heard from Dr Stobbs. But I thought he only took out appendixes in Harley Street.'

'So he did,' said Lockhart, 'but he was a damn good doctor and a very bright man, and what I was doing fascinated him. So when he treated Colley – you and he together I should say – he thought I might be interested, and wrote to tell me about it. Colley's an interesting case, of course – '

'Because of the way he can control it?'

'I doubt if it's control exactly. But yes. And he asked for my advice and of course I've given it, but that isn't the point.'

'What is then?'

'You,' said Lockhart.

'*Me?*'

'Stobbs doesn't know about our professional relationship of course – and he most certainly doesn't know, anyway from me – that you had been ill. But it seems the whole town knows it.'

'Knows that I was mad?'

'We had agreed you wouldn't say that – '

'I'm sorry,' said Jane.

'And anyway they have no idea of the exact nature of your illness. They think it was – '

'Was what?'

'Stobbs said the people he talked to got extraordinarily coy when he tried to pin them down. The best he could get was something they called women's problems.'

So Grandma had not betrayed her. But she must have said something to Bet and Bob and Andy and Stan. . . . It must have been Andy. She was sure of it.

Aloud she said, 'So that's all right then?'

'Is it? You've made yourself quite a reputation in Felston. Up to your old tricks. Driving an ambulance. Just like the war.'

'Making myself useful.'

'*Exactly* like the war. And getting mixed up in poverty and degradation. Trying to help a man who suffered as you suffered – '

'I didn't try. I succeeded. And anyway why shouldn't I?'

Lockhart said, 'I'll tell you. Because that man could drag you back into your nightmares. And not just him. *All* the things you're doing – '

'All I did was help Dr Stobbs.'

'And involve yourself in poverty and grief. Work too hard and worry too much and suffer because the people you help are suffering. It won't do, Jane.'

'*Won't do?*'

'I have to tell you this,' said Lockhart. 'What you are doing is as near as it's possible to get to what you did in the war – and in the end it almost destroyed you. It could do so again. And I sent you up there because I thought it might distract you, God help me.'

'There is one difference,' said Jane. 'John is dead.'

'He's all around you up there,' said Lockhart. 'Stobbs told me that, too. Just as he told me that you'll be going back there. Will you?'

'I must,' said Jane. 'Don't you see? It's *because* John's all around me there. I have no choice. . . .'

And not just John. Grandma and Dr Stobbs and Laidlaw and Bella Docherty. All of them. Waiting for her and needing her, and the money she could raise.

Lockhart sighed, 'All right,' he said. 'Stobbs said you were a marvellous help up there, and Stobbs didn't use words like "marvellous" for less than a fifty-guinea fee, not when I knew him. So he values your help. Of course he does. I know you. If you give at all you'll give the lot. But I really must warn you. If you go over again, you may not find it possible to come back.'

'Private Colley came back,' she said.

'And he's more important than you?'

'Not on his own,' she said. 'But put them all together – of course they're more important than me.'

'Then I wish you luck,' he said.

'But don't go crying to Jabber if things go wrong?'

'No!' He strode from the window and stood in front of her, glowering down into her face. Foch growled, disturbed, but her eyes still on Lockhart she touched the dog and he was silent. 'Of course come crying to Jabber,' he said. 'That's what I'm here for. I thought you knew that.'

The Erté dress again, she thought, because it really was her best and she was going to need all the money she could get – and looking her best would certainly help with *that*. Jabber had coughed up five guineas, which was really rather decent of him. He wasn't exactly rolling in riches and never would be – far too nice to drum his patients, so that really five pounds five shillings was awfully decent.

She examined the dress for marks and stains, found none, and began to ponder the fact that Jabber, Dr J.A.B. Lockhart, was very much in love with her. Never mind how, never mind why.

She just knew for a fact that he was, and that she didn't care for him at all, not in 'that way'. That's how one put it when one didn't want to be vulgar. Not in that way: i.e. she didn't want to go to bed with him. She didn't have to, either. Couldn't. What with the Hippocratic oath and all that. But sooner or later she'd want to go to bed with somebody, and what price Felston then? In the meantime she had to get her hands on a lot of money. Aunt Pen's wouldn't support Felston single-handed, and anyway that wasn't why Aunt Pen had left it to her. Other people would have to fork out too: and so she chose the Erté dress. It was nice to know that Lockhart was in love with her, but all she could do was feel sorry for him, and what was the use of that? The doorbell rang and it was Bower, punctual as always, but this time without his chauffeur.

The Erté dress was much admired, which was what it was for, that and arousing the envy of other women perhaps.

'But you aren't wearing your leopard,' said Bower.

'Leopardess – or so I'm told. No. She's having a night off.'

'You feel safe without her then?'

'The question doesn't arise,' said Jane. 'There just wasn't anywhere practical to pin her.'

'How on earth can you look and talk like that and spend time in Felston?' said Bower.

'That's simply asking how can I be Jane Whitcomb,' said Jane. 'But I manage it – and without undue difficulty most of the time.' Then the band played 'My Blue Heaven' and they danced.

They danced rather a lot, and there was rather a lot of champagne, and very little further talk of Felston, except for a brisk five minutes' cross-examination on the progress of her article. In fact there had been none, but she couldn't tell Bower that, not when she was after his money.

'I finished it,' she said, 'but the style was too florid so I tore it up. I didn't want to waste your time.'

'You were probably right,' he said, 'but I want to see something soon. Newspapers never wait. It's the one thing they can't do for you.' The band played 'Tea For Two'. They took to the floor again and Georgina Payne danced by her, in a blue dress so unsuitable Jane knew at once that it had belonged to someone else. The man holding her, and delighted to be doing so, was Michael Browne, sober this time, but still in his ancient dress-suit.

When they were seated once more, Georgina looked across to

Jane, a look that to a woman was as obvious as a firework display, but to a man non-existent. Obediently Jane followed the blonde girl to the powder-room, which was empty except for a fat girl sobbing in a corner while the attendant hovered with eau de cologne.

'What on earth – ' said Jane.

'Too many Manhattans probably.' Georgina sat at the mirror, took out powder compact and puff, and examined her complexion pitilessly. She could well afford to, thought Jane, as she joined her. Georgina's complexion was flawless.

'I love your dress,' said Georgina. 'Poiret?'

'You're close,' said Jane. 'It's Erté. . . . It would look wonderful on you.'

'Better than this, you mean?' said Georgina. 'It's borrowed. But of course you'll have guessed that anyway. I hadn't a thing to wear that I hadn't worn five hundred times already. It's different for men. Mike still goes around in that dreadful old ruin of a suit he bought before the war, and people merely think he's eccentric. Which is true enough, I suppose. He sold a drawing last week, which is why we're here. Celebrating.'

'I'm glad for you,' said Jane.

'Are you?' said Georgina. 'You never came to see me. After you *promised*.'

Jane decided that this time it was Miss Payne's turn to be not quite sober, and wondered how Michael Browne would cope.

'I've been away,' she said, 'for rather a long while. But I'll call on you soon. I promise.'

'Oh how gorgeous,' said Georgina. 'Now promise me again – you won't forget. Has Bower got his chauffeur with him?'

Jane separated the sentences.

'I won't forget,' she said. 'Bower drove me here himself.'

'I've never been one of Bower's girls,' said Georgina, 'apart from parties and things, but from what I hear – no chauffeur is a bad sign. Unless you think it's a good sign, of course.'

'I'm obliged to you,' said Jane, and rose to her feet. 'Ready?'

'You go back without me,' said Georgina. 'We don't want the chaps to think we've been talking. And in any case, a little pause for quiet reflection would do me no harm at all.'

Jane went back. The wine waiter had poured more champagne, but she wasn't with Cuthbert Pardoe after all: she didn't *have* to get sloshed. Instead, she sipped.

'Dessert?' Bower asked.

'Strawberries please, and lots of cream. I'll starve tomorrow.'

Bower gave the order. 'How's the fund doing?' he asked.

'It isn't,' said Jane, then remembered Lockhart. 'Well only just. I'm relying on you to really get things going.'

'Split infinitive,' said Bower.

'Which just goes to show how much I mean it,' said Jane. 'And in front of my publisher too.'

'Don't be too sure,' said Bower. 'I never buy until I've seen the goods.'

'Very wise,' said Jane. 'I'm rather that way myself.'

He looked at her; waited until the strawberries were gone. Her champagne glass was almost full, but she made no move to reach for it.

'Shall I take you home now?'

'Unless you would like to dance some more.'

'No more dancing.'

The flirting stage it seemed was over. 'Then home it must be.'

'Coffee,' he said. 'I forgot coffee.'

'I feel no need for it,' she said. 'And if you're feeling tired – '

'I am *not* tired.' He took a folded piece of paper from his wallet and passed it to her. It was a cheque for five hundred pounds.

'That's for Felston,' he said. 'No strings and no provisos.'

'You mean you'll still pay me for my article?'

'Well of course I will,' he said. 'If it's any good. But that isn't it. What I mean is that money's for your charity and I want you to have it because I believe it's a good thing and it sure won't hurt the paper – '

'Altruism like yours is so rare these days.'

'Now you just stop that,' said Bower amiably. 'And never let me catch you using that word when you're writing for me. Even the people who know what it means don't like to see it. They're afraid it might be catching. . . . That cheque's for your fund, OK? It's over and finished with, no matter what.'

'I understand,' said Jane, who understood not at all.

'Fine,' said Bower. 'Now when I said I was ready to take you home I meant that too, but I didn't necessarily mean your home.'

Now she understood. He looked at her closely. That he was a clever man she had never doubted, but that look told her he was a perceptive one too.

'I guess I'm rushing things,' he said.

Cuthbert Pardoe, Jabber Lockhart, and now Bower. Things were certainly looking up, even if she had turned down two lordlings.

'Just a bit,' she said.

'You're a very attractive woman,' said Bower. 'I don't believe for a minute you realise just how attractive you are – and that's part of it.' He signalled for his bill.

'You can sit in the back if you like,' said Bower.

'What nonsense,' said Jane, and got in beside him. On the way home Bower talked of Russia and the gold standard and whether Winston Churchill had a future, until Jane interrupted to say that it all sounded terribly worthy and informative, but she'd much sooner hear about Hollywood. So then he told her about Charlie Chaplin, and Douglas Fairbanks and Mary Pickford, and Clara Bow, all of whom he knew: talking about them as if they all lived just round the next corner, and to drop in on them for a drink would be the most natural thing in the world.

'How marvellous to know them like that,' she said.

'Marvellous? I never thought so, but maybe you're right. They're in the marvel business after all. The best thing is for you to meet them and judge for yourself.'

'You think I will?'

'Oh sure,' he said. 'It may take a little time, that's all.'

Then he pulled up at her door, and leaned across and kissed her, a smooth and easy flow of the body of a kind she'd seen a hundred times at the cinema, or what he would call the movies.

His lips were gentle, and there was no pawing. Really a most civilised embrace, she thought, and found her arms wanted to be around his neck as she thought it.

'I'll ask again,' Jay Bower said. 'Maybe not tomorrow, but I'll ask again,' then got out of the car and escorted her to her door, waited until she produced her key, and left her after an inclination of the torso that in anybody else would have been a bow. Jane realised that Pardoe was not the only amorous tank of her acquaintance; realised too that a certain kind of tank, if not watched very carefully, might gain its objective.

29

THE HOUSE WAS between the King's Road and the Fulham Road, not exactly the best part, but with big and airy attics with a north light, which was just as well, as Michael Browne appeared to have moved in there and used the place as a studio. It should have looked very artistic, thought Jane, or rather Artistic, with a capital 'A', easel and brushes and unshaded windows, and a battered upright piano and piles of sheet music. But it didn't look like that at all: merely easy and lived in, with its cheap and cheerful furniture, coffee mugs and bottles of wine. Both of them had been working when she arrived; both of them stopped at once.

'It was sweet of you to come so soon,' said Georgie. 'Michael darling, this is Jane Whitcomb.'

They shook hands. Jane could sense the contained power in the man: the first thing that she had noticed about him.

'How do you do?' he said. 'I'm told I should have seen you at Hugh Lessing's party – always assuming I could see anything. But I couldn't.'

'Go and put the kettle on,' said Georgina, 'while I show Jane around the place. It'll only take five minutes.'

'If that,' said Michael Browne.

Most of the flat was the studio: that was where they ate, lived, worked. The rest was simply a kitchen with a gas-ring, sink and stove, a cupboard of a bathroom, and a bedroom that showed the only signs of luxury in the place: elegant white furniture, a canopied bed. A lover's room, thought Jane, which was all very right if not proper, since lovers they were.

'Did you have problems last night?' Georgina asked.

'I might have done,' said Jane. 'But I didn't. It was sweet of you to warn me.'

'Forewarned is forearmed and all that,' said Georgina. 'I wouldn't want you to be embarrassed.'

'I wasn't. Not last night anyway. I like your Michael.'

'Isn't he scrumptious? But he isn't. Mine I mean. He's married.'

'It doesn't surprise me.'

'It was the war,' said Georgina. 'Everybody was getting married. Everybody.'

'I nearly did myself,' said Jane.

'Oh!' said Georgina and her hand went to her mouth: a gesture at once endearing and contrite. 'I didn't mean – '

'On the shelf,' said Jane. 'Spinster. Old maid.'

'You mustn't say that,' said Georgina fiercely. 'You mustn't think of yourself like that.'

'I don't,' said Jane, and after a second Georgina began to laugh. Even her laughter, thought Jane, was pretty.

'That's all right then,' she said. 'Let's go and see what hell brew Michael's making.'

But it was only tea the way the army made it, hot, strong and sweet. Browne poured her a cup and said, 'You were in it, Georgie says. The war I mean.'

'I drove an ambulance.'

'I rode in one once,' said Browne. 'But you weren't driving. I would have remembered.'

'A bad one?'

'First day of the Somme,' said Browne. 'Got me six weeks' sick leave. Probably saved my life, though.'

Georgina said, 'I don't want to talk about that.'

'No reason why we should,' said Browne. 'What do you do now, Miss Whitcomb?'

'Good works,' said Jane. 'The proper occupation for unmarried ladies of an uncertain age. But please call me Jane.'

'You never fancied becoming an art collector?'

'Never,' said Jane.

'Pity,' said Browne. 'There's a lot of art in this place going cheap.'

'But I might,' said Jane. 'I just bought a house in South Terrace.'

'Off the Brompton Road?' Browne asked, and she nodded.

'How dashing,' said Georgina.

'Pooh that's nothing,' said Jane. 'I used to have a house in Mount Street. Show me some of that art you've got.'

He had oils and drawings, and both were of two kinds: the war, and his celebration of the fact that he had survived it: a celebration that involved Georgina a good deal. The war was portraits of soldiers: mostly privates and NCOs and an occasional young officer to remind her of John. Together with the mad, smashed landscape of the trenches, guns and limbers, horses that were still alive and unhurt to remind her of Mavis and Bridget O'Dowd, and then a gun team that was dead: men and horses both.

Jane looked away at once to the postwar pictures and sketches, that were a kind of hymn to survival and more than survival: to life itself. Pictures of flowers and still lives of fruit and bread and wine that somehow throbbed with vitality, sketches and portraits of Georgie that praised her beauty like love sonnets. But always her glance went back to the dead horses, the dead men.

'It's all so morbid,' said Georgina. 'Don't you think it's morbid?'

Jane heard her voice say, 'No, my dear. That's pretty well the way it was.'

In her nightmares it had always been the horses: it was only now, when she was awake, that she was shown the image of dead men. Soon, she knew, she would begin to scream.

It was the noise from outside that saved her: feet stamping on the stairs and then the pounding of a fist on the door, and a voice made hoarse by anger shouting, 'Michael, Michael, I know you're in there so don't try to hide.'

Browne looked at Georgina Payne. 'Oh Lord,' he said.

'Lilian?' she asked.

'I'm afraid so.' The pounding intensified.

'I'm most awfully sorry,' said Georgina to Jane, 'but it's Michael's wife.'

'I'm afraid I'll have to let her in,' said Browne. 'We'll have the whole house here if we don't.'

The hoarse voice rose louder. 'Don't try to hide behind that bitch's skirts – if she's wearing any skirts that is.'

Browne got up and moved to the door, and Jane rose. This

was a private quarrel, and one that guaranteed the maximum quantity of embarrassment. Not her kind of thing at all. She handed the drawings and oils to Georgina.

'I should hide these somewhere,' she said, and Georgina did so, and Browne opened the door.

The woman exploded into the room, an entrance as dramatic as a demon king's at a pantomime, and perhaps she knew she was doing it, perhaps it gave her pleasure, but the overwhelming effect that she created was one of grief. Heartbreak. She stood just inside the door, kicked it shut with her foot, then posed with arms spread wide as if determined that no one should leave: an effect even more dramatic: even more heartbreaking, too.

'So there you are,' she said, and looked from Browne to Georgina. Jane might not have existed. 'Decent for once.'

'Lilian, for Christ's sake – ' said Browne.

'Go on,' said his wife. 'Blasphemy as well as fornication. Where is it?'

'Lilian!'

She ignored him. 'That tart's picture. . . . Where is it?'

Of medium height and with a good figure. Fair and not too badly dressed. She would have passed for a pretty enough woman if Georgina had not been there.

She darted away from the doorway, and Browne made a grab for her and missed. His wife headed straight for an easel covered with a cloth and swept the cloth aside. It was a nude of Georgina, and she had a magnificent body, or at least Browne had made it so, a body that proclaimed its joyful eroticism because it was alive, and to be alive was in itself a kind of miracle to be celebrated by love.

The most wonderful body she had ever seen, thought Jane. But Mrs Browne did not seem to agree with her.

'Bitch! Harlot! Whore!' she screamed, and grabbed a bread knife, swung back to lunge as if it were Georgina's body. Browne grabbed for her and swung her away from the picture. He needed all his strength. His wife struggled with a kind of hysterical force that he could only just contain, until at last he managed to grab the wrist of the hand that held the knife and forced it back, twisting as he levered until Mrs Browne screamed out loud.

'Oh please,' said Georgina. 'Please.' Then the knife dropped and Lilian Browne was still. Jane leaned forward and scooped it up, hid it under a cushion, but there was no need. The woman put her hands to her face and sobbed, then the sobs became moans, the moans great bellows of despair.

Almost apologetically Browne took her hands from her face, then struck her open-handed, hard enough to rock her on her heels.

'Stop that!' Georgina called, but he had no need to do it again. The noises ceased.

Lilian Browne said, 'I need a handkerchief' and Jane opened her bag and gave her hers, a scrap of linen with perfume by Worth. One of Jabber's bath towels would have been better, she thought, but Mrs Browne dried her eyes, then looked at the handkerchief.

'Very pretty,' she said, then her hand went to her cheek. She turned to her husband. 'You hurt me.'

'You wouldn't stop,' said Browne.

'I never will. You might as well come home, you know.' Browne shook his head, and she looked at the nude painting.

'Does she really look like that?' Lilian Browne asked, and then, 'Not that it matters. You'll come back to me. I'll make you.'

She went to the door and opened it. Outside, a group of spectators waited: some neighbours, mostly women, a milkman, and a grocer's delivery boy.

'Oh dear,' said Georgina.

A policeman came up to join them. 'Oh sod it,' Georgina said.

'Bit of trouble?' the policeman asked.

'I came to have a word with my husband,' said Lilian Browne. 'He's Michael Browne, the artist. At the moment he's cohabiting with this young lady. Miss Georgina Payne. That's P-A-Y-N-E.'

The policeman, who had produced a note book, put it back in his pocket. 'Matrimonial,' the policeman said. 'I see.' Then he saw the mark of the blow on Lilian Browne's face.

'Who hit you, Mrs Browne?' he asked.

'My husband.'

The policeman accepted this as very much part of the scheme of things, but turned to Browne even so, because the rules required it, thought Jane.

'Clocked her a bit hard, didn't you, sir?' The note book reappeared, and this time the policeman wrote in it.

'She was hysterical,' Browne said. 'Trying to destroy a picture of mine.'

'You got a witness, sir?'

'This lady,' said Browne, and Jane supplied her name and address. The policeman turned to Mrs Browne.

'Is it true what your husband says?'

'Of course it's true. It was a picture of his trollop with no clothes on.'

The spectators sighed. Their wait had been rewarded.

'Does either of you wish to charge the other?'

'No,' said Browne.

'I want him home,' said Mrs Browne. 'Not in one of your beastly prisons.'

'I'm assuming that means no,' said the policeman. 'Where do you live, Mrs Browne?'

'Acacia Avenue,' Lilian Browne said. 'Number 37.'

'And where's that?'

'Clapham,' she said.

'You take my advice and go there,' said the policeman. 'No sense in hanging about here.'

'*Sense*!' said Lilian Browne. 'There was no sense in coming here, no sense in marrying *him*.' Her head flicked like a hawk's towards her husband. 'Sense is for the lucky ones. All the same I *would* like to go home, but I don't think I can. Not on my own.'

The policeman, and the spectators, waited. Jane said at last, 'I have my car outside. I'll take you if you like.' The policeman looked relieved.

'That agreeable to you, Mrs Browne?'

'Certainly. Most kind,' said Lilian Browne, as if she were accepting a lift home from a bridge game.

'Then I'll ask you all to leave,' said the policeman, and waited with a massive yet threatening sort of patience until the spectators had gone, then asked, 'You're sure you'll be all right, Mrs Browne?'

'For the moment,' said Lilian Browne.

The policeman sighed. 'You'd best hop off then, miss,' he said to Jane, and then to Browne, 'I'd like a word with you inside, sir.'

He wants to see Georgina without any clothes on, thought Jane. But then what man wouldn't?

It didn't take long. Over Battersea Bridge and on to Clapham Common, and Acacia Avenue was just five minutes' walk away: near enough to take one's dog for a run, then return to the neat and shining little house that had a kind of gentility that would, Jane felt sure, have delighted Hawkins. All the way to it, Lilian Browne talked of Georgina Payne: the wicked soul in the beautiful body that had enticed away her wonderful man and left behind an emptiness that nothing could ever fill. On and on she went, until the Riley drew up at Number 37, and then the social manner returned.

'You have been most extremely kind,' she said, and then: 'Who did Mike say you were?'

'My name is Jane Whitcomb,' she said, and left it at that. No point in saying she was a friend of Georgie's. 'I came to buy a picture from Mr Browne.'

'You think he's good?'

'Very good,' said Jane.

'My father was a bank manager,' said Lilian Browne. 'He left me this house. He could never understand why I married Mike. He won't do anything else, you see. Except draw and paint I mean. My father could never understand how a grown man could go through life like that. I can't always understand it myself. All the same I tried. Honestly. I even built him a studio at the bottom of the garden.'

'You did?'

'Metcalf and Richards,' said Lilian Browne. 'The best builders for miles. Cost me three figures. But all he said was the light was wrong. No pleasing him. . . . It was the war.'

'I beg your pardon?'

'The reason I married him. You should have seen him in uniform.'

'You've no children?' Jane asked.

'No, thank God. Though we tried hard enough. – Oh I'm sorry.'

'Quite all right,' said Jane.

'But I heard Mike tell that policeman – you're *Miss* Whitcomb. He never – '

'Never what?' asked Jane.

'Tried it on with you?'

'I told you,' said Jane. 'I merely wanted to buy a picture.'

'That wouldn't stop him,' said Lilian Browne. 'A pretty woman like you. You're like pollen to the bees. Not that he can help himself any more than a monkey can. All the same it isn't easy when you're married to him.'

'You make it sound impossible,' said Jane.

'No!' Lilian Browne yelled aloud. 'It isn't impossible. How can it be? We're man and wife.' She fumbled for the car door. 'I've taken up too much of your time already. I'd better go. I'm sorry but under the circumstances you must excuse me if I don't ask you in.'

'Of course,' said Jane, and watched and waited until Lilian Browne closed the door behind her. It was inexcusable to have said that her marriage to Browne was impossible, though obviously it was. All that suburban gentility ranged against the painter's singlemindedness. But she should have kept her mouth shut, especially as Mrs Browne had just called her pretty – and done rather more than that. She'd helped her forget her husband's picture of the shattered gun team. Jane discovered that she could think about it without wanting to scream. All the same she didn't buy it when she went back to the Fulham flat to report Mrs Browne's safe return. She bought the pencil sketch of the infantry officer instead, paying cash there and then, which almost certainly meant that Georgie would dance at the Café de Paris that night.

'How was she?' Browne asked, when the notes were handed over.

'Calm,' said Jane. 'For the time being anyway.'

'It won't last,' said Browne. 'It never does.'

'You've left her before?'

'Not like this,' he said, and looked at Georgina. 'We were married during the war when I was an officer. I told her from the beginning that I was a painter in civilian life, but I don't think she really believed me. I mean she probably thought I went sketching on Sundays and worked in an office during the week.

'I don't think she believes that anybody could ever be a painter full-time. To her it just doesn't make sense. She wanted me to get a job in a bank. I went off and started painting instead – then she came to my digs and yelled and screamed till I went back to her and she had a studio built for me in the back garden. At least she called it a studio. It's more like a potting-shed.

'Then she got the idea I should be an art master at a school and I left her again.' Browne shook his head.

'It didn't make any *sense*,' he said. 'We'd made a mistake and she wouldn't admit it. Better for her if I'd been killed – she'd have made a marvellous widow – but I wasn't. God knows why.'

'So you could live with me, silly,' said Georgina.

'I meant it's not even as if we had any kids,' said Browne. 'She just won't let go.'

'There's no rush,' Georgina said. 'If she let go everyone would be telling us to get married – and I'm not sure it's such a good idea. Not yet.'

'I am,' said Browne, 'but we won't bore Jane with that one. And there's another thing.'

'What?' Jane asked.

'If Lilian doesn't let go she'll be back, shrieking about harlots and trying to slash my pictures.' He looked at the nude portrait, and Jane looked again, too. Really a quite extraordinary body, she thought.

'Bit of all right, aren't I?' Georgina said.

'We'd have to move,' said Browne. 'And she'd hire detectives to find us so that she could do the whole thing again.'

'Not today,' said Georgina. 'Today we'll be quite safe.'

She went up to him and put her arms about him as if he were her child.

30

JANE WENT TO call on Lionel. He would enjoy the whole story enormously she thought, and she was right.

'I was always one for a bit of drama,' he said. 'Only do keep your voice down, my dear. I daren't for the life of me upset Pott.' Jane told it all.

'The gorgeous Miss Payne in the altogether?' he said.

'About as altogether as you can get,' said Jane.

'And really gorgeous?'

'Almost impossibly so – except that Michael Browne isn't that kind of painter. I've never seen a body quite like it, which isn't all that surprising really. The only naked women I've ever seen were at the Folies Bergères.'

'Will they stay together?'

'He will,' said Jane. 'I'm not too sure about her. Domesticity's the least of her wants. . . . Can we talk about my house?'

'You'll buy it then?'

'Yes, I think so. Hawkins approves – subject to certain modifications. Can you find me a good builder?'

'Easily.'

'Anybody except Metcalf and Richards,' said Jane. 'They build studios that look like potting sheds.'

'And an interior designer?'

'I was hoping you'd do that,' said Jane.

'I'd adore to,' said Lionel. 'How sweet you are.'

The telephone rang, and Lionel picked it up at once, 'to save Pott's poor feet'. It quacked ominously for a moment, and Lionel covered the mouthpiece. 'It's Bower,' he said. 'He wants to know if you're here. Are you?'

'Well of course,' said Jane.

'The thing is he seems to be in rather a tizz,' Lionel said.

In fact he was furious, and shouting so loud that at first Jane had no idea what she was supposed to have done. At last, Pott or no Pott, she began shouting back. Dear Lionel was in agonies, but it worked very quickly, especially when she swore.

'Oh,' said Bower, and then: 'Was I yelling?'

'Very loud,' said Jane, 'and quite incoherently.'

'All the same you shouldn't have done it.'

'For God's sake,' said Jane. 'Done what?'

'Gone to see Georgina Payne and that lover of hers. That Browne.'

'Why on earth not?' said Jane. 'She's a friend.'

'Because Mrs Browne came calling, that's why not. Tried to stick a bayonet into some nude painting or other.'

'It was a bread knife,' said Jane, 'and the nude was of Georgie.'

'That must have been something,' Bower said.

'Stick to the point,' said Jane.

'You shouldn't have been involved.'

'Who told you I was? And who said it was a bayonet?'

'The *Daily Express* got it first. Then my man got to hear of it. It was an eyewitness who said it was a bayonet. More exciting than a bread knife.' He sighed then, and his voice became reproachful. 'You're making trouble for me, Jane. You gave your full name – '

'I spoke to a policeman.'

To her fury, Jane realised that she sounded apologetic, but he continued unheeding.

'I had to phone Beaverbrook personally,' he said, 'and that is one guy I do not want to owe a favour to.'

'But why on earth should you? I mean what business is it of yours?'

'We have a deal, remember? You're doing an article for me, remember? All about the misfortunes of Felston and how we all have to help. And the *World* is building you up as some kind of Florence Nightingale who knows how to drive. Believe me that does not belong with artists and bayonets and pictures of naked ladies.'

'It was a bread knife.'

'I don't care if it was a meat axe,' said Bower. 'You keep your nose clean. And get that copy over here. I need it Friday.' He hung up on her then, and she turned to Lionel. She was spluttering with fury.

'Darling *please*,' he said. 'Think of Pott.'

She breathed in deeply once, then again, and realised that Bower was right. All the same, she thought, there were ways of being right, and Bower's way was awful.

'I have to leave you, darling,' she said. 'I have my composition to do, and my teacher's ratty enough as it is.'

But when she went home the first thing she did was write to Grandma, in John Bright Street, then she attacked the article the way Vinney had taught her: outline, then rough draft, then polish, and then, remembering her father's conversation with a friend in India which began with Kipling and ended with the iniquities of the gutter press, went through it all again and took out all the adverbs and adjectives she could find. He had asked for a thousand words and she had produced, at her final count, an irreducible twelve hundred and four. She rang Bower and got his secretary. She was expected, the secretary said, at precisely half past ten. Once again she felt the anger rise, and once again shrugged it away. He employed her after all.

Next day brought another communication from Mummy; a letter this time. Miss Gwatkin continued in good health, and continued to gain weight despite the heat. Indian sweets were so fascinating, and she had developed a passion for pistachio burfi. Her mother too continued in good health, and after the discovery of a small sum deposited by Papa at Cox and King's in Calcutta, had determined to accompany Gwendoline on a visit to Kalpur, the scene of that momentous cricket match. Gwendoline's cousin, it seemed, was now resident there. It would involve a change of ships, but the P and O people had been most helpful. She hoped that her daughter was in good health, and not exhausted by the demands of whatever passed for the season these days. In a PS she added that she had written to Francis, because Francis was one of those weaker vessels who required support. . . . Then I'd better go and support him, thought Jane, and take a few quid from his chums while I'm

– 303 –

doing it, though she doubted whether Pardoe would be good for as much as even half a crown.

Bower was at his desk and talking hard on the telephone when she was shown in. A spokesman for the coal-mine owners had just issued a statement saying that the miners' wage demands were totally unacceptable, the world price of coal being what it was, and the miners' leaders had reacted with even more anger than had been assumed. A strike was more than possible, which meant more column inches, a leader, and at least one photograph. As he spoke he held out his hand to Jane, then scowled as she took it. It seemed he wanted her – what was it? – copy. She gave it to him, and he blinked, then covered the telephone.

'But this is hand-written,' he said.

'It's perfectly legible.'

He began to talk into the telephone about a man called A.J. Cook, a miners' leader apparently, then ran his eyes down her article as he talked, and reached for a pencil. Jane watched in horror as he butchered her careful prose, transposing, eliminating, deleting semi-colons, then he said goodbye to whoever it was, hung up the phone, and read her piece again.

'Not bad,' he said. 'For a beginner not bad at all.'

'I thought you hated it,' she said, 'the way you hacked it about.'

'Not at all,' he said. 'It happens all the time.' He took out a cheque book and began to write. 'Want to do me another?'

'I can't go to Paris just now.'

'Paris is for later. What I need now is Felston,' said Bower. 'And why can't you go to Paris now?'

'Because I'm going to Cambridge.'

'Best place for you,' said Bower. 'All that culture. Phone the "Wicked World" desk when you get there. They'll do a paragraph on you.' He handed her the cheque. 'There you are. Ten guineas.' She took it with an altogether disproportionate feeling of pride. Composition – eight out of ten.

'Now what's the next one going to be about?'

She and Bob had walked past a pub, she remembered. Inside, a group of men had been singing softly together, making the beer last longer:

If you want to find the sergeant, I know where he is,
I know where he is, I know where he is.
If you want to find the sergeant, I know where he is.
He's hanging on the old barbed wire.
I *saw* him, I *saw* him,
Hanging on the old barbed wire.
If you want to find the sergeant, I know where he is.
He's hanging on the old barbed wire.

On and on, over and over: the saddest, most defeatist song of
the whole war. She'd first heard it in 1917, and John and every
other officer had done their best to discourage it, but without
success. The men fought on, but they were telling John and the
rest that they'd had enough. The whole thing had better end
soon. 'Soon' meant another year. . . .

Then Corporal Laidlaw had come out of the pub – The Boilermakers' Arms was it? – and begun to talk about the riot of a
couple of years before when a group of the unemployed had
demonstrated in the market place, and a Tory JP had read the
Riot Act, the police had charged, and the crowd had retreated,
until, steadied by ex-NCOs like Laidlaw, they had counter-
attacked and were actually winning, until the police reinforce-
ments arrived. 'The Royal Northumbrians' Last Battle', Laidlaw
had called it: the only one the regiment had both won and lost,
because its members fought on both sides.

'That's great,' said Bower. 'You can have fifteen hundred
words.'

'Fifteen guineas?'

'If you make it quick,' said Bower. 'Spend some of your money
on a typewriter will you? Your handwriting's very nice but it
makes me feel silly.'

Then the phone rang and he began talking as soon as he picked
it up. This time it was about boxing and a man called Jack
Dempsey. She left him to it.

On the train to Cambridge next day, she checked that Bower
had mentioned Felston in the *Daily World*, then read her piece
and counted the words. There were nine hundred and eighty-
three, and all of them relevant.

Grandma held the letter about three inches from her eyes, and slowly and painstakingly read it with the aid of a magnifying glass. Her son and grand-daughter pegged away at the clippy mat that they were making, Andy struggled with a book by Sidney and Beatrice Webb, and Bob tinkered with his crystal set. All of them were impatient for Grandma's news.

'She writes a lovely fist,' the old woman said.

'But what does she say, Gran?' said Bet.

'She's missing us.'

'It took her three pages to tell you that?' said Bob.

'No it didn't, impiddence. But I thought it was nice of her so I told you that first. She says she's raised five hundred and fifteen pounds fifteen shillings for the Felston Relief Fund. . . . So far, she says.'

'But she can't have done,' said Andy.

'It's here in black and white,' said his grandmother.

'I mean she's only been gone a few days,' said Andy. 'Nobody can raise money that quick.'

'Of course she can,' said Bob. 'She's rich. All she knows is other rich people – and us.'

'Rich is right,' said Andy.

'You none of us say you're pleased, I notice,' said their grandmother. 'Or grateful.'

'I think it's wonderful,' said Bet.

'Well I don't,' said Andy. 'I think it's charity.'

'And we all know what you think of charity,' said his father. 'But I know what St Paul thought of it an' all, and I'll stick with him. She didn't have to do it, and I bet it won't be always easy for her – asking for money.'

'Begging,' said Andy. 'Begging for the poor unfortunates in the North East – so far away from Mayfair.' He tried and failed to mimic Jane's accent. 'Well we don't want begging. We want what's due to us. Our rights.'

'You speak for yourself,' said Bob. 'I'll take my share of five hundred and fifteen pounds fifteen shillings.'

'You'll take nowt,' said his father. 'That money's for the needy.'

'And just what do you think I am, Da?'

He smiled as he said it, but the old woman reacted to the bitterness in his voice, her almost sightless eyes searching for his face in vain.

Foch approved of Cambridge: its sedate and dignified masculinity held great appeal, Jane was certain. For herself she enjoyed the beauty of the Backs, the Cam still glowing in the autumn sun, the college buildings still not chilled by the wind off the fens: warm stone, rosy birch. She enjoyed the streets too, narrow for the most part, and leisurely, their most constant hazard the onrush of bicycles as she crossed. (Not yet at their worst, her hotel porter told her. Just you wait until the young gentlemen come back in a week or two.) Well, maybe she would, though she doubted it. But she did rent a bicycle, and coaxed Foch into travelling in the basket in front of the handlebars. He wasn't very gracious about it; he much preferred the Riley's padded leather.

Her first job, she supposed, was to seek out Francis and support him, though how she had no idea. As if he were a leaning tower, she thought. Or a political party. All the same Francis could be put to use: introduce her to the sort of people who might want to hear about Felston, and the sort who had money. She left a note at his college while she did her sightseeing, and he phoned her at her hotel at the time she had suggested. She was staying at the Baron of Beef, which was much more co-operative in the matter of telephones than the Eldon Arms.

'Jane?' He sounded incredulous, perhaps even appalled.

'Francis. . . . How *nice*.'

'But why didn't you tell me you were coming up?'

So that you could dream up all sorts of lovely excuses for avoiding me?

'It was very much a spur-of-the-moment thing,' she said.

'But why?'

'I've never seen Cambridge, which seemed rather remiss. What's wrong? Don't you like my being here?'

'Well of course,' he said, 'but – '

'Then let's meet,' she said. 'I have news of Mummy.'

'I can't come over this evening, I'm afraid,' Francis said. 'I'm giving a sherry party.'

'Then I'll come to you,' said Jane. 'Such fun to see your college.'

'There won't be any other women, I shouldn't think,' Francis said.

'Then I can hardly fail to be a success,' said Jane. 'And I promise you I can hold my sherry better than my champagne.'

Somewhere in that sentence a threat lay buried, and Francis knew it and surrendered.

'Six o'clock,' he said. 'My set is in the front quad. The porter will show you. And Jane – '

'Yes, Francis?'

'You will watch how you dress, won't you? I mean it won't be the Savoy.' He hung up.

And just who, Jane wondered, has been telling you that I went to the Savoy quite recently? A *Daily World* reader, no doubt, but certainly not Francis himself. Francis, she was sure, would never read the *Daily World*, was almost incapable of doing so. She went upstairs to change.

The Chanel suit, she thought. Neat and yet worldly, smart, and yet not too feminine. A chum's suit, perhaps even an equal's, though not in Cambridge, not yet. And over it for contrast a vast and swirling coat in red and green that seemed to have come out of the depths of central Asia, a hat with an osprey feather curled to its crown, and Foch on a scarlet lead. All very well for Francis to say that his college wasn't the Savoy, but what did Francis know about what clothes men wanted women to wear?

He was a fellow of Dorset College, which was neither as vast as Trinity nor as exquisite as King's, but charming enough, she thought. On her way across the quad she inserted a cigarette into a jade cigarette holder. The porter went ahead of her like an escort of cavalry, and a couple of ageing dons stopped to stare, though not in rebuke, and she followed the porter up one flight of stairs (and one was quite enough, given the shoes she was wearing: dyed kid and French, but ruthlessly tight, and Foch disliked stairs anyway), then stood as the porter tapped at Francis's door, and waited until he had observed her brother's reaction, then left with the air of a man for whom that day at least had achieved fulfilment, for Francis had taken one look and was appalled.

'Francis, my dear,' she said, 'how sweet of you to invite me,' and then, as he made no move: 'You *did* invite me, you know.'

'Oh yes,' he said. 'You'd better come in.'

Not exactly my house is yours, she thought, but at least he'd allowed her inside. And Foch. And why not? she thought. Foch's company manners were excellent.

Francis's set of rooms contained a study and a sitting room,

- 308 -

both austere, and both book-lined. It was in the sitting room that his party was being held: a room, she thought, from which every hint of frivolity had been ruthlessly removed, a grey and brown room with only one picture, Courbet's 'Reapers', a painterly enough expression of peasants exploited by the capitalist system. Even the ranks of sherry bottles and glasses did little to dispel the gloom, though here and there a guest did his best: a pink tie, long hair languidly waved, a sapphire-blue waistcoat. And there *were* other ladies there, after all: three of them, in identical cloche hats and dresses which showed that they at least had obeyed her brother's instruction not to confuse his rooms with the Savoy. One of them was Marigold Ledbitter, and the man standing next to her was inevitably Pardoe.

Jane stepped across the threshold of the living room and all conversation ceased. It was an agreeable sensation, she discovered, to have eleven men and three women stare at her in precisely that way: a really delicious mixture of envy, admiration and carnality. Sarah Unwin must be used to it she thought, but for me it's the first time and I *love* it.

'Everyone, this is my sister Jane,' said Francis, and then to Jane: 'Best if you just mingle, I should think. There are far too many names for you to remember.'

'Yes, of course,' said Jane. 'If I might just be given the minutest glass of sherry. . . .'

Half the men in the room, including Pardoe, rushed to obey, but the winner was a squat and powerful man with the look of a games player.

'Fino or medium sweet?' he said, and she chose the amontillado. The squat man had brought both.

'My name's Robins,' he said. 'Tony Robins.' He sipped at the fino.

'Jane Whitcomb.'

'So I heard Francis say. He never told me he had a sister before. Pleased to meet you.'

He offered his hand, and she juggled with her cigarette holder, her glass and Foch's lead, and took it at last.

'I must say,' said Robins, 'that even if he had told me I wouldn't have been prepared for quite such a sister.'

'You don't approve?'

'Of course I approve,' said Robins. 'I wouldn't have believed it possible for one human being to light up this room the way you do. Believe me, we poor scholars are grateful.'

The man with the pink tie joined them. 'My very words,' he said, and Robins scowled. They had been his words after all.

'Do I detect the influence of Bakst on that *exquisite* coat?' the man in the pink tie asked.

'I expect so,' said Jane. 'He seems to have influenced everything else.'

'Flamboyant,' said Robins, 'and yet not in the least outré. How is it done, do you suppose?'

'By design of course,' said the man in the pink tie, and waited for applause. He didn't get it.

'What brings you here, Miss Whitcomb?' Robins asked.

She shrugged. 'The desire to see Francis in his native habitat,' she said.

The man in the pink tie giggled. 'How intrepid of you.'

'Wasn't it?' said Jane. 'But worth it. Such a lovely habitat.'

'It isn't fashionable to say so at the moment,' said Robins. 'The Backs and King's College Chapel are all very well in their way –'

'Their very much outmoded way,' said the man in the pink tie.

' – but we must be concerned only with what is real, functional, productive.'

'It all sounds rather bleak,' said Jane.

'It *is* bleak,' said Robins.

'And not in the least like my coat.'

'It could be argued – in fact it probably will be argued over Senior Common Room coffee for many days to come – that your coat is outmoded too,' said Pardoe. He had crept up on them, Jane noticed, and deserted Marigold Ledbitter.

'Then I'd better remove it,' said Jane. 'I simply cannot bear to seem outmoded.'

She left the three men and went to what she guessed was Francis's bedroom, took off the coat and hat. Foch snorted.

'I quite agree,' she said, 'but they've served their purpose. They got me noticed, which is why I brought them. Now let's see what the plucky little pal can do.' She straightened the Chanel suit – scarlet skirt, scarlet and white top – and went back to the party. In one corner the man with the languidly waved hair was listening to what Francis was saying. Suddenly he smiled, and Jane knew at once that he was the one who'd gone to Germany with her brother.

Pardoe the Tank crashed his way over to her, and Foch glowered. Pardoe bent to pat him and Foch was outraged.

'You are looking singularly well-clad this evening,' Pardoe said.

'I'm delighted that you noticed,' said Jane.

'I shall always notice you,' said Pardoe, 'despite your absurd misapprehension over that housemaid of yours. You did not dismiss her, I trust?'

'On the contrary,' said Jane. 'I promoted her.' Pardoe did not seem pleased.

'It has come to my notice,' he said, 'that you have been busy in a – how shall I describe it? – literary seems too beneficent, journalism too dismissive – in a socially aware kind of way, should I say?'

The man next to her joined them at that.

'So you're that Jane Whitcomb,' he said.

'Which Jane Whitcomb?' she asked.

'The one who wrote that piece in yesterday's *Daily World*.'

'That's the one I am,' she said.

'And presumably meant every word. . . . I'm Myers, by the way.'

And even I have heard of you, thought Jane. The Honourable Frederick Myers – Freddy: savant, mathematician, philosopher, atheist – and above all philanderer: which was why she had heard of him, she and every other reader of the *Daily World*, the *Mail*, the *Express* – any and all of them. Small, neat in build, with the most frankly disrobing eyes she had ever encountered.

'You're right. You must be right,' he said. 'You must allow me to make a contribution.' He pulled a cracked and ancient wallet from his pocket, and his fingers explored among tram tickets, laundry lists, a pageful of mathematical symbols, and emerged with a note that Jane thought could be twenty pounds. He offered it to Jane, but Pardoe stepped between them, pushed Myers's hand gently to one side.

'Freddy, I must beg you to think again,' he said.

'I never think again,' said Myers. 'Miss Whitcomb is right and there's an end on't.'

'Miss Whitcomb is not in the least right,' said Pardoe. 'Come. . . . Let us consider.'

'Consider away.' Myers put away the note, to Jane's dismay, but in his pocket rather than his wallet. There was still hope.

The other men in the party refilled their glasses and stood around Freddy Myers and Pardoe, rather like a circle of Regency bucks round a couple of prize-fighters, thought Jane, and at last even the three other women joined them.

'Consider the facts,' said Pardoe. 'The good people of Felstone – '

'Felston,' said Jane, and Pardoe winced. He was not used to being interrupted quite so early in the proceedings.

'Felston then,' he said. 'Let us try not to impede this discussion with unnecessary pedantry.'

'It isn't pedantry to them,' said Jane. 'It's the place where they live. It's important to them.'

Francis clicked his tongue at his sister's persistence, and some of the other men too seemed annoyed, but not Robins.

'She's right, you know,' he said. 'The place where we belong is almost as important as the name we bear – whether we like it or lump it.'

'Oh agreed, agreed,' said Myers, 'but do let Pardoe get on with it.'

He produced a large, curved pipe half filled with shag tobacco, which, when lit, smelled even nastier than it looked, but Jane noticed that Pardoe got most of it. Not that it put him off.

Pardoe's argument was simply Andy's after all, but with longer words. The 'good people' of Felston were ignorant of the fact that they were part of an inevitable historical process – and who could blame them for that? Starvation and despair were their destiny so long as the present system existed, and their only hope of betterment was to change the system, and the only way to do that was for them to overthrow the capitalist class. Charities and subscriptions and articles in the *Daily World* were at best an irrelevance, a way of postponing the inevitable.

Very violent the inevitable was going to be, according to Pardoe, thought Jane. And there seemed little doubt that Pardoe was looking forward to it. Words like 'smash' and 'crush' and 'overthrow' were in pretty frequent use. She looked at her brother, who was nodding in agreement each time they were uttered.

'Their position in life is awful,' said Pardoe, 'but it must be seen as a sacrifice: one that they must make for the unborn generations who will succeed them into a kind of world which to us would be a paradise – were we to believe in such places: a world where there is neither crime nor poverty, hatred nor hunger: a world where there is enough for all and superfluity for no man. We have to hurry towards that day, Freddy, not hold it at bay with bank notes.'

Not bad, thought Jane. In Felston market place he could always be sure of an audience, but his voice lacked the fury that Andy's had, that terrible intimation of the wrath to come.

Myers blew more smoke at Pardoe, who began at last to cough.

'Good stuff,' said Myers. 'Quite powerful stuff too – from time to time. But I deny your major.'

'Freddy, *please*,' said Pardoe, choking still.

'Eh? Oh, sorry.' Myers blew more smoke, slightly to Pardoe's right. This time it was the turn of Francis's friend.

'It's that word inevitable,' said Myers. 'Not an easy word for mathematicians. We tend to restrict its use – to mathematics. Anything living, anything that is born in fact, including homo sapiens, has only one claim to inevitability and that is the certainty that it will die. Now this being so –'

'I was talking of the theory itself: not its exponents,' said Pardoe.

'To be sure you were,' said Myers, 'and who created the theory but a finite being who was born, then died? All flesh is as grass you see, Pardoe. And I note that you used the word "theory" rather than "law". You fail, my dear fellow. Fail utterly. . . . To convince me that is.'

Once more it was Pardoe who received the tobacco smoke, rather as a much younger Pardoe might have received a stroke of the cane for failing to use π to three decimal places, thought Jane, and held out her hand to Myers.

'To be sure,' said Myers, 'I win, therefore I lose.'

His hand went to his pocket and came out with the bank note. It was for a hundred pounds. The way in which he pressed it into her palm seemed to cause him a certain amount of pleasure.

'We must talk some more about this,' he said. 'Over tea in my rooms, perhaps.'

'Perhaps,' she said, and thought: Not bloody likely. And then: I can do quotations, too.

'Tell you what,' said Myers. 'I'll pass the hat round. Do my own bit for Felston.'

He went to where Francis's academic square hung above his MA gown, and thrust it determinedly at one guest after another, refusing all offers he considered inadequate.

Pardoe said to Jane: 'I expect you took my intervention personally.'

'No more than you did,' said Jane. 'And anyway it doesn't matter. You lost.'

'I did not lose,' said Pardoe. 'It's just that I find tobacco smoke distracting. I shall not subscribe, of course.'

Jane said nothing, and in the silence that followed Marigold Ledbitter's voice rang out clear and shrill.

'More like a fashion show than a civilised party,' she said. 'Will she take off anything else, one wonders?'

Jane walked across to her and smiled. 'I will if you will,' she said, then looked once more towards Francis. The poor boy was sweating visibly.

31

J ANE AWOKE NEXT morning and found herself famous. More quotations, she thought, but after all, Lord Byron had been there too. There were notes and telephone calls, there were even flowers, and there was money to be counted yet again. Two hundred and four pounds seven shillings. Half a crown apiece from Marigold's companions, and two bob from the lady herself. All the men had given notes, except Pardoe of course; even Francis had managed a quid. He'd sort of hinted that he could do with it back when she took him out to dinner, but she'd been firm about that. Francis's well-being stood in need of such a sacrifice, and anyway the dinner had cost far more, what with his passion for Château Gruaud Larose when his rich sister was paying. Though maybe that was unfair. After all she *was* his rich sister.

She lay on the bed and took tea and biscuits, then saw she'd reached the last one and it was promised to Foch, and gave it to him.

'I hope you realise what a privilege it is sharing my bedroom,' she said, 'and I don't mean because you're a dog. That only took bribery. But when I think of the number of gentlemen eager to take your place. . . .' Freddy Myers of course, and quite a few of the others. When she'd offered to undress in competition with the Ledbitter, contributions had rocketed. And even Pardoe, when she left, had said that he still held himself in readiness for a certain delightful day. In some inexplicable way he'd acted as if she owed it to him because he'd lost an argument.

Francis had waited until the coffee before he'd begun to complain. Until then nothing must upset the texture and bouquet of the wine, and so she'd told him of their mother, and the decision to visit Kalpur.

'Kalpur?' Francis asked.

'Where Papa played cricket and the maharajah cheated.'

'I don't remember,' said Francis. 'Why has Mummy gone there?'

'Because the resident is a cousin of Miss Gwatkin's.'

'That ghastly old gammer who came to the funeral? The one who never stopped talking?'

'The very same.'

'Poor Mummy,' said Francis. Jane rather liked him for that.

Over coffee he said, 'I say.' Jane waited. 'You rather upset old Cuthbert.'

'Old Cuthbert must learn to get used to it,' said Jane. 'I have no intention of making him a present of my virtue.'

Not that I have it to bestow, she thought, but Francis is not one of those I can tell. Not like Harriet Watson.

'You mustn't say things like that,' said Francis. Jane looked up and saw that he was blushing.

'Why on earth not?' she said. 'Don't tell me you're a prude.'

'Oh dear,' said Francis, 'I'm afraid I must be. And me a you-know-what.'

'I like the look of your new friend,' said Jane.

'Dennis? He's an art historian. Doing research at the Fitzwilliam.'

'And rather sweet.'

'Well I think so,' said Francis, 'obviously.' And once again Jane liked him, but it didn't last. 'All the same – ' Francis began.

'Do go on.'

'I wish I knew what you're *doing* here.'

'Raising money,' she said. 'You saw me in action. I did rather well.'

'I'm sure you did,' said Francis. 'Where on earth did you learn how to do it? Papa?'

'It's mostly because I have to,' said Jane, 'but if there is any heredity involved I rather think it's Mummy.'

'You see,' said Francis, 'I happen to agree with Pardoe – about the charity thing. But then I think you knew that?'

'Suspected it, shall we say?'

'But that didn't prevent you from coming here and wrecking my party.'

'Like you,' said Jane, 'I can accept present suffering if it leads to future happiness. And besides – how can you think your party was wrecked? I thought it rather a success.'

'For you perhaps,' said her brother, 'but not for me. My parties are all earnestness and sherry. The instant you appeared one thought of champagne. Why on earth did you choose Cambridge? Surely you could raise far more money in Mayfair.'

'Oh I can,' said Jane. 'I do. But Cambridge has rather begun to take an interest in the Felstons of this world, wouldn't you say? Which means there'll be lots of useful talk. Cambridge can make Felston a cause for concern.'

'That's true enough, I suppose,' said Francis. The thought pleased him. 'But why on earth should you bother?'

'Because I was once engaged to a man from Felston.'

'*You*?' said Francis. '*Engaged?*' And then: 'Does Mummy know?'

'The way you said that was hardly flattering,' said Jane, 'and Mummy doesn't know – though you can tell her if you want to. The reason we're not married is that he was killed.'

'In the war you mean?'

'Of course in the war.' She pushed her left hand towards him. 'I'm wearing his ring.'

'And that's why you're doing all this?'

'That's why.'

'Sentimentality?'

'You could call it that. I went there to see how John had lived and didn't like what I saw and decided to do something about it. I'm sorry if you think I spoiled your party, but it's all in a good cause.'

'It's never occurred to you that Cuthbert may be right I suppose?' said her brother. 'Oh I realise that he may be a bit over-enthusiastic when it comes to sex and a lot of people find him funny, but he has a really first-rate brain. Alpha plus in fact. Have you *never* thought he might be right?'

'I couldn't be so cruel.'

Francis sighed. 'Cruelty doesn't come into it,' he said, 'just as love doesn't come into it. It's just what's going to be.'

'Let's wait,' said Jane, 'and see, and if you're right and it all comes to pass I'll apologise – if I'm not hanging from a lamp-post in Grosvenor Square.'

'You were always good at jokes,' said Francis. 'You and Guy and David. Not like me.'

You have only to add that Mummy never saw a joke in her life and you've split the Whitcomb family down the middle, thought Jane.

'Jokes can be useful in some ways, I suppose,' Francis continued, 'but I've never felt the need of them.'

'Does Dennis?'

'Well yes,' said Francis. 'He does – but then – ' He hesitated.

'But what?'

'He has other friends,' said Francis. 'Friends he can go to when he needs laughter.'

Not her most successful dinner party thought Jane, and looked down at the floor for crumbs, but Foch had left none at all, not even on his whiskers. The telephone rang. It was Freddy Myers, with offers of tea or lunch in Trinity, or even dinner in a discreet little place he knew of on the road to Ely. Jane pleaded pressure of work for the *Daily World* and indeed there were fifteen hundred words to be written. There were calls from other optimists at the party she could only just remember, then Robins whom she agreed to meet for cocktails, and then to her surprise, Dennis, Francis's Dennis, who wanted very much to take her out to lunch. Warily she accepted.

He arrived in a Daimler she was quite sure was hired, and took her to an hotel on the road to Ely. Jane hoped against hope that Freddy Myers always chose to dine there. The lunch was good, though expensive, far too expensive for a post-graduate student doing research at the Fitzwilliam, but Dennis was a good host, charming and relaxed. The lunch was good, too. The last of the season's asparagus, Dover sole, queen of puddings, and with it a hock that made even her relaxed and charming host blink when he saw the price. But he recovered almost at once, and Jane began to wonder whether it was her brother who was paying for the lunch, however unaware he might be, and if that were so how long it would take him to transfer the debt to her.

'Jolly nice of you to accept at such short notice,' Dennis was saying. Dennis Willis, she remembered. A most inappropriate surname.

'Sweet of you to ask me,' said Jane.

Dennis made a gesture at once graceful and deprecating.

'One could but hope, but I don't mind betting you've had all kinds of invitations.'

'One or two,' said Jane, and thought: And almost all of them improper, which yours most definitely is not.

'You see I've been longing to meet you for absolutely ages.'

'Good gracious,' said Jane. 'Where on earth did you hear about me?'

'From Lionel Warley,' said Dennis.

Of *course*, she thought. Where else would one go for jokes and laughter?

'I hope you'll treat that as confidential,' Dennis said. 'Your brother doesn't really approve of people like Lionel.'

'I expect a lot of people don't,' said Jane. 'But I do.'

'Well of course,' said Dennis. 'You're so like him in a way. And not like your brother at all.'

'I hope that's a compliment?'

'I hope so too,' Dennis said. 'It's meant to be. But the thing is I rather need your help. No. Not that exactly.'

And just as well, thought Jane. All the help I have belongs to Felston.

'What then?' she asked.

'I need to tell you something. I mean when I've told you I don't expect you to do anything about it, but I need to tell you. If you'll let me.'

'Go ahead.'

'Well. . . .' Dennis swigged at his hock, then leaned forward, lowered his voice: 'Your brother and I are lovers.'

'Obviously.'

'Oh Lord,' said Dennis. 'Is it as plain as that? Well we are, and I went to Germany with him. No problems there, thank God. Not about being queer, anyway. At least not in a general way.'

'What then?'

'Francis is – difficult. I mean he has these ideas. These Communist ideas.'

'And you don't share them?'

'No,' Dennis said. 'I don't. I'm not rich, but I like being with people who are. And I like eating in places like this and wearing nice clothes. All that.'

'So do I.'

'*You* do – but Francis doesn't. I mean in Germany he was weird

– 319 –

'– always going into cheap cafés and workers' restaurants.'

'Did you go with him?' asked Jane.

'No fear.' Dennis realised that for once his carefully cultivated speech pattern had slipped, and added: 'Certainly not.'

'You don't like the workers?'

'My father's one,' said Dennis. 'In Wallasey. I can't stand them. I made Francis take me to nice places on the Kurfurstendamm and nightclubs with our sort of cabaret and real champagne, and in the end he always did, but there were the most tremendous rows. Still are, as a matter of fact. But I can't feel the way he does about the workers. I simply can't.' He divided the last of the hock between them. 'What I want to ask you is – do you think Francis will ever change?'

'I doubt it,' said Jane.

Dennis nodded. Suddenly he seemed much more mature, the languid hair an irrelevance.

'I was afraid you'd say that. Francis is awfully sweet you know – besides being rather good at making love – but he has this idée fixe. He simply won't let go, and he just can't believe that I won't change either. I shall have to leave him. I know it's what people always say – but it really is for both our sakes.'

'You want me to tell him so?' asked Jane.

'Good heavens no. That's my job,' said Dennis. 'I just wanted you to know. After all, he's bound to be upset.'

'I'll do what I can,' said Jane, 'but I doubt if it will do much good,' then added: 'Handling it yourself – it's the only way in the end. But it's never easy. I admire you for it.'

He paid the bill, and while they waited for change said, 'Thank you for coming. You certainly know how to put a poor bugger at his ease.' It was a bon mot carefully polished but badly delivered. Even so Jane smiled appropriately.

On the way out they passed Freddy Myers, taking an early tea in the hall. Marigold Ledbitter was with him, eating cucumber sandwiches. Dennis went ahead to speak to the Daimler's chauffeur, and Myers called out to her, then followed her to the doorway.

'Shouldn't think you'll do much good with your young friend,' he said.

'On the contrary,' said Jane. 'I think I have already.'

'You turned me down.'

'I said, "Perhaps".'

'Perhaps always means no. I learned that years ago. You turned me down after I gave you a hundred pounds.'

Bower had given her five hundred, yet he'd never made a remark like that. But then, she thought, Bower wasn't a philosopher, and anyway with Bower 'Perhaps' could turn out to mean almost anything. She went into the sunlight to join Dennis in the Daimler.

Back to the hotel in time to meet Robins for cocktails, but first she had to telephone the *Daily World*, ask for the 'Wicked World' desk and tell them what she'd been up to. They were delighted. Freddy Myers alone had made the call worthwhile. She changed then, into a little confection in black and silver by Paquin, which turned out to be not nearly so demure as it first seemed, then spent the time until Robins arrived blocking out the story of Corporal Laidlaw and the Royal Northumbrians' last battle. 'If You Want to Find the Sergeant', she called it.

Robins. Anthony Dempster Robins. Clever and quick, despite his bruiser's face, neat if not elegant in a dinner jacket. His appreciation of the Paquin dress included the girl inside it, she thought, and together they went out to his car, an ageing Jowett that needed cautious driving. It didn't get it. Robins was a terrible driver.

'We have to go out of Cambridge for cocktails,' he yelled, over the car engine's all too audible resentment of the treatment he gave it.

'So long as it isn't a little place on the road to Ely,' said Jane.

'Whyever not?'

'I just had lunch there. And I rather think Freddy Myers is there for dinner.' With Marigold Ledbitter for dessert, she thought.

Robins's car did an abrupt right turn, barely avoiding an oncoming van, and Jane decided that if she survived the night she would go back to London next day.

'There's only one other place,' said Robins. 'Roadhouse half way to London. Ghastly décor but the cocktails are good.' He put his foot down and the Jowett accelerated viciously. Jane contemplated closing her eyes but decided that she preferred the horrors she could see to those her imagination would create.

The roadhouse was a converted barn that had been whitewashed and spangled with gold paper stars. There was a bar, some tables for eating and a dance floor, and that was about it. When they arrived a band – piano, banjo, saxophone, drums – were doing their best with 'Varsity Rag', but Robins went at once to the bar, studied the cocktail list and suggested 'White Ladies'.

'It *is* ghastly, wouldn't you say?' he asked when the drinks arrived.

'Yes,' said Jane. 'But the drinks are good.'

'Mm,' said Robins. 'Do you like to dance?'

'Yes.'

'Me too,' he said. 'But I'll need at least one more of these before I have the nerve to ask you. Do you like this sort of place?'

'Sometimes,' she said. 'Do you?'

'Not often,' he said, 'but tonight I'm loving it. You see I've never held a dress by – ' he raised his eyebrows.

'Paquin,' she said.

' – by Paquin in my arms before. It will be something to warm my old age.'

'Where on earth,' she heard herself asking, 'did you meet my brother?' And then added, 'But that's silly. I suppose you work together.'

'Good heavens no,' said Robins. 'I'm not an economist.'

He said 'economist' as though it meant 'male prostitute', she thought.

'What then?'

'I'm an experimental physicist.'

'A colleague of Cuthbert Pardoe?'

'That's it.'

Jane found this even more extraordinary than the fact that he'd known her brother.

'Cuthbert's all right,' said Robins. 'If you can think of him solely as a scientific mind.'

Jane tried and failed to do so.

'You're working with him on this atom thing?'

'Now where on earth did you hear about that? Because that's exactly what we do. Cuthbert and the humble servant who stands here before you are the devoted slaves of Sir Ernest Rutherford and Peter Kapitza.'

'Of whom?'

'The New Zealander and the Russian who are really going to do the thing.'

'What thing? Blow up the world?'

'That's what the papers say, I agree. Your *Daily World*. All of them. But it won't be that.' He signalled for more drinks.

'What will it be then?'

'Power,' he said. 'The greatest power since Prometheus stole fire from heaven. More than all the big bad bangs in that big bad war.'

'You were in it?'

'Briefly and ingloriously,' he said. 'Not like you.'

'I think it's time you stopped remembering all the things you read in the *Daily World* and asked me to dance,' she said.

He danced rather as he drove, she thought: struggling with the concepts of rhythm, music, movement as though they were enemies, and yet he appeared to enjoy it. After a while they went back to the bar, and their drinks.

'You know I enjoy these things,' he said. 'Probably because I first came across them in America.'

'But aren't they illegal there?'

'That's probably why I enjoyed them,' he said. 'I was at MIT – the Massachusetts Institute of Technology. What a place. Everything I ever needed. Like Christmas. Every boy his own train set.'

'And yet you came back.'

'The atom bug hit me,' he said. 'For some reason the Yanks aren't ready for it yet. To them it's either crazy or the defiance of God.' He looked at his empty glass and signalled for more.

'I hope to God they're wrong,' he said.

Within another half an hour he was drunk. True he'd had five 'White Ladies' to her two, but even so he was much more drunk than he should have been.

Jane said, 'I'm rather hungry. It must be the country air.'

'No doubt, no doubt,' said Robins. 'I wrote to Rutherford you see, and there was a research fellowship going at Trinity and for once my face fitted and so here I am with the most beautiful girl in Cambridge. The one they all adore so. Just like Zulu what's it.'

'Zuleika Dobson,' said Jane. 'And anyway she was Oxford. And I wish you'd stick to the point.'

'Your point being?'

'*I want to eat.*'

She didn't in the least want to eat, not after the lunch she'd had, but it was the only course of action she could think of.

'Eat?' said Robins. 'Oh – eat. You know I rather think I want to eat, too. Of course I do. I haven't eaten all day. Come to think of it I don't think I ate anything yesterday either, apart from some cheese things at your brother's party, and I must say they were pretty ghastly.'

'You haven't eaten for two days?'

'Nothing of any significance. One can hardly count the cheese things.'

'But whyever not?' Jane asked.

'Busy,' said Robins. 'Busy busy busy. In the lab all day and up half the night writing the notes, doing the sums. I say. . . .'

'Yes?'

'I think we should have something to eat, don't you?'

The roadhouse could manage soup and a steak and crème caramel and cheese, and Robins ate the lot, and most of Jane's. She declined the wine list for both of them, but called for black coffee and watched as Robins drank it.

'How drunk was I?' he asked her at last.

'Well on,' she said. 'You really should eat from time to time.'

'That's one thing all the nutritionists agree on,' he said. 'I'm most awfully sorry.'

'Why?' she asked. 'I said you were drunk, but you were never nasty, so please don't apologise.'

'Will you marry me?' he asked.

Oh dear, thought Jane. It doesn't seem to have worked all that well.

'Are you sure you want to?'

'Of course I am,' he said. 'No other woman in the world would have let me off the hook the way you just did. I'd be all kinds of a fool if I didn't even *ask*.'

'Perhaps when I've had time to think about it,' she said.

'"Perhaps" is the word you used to Freddy Myers,' he said. 'I heard you. Not eavesdropping – word of honour. Just very sharp hearing. I deserve better than perhaps.'

'It's all you get at this time of night,' said Jane.

'The trouble is one works so hard,' said Robins. 'So hard one doesn't eat so that one can't drink and therefore disgraces oneself before a lovely lady. But it's so wonderful, you see.'

'What is?'

'The work. The things we do. Rutherford and Carr and Bell and Kapitza and Pardoe and me. It has a sort of pure beauty about it and yet it's so exciting, too. Do you suppose nuns feel like that?'

'Some might,' said Jane.

'Not the ones in Casanova,' said Robins. 'Have you ever read his memoirs?'

'Not yet,' said Jane.

'Not yet! Oh bliss,' said Robins. 'I do wish you'd marry me.'

Jane signalled for more coffee, and Robins appeared to go into a trance. When he emerged he said, 'I was considering something.'

'I'd love to hear it.'

'I was considering,' said Robins, 'that your brother is putting under the microscope of his mind the means whereby the world will be changed. Workers of the World Unite. Nationalisation. Everything in Common. A long and arduous process, preceded by a short and violent one. Overthrow Capitalism. Arm the Workers. The inevitable Upsurge of the Masses. Power to the People. It will take years for Francis Whitcomb MA to change the world. Years and years and years. And even then he's supposing that all his preconceptions are correct whereas I or rather Rutherford and Kapitza and Pardoe and all the others and I – could change the world in weeks. All we have to do is get one experiment right.'

'You're quite serious, aren't you?' asked Jane.

'Never more so. One successful experiment is all it would take.'

'About my brother, I mean. He wants to change the world?'

'We both do,' said Robins. 'I say I'm most awfully sleepy. I'd better drive you home before I nod off.'

Getting the right money to pay the bill then walking him to the car were major challenges: coaxing the car keys from him and putting him in the passenger's seat an achievement, but she did it at last and the Jowett fired first time, which was as well. Carefully she explored her way back to the Cambridge road.

'I've never been driven by a woman before,' said Robins.

'I've driven dozens of men. Hundreds,' said Jane.

'Ah yes,' said Robins. 'The war to be sure,' and promptly went to sleep.

The car knew how to move when it was handled properly, and Jane had no difficulty in finding her way back to Cambridge. She stopped the car at last near the great gate of his college, and gently shook him awake.

'Tony we're here,' she said, and he opened his eyes.

'Why did you call me that?'

'It's what you asked me to call you.'

'How sweet you are. . . . Did you like driving my car?'

'Very much.'

'You drive much better than I do,' he said. 'It's humiliating I suppose.'

'Why is it?'

'Male authority. All that.'

'Such nonsense.'

'You would naturally think so but then you haven't met my mother. My all-conquering mother.'

'Is she all-conquering?'

'She does it by giving in all the time and making one feel guilty.'

'Hardly the ideal mother-in-law,' said Jane.

'You said perhaps,' said Robins. 'Not very flattering – but I shall ask you again.'

'Can you get out of the car?' Jane asked.

Robins considered. 'I think very probably,' he said at last. 'But what about you?'

'I shall walk home,' she said. 'It isn't far. Will the car be all right?'

'Much safer than with me behind the wheel.'

He turned towards her and kissed her, a swifter, much clumsier kiss than Bower's.

'Forgive me for that,' he said. 'But these have been far and away the happiest hours of my life I ever spent outside a lab.'

'I forgive you,' said Jane. 'I had a happy time too. Shall I help you out of the car?'

'No,' he said. 'Please go. Watching me emerge will not bring back memories of Nijinsky.'

She left, and did not look back.

32

HARRIET WATSON SAID, 'Keith reckons he's good. In Pardoe's class even.'

'He's not in the least like Pardoe,' said Jane.

'I don't think that's strictly true,' said Harriet. 'They're both big and burly and first-rate scientists.'

'At least Tony Robins is human.'

It was lunchtime. They were eating poached eggs and drinking gin in the sitting room of Harriet's surgery.

'He asked me to marry him,' said Jane.

'Which is more than Cuthbert Pardoe ever did,' said Harriet.

'*Or* Freddy Myers,' said Jane, not without pride.

Harriet Watson goggled.

'Good Lord,' she said. 'You have been busy.'

'No I haven't,' said Jane. 'Not in that way. But what gets into these Cambridge fellows? Is it because they're shut off from us females so much?'

'Urges,' said Harriet. 'All men have them – you know that. Only at Cambridge they talk about it more because talking's what they do best. You didn't accept him, I suppose?'

'Tony?' Jane knew that she sounded surprised. It was unfair. 'No. But I liked him.'

'Then you haven't come to ask me to be your matron of honour?'

'Not yet.'

'Then what have you come for? Forgive me, that's rude, but I'll have to fly soon – '

'It's *mostly* about Felston,' said Jane.

'I thought it might be. How much have you got now?'

'With your ten bob I've passed two thousand three hundred quid.'

It was incredible, but it had happened. Already the cheques and postal orders had started coming into the *Daily World*, and often letters came with them. 'I was touched by your reference to the cart-horse, Mavis.' . . . 'I remember the Royal Northumbrians' gallantry at the Somme.'

'And how will you spend it?'

'Medicine mostly.'

'I can't advise you on that,' said Harriet. 'Your Dr Stobbs would skin me alive if I did, and quite right too.'

'I realise that. This is something more personal. John's grandmother.'

'The one you call Grandma?'

'She's going blind,' said Jane. 'At a guess it looks like cataract – I only say that because I saw a lot of it in India, and I wondered if anything could be done.'

'Who would pay?'

'Me.'

'Then the answer is probably yes. How old is she?'

'Mid seventies, I should say.'

'In good health?'

'Exhaustingly so.'

'There should be no major problem, if her heart's strong. Normally one would look to Harley Street – but there might be difficulties – '

'Naturally I would pay for a clinic,' said Jane.

'Of course you would, silly, but these old ladies who've got into the habit of ruling the family roost don't take kindly to moving away from it. It's the only pleasure they have in life. Better let me make enquiries. See if I can find you someone in Newcastle.'

'Will he be all right?'

'If I find him he will be,' said Harriet, and then: 'Good gracious. I never thought you'd turn into an intellectual snob. When will you come and dine with us?'

'As soon as you ask me.'

'The sooner the better. Now I simply have to go. Can I cadge a lift to Kensington?'

'Be a pleasure.'

Foch, Jane noticed, had no objection to squeezing up to make room for Dr Harriet Watson. He approved of her: considered her a serious person.

After she had dropped Harriet she moved on to Falcon Court, and Mr Pinner, neat and dapper and discreet as ever.

'It's about your horse, miss,' he said.

'You've found her?'

'I thought I had, miss – almost certain – but when I got there the description was wrong. Somebody had heard there was a bit of money in it, I reckon.'

'When it comes to horses somebody always does,' said Jane. 'I want you to keep looking.'

'The thing is, miss, it's going to cost you forty-eight pounds nine shillings and fourpence already, what with train fares and so on.'

'That doesn't matter,' said Jane.

'Nearly fifty pounds and nothing to show for it,' Mr Pinner said. 'That's a lot of money when there's nothing to show. I reckon you should try somebody else, miss.'

'Please go on looking, Mr Pinner,' said Jane.

'Very well,' Mr Pinner sighed. It was obvious that he now regarded Jane as a moral obligation rather than a source of income.

'There's one report I got,' he said, 'that just might get us somewhere. Oxfordshire. Did anybody who had anything to do with that mare have connections in Oxfordshire?'

Jane thought hard, and then remembered. . . . Goosey. . . . Captain Gander, the third officer to own Bridget. Hadn't John said something about being brought up by relatives who lived near Banbury? Pinner listened and made notes.

'That fits in pretty well with what I've got, miss,' he said. 'At least there's enough for one more try. But I shouldn't be in a hurry, miss. Oxfordshire's a big county.'

'I can wait,' said Jane.

She had waited for seven years, after all.

On to Fleet Street then, which Foch deplored as being irredeemably frivolous, though like Jane he took pride in the fact that he was the only dog allowed in the building.

Bower very much resented this. He took the view that during working hours Jane was a reporter and that reporters did not bring their pets to work. Jane's position was that if Foch wasn't welcome then she wasn't either. Since Felston was, in Bower's phrase, a bandwagon beginning to roll, they were both allowed in, for the moment. Felston, Jane realised, must be big news indeed, and Bower made no attempt to hide it.

'It's an angle,' he said. 'And a good one. Everybody knows the working class is in. Beaverbrook, Rothermere – everybody. Even *The Times* is beginning to admit they exist. But for them it's an abstraction. We've got a personal view, a place to identify with.'

'You've also got me,' said Jane. 'And I'm not exactly working class, now am I?'

'You're their guardian angel,' said Bower.

'I thought I was their Florence Nightingale.'

'You're anything that sells newspapers,' said Bower.

Jabber had once told her she might have something he called an identity crisis. It seemed that Bower had just solved it.

'And how do I sell newspapers today?'

'By helping Felston.'

'And how do I do that?'

'By being talked about. That needn't worry you. You've a natural flair for it. In Cambridge you knocked them out of the ball park.'

'The what?'

'It's what we Americans have to say because we don't play cricket. You were a hit. A smash. Like that girl at Oxford Max Beerbohm wrote about.'

'Zuleika Dobson,' said Jane, rather wearily this time. If comparisons had to be made she would have preferred someone rather more intelligent.

'I don't know how you do it,' he continued.

'Neither do I,' said Jane.

'It doesn't matter. You can't help doing it, and that's just fine. So you go about and do things and it helps sell my paper.'

'And what do I get out of it?'

'Money for Felston,' he said. 'Big money.' It was what she wanted after all.

'And what do I have to do today?'

– 330 –

'Two things,' said Bower. 'There are a lot of women who talk too much out in Hampstead. They run a thing called the Tea Club. Their speaker let them down today. You're going to take his place and talk about Felston.'

'I've never addressed a tea club in my life.'

'Now's a good time to start,' said Bower. 'Just tell them the way you told me. They'll eat it.'

Jane looked at him more closely. 'Whose place am I taking?' she asked.

'Mine,' he said, and grinned.

'I might have known,' said Jane.

'Sure you might,' said Bower. 'But whose is the greater need?'

Jane let it go. Talking at tea clubs could hardly be worse than dreams of the Somme.

'And the second thing?'

'There's a charity ball tonight,' said Bower.

'Disabled ex-servicemen,' said Jane. 'At the Piccadilly Hotel.'

'Are you going?'

'I'd thought about it,' said Jane, 'but I was too busy at Cambridge to arrange a partner.'

Coo hark at me, she thought. A year ago I'd no more have thought of going to a charity ball at the Piccadilly Hotel than of wearing an Erté dress. But it was true. . . .

'You'll go with me,' said Bower.

'Is it in company orders, sir?'

'Look,' said Bower. 'This isn't fun, it's work, and when I'm working I talk like this because I don't have the time to be polite. You want to work tonight?'

'I'll be delighted.'

'Pick you up at seven. Wear something that'll photograph well. They're still describing the coat you wore at Cambridge. Oh and about the Tea Club. You can use all the stuff you put in those two articles. None of those women ever opened a *Daily World* in their lives.'

She found herself thanking him as if he'd been the soul of generosity, then Foch dragged her to the door. Bower was already flipping through copy, but he called out to her, 'Hey wait a minute.' She paused. 'Is it really true you offered to strip against some bluestocking girl?'

'Marigold Ledbitter,' said Jane. 'Certainly it's true.'

'Don't try it with the tea-club crowd,' said Bower. 'They'd call you.'

She had three hours to prepare a speech, change her clothes, and drive to Hampstead. The clothes took rather a long time, even with Hawkins to help her. In the end she settled for a severe Paquin suit, a silk blouse cut like a shirt, and Aunt Pen's Cartier leopardess. And a hat of course. Rather a nice hat from Paris.

The Hampstead Tea Club ladies were not at all like that. It was all either folk weave and sandals, or brogues and woollen stockings and tweeds like barbed wire. Writers and the wives of writers, professors and the wives of professors, architects and a doctor or two, teachers of the superior sort. They drank their terrible tea and talked about Virginia Woolf and a German called Spengler, then waited ominously as Madam Chairman told them that Miss Whitcomb would now address them. When Jane rose, they produced note books to a woman.

Jane looked about her wildly. I'm dressed all wrong, she thought. Silk suit in that incredible kingfisher blue, half a lifetime's wages of a working man pinned to my lapel. I should have worn the clothes I bought in Felston – but I gave them to Bet instead. . . . She had been silent too long. The big drawing room where the meeting was held rustled in unease, and somewhere a woman tittered. Definitely not on her side. Say something. Say *anything*.

'I'm afraid,' Jane began. Well God knows that was true. The trouble was she couldn't even begin to explain why she was afraid. The pause went on. And then suddenly Harriet Watson came into the room, sat at the back, and winked at Jane, and Jane heard herself saying: 'I'm afraid I must be a sad disappointment to you after your promised treat. All I can say is I know precisely how much Mr Bower regrets not being with you this afternoon.'

And that also is true, she thought. How much Mr Bower regrets is not at all. He only accepted in the first place so that he could cancel and offer me in his place as sacrificial victim.

'But since I have been so very kindly accepted here,' she said, and two other women at once turned to scowl at the titterer, 'I'd like to tell you about a place I know. A place called Felston.' And out it all came. The Pattersons, Dr Stobbs and George Habbershaw, Private Colley and the cart-horse Mavis, and then, because these were all women who thought a lot, thought in abstractions, Manny Mendel and Andy on one side of the market square and the Salvation Army on the other. Compare and contrast, as the exam papers say.

She was amazed at how quickly the half hour went by, and even more amazed that she should be applauded. Really, she thought, one could develop quite a taste for this sort of thing. No wonder Francis wanted to spend the rest of his life doing it. And then the questions began, and Jane discovered that tweeds or no tweeds, folk weave or no folk weave, these women knew their stuff. To begin with they had read all the books, because for the Hampstead Tea Club, to read all the books was mandatory, and Jane hadn't read one except for *Felston* – by Stobbs and Messeter. In fact she scored high marks for that, since no one else had read it, but her background reading was abysmal, non-existent in fact. *She hadn't even read Marx's* Capital. Eyewitness accounts, Jane gathered, were not to be compared in value with what one read in books. Then Harriet got up.

'Would the speaker tell us,' she asked, 'how she first became concerned with the town of Felston?'

Harriet was throwing her a lifebelt, letting human emotion back in if she chose to do it.

'Certainly,' said Jane. 'I served as an ambulance driver in the war.'

There was a purr of approval at this, for many of her audience had been suffragettes, and success in a man's job had to be taken seriously. 'As a matter of fact,' Jane continued, 'I was able to use the skills I'd learned at the Front when I drove an ambulance for Dr Stobbs in Felston.' The purr deepened to a contented growl of approval.

'When I was in the war,' Jane continued, 'I met a captain in the Royal Northumbrians. We were engaged to be married. Unfortunately he was killed. On the 10th of November, 1918.'

That got through to them, bang on target. There was not a woman there who had not lost a relative or friend, and the monstrous ill-fortune of the date of John's death was a disaster they could all share, and Jane continued her explanation. When she sat down there were no more questions, only a vote of thanks proposed and seconded, to more applause before Jane stood up for the last time. ('Don't forget to pass the hat,' Bower had warned her. 'If you don't nobody else will.') And so the hat was passed, and another seven pounds six shillings and sixpence, mostly in silver, raised for Felston, before Jane found herself shaking hands with Madam Chairman and assuring her what a pleasure it had been.

And so it was, Jane found herself thinking. You enjoyed all that showing off and spouting good works. You even enjoyed all that Hearts and Flowers stuff about poor old John – not that he would have minded, not if it had helped Felston, but it was the sort of sneaky newspaper's trick you learned from Bower, and John most certainly would have minded that.

All the same, when she met Harriet on the way out, she thanked her. 'Lord knows how I'd have managed if they'd continued to assess my reading,' she said.

'We're a hard lot to cut your teeth on,' said Harriet. 'Did you enjoy it?'

'I think rather too much,' said Jane. 'But I wish I could have you in the audience at all my meetings. . . . Just in case.'

'There will be more then?'

'I have a feeling Bower's set on it,' said Jane. 'As a matter of fact I think I am, too.'

Wear something that'll photograph well, Bower had said, but that was a man's remark. Everything she wore photographed well – inside the covers of *Vogue*. It was what the clothes would look like when they covered her that was important. She went through her wardrobe once, then again, and settled at last on a dress by Fortuny: charioteer dresses, as the fashion critics called them, modelled on the robe worn by the charioteer at Delphi. The one she owned was in white, heavy Chinese silk, pleated all around the skirt, each pleat weighted with a bead of Venetian glass to hold it in place. Not much on top, bare arms and shoulders, and so she chose a necklace of heavy gold, golden sandals, and Papa's ear-rings because she knew he would have enjoyed what he saw. . . . And the yellow silk evening coat, she decided; Hawkins agreed with her.

'I don't know how it is, miss,' said Hawkins, 'but it has the same à la Grecque touch as the dress.'

What on earth was Hawkins up to? Now was not the time to ask, not before a charity ball, but she really must find out, and soon.

For the moment she settled for a glass of cold milk (there'd be far too much champagne at the ball) and asked Hawkins if she intended to go to the pictures as she had the night off. Hawkins said severely that she had far too much reading to do to bother with Theda Bara. Tomorrow, Jane told herself. Tomorrow I shall ask her. Or the day after at the latest.

Bower was prompt, as he was always prompt. The politeness of princes, she thought, or at any rate newspaper tycoons. He looked at the coat and what he could see of the dress, and liked what he saw, then handed her into the car. He'd brought his chauffeur, she noticed.

'I hear you did well at the Tea Club,' he said.

'Like that man in the French Revolution, I survived,' she said, 'though you could say even that's doing well.'

'Not a dry eye in the auditorium, they tell me.'

'You had a spy there?'

'I like to think of her as a woman reporter,' said Bower.

'No doubt she's that too,' Jane said affably. 'Did she tell you how cerebral they all were – the books they'd all read? The only card I had was my womanly courage in the face of adversity.'

'You played it well.'

'If I did,' said Jane, 'it was because you taught me how. Who's giving this ball by the way?'

'The Countess of Twyford.'

'She does a lot of that sort of thing.'

'She has to,' said Bower. 'Twyford's just about broke. But she makes a living because she's good at it. As a matter of fact I thought she might organise your ball, too.'

'Mine?'

'The Felston Charity Ball,' said Bower. 'Around Christmas, I thought. To raise the money for toys for all the Tiny Tims. Beer and plum puddings. It'll have your name on it but Bella Twyford will do all the organising. You'll be far too busy.'

'Doing what?'

'You'll think of something,' said Bower.

They arrived at the Piccadilly, and the flash bulbs began to pop. ('Open your coat,' said Bower. 'Let them see the dress, too.' And open her coat she did.) Then off she went to the cloakroom, and came back without it. Bower looked at her and blinked, and she knew that she wore the right dress, then she joined the queue to shake hands with their hostess, the wife of a general Papa had once clean bowled for a duck, and Lady Twyford. The general's wife was the usual pouter pigeon, but Lady Twyford looked like an avaricious lawyer in an American film comedy who for some reason had decided to wear a dress in the wrong shade of green.

After that they went to their table: millionaires and their wives, a duke and his wife, a distinguished actor with his equally distinguished actress wife. Among the millionaires was Sir Hugh Lessing. His wife again wore a dress that looked as if it had been made from fragments of Bakst's scenery. Jane wondered if she had any other kind. The band struck up 'Get Out And Get Under', but there would be time enough for that. She accepted a glass of champagne instead.

Lessing said, 'We've met,' in a voice of absolute certainty, but he gave no indication that he remembered where.

'At a ball,' said Jane. 'Just like this – except that it was at your house. You and your wife gave it.'

'I remember,' said Lessing, though she doubted whether he did. 'But it wasn't a *ball* exactly. More a party with delusions of grandeur. We gave it for Mirova. Michael Browne was there.'

'And Georgina Payne.'

'Good Lord, yes. The poor chap's potty about her. Do you think he paints well?'

'Very well. I bought some of his stuff the other day.'

'Did you indeed? He was my company commander. All I ever managed was bad verse – rather in the manner of Baudelaire, I used to think – but bad. Quite ghastly, sometimes. Are you sure you wouldn't care to dance?'

'I think perhaps I will,' she said, and found that Sir Hugh danced rather well, as behoved a man who had had Mirova as a house-guest, but all he would talk about was Michael Browne. Browne, it seemed, had saved his life and wouldn't take a penny for it. When Lessing had asked to buy some pictures he'd given him one instead. And yet the poor fellow had to be helped.

'Endow an arts scholarship,' said Jane. 'Give it to him. He's good enough.'

Lessing wasn't sure.

'That wife of his would be after him,' he said.

'Make it a travelling scholarship.'

'Good Lord.' Lessing was so impressed he stopped dancing and couples swerved wildly round him as if he were a stray boulder on a roadway, thought Jane. At last Lessing apologised and led her back into the stream.

'But that's a marvellous idea,' he said.

'It'll get him away from his wife.'

'You don't think that's – well – an immoral thing to do?'

'I've met her,' said Jane.

'So you have,' said Lessing. 'You were in all the newspapers.'

Jane was glad to be led back to the table.

It was rather that sort of dance: predictable food, too much champagne, and foxtrots and tangoes with men who didn't know which was which; being presented to the inevitable royalty (a dumpy and very deaf old lady), and prizes for the raffle tickets. Bower spent fifty pounds and won a spray of gardenias, which he promptly gave to her. She detested gardenias – for some reason they made her look diseased – and promptly left them on an unoccupied seat. Lady Lessing returned and sat on them with her Bakst bottom and didn't even notice. Rather that sort of dance.

Just after midnight Bower said to her, 'Are you enjoying yourself?'

'Only if you are,' said Jane.

'No more than you. Want to get out of here?'

'Can we?'

'Sure,' said Bower. 'We're newspaper people. We have deadlines to meet.' Suddenly for Bower he looked furtive, shifty even. 'Just one thing,' he said. 'My chauffeur – '

'Has left?'

'He's had a long day,' said Bower, 'and his wife's not well. He asked if he could go early and I said OK. But I don't want you to worry. I can phone the newspaper and they'll send an automobile if you don't want a taxi – or else I could drive you somewhere if you're not too tired. I shan't – embarrass you or anything. You have my word on that.'

'I'm not in the least tired.'

'Then let's go,' said Bower. 'And remember to be nice to Lady Twyford on the way out – we're going to need her. And if there are any more photographers around be sure you give them your left profile.'

As if he were my manager, thought Jane, or even my husband.

33

S HE SAT BESIDE him in the Rolls-Royce, and absorbed again
the familiar scent of leather and eau de cologne and Havana
cigars. They drove through London and headed north, through
sleepy Hampstead, slumbering Highbury, and on at last into
Berkshire, and the sort of country where Uncle Walter and Aunt
Pen liked to hire a house for the summer: rich and lush and
sheltered and discreet. As they drove, Bower talked: Bower could
no more help talking, thought Jane, than a bird could help
singing. This time it was all about strikes, miners for the most
part, but railwaymen and engineers too, then on to the royal
family, and what possible use they were in a country that might
soon be following Russia. And yet they seemed to escape resentment, mused Bower. People actually liked them. So how could
a foreigner hope to understand a country where the people
didn't even understand each other?

Deeper and deeper into Berkshire, from a main road to a
by-road, and at last to a track that the big car waddled along
comfortably enough, until they rounded one last corner and
Bower stopped, put on the brake, and Jane looked in front of
her and gasped.

Ahead of her was a stretch of water and a stone bridge with a
single span, beautiful at any time, but now with a magical quality
because of the light of a half moon filtered through clouds like a
lamp through gauze. And beyond the bridge a water meadow,
and beyond that, formal gardens, and beyond the gardens a
house – William and Mary? Jane wondered, or as late as Queen